W9-AEU-644

WITHDRAWN
FROM THE DOOHAN PUBLIC LIBRARY

Far From Home

Far From Home

Charlotte Hardy

St. Martin's Press ≈ New York

RODMAN PUBLIC LIBRARY

38212002453675
Main Adult Fiction
Hardy, Charlotte
Far from home

FAR FROM HOME. Copyright © 1996 by L. B. Carter.
All rights reserved. Printed in the United States of America.
No part of this book may be used or reproduced in any manner
whatsoever without written permission except in the case of
brief quotations embodied in critical articles or reviews.
For information, address St. Martin's Press,
175 Fifth Avenue, New York, N.Y. 10010.

Library of Congress Cataloging-in-Publication Data

Hardy, Charlotte.
    Far from home / Charlotte Hardy.
        p.   cm.
    ISBN 0-312-15289-2
    I. Title.
PR6058.A6736F37   1997
823'.914—dc20   96-43078
                                            CIP

First published in Great Britain by
Judy Piatkus (Publishers) Ltd

First U.S. Edition: January 1997

10 9 8 7 6 5 4 3 2 1

Author's Note

Bríd is a very common Irish name and St. Bríd
(or Brigid or Bride), said to have been baptised by
St Patrick himself, is one of Ireland's patron saints.
It is pronounced to rhyme with 'reed'.

A poor girl who in her innocence is drawn
into error loses character for ever when
her sin, for such it is, becomes known.

Entry for 4 February 1843 in *The Irish
Journals of Elizabeth Smith* 1840–50

Far From Home

Part I
1865

Chapter One

Danny Keogh. What could he want with her?

Bríd stared away to the west, where the sun was now resting on the brink of the mountains.

Danny Keogh, that funny little man with a face like a walnut, and a tall hat destroyed with age; in a long-tailed coat, once black, now faded to green, its silver buttons tarnished, and stockings hanging down his shrunken calves.

She stood with her back to the stone as the sun perched on the very rim of the world, a ball of incandescence in a sky of emerald green merging into glorious pink.

Danny Keogh in there now, even now. She drew a deep breath and looked up into the vast bowl of the sky which was gradually deepening into night above her, then turned and wandered slowly through the wide circle of standing stones which crowned the summit of the hill. Grey and mossy they stood, the companions of her solitude, one or two leaning in as if to catch her thoughts. In summer cows browsed among the stones, rubbing their backs against them. She often came here to be alone or to talk with her friend Molly. They called it the Fairy Ring.

She stopped again. She had known Danny Keogh since she was a child, seen him trotting about the village, always in a hurry; a joke really, to a child. Danny Keogh, the matchmaker.

And now, this minute, he was in the cottage talking to Uncle Patsy and Aunt Nora.

She pulled the long, blue cloak round her with a natural dignity, a tall, stately girl who walked through the village like a queen; a proud girl who scandalised her friends by her behaviour, who had a way of kicking her skirt round her legs as she walked or turned which excited the boys and made the girls envious of her – though none would come near her. Bríd was too sure; there was too much of her – and

3

they could see she didn't think too much of any of them. A girl with a heart-shaped face and a glance in her wide, dark eyes that had disconcerted Uncle Patsy lately, made him realise she was no longer a girl but a woman.

She looked down towards the cabin nestling against the side of the hill below her, saw the thatched roof and from it a line of smoke rising straight up in the crystal-clear air.

What could he want with them? Only one thing – some man had seen her, and wanted her as his wife. They were talking about this man now, this man whom she did not know, could not even guess at.

Her gaze moved away from the cottage towards the village stretching down towards the river in two thin lines of cabins, and the grey mass of the new church rising among them. She knew every one of those cabins, could name every tenant; in one of them, at this minute, was sitting a man who wanted to marry her.

Danny Keogh had come into the cabin that afternoon, and Uncle Patsy had offered him a glass of spirits, sat him by the fire. They'd talked about nothing much, then Uncle Patsy had turned to her as she stood by the table folding petticoats and said, ''Tis a pleasant afternoon, Bríd. Would you not like to take a walk in the air?'

And Aunt Nora, without looking up, said, 'Run along, Bríd. Your uncle and Danny must be having a conference.'

So she'd pulled her long, blue cloak round her shoulders and set out, up here on the hill among the old stones, while down below her future was discussed.

Bríd drew a deep breath. She felt a sudden heat of anger that that shrivelled little man should discuss her future with Uncle Patsy, and she not by.

Uncle Patsy was not her father, it was true, but he was a good man, a kindly, soft man, whom she could throw her arms round and hold, a safe man. He would never marry her to a man not of her choosing; of that she was sure.

She shivered, suddenly cold in the needle-sharp air, turning again towards the west. And Aunt Nora? Would she look after her? Bríd believed Aunt Nora loved her. But could she be sure? Aunt Nora was so sharp, so certain, so clever; you never knew what she was thinking. Did Aunt Nora really love her? Bríd was not of her family. Bríd's mother had been Uncle Patsy's sister. She'd died when Bríd, her only child, was small; her father had died when she was eleven, of the cholera, and Uncle Patsy and Aunt Nora had taken her in. They'd always been kind to her, especially Uncle Patsy. She had always been able to tell him everything. He wouldn't make her marry a man she didn't want. Or would he be ruled by Nora? What did Nora want?

Bríd could never fathom her. She felt sorry for Nora, because Nora had no children of her own. God had inexplicably withheld his favour from her. Bríd, when she had come to them, had tried to be a daughter to her – how successfully, it was impossible to know.

Bríd had not thought to marry yet, though she was seventeen and many girls of that age were already married. She turned again; her gaze swept across the countryside towards the distant mountains, towards Mayo and Sligo, took in this little corner of Roscommon. To marry?

She knew what it meant. Some of her friends were already married, already expecting children. She knew what it was to take a man for ever, to be true to him, to have babies, to feed the chickens and pigs, to be always washing clothes, cooking, endless days stretching out, there, fixed in the cabin, fixed in Ballyglin.

Looking down again over the roofs of Ballyglin, she knew there must be more for her than this. God had not put her on earth just for this.

And now, as always, her imagination took over. She forgot the cold, the darkening sky, the little fields there below her, and all the old stories which Uncle Patsy had poured into her came rushing back, stories of heroes and fairies, of Finn McCool, of Cuchullain, of Diarmid and Grainne, of Ailil and Maeve. Grand stories, wild deeds, bold men and beautiful, headstrong women. She could have been a queen of old, in her chariot! She saw herself as Queen Maeve, tall, bold and imperious, in her cloak of scarlet and gold, her long hair braided with golden threads, golden slippers on her feet, dashing through the battle in her chariot, a spear in her hand, urging on her men, seeing the enemy falling beneath her wheels.

Queen Maeve on her throne where men would do her homage, and where one day a prince would kneel before her, tall, slim as a young birch tree, modest yet bold, who would come to her, offering her his devotion, and raising his head would look up into her eyes, straight, deep and true, and she would know he was her prince, and he would take her and lead her . . . The dream became unclear; she knew only that it must end in bliss unimaginable.

She shivered. It was nearly dark. She turned and slowly made her way down the hillside into the lane – the *bohreen* – and picked her way along the rutted track, frozen hard, until she stood before the cabin. For a moment she paused there in the lane and looked at the house – her home – its long, low shape silhouetted against the sky, the wall, whitewashed, nestling under a low, deep thatch. A light glimmered from the one small window on this side. She could hear the cows in the byre up to the right, hear the snuffling, breathing and

5

stamping of Uncle Patsy's eight cows, and thought of them, warm together in the darkness, hearing each other, recognising each other's sounds and smells. Was that to be her life too here in the village, safe, cosy, bound in? The life of a cow, milky, soft-eyed, treading her daily round?

She bit her lip. That should not be her life, not if she could prevent it.

Danny Keogh had gone. Uncle Patsy was sitting in his rocking chair and Nora was tending a pot hanging over the fire, prodding potatoes. Bríd stood for a moment in the doorway looking at them both as she pushed back the hood of her cloak. She was about to speak when Nora straightened up and turned to her.

'Look at you! 'Tis a wonder any man would think to marry such a scamp! Your hair is a haystack, and your stockings falling down –'

Bríd's hand instinctively went to her hair, pushing it away from her face. She took off her cloak, went through the kitchen into her little bedroom and hung it on a nail behind the door, and there, in the half-dark, bent and pulled her woollen stockings straight. As she came back into the kitchen, she was tidying her hair, thick and dark, back from her face, tying it behind her head with a ribbon. Uncle Patsy was looking at her. He smiled.

'Well, Bríd –'

Nora interrupted him. 'We'll discuss it after dinner.'

Later, when they had eaten their evening meal and Nora and Bríd had cleared away the dishes, Patsy opened the subject.

'You see, Bríd,' he said, leaning his elbows on the table. He smiled at her for a moment, then his face lapsed into perplexity. He looked at Nora.

'The long and the short of it is that Garrett Doyle asks if he might come courting you,' she said abruptly.

Garrett Doyle. That was it. Garrett, not a quarter of a mile away, their near neighbour. His father had died a month ago and he had sent Danny Keogh to speak on his behalf. Bríd knew him very well; he used to follow her to school and after church, though he was a few years older than she. Garrett, a serious boy with a mop of curly hair above hard eyes that burned into her. A boy who never seemed to laugh, who made her feel slightly ill at ease. She sat silent, thinking.

'Well, Bríd?' said Patsy doubtfully.

Bríd didn't know what to say.

'Will you hear him?' said Nora. 'Shall we say he's to come?'

Bríd looked down.

'Aunt Nora, Uncle Patsy, I didn't, you know, I didn't think to marry yet awhile,' she said quietly, looking up at them both.

6

Patsy reached over and touched her hand. 'We understand, Bríd –'

'Shall we say he's to call, at any rate?' Nora interrupted. 'You'll find no better husband in Ballyglin, and him with twenty acres and twelve cows.'

Bríd looked up, her mind reaching out for something, she knew not what. Her eye caught a little woollen sampler, framed on the wall opposite, which she herself had worked when she was small. 'Love God above all and thy neighbour as thyself.' Was there no more to it than this? Was this to be her life? Auctioned off to the highest bidder? The most comfortable farm Nora could bargain for? Bríd could not believe that this great miracle, her life, this indescribable glory and mystery, was to be no more than to live as a farmer's wife in Ballyglin. Never to see the great world. Never to know danger and adventure. Never to find a great love. Was she, the Maeve of her dreams, the Queen of Connacht, never to find her prince? Was her life to wear away in babies, in chickens and pigs?

'He says maybe you'll have a gig to ride in.'

This had been to Nora a strong attraction in Garrett, and she had been well disposed to the idea when Danny Keogh had proposed it. Garrett Doyle was a good match – for someone. Many of the girls in the village had flirted with him. Garrett was hard-working, no rain leaked in his roof, his walls were all repaired and made good. He drove a shrewd bargain at Boyle Fair. He didn't drink overmuch. And yet, and yet ... there was his mother, a jealous, hard woman, what would she say to Bríd in the house? And then again, Nora thought, Garrett was a man not at peace; a man with a grudge, strong, yes, brave, yet uncaring, not a man to make a woman happy, she thought. But that was a matter for Bríd to decide.

'Well, Bríd,' she said, 'will you hear him? Shall we say he's to come?'

Bríd felt the room turning round her. Was this it? Was she bestowed? Spoken for? Finished with? Yet how could she reject their advice, their wishes? They who had taken her in and cared for her, gladly, willingly? Who was she to do that?

Nora was speaking.

'Do you think husbands do grow on trees, child? You might not find another such. The young men here do be going to America, Bríd. Times now are hard. If you wait ...'

She paused. Bríd looked up at her.

'If you let a chance like this pass you by, you'll find yourself in a few years stuck maybe with some old man of fifty and a couple of cows, and the smell of the bottle on him.'

She looked very hard at Bríd.

The thought made Bríd go cold. She could imagine such a thing. And so, quietly, she gave her consent for Garrett to call.

The January day had dawned bright and clear, and the ground had been frosty, but during the morning it had slowly warmed, and the earth was softer underfoot. In the early afternoon there was a knock at the door. Bríd and Nora had been waiting, but at the sound Bríd rose and went into her room. Nora opened the door. There against the light stood Garrett, relaxed, his hat in his hand. He was in a smart corduroy jacket with a cheerful red scarf knotted round his throat. Nora quickly invited him in.

'She'll be ready directly, Garrett. My, but you're looking smart today, quite the gentleman, I'd say.'

'God save you, Mrs Byrne.'

He seemed a large presence in the room.

Nora lowered her voice. 'She talks of nothing but you, Garrett. Don't be bashful now. Play the man with her, you understand.'

Garrett looked down into her eyes calmly. 'I'm thankful for your advice, Mrs Byrne.'

In her room, Bríd could hear their voices. Her heart was beating. What would he say? What would he be like? Was this the man who might one day be her husband? She took up her cloak, drew it round herself and fastened the drawstring, then went quickly and opened the door.

'God save you, Bríd.'

She had known him since a child, had seen him a hundred times in the village. But here he was taller, bigger; no longer a child, he had grown into a man – and he was here in the dim room, looking directly into her face. She wanted to draw back, away from the strength of his gaze. But she moved forward and held out her hand.

'Garrett Doyle, 'tis pleased I am to see you well.'

Then they were together walking up the *bohreen*. He was talking, asking her questions, and she was making answers; she couldn't remember afterwards what she'd said. She couldn't think clearly, only felt his presence there beside her, and all the time he was talking, she was thinking, was this man to be her husband? And how strange that the boy who had followed her once, and stared at her across the crowded church on Sunday, the boy who fought once for her when Micky O'Sullivan had pulled her hair, that that boy was now this serious man, who looked hard at her and asked questions, probed her, looking into her as if to understand her, to take charge of her, to make her part of himself.

Well, he should not. She could feel that hardness in him, that deci-

8

sive will that would take control; she could feel it, but she knew instinctively he should not take control of her.

The afternoon was warmer, the lane was no longer frozen, and they picked their way through the muddy, rutted way. As they came out into higher ground, the hill opened up away to their right, the hill where Bríd had walked among the old stones. She would not take Garrett there. It was her place, to go alone or with Molly.

The lane became more open, with low hedges on either side, and the fields stretching away on their left. Then their attention was distracted.

Distantly they heard a huntsman's horn, and then another answering it. They looked down to their left, to the woods that ran along by the river, a mile away. They heard the horns again, and the belling of hounds, and as they stood in the lane, hounds began to emerge from the woods, and then huntsmen, in their bright red and green coats, streaming out and up the field towards them. Other huntsmen emerged, clear to see, then ladies too, in black and all coming up towards them.

Bríd and Garrett stood watching as the hunt came closer. The horns sounded; now they could hear the noise of the hooves thudding on the earth, the belling of the hounds, and then suddenly the fox was there in the lane before them, the most beautiful russet red, with white breast and bushy tail, its eyes bright, staring with panic. Bríd could hear its quick breathing as it stopped there in front of them, momentarily surprised, for one second only before it was gone, but her mind took it in as if it had been a photograph.

Already it was away through the hedge and up the hill, and only seconds later the hounds were streaming through a gate, through gaps in the hedge, and the lane was full of them, vicious, baying dogs, pushing, climbing, thrusting on, finding holes in the hedge, and then off again, up the hill after the fox. Bríd could feel their excitement, the unthinking instinct to kill, to destroy.

But now the huntsmen were upon them, and as she stood in the lane, forgetting Garrett, above her, arching over, the huntsmen came hurtling over the hedge, and oh, the strength of the horses, gleaming, strong, majestic animals, and on them, like gods in their red coats, the huntsmen, oblivious of hedges or walls, only exulting in the chase, hurtling onwards, flying through the air above her, as if immortal, unearthly beings.

And the ladies too: Bríd had never seen anything so elegant, in their black riding habits, their tall hard hats, their hair taken up in a net behind their heads, their gloved hands, their tight jaws, the fire in their eyes – for in that moment Bríd saw everything, especially the

9

vicious way they lashed their horses, and heard their incoherent cries of excitement.

Then they were gone and streaming up the hillside with the hounds, the horns and the hounds fading as they grew distant and came to the brow of the hill and were gone.

Bríd stared after them in silent wonder. Her heart was beating violently within her, Garrett forgotten, all forgotten; she saw only the heavenly beings who had flown over her, that vision of power and grace and speed flying past.

'Our lords and masters.'

After a moment, Garrett had spoken, his voice level but with a flick of sarcasm. Bríd turned slowly, still feeling the blood flooding through her.

'Our noble lords and ladies, set over us by a higher Providence to rule and exploit the Irish people.'

Bríd looked at him, not understanding. Garrett maintained his attitude of calm understanding.

'The noble Englishman at his sport, Bríd. The Earl of Elphin and his friends. Our landlord, taking his pleasure across his broad Irish acres.'

He imitated an English accent. 'Over here for the huntin', don't you know, old feller. What?'

Bríd was about to exclaim how wonderful it had seemed, but Garrett's tone stopped her. He looked into her face again.

'One of these days, Bríd, we'll drive them out of Ireland, drive them back where they came from. One day this will be a free land, Bríd.'

There was something about his expression that she felt a flicker of fear run through her.

Chapter Two

Bríd would not allow herself to seem impressed with his words.

She knew of the Earl of Elphin, had seen him ride through the village with his friends and his sons. 'The gentry,' people said as they went past. No harm in that. She'd never given it a thought. She had seen his home too, Castle Leighton, three miles away – not a castle at all but a grand, big place with a long drive up to it.

'They're over at this minute for the election,' said Garrett as they turned back down the lane.

'Yes.' She'd heard something about it.

'The young Lord Leighton, the son and heir, is down from Oxford, and must have his seat in Parliament.'

Bríd resented his schoolmasterly manner.

'I dare say he's a gentleman,' she said.

'Oh, I dare say he is.'

'And who better to sit in the Parliament, then?'

'Well, Bríd, I dare say a true Irishman would be better to represent the Irish people. A man of the people, too, not an English lord who only comes over here for the hunting. Who doesn't even bother to collect his own rent.'

He seemed very bitter as he spoke. Bríd refused to be impressed.

'And what would you rather have?'

'I'd have us pay not a penny in rent. When the half-year comes, I'd have us all go to Kemp the agent and tell him we'll not pay rent for our own land.'

'What do you mean? 'Tis the Earl's land.'

'No, Bríd! 'Tis ours. Stolen from us years ago, back in the days of King William. Their ancestor, the first earl, was given this land by William for helping to beat the loyal Catholics who fought for King James. It was taken from our own ancestors, yours and mine.'

Bríd was astonished to hear this.

'Stolen? But if the King gave it –'

'King? What king? The King of England, Bríd. He gave away land he didn't even own. 'Twas Irish land, not England's.'

'Well, but wasn't he king of Ireland too?'

'But how? Answer me that. By thieving and robbery.'

Bríd had nothing to say. As far as she knew, kings were kings, and that was that. Garrett went on, his eloquence flowing.

'They make us pay rent for our own land. Every penny the Leighton family possesses is our money, taken from us by force. In the days of the famine, my father told me, the Earl would evict any family that couldn't pay rent. Is that fair? A starving family, little children, old grandparents, all thrown out in the depth of winter to starve under a hedge. Many and many a time. Thrown off their own land.'

He lapsed into silence, staring moodily at the ground before him. Bríd had never heard anything like it. She never thought about the castle, but if she did it was as something that was just there, set above them by Providence or fate.

Garrett's words turned in her mind. She knew of families being evicted. It was hard and cruel but it had never occurred to her to doubt the Earl's right to do it. Garrett disputed that right. Still she couldn't understand.

'But if there were no kings or earls, who would rule over us?'

'We'd rule ourselves. Why not? Have our own parliament in Dublin, instead of Englishmen deciding for us in the Parliament of London. There's nothing in the Bible that says Queen Victoria must rule over Ireland. We'd be free, Bríd! Free! An independent Ireland.'

'And you'd have no landlords or rent at all?'

'None.'

She saw in a flash that everything could be utterly different. No landlord, no rent. No more Uncle Patsy and Aunt Nora counting out the money on the kitchen table. No more a basket of eggs or a goose to make up the amount, as sometimes happened. It was an astonishing revelation. The English, the strangers, the conquerors, would simply disappear, and everyone a free man on his own land.

'Oh, but it could never be!'

'It could be. And maybe one day it will be.'

He looked into her face as he spoke and she saw his absolute conviction. She believed him.

'Uncle Patsy, our landlord – that's the Earl of Elphin, isn't it?'

It was a bright day, still cold, in the middle of January, and Bríd was helping Patsy open a clamp of turnips for the cows. They were in the field that stretched up behind the cabin. The ground was hard, and it was difficult work to break the earth heaped over the turnips. Patsy straightened his back and leaned on his long spade.

'He is indeed. He owns the whole village, Bríd. He owns most of the County Roscommon too. You might as well say he owns us, for he could throw us out if he chose. And then what would we do? Oh, he's a great man, Bríd, with a house in London, and goes over there on important business of state, no doubt.'

'That's why we hardly ever see him, I suppose. And that's why he has Mr Kemp to collect the rent for him too.'

Bríd knew Kemp well. He often rode through the village on a grey horse. A thin, stringy sort of man, bent-backed and bald-headed, in a tight suit of black.

'And why do we pay rent to him, Uncle Patsy?'

Patsy laughed.

'He owns the land, Bríd. We pay him for it.'

'Did he always own it?'

Patsy turned again to the difficult work of prising off the frozen earth from the turnips.

'Of course not. Time was, we ruled ourselves with no assistance from the English.'

Bríd had been thinking over what Garrett had told her. She returned to the work of clearing the turnips.

Garrett was a strange man. He had such a fixed view of things. On their way back to the cabin, he had talked about the English and the Earl and his family, and all the time with a steady look in his eyes that sometimes frightened her and sometimes almost repelled her. She didn't know how to take him.

And when they were outside the door and she had turned to him to say goodbye, she had expected – she didn't know what exactly. She had never been kissed by a man, never been held in a man's arms. But if she and Garrett were walking out together, and he was her young man, well, she supposed, she'd heard, they did things like that – held hands, kissed and so on. When she sat with Molly and the other girls by the river on summer evenings, they talked about the boys in the village and things they did together. Some of the girls were more daring and told of their adventures, in whispers, giggling, discussed the way boys would want to hold them and kiss them. Bríd had listened to the talk, but had never had anything to contribute. She had had no adventures with any boy, never been pursued, never flirted. She longed for – she could not exactly say what it was, but something grand, something glorious it must be, something to sweep her away, to carry her into some wonderful world. And it would be a

13

world she had never seen, yet knew she would recognise at once, just as she would recognise her prince when she saw him.

When they were standing outside the cabin door, she had turned and stood looking at him, looking into his eyes, and waited.

Now he changed. He was, it seemed, polite, respectful.

'Bríd,' he said, after a moment, 'I'm hoping that you'll find me a fit man for a husband. I've never wanted any other girl but you, ever since I can remember, since I was a boy. We'd make a good husband and wife, I'm thinking, and you'd never want. I hope you'll maybe give me your answer before long.'

Bríd's heart swelled. Garrett had such dignity, such quiet strength. She was within a hair's breadth of saying yes there and then. Yet something, she knew not what, prevented her.

'Garrett, I'm thankful to you for your kind offer.'

She looked down.

'I'll try to give you an answer soon.'

'Well, I'll call again to see you.'

'Oh yes, do so, Garrett.'

He gave a slight nod of his head, and turned and walked away down the *bohreen* towards the village. She watched him. He did not look back, but walked with a steady, solid tread. She thought, I'll never get another such offer. Why didn't I say yes right away? The answer was in her mind, but it was unclear, and she couldn't see it at that moment.

Bríd was puzzled by the things he had said. Of course she knew about the Earl, had seen him and his sons and friends riding through the village sometimes. She knew they lived at Castle Leighton, three miles away. Several of her friends worked there in service. There was one girl who had been sent home in disgrace. She had a little boy now, and was living with her mother and father.

'They'll be over just now for the election.'

They were carrying turnips across to the byre. The little wooden hut had been built by Patsy himself. Inside it was warm, and the cows greeted them loudly as they threw the turnips on the earth before them.

'Young Lord Leighton is standing for the county seat in the by-election. Old Mr Shaunessy died. You'll maybe not remember him.'

Patsy leaned on the cow's back and looked across at her.

'Will you vote for him, Uncle Patsy?'

'Sure, haven't I always voted with the family?'

Bríd didn't know what to think.

'Do you have to vote for him?'

14

'I always vote for the family, Bríd. What do you suppose the Earl would say if I was to vote for some radical fellow?'

'I don't know. What would he say?'

'He'd say, I'll need your farm next year, Byrne.' Patsy laughed.

'Oh.'

Resting her arm on a cow's back, Bríd felt her warmth, her live, solid bulk.

'I saw them out yesterday fox-hunting.'

'Ah. They don't often come over this way.'

They were to come over that way again that very afternoon.

There was a violent knocking at the door. As Bríd lifted the latch, it flew open and a tall figure in a red hunting coat and mud-spattered boots was upon her urgently.

'Sorry to trouble you, Mrs Byrne –'

Nora was there, behind Bríd's shoulder.

'It's an emergency. My younger brother's taken a fall.'

Already three men were carrying a young man into the room, and others were crowding in behind. Outside, the *bohreen* was filled with hunt servants; Bríd could hear their horses whinnying and stamping, and the jingle of bridles.

'He's still unconscious. Haven't had a chance to find out if anything's broken.'

The tall, blond man turned and spoke sharply to a man in the doorway.

'Has Murphy gone for the doctor?'

'Yes, Sir.'

'Peter, run up to the house and fetch Thomas with the carriage.'

Nora and Bríd were helping the men to lay the young man carefully on the table and put a rolled-up blanket under his head.

'There's a terrible bruise on the side of his head,' said Nora, who had taken charge of him. 'Bríd, there's an old petticoat in our room. Tear it in strips and bring it here.' She turned to the groom beside her. 'That bowl – take it out and fill it with water, and bring it to me.'

Bríd had the old, red flannel petticoat in her hands and was tearing at it, and in a moment Nora was bathing the pale young face, which was caked with mud from his fall. He was still deeply unconscious.

As Nora bathed his face, the others looked on anxiously, crowding close round her. Bríd knew who they were. The blond young man opposite her, bending anxiously over the body on the table, was the Earl's eldest son Lord Leighton, who was standing in the election. She didn't recognise the one lying unconscious on the table.

Nora had taken charge immediately with instinctive authority. She

15

moved his head carefully as she washed him, then looked up seriously.

'I hope his neck's not broken.'

Bríd's hand flew to her mouth. His neck! She had never seen anyone so beautiful, and now so shattered and helpless. Without thinking, she reached for the cloth.

'Give it me, Aunt Nora, I'll bathe his head.'

Nora gave her a strange look, but handed her the cloth.

'Set the bowl there, so I can reach it.'

Bríd looked into his face for a moment, then undid the stock from his throat, so carefully tied that morning, now twisted and thick with mud. As his head lolled to one side, she freed his collar and opened it to his white throat. Nora looked on, then turned to Lord Leighton.

'That's a terrible bruise, your honour.'

He looked at her, trying to glean some meaning from her tone.

'It's nothing worse?'

Nora shrugged.

'I'm not a physician. Who can tell?'

Bríd was wiping his face. Oh, the poor man, would he ever wake up?

'He took the most appalling fall. Came over a bank up in the field behind your cabin, and didn't see the ditch on the far side. Poor mare crashed into the ditch and he went flying.'

'Ah, that ditch! 'Twas me that dug it!' Patsy exclaimed. He had been there all the time, watching, seeing nothing he could do. 'And now the young gentleman's hurt for it!'

Leighton glanced at him. 'It's not your fault, Patsy,' he said mildly.

Patsy looked round wildly for a moment. ''Twould have better to have let it alone, so it would,' he muttered.

Bríd was staring down into the unconscious face on the table beneath her.

The door crashed open again, and there was a thickset man of sixty, a top hat on his head and a black bag in his hand. He came directly to the table. The others moved quickly out of his way. He was Dr Fitzgerald.

He set his bag on the side of the table and ignoring the others, looked hard into the young man's unconscious face. Without taking his eyes from the face, he took his hand and felt for the pulse.

Bríd on one side and Leighton on the other watched the doctor anxiously. Fitzgerald put his hand to his patient's forehead, looking still into his face, thinking. He looked up at Leighton beside him.

'He took a fall?'

Leighton nodded silently.

Fitzgerald took the head in both his hands and began very gently to move it from side to side. Then he turned the head and examined the bruises at the side. He stood back for a moment, while the others watched him with intense and silent anxiety.

'Neck's not broken at any rate.'

This seemed astonishingly good news. Bríd felt relief flood into her. By then the doctor was feeling the arms, gently lifting them, moving the elbow, watching the face all the time for any sign, then lifting his legs one at a time.

He was back at the head, moving it slowly about, looking into the eyes. It seemed agonisingly slow; Bríd wanted some news; wanted to know that the young man was safe. Wouldn't Dr Fitzgerald tell them?

The doctor straightened up. At last he turned away from the patient and looked at Leighton.

'My lord, as far as I can see he has no bones broken, but he has received a very severe blow to the head, and his whole system has sustained a most appalling shock.'

He paused and looked round the room.

'He can't be moved for the moment. He's deeply unconscious. I've no idea how long it will be before he comes round. Even then he'll be very weak. It may be days.'

He paused again. Lord Leighton interrupted him.

'I've sent for the carriage. We can get him home to his own bed.'

'No, he can't be moved. Can a bed be made up here for a couple of days?'

He looked round at Nora. But Bríd spoke.

'He can have my bed and welcome. If he'd accept of it, my lord.' She looked across at Leighton opposite.

His lordship was looking round the room, thinking fast. A tenant's cabin; a poor farmer's home, the flagged floor, the peat smoke in the chimney – he didn't know what to think.

'Let me see the bed.'

Bríd opened the door and he walked into the little room. He looked round. Whitewashed walls, a small window. A chair and a bit of broken mirror on the window sill, a crucifix hanging on the wall. Clothes hanging on a nail behind the door. And a bed, small but neatly made, with a faded patchwork cover. It was warm and dry, he could feel that, and it had a charming innocence in a way . . .

The doctor was behind him.

'Yes, this will do admirably.'

He turned at the door.

'You men, give me a hand to bring Lord Harry in here.'

17

Lord Harry, still unconscious, was lifted by four huntsmen, carried slowly and gently into the room and lowered on to the bed.

'Now all of you get out. Mrs Byrne, give me a hand to undress him and get him warmly tucked up.'

Bríd was left by the fire among all the huntsmen and servants who still crowded the room. She looked into Patsy's face.

'Lord Harry?' she whispered.

''Tis the younger son of his lordship the Earl.'

There was another rap on the door. It opened and another young man in muddy hunting clothes came in, behind him there was a lady in a hooped skirt, a cloak and bonnet, and servants in plum-coloured livery. Leighton turned.

'Don't fret, Mother. He's being taken care of. Fitzgerald's with him.'

'Edward, where is he?'

Lord Leighton was about to show her, but already she had crossed the room and gone through the door.

Patsy and Bríd watched the open door.

''Tis her ladyship,' whispered Patsy.

There was talking inside. They waited. It seemed an age. What were they saying? Then the lady came out with the doctor behind her.

'I'll have some proper bedding brought down, and some broth sent –' She glanced in a distracted way at Nora. 'Can she be trusted to –'

'I think we may trust Mrs Byrne, your ladyship,' the doctor reassured her.

Then Bríd found her voice, strangely and unexpectedly. 'Your son will be quite safe here, your ladyship.'

Lady Elphin looked up, surprised at the dignity in her tone. 'Oh, very well.'

The doctor looked round at the crowded room. 'I want the room cleared. Thank you, gentlemen, but there's nothing more to be done. Lord Harry must lie still, that's all.'

The room was emptying. Lord Leighton was with his mother.

'Fitzgerald knows what he's doing, Mother. We can come down again later. It's better to leave him for a while.'

They were going. The doctor took Bríd by the elbow and drew her towards the fire.

'Now, young lady, I shall need you to nurse our patient. Have you cared for a sick man before?'

Bríd looked at him with a level gaze. 'I have, sir.'

'I'm glad to hear it. You must send for me when he comes round. I have no idea how long it will be. After that – well, he won't want a lot to eat. Her ladyship will send down some broth from the house. Just keep him warm and comfortable, and feed him the broth and maybe a biscuit now and then. And in a couple of days he'll be himself again. I'll look in again tomorrow, whatever happens.'

He went out and the room suddenly seemed empty. Bríd, Nora and Patsy looked at each other while they decided what to do next. Bríd was thinking of the man lying next door. They sat by the fire. Patsy was saying something about the rest of the family but her thoughts kept returning to the room there, and the young man lying alone, unconscious. A little later, as soon as she thought she decently could, she rose.

'I'll just take a look at the young gentleman.'

It was growing towards dusk and, as she gently pushed open the door, the room was already in the gloom of a winter's afternoon. The room was silent, but there was the shape of a body in her bed. She crossed on tiptoe and looked down to where Lord Harry lay. His face was pale, and he seemed asleep. The doctor had bound some of Aunt Nora's old flannel petticoat round his head as a bandage. What delicate features he had, she thought, seeing his eyelids and soft eyelashes. What fine skin, almost transparent, She could see a vein in the side of his forehead through the skin. And his nose and lips were so finely moulded. She gazed into his face, trying to absorb the wonder of it, the mystery of another presence, hearing all the while his regular breathing.

19

Chapter Three

That night Bríd made herself a bed in the loft out of some sacks and blankets, so as not to disturb Patsy and Nora who slept in the other bedroom. She rose several times during the night but every time found the young man still unconscious. She wondered if he would ever recover. Perhaps he would lie there for ever, unconscious. Was it possible?

At dawn she rose and dressed herself quickly, rolled up the sacks and bedding, and climbed down the ladder in the corner of the room.

She went quietly to the door, opened it silently and entered. The room was light, and the young man was lying there still as he had been last night, but his eyes were open. She went to him.

His eyes registered her and he tried to move his head. He winced and closed his eyes for a moment. She bent low over him and spoke in a soft voice.

'Don't try to move. You'll only hurt yourself.'

He stared up into her face. He seemed to be summoning up strength to speak. His voice came out in a sort of croak.

'I say, would you mind telling me –'

'What?'

'Who are you? And where am I?'

She smiled. 'My name is Bríd Flynn. At your service.'

'I see.'

He looked up at her for a moment.

'And where am I? What place is this?'

'Hush now, and don't talk so. You're in my uncle and aunt's house in Ballyglin.'

'Ah. Ballyglin.'

His face was deathly pale. For a moment she felt helpless in the face of his affliction, did not know how to aid him. She fluttered about the bed, adjusting and straightening the covers. Then she looked into his face again.

'Will you take a little broth?'

The previous evening Lady Elphin had returned with two footmen carrying bedding and some dishes and boxes. They had spread this lovely bedspread over him, and then her ladyship had entrusted to Nora pots and saucepans containing food, in particular the beef broth which the doctor had specified. It was standing by the fire. Bríd went to the fire, raked it up and blew it into life. She hung the little pot over the fire and poured some of the broth into it. The room was barely light and the house was quite still. Aunt Nora and Uncle Patsy were still asleep.

He hadn't moved when she returned. She took up a chair and set it by the bed, then contrived to prop his head a little higher on the pillow.

'I say, Miss Flynn, I must know, can you find out – Miss Richardson, in difficulties, might have been thrown. Ask my brother, I beg you.'

'Hush now.' She was propping a pillow behind his back. 'I've brought you some broth.'

'You don't understand. I was supposed to be taking care of her, and I think she may have been thrown, don't you see?'

She sat with the bowl in her lap.

'I expect you'll hear soon. Your brother will know, he's bound to. Calm yourself.'

'Ask him when he comes, I beg you.'

She was spooning broth into him. He was able to take it, thank God. He sank back, strengthened. And who was Miss Richardson? His betrothed? Like as not. Him, such a handsome young man, he'd have a host of girls round him.

Later his mother called. She swept in, her great skirt billowing round her, her beautiful cape and her bonnet, followed by servants – a woman close behind her, and two footmen. She insisted on Bríd leaving her alone with Lord Harry.

Then the doctor called. After he had been with Lord Harry, he came out into the kitchen where Bríd waited with Nora and Patsy.

'He's mending well. I think we may be able to move him tomorrow or the day after.'

Later still, there was another rap at the door. Bríd answered it. A footman was there, and behind him, on a very large horse, sat a pretty young woman in a long, black riding habit.

The footman was Irish.

'Begging your pardon, miss, but is this Mrs Byrne's, where the young gentleman is laid up?'

21

Silently Bríd nodded. As the man turned, the young woman said, 'Take his head, Cavanagh.'

She slid to the ground and, gathering up her habit over her arm, she came quickly to the door.

'Show me where he is.'

She was English.

Bríd stood aside, and the woman quickly crossed the room and went in to where Harry was lying. Bríd followed her.

'Harry! I couldn't believe it! Heavens, you poor fellow, how are you?'

Harry turned his head and tried to lift himself a little. Bríd was in the doorway.

'You shouldn't try to move, sir,' she said.

'I say, are they looking after you? This is a bit of a hole, isn't it? Couldn't they get you home?'

'They've been taking good care of me, Stella,' Harry said weakly. Bríd stood at the door watching.

'But, I say, Stella, what about you? I saw you in difficulties –'

'Me? In difficulties?' She laughed merrily. 'I should say not. What do you mean?'

Harry looked up dismayed.

'Weren't you? I mean, just up from here, in that patch of bog –'

'What? Never. No – oh, wait a minute, you must mean – up there, oh, I was checking him a moment, wanted to take the stirrup up a notch. Get a snugger grip, that's all. No, old Starlight was a treasure. Went like a rocket.'

Harry leaned back relieved. Bríd watched the young woman. Stella was a little shorter than Bríd, auburn hair in a net under her tall hat, strong colour in her cheeks, bright-blue eyes and gleaming teeth as she laughed.

'So you're unhurt?'

'Goodness, yes, right as rain. But you, you poor soul, you practically broke your neck, I heard.'

'No, honestly, I was rather shaken about, that's all.'

'That's a relief.'

Stella looked about her.

'How long have you got to stay here?'

'I don't know, a day or two.'

'Well, get well soon. I want you to dance with me at your brother's ball.'

'Oh, yes.' Harry smiled weakly. 'The election ball.'

'Quite right. The whole county's going to be there. Edward's invited *everybody*. And no one does the polka like you, Harry. And I

22

love the polka. Must rush now. I'll look in again and see how you are.'

She was about to go out of the room, but stopped as she passed Brid. For a moment the two women looked into each other's eyes. They made no sign to each other. Then Stella was gone. Brid remained by the door. So that was Miss Richardson? A fine lady. But Brid had seen the contempt in her eyes as she went out.

Harry was lying, his eyes open, staring upwards. He was smiling. Brid was surprised to feel a pang of pain.

Harry looked up at her as she stood over him.

'Father would have roasted me alive if anything had happened to her. I needn't have worried. She's made of cast iron, if you ask me. Irrepressible, wasn't she?'

As he smiled up at her, she couldn't help herself smiling back at him.

She washed his face. She had a bowl of water and a cloth, and she carefully wiped it across his forehead, down his cheeks and round under his neck, studying his face carefully as she did so. He seemed so finely made, like a piece of expensive china. His eyes followed hers. Then she combed his hair. It was fine and delicate too, almost like a baby's.

For a long time there was silence between them. At last he said,

'I say, you're being most awfully decent to me, Miss Flynn. I really don't deserve it. After all, I only took a tumble from a horse. Oh, my goodness, that reminds me – you must ask my brother when he comes, what became of Mignonette?'

She looked into his face.

'My horse, you know. Capital creature. Best-hearted mare in the country. I wouldn't lose her for anything.'

She combed his hair carefully.

'Your brother will know. She will be taken care of.'

She paused. She couldn't resist continuing the conversation.

'Are you fond of riding, sir?'

'Fond? I should say so. I'd rather be in the saddle than anywhere, I believe. Do you ride?'

'No, sir.'

'No? Oh, I see. No, I suppose not. Well, really, Miss Flynn, there's nothing like it, I assure you.'

She was still combing his hair.

'I'm going into the cavalry, you see. Father's supposed to be buying me a commission. At the moment he's rather taken up with this election, getting Edward into Parliament, so he hasn't got much time for me.'

23

'I see.'

'I've just come out of Sandhurst. That's why I haven't been over lately.'

'And how do you like it here, sir?'

'I love it. Can't stand London, Miss Flynn. But here, there's all the space in the world, the most wonderful country. Never want to go back.'

'I should like to see London.'

Bríd could scarcely comprehend the freedom of being able to come and go across countries with such ease.

'Would you?'

He looked into her eyes. She stopped combing.

'More than anything in the world.'

'I say, Miss Flynn, do you know, you are the most beautiful girl I ever saw.'

Bríd felt an intense blush fill her cheek. There was silence as they looked at each other.

'I mean – that is to say – you must excuse me, perhaps I shouldn't . . .' He turned his head on the pillow. 'Shouldn't have said it, I know. It's just that . . .'

He looked out of the window, lying there in the bed, with the beautiful cover up to his chin, and his pale face catching the afternoon light.

Bríd felt the heat of the blood in her cheek. Beautiful. No one had ever told her that. Instinctively, she drew back a wisp of hair from her face.

He turned his head again towards her. She felt helpless to break his look. At last she took herself in hand, and collecting together the bowl of water and the comb and cloth, she rose.

'I'll bring you a cup of tea,' she said and went out, her mind in a whirl.

Next day, Patsy had come into the sickroom for some reason and they were sitting talking. He said, 'Bríd, why don't you sing his lordship a song with your harp? He'd love to hear you.'

And to Harry, 'She sings like an angel, sir, to charm the birds off the trees. Bríd, fetch your harp, girl, and sing Lord Harry a song'.

'Oh, I don't think his lordship –'

'I beg you!' Harry burst out. 'I should like it of all things.'

For a moment Bríd had been thrown by the suggestion, but then a voice within her told her she'd love to sing to him. Without speaking, she took up her harp, which was standing in the corner, placed it by the bed, and sat by it. She made no preamble but took the harp, and after wrestling a moment with some of the pegs to tune it, she ran her fingers over the strings twice, then began to sing.

From as early as she could remember, Bríd had sung to her harp. The harp had been her mother's, and when she had died, it had become Bríd's. In the last days of her father's life, she had sung to comfort him, songs of home, sad songs of loss and separation, which had been almost the last sounds he had heard. He'd always liked the old songs, the ones he had himself learned as a child, the songs he had taught his daughter.

Now, as she ran her fingers over the strings, she began to sing one of them for Lord Harry, conscious that he would understand nothing of it, for it was in Irish, but that even if he had understood the words, little of it might make sense to him. And yet, she thought, he might understand something after all; we are all mortals, and suffer the same ills and misfortunes.

Harry had no idea what to expect. Once or twice he had had to endure a recital in the drawing room at home, an afternoon of excruciating boredom as some stout lady had stood by the piano and bellowed, or warbled, as it might be, inexplicable songs. And why everyone should have sat round in such reverent silence, he could never understand. What he chiefly remembered from those afternoons was an overwhelming desire to get out into the fresh air.

But now Harry was surprised. Bríd's low voice held a baffling, intense quality, cloudy and troubled. He felt she was getting beneath his guard in a way he did not understand. As she played, she lifted her eyes once from the strings and there was such a passionate light in them that he felt disturbed to the depth of his being. What the song was about he had no idea, but mere words weren't the point. It was that sound, the unearthly sound of her voice, reaching into him in a way that he could not begin to comprehend, let alone control.

Music was a passion with her. She could not remember when or how she had learned to play the harp. It had always been there in the house, she couldn't remember a time when she had not played it.

She surprised herself when she sang. Something came out, not just the words or the music but some force of which she was unaware; something strong and compelling which took hold of her and would have run away with her if she hadn't struggled to control it. Yet she was never so truly herself as when she sang.

As the song came to an end and the last notes of the harp faded, Patsy clapped his hands and said, with a sigh, 'The voice of an angel.'

Harry was looking at Bríd and could think of nothing to say. Her head was bowed over the harp, and she could not for a moment bring herself to look up at him. But then she did so and as their eyes met he

25

saw in hers the same troubled intensity she'd had as she sang. His head seemed more than usually clear; her song had bypassed all the filters of common experience and entered directly into his soul. He had been moved by her song as he'd never been moved by anything in his life. He simply didn't know what to say to her and, having nothing to say, he was silent. But he couldn't stop looking into her eyes.

Why didn't he say something? She couldn't make it out. Oh, it was such a stupid idea of Uncle Patsy's! The young man was embarrassed and she'd made a fool of herself. She wanted to put the harp away and forget it had happened. Anyway, wasn't there other work to be doing?

She rose abruptly and carried the harp to the corner of the room.

'Come now, Uncle Patsy, we'll let Lord Harry rest. Her ladyship will be coming for him this afternoon. What will she think if we've worn him out with all our chatter?'

Patsy went out, but Bríd returned for a moment to Harry's bed, and, without looking at him, eased him down and fussed round him, arranging the covers. Once, quickly before she went out, she looked into his eyes again. He was looking at her still but she could not make out his thoughts. Confused, she went back into the kitchen.

That afternoon a black carriage with a coat of arms on the door drew up outside the cabin. The room was again full of servants, and Lady Elphin was among them, fussing, ordering everyone about in a distracted way. Harry was dressed and, though a little light in the head, was able to walk out to the carriage. As he was about to be helped into it, he stopped and looked round. The servants were there, his mother was beside him; Patsy, Nora, and Bríd were standing by the door.

He turned back to them.

'Mrs Byrne, I'm deeply obliged to you. You saved my life, I do believe.'

Nora dropped a curtsy.

'Sure, 'twas nothing at all, your lordship. Wouldn't anyone do the same?'

'No trouble at all, your honour, and 'twas our duty,' said Patsy, nodding as he spoke.

Bríd stood silent, upright. Something in her would not curtsy. She looked at Harry and his mother, and back to him. Would he notice her? Wouldn't he rather be glad to get back to the big house, among his own people? To see his family? To see that Miss Richardson?

She was right. He did not look at her. He turned his back and got into the carriage with his mother. The footmen leaped up on the back, the coachman cracked his whip, and the carriage heaved and swayed up the narrow *bohreen*. Soon it was out of sight. The three of them returned to the cottage.

He had not looked at her. Well, why should he? Him, a fine gentleman, a lord.

It was just as Garrett had said: 'our lords and masters'. She felt sick. What a fool! Shame filled her when she thought of them together and her playing the harp and singing. It was something precious she had given him then, not meaning to, but it had come out unexpectedly.

It had meant nothing to him. An embarrassment only.

Chapter Four

'So you've been nursing the young lord? They'll never pay you for it, I believe. All your pains, all for the honour of serving their lordships.'

Bríd would not be drawn into the discussion. Garrett was right, and she felt low, depressed by it. As Garrett was speaking, there had come into her mind suddenly the vision of that face asleep on the pillow, the delicacy of his skin, his finely moulded features. Thinking of herself as she bent over him, hearing his breathing, she felt ashamed, betrayed. Made a fool of.

Garrett was right. But she couldn't bring herself to say anything. In a way she ought to feel angry, but she couldn't. At last she began to find his certainty irritating, and said,

'He was hurt, unconscious. What should we do? And why should we expect payment?'

'That is not the point, Bríd. The gentry, the English, *expect* you to come running at their bidding. They *expect* you to serve them, and fetch and carry for them, as if it was the most natural thing in the world. Well, it is *not* the most natural thing in the world. They despise you for it, and so do I.'

Something in Garrett's cool superiority suddenly angered her, and she found herself forced to defend the Englishman.

'You attribute your own base feelings to people who are your betters. He was a perfect gentleman, and that's something you'll never be, I think.'

Garrett remained seated, unruffled.

'A gentleman, is it? And you in love with him, I dare say? A native Irishman is no longer fit company for you, Bríd, is that it? You must be keeping company with the gentry. He's turned your head with his lordly ways. You're a fool, girl.'

'You will not call me a fool in this house, Garrett Doyle!'

She could feel the heat in her face. She was on her feet.

Patsy stood up, took her by the shoulders and made her sit down again.

'Hush, Bríd my dear. Of course Garrett meant no such thing, did you, Garrett? He spoke only in the heat of the moment, isn't that it, Garrett?'

Garrett looked her with his cool, level gaze. 'Let Bríd answer that.'

'You are the fool, then. Is it likely I should fall in love with the Earl's son? Just because he spends two nights under this roof? Where would be the sense of it? He's very likely to marry me, I should think.'

They had been out walking again, and Garrett had accepted her invitation in for a cup of tea when they returned. All the time he had been very respectful, kind and solicitous. Still she could feel herself hedged about in a fatherly way, as if Garrett were determined to care for her, but he was certain of what he thought, and was going to make certain she thought the same too. She could feel herself drawn into his shadow.

She didn't mean to argue with him, because he was right after all, but in a way it seemed to her she was drowning, and she had to struggle to stay afloat. Their talks tended to become wrangling arguments.

There was a knock at the door. Nora went to answer it. In a moment a tall, stooping man of about sixty, in a dark coat and riding gaiters, came in, and she closed the door behind him. He was very nearly bald and his hair formed a sort of halo around his head.

Patsy sprang up, and Bríd rose too. Garrett remained seated.

'Oh, Mr Kemp, sir.'

'Sit down, Byrne, 'tis no great matter.'

'You'll take a cup of tea, Mr Kemp?' said Nora.

'I will, and thank you, Mrs Byrne,' said Kemp and sat at the table. He was an Irishman.

'Well now, Mrs Byrne,' he said, after he had taken a mouthful of tea. 'There's great to-dos at the castle, you may be sure. The election is coming up, and we must do all we can to get his lordship elected.'

'Oh, right enough, Mr Kemp,' said Patsy.

'There's to be a great ball, you heard, I dare say?'

''Tis the talk of the village, Mr Kemp.'

'All the county will be in it. The Earl is sparing no expense to get his son in. No expense. There'll be guests by the score, all the quality, all the titled folk of the county, the gentry, dragoon officers from Athlone barracks; 'twill be the most elegant thing imaginable. There'll be bands playing, dancing all night, feasting and merriment, hot dishes, cold collations, fireworks –'

'Fireworks!' Brid couldn't help exclaiming.

'Oh, 'twill be the grandest thing these ten years. Of course the tenants won't be forgotten. There'll be dancing, and beef and porter in the barn . . .'

Brid noticed Garrett's expression at this news.

''Twill be a grand occasion, no doubt!' said Patsy.

'Now, Mrs Byrne, here's his lordship with his guests. How are they to be provided for? Where are we to find the pretty young girls who will look after them, eh? Who's to make sure that all goes with a swing, who's going to hold the trays of champagne, to trim the candles, to take the ladies' mantles, eh? Eh?'

He was looking at Brid.

'In short, Mr Kemp, you'll be wanting Brid here to wait on their lordships for the occasion?' said Garrett, with a light, sarcastic tone which Kemp didn't notice.

'Quite right. We shall need extra staff for the evening and if Miss Flynn would care to earn a shilling –'

'She would be delighted,' said Nora firmly. Brid turned abruptly to her.

'Wouldn't you?' Nora said, looking at her.

'I have not the slightest intention of going into service at the castle, Aunt Nora, if you please!'

'If I please?' echoed Nora, and turned to Kemp again. 'She'd be delighted to accept, Mr Kemp.'

Kemp looked suspiciously between them.

Brid was about to speak, but Nora repeated, 'She'll come.'

Brid was furious. 'Aunt Nora, shall I decide for myself? Is it me to earn a shilling or you?'

'Brid, Mr Kemp has very kindly called to offer you an evening's work. You'll take it, or look for somewhere else to lodge! Will you be for ever contradicting me, girl? She'll come, Mr Kemp.'

Kemp seemed unsure. Garrett smiled at Brid.

Brid thought, Lord Harry will be there and he'll snub me again.

Garrett spoke up. 'Is there to be such expense, Mr Kemp? The talk in the village is that the Earl has fallen on hard times. That he's had to mortgage most of his land.'

Kemp looked uncomfortable. 'Devil a word of truth in it!' he exclaimed. 'And who's the dirty little scoundrel been spreading such lies, I should like to know!'

Garrett remained imperturbable. 'Who's to say?'

Kemp turned businesslike. 'You're to report to the castle kitchen at two in the afternoon. You'll be wanted to help with the preparations.'

Kemp left soon after. Brid couldn't decide whether she wanted to go or not. Suppose she saw Lord Harry again? Like as not, he'd ignore her, as he had done outside the cabin. Wasn't it his privilege? And wasn't she the great fool, thinking about him and looking out for him, knowing he'd only snub her again?

Garrett was shaking his head slowly. But this time Nora spoke up.

'Everything you say is quite true, Garrett, don't we know it? And one day, maybe in five hundred years, the English will leave Ireland. But in the meantime the world must go round. The Earl is our landlord, and if it is his wish that Bríd should lend her assistance at the ball and earn her shilling, so be it. There's no disgrace in it.'

'Oh, but there is disgrace in it!' said Garrett.

Bríd was watching him. Garrett had a kind of nobility. Maybe it would be five hundred years before the English would leave, but she knew Garrett would live and work and fight for that day. She respected his integrity.

After Lord Harry had gone and never looked at her, ridden away in the great black carriage, Bríd had wandered into her little room and taken up the piece of mirror that stood on the windowsill. Was she beautiful? She looked at herself. He had said so. For a long time she had stood there in the light of the window, staring into her own dark eyes, until she heard Nora shout, and she'd had to go out to fetch a pail of water.

This evening as she stood with Garrett outside the door to say goodbye, he looked into her face in the half-light from the kitchen and, speaking low, asked her again for her answer. She put him off, evaded his thought, his intention, and knew that between her face and Garrett's, it was now Lord Harry's face that intervened.

Later as they were eating together at the table, Nora suddenly said, 'If you'll be for ever contradicting people, you'll never find a husband.'

She knew Nora was talking about Garrett.

'But Aunt Nora, you yourself didn't agree with him!'

'I don't want to marry him.'

'Honestly, Aunt Nora, I don't mean to, but somehow it always comes out that way. I agree with him, I swear I do, but he says everything with such certainty I can't resist objecting. I can't explain.'

'He's a man. He's entitled to his opinions, if he wants. It's no business of yours. Anyway, it doesn't make any difference.'

'If I'm to live with him for the rest of my life, I should think it is my business. And it does make a difference. It tires me out to hear him.'

'If you'll take my advice, you'll learn to like him. You'll find none better, that's certain. You'll not hang around here for ever. Do you want to go into service?'

On the morning of the ball, Bríd went into the village to see her friend Molly, who was also going to the castle that afternoon. Kemp had said nothing about what they were to wear, but Molly said they would be given uniforms when they got there. Then Bríd went into Mrs Carruthers's shop and bought two bottles of porter for Uncle Patsy, and set off towards home.

The weather had turned cold again; there was frost on the branches, the rutted track was hard as iron, and as she walked her breath was visible in the clear air.

Coming up the *bohreen*, she saw a man outside the cabin, high up on a lovely grey horse, and wearing a long tweed riding coat. It was Lord Harry. He started down towards her, and the mare picked her way carefully over the uneven track.

As they came close, he seemed taken by surprise, awkward, and words tumbled from his mouth.

'Oh, Miss Flynn, I was just passing, and called on Mrs Byrne to thank you all again for your hospitality . . .'

His words faltered. Bríd bent to put down the basket she was carrying. As she straightened, she looked up into his eyes. Her cheeks were pink and her eyes bright in the cold air, and, framed in the dark-blue hood of her cloak, she looked more beautiful even than his memory had made her. She smiled.

'Lord Harry! Sure, wasn't it the gentleman you were to ride over this cold morning, and the roads like iron, the way your horse must slip and stumble in the rutted ways. How is yourself? Are you recovered from your fall?'

'Really, that was nothing – nothing at all. You were most kind . . .'

He was again at a loss for words. There was silence for a moment, their eyes were locked, and she felt almost a kind of panic. Then she said,

'And your horse is safe from her fall?'

Harry rubbed the horse's neck.

'Yes, dear old Mignonette was safe and sound, thank God.'

She smiled again. Lord Harry got down from his horse.

'May I carry your basket?'

But as he leaned down towards the basket, he unexpectedly found his face passing near to hers, and without intending it, and without knowing how, and without remembering the exact moment, he kissed her, gently and respectfully. Silently they looked into each other's eyes.

32

'Lord Harry –'

'Call me Harry. Oh, Bríd, you're so beautiful!' He took her by the shoulders and kissed her again, hard and earnest.

Bríd was shaken, and stepped back. She waited a moment, as they both looked at one another, then she regained control of herself and reached down for her basket.

'Is it this way you are with all the girls?'

Her heart was racing, she could feel the blood in her cheeks and in her ears. And he seemed to have difficulty in speaking, but after a moment he said,

'I swear I never did such a thing before. I never spoke such a word before. You are the most beautiful girl I ever –'

But Bríd had picked up the basket and was walking, almost running up the lane. Harry ran beside her, pulling Mignonette by the bridle.

'For God's sake, Bríd – Miss Flynn – don't be angry with me. I swear I wasn't thinking what I was doing.'

'Wasn't thinking is right,' said Bríd, not looking at him, remembering Garrett's words again, and ashamed of her own folly. 'Fine gentlemen don't think when they flirt with girls.'

'Bríd, I wasn't flirting. Why do you say that? I wasn't flirting. Why are you so angry?'

'Angry, is it? And shouldn't I be angry, you from the Castle Leighton and me just a country girl? What sense is in that?'

She seemed destined to be insulted and humiliated by the gentry.

'Oh, Bríd, I don't know. But don't be angry with me. I tell you I didn't think.'

They had reached the cabin, and Bríd went inside before Harry could say any more.

'There was that Lord Harry here just now, asking after you,' said Nora, who was cutting vegetables on the table.

'I saw him in the *bohreen*,' said Bríd, putting the basket on the table and going into her room as she undid her cloak.

Inside she stopped, and with her hand still on the drawstring, she leaned against the wall. For a moment she could see nothing, her mind was full of Harry's presence, himself there suddenly kissing her, not once, not calmly or in a gentlemanly way, nor like Uncle Patsy, but suddenly, with a man's passion, a force that had utterly capsized her, taken her breath away, set her heart racing and confused her mind.

But what had she said to him? She leaned against the wall, racking her brains to recall her words. She had been unkind, she had scolded him for kissing her. Why? She felt tears of vexation in her eyes. Why

33

had she been so unkind? That lovely, sweet man had descended from his horse, like a knight of old, had gently saluted her, and then had taken her in his arms and kissed her with such force, she could feel it still. Yet she had dismissed him with harsh words; he would never speak to her again.

Chapter Five

Bríd was walking up the drive to Castle Leighton with Molly, her closest friend, from whom she had no secrets, and who was also going to earn her shilling at the ball.

They came out from the long avenue of elms into the space before the house and stopped a moment in awe. It was a white stone mansion with rows of long windows along the front and a columned portico in the centre with a broad flight of steps running up to it. Wings curved round on either side.

As they set forward again, Bríd was about to mount the steps to the front door, when Molly tugged at her and laughed.

'Very likely we should go in the front door, Bríd! Come on, 'tis the kitchens for us.'

But Bríd took her arm and together they began to walk up the steps.

'And why shouldn't we be admitted the same as other folks? We're as good as they are, anyway!'

On the steps with the great façade towering above them, the two girls stopped, looked at each other and burst into a fit of giggles. A window opened suddenly above them, and a man leaned out.

'Are you girls for the ball? Away round to the kitchens with ye, ye *umadauns!*'

Still giggling, they made their way round past the stables and already could hear shouting, bustle and doors slamming. The kitchen door was open, and servants were hurrying out past them towards the great barn which stood away to one side, hidden from the front by the bulk of the house. Men were carrying trestle tables, and maids carried trays of pewter tankards. Molly and Bríd watched these busy preparations, and as a footman passed them they told him who they were and asked whom they should report to.

'You'd best look for Mr O'Flaherty,' he said breathlessly and hurried on.

They followed him into the kitchen. It was a large high room, hot, steamy and crowded with cooks and helpers. Bedlam reigned as far as Bríd could see. They did not dare go too far in lest they should be knocked over as women flew back and forth in their preparations.

A solid-looking woman in her fifties with an authoritative manner spied them.

'You'll be the girls from the village,' she said, coming towards them. 'Follow me.'

She led them down a corridor paved with brick, cool and dark, with rooms leading off in which Bríd caught glimpses of servants busy unpacking boxes, polishing cutlery or folding linen. The woman turned into a room with a window high up in the wall, giving a gloomy light, and threw open a tall cupboard against the wall. There were stacks of folded clothes. She gave a glance at the two girls, then rummaged down through the neatly folded and piled things till she pulled some out and held them up.

'Try them for size.'

Before long Bríd and Molly were dressed as housemaids, with starched white aprons and white caps on their heads.

'Now run upstairs and find Mr O'Flaherty, and he'll give you your duties.'

Giggling, they paraded before each other in their unaccustomed clothes, and then found their way upstairs. Bríd found the feeling of the stiff clothes exciting, and thought she looked rather good in them.

Her misgivings about coming had entirely melted in excitement at the thought of the ball, the glamour which she could share vicariously. Of course Garrett was right, but still . . . it would be fun! And if she saw Lord Harry, well, no matter.

They ran up stone steps and emerged unexpectedly into the hall, behind the front door they had nearly entered. It was plastered dazzling white, with elegant twin staircases leading up to a balcony, and beneath the staircases niches sheltering life-sized nude sculptures. Above hung an enormous crystal chandelier, and on either wall were long looking glasses. The white surfaces of the walls and ceiling were decorated with slender trailing designs. Through open doors they saw spacious rooms decorated with no less magnificence.

They both stopped for a moment, open-mouthed at the magnificence of it all. The air was thick with the noise of preparations. Servants were cleaning; furniture was being carried in and out, and carpets were rolled up; a grand piano was being pushed past; there

36

was the noise of hammering, shouts and talk, a baffling cacophony on all sides.

They looked about them, and asked again for O'Flaherty. As they were peeping into a great hall where chairs were being arranged along the wall, the floor was being washed, and a girl was laying a fire, a florid man of sixty in his shirtsleeves caught sight of them.

'Ah, girls, you're very welcome! And not a moment too soon!'

From then on for three hours they did not stop: fetching, carrying, cleaning, arranging, helping, holding decorations as they were fixed on the wall, laying fires, dusting, polishing. And all the time, Bríd looked about her in wonder at the great rooms, the elegant proportions, the lofty ceilings, the chandeliers and the swirling decorations.

As she was holding one end of the decorations in the Grand Saloon where the dancing was to be, Bríd looked out of the window and saw men setting up wooden frames on the grass in front of the house. Edward was supervising them. In a flash she remembered – fireworks! She prayed she would be in a position to see them when they went off at midnight.

Upstairs a room had been set aside for the ladies when they should arrive, where they could disrobe and prepare themselves, and everything was ready for them, a fire lit, hot water, toiletries, scents, brushes, work baskets and pincushions, all that could be wanted. Real ladies' maids would be here to lend assistance.

'Which isn't you or me, Bríd,' said Molly, as they looked wide-eyed around the room. 'Imagine the finery, and everything here so perfect.'

They were chased out by a haughty English maid, who told them curtly to 'Get orf aht of it, downstairs.'

At six they all sat round the long table in the kitchen eating their dinner of stew and potatoes, while O'Flaherty gave them his final instructions.

'Keep their glasses full, girls. And no flirting with the guests!'

As Bríd listened, she thought again of Lord Harry. She had been looking out for him all the afternoon, thinking what she would say if he noticed her. But there would be little chance of that, after the way she had spoken to him. She was still vexed with herself for her rudeness to him. She didn't care any more if he was gentry or anything else, she only wanted to make amends with him somehow.

She didn't see him. She saw the Countess once, but she didn't appear to recognise Bríd. In her distracted manner she had looked right through her.

The guests were already arriving. The men's topcoats were taken by servants, and the ladies were led upstairs to the White Room, which Bríd and Molly had discovered earlier that afternoon. Bríd was sent down to the wine store, a cold, dank room in the basement, where bottles of champagne were being opened. She thought she had got over the novelty by this time, and was feeling quite at home in Castle Leighton, but when she saw the dozen upon dozen of champagne bottles standing on the table, and two footmen busily opening them, her astonishment was renewed.

'Never tasted champagne?' One of them winked at her. 'Go on, have a sip.'

The bubbles went up her nose and made her eyes water. Soon she was taking a broad silver tray heavily laden with fizzing glasses up the narrow staircases. Servants rushed past her on both sides, making her terrified lest she be knocked and drop the tray.

Then she was in the throng of guests, as they called to each other, kissed relatives long not seen, and exchanged news. There was a buzz of excitement and anticipation.

She could hear the band tuning up, and in a moment, O'Flaherty, who now looked imposing in evening dress, announced loudly,

'Dancing will be in the Grand Saloon.'

Bríd was stationed by the doors there, and as guests came in, chattering and laughing, they took glasses from her tray. It was not long before she was hurrying down to the basement for more. In all this rush and excitement she had completely forgotten Lord Harry again. The high spirits were infectious and she felt she had never had enjoyed herself so much in her life. Molly tore past her in the opposite direction, and they laughed to each other.

'Did you ever see the like?'

She took her tray of fresh glasses and went back to the ballroom door. The guests were just lining up for the first dance. There seemed such a crowd; she counted twenty-five couples down the centre of the room. The band struck a mighty chord, and they all launched into a country dance. The music of the old tune swirled and swooped, and the lines of partners came together, parted, then whirled round, ducked in, passed and repassed, up and down. Their energy and enjoyment washed over Bríd. She would have loved to join in the dancing, but even from behind her tray of glasses she could sense the dancers' infectious fun.

Watching them, she thought again of Lord Harry, and then, even then, she saw him in the middle of the line, with the same young lady who had come to see him that day. And at the very minute she spotted him, it seemed, he turned and saw her.

She had never seen such a look of surprise on anyone's face. She read his thought instantaneously: dressed as a housemaid! She saw herself through his eyes, as a servant.

In that instant, all her pleasure in the entertainment was ashes in her mouth.

For one moment their eyes were locked. He had stopped in that one look of sheer astonishment until almost knocked over by the man behind. Forced on, he had stolen another look over his shoulder before going on up the line. But by that time, she had left the room.

Her head was in a turmoil, she felt shame and embarrassment. What must he think to see her there, dressed as a housemaid? She should never have agreed to come. Their positions were suddenly and cruelly reversed. Before, she had been his nurse, she had fed him and he had depended on her, looked up to her, thanked her. And in the lane she had felt herself his equal. But now what was she? A housemaid. In a burst of fury with herself, she vowed that never again would she be seen in servant's clothes. Never. She turned quickly and moved away into another room. She was angry, shaking, and irritated with this tray of glasses. What could she do? She was doomed to stand there like a great fool while the gentry came and went past her ignoring her, except to take a glass or put an empty one on the tray.

She was in the card room. The elderly folk were arranged at their tables and whist was in full swing. Chatter flew back and forth across the tables, county gossip. Bríd heard none of it; again and again she saw the astonished look on Harry's face. What must he have thought? Why had she come?

She was in the billiards room. The atmosphere was thick with cigar smoke. A crowd of dragoon officers were gathered round the table watching a game. They greeted her with loud cries and helped themselves to fresh glasses. They wanted to talk to her, chaff her, asked her her name. She lied. None of them should know her name. One of them put his arm round her waist. With her hands full there was nothing she could do, but she snapped at him so fiercely that he was deflated like a little boy, and looked apologetic. The others only laughed louder. She went out again into the great hall.

Her tray was nearly empty. She went downstairs, through the cool corridors below, to the wine room. She could breathe awhile. She set down the tray, leaning on the sideboard, staring at the rows of empty bottles. What could she do? And the answer was, nothing. She had to stay, to see it out. Maybe they could give her a job down here, washing dishes or something.

O'Flaherty rushed into the wine store.

'Come on, Bríd, daydreaming? They'll be having the fireworks soon, and afterwards we're serving supper. Up you go!'

She turned toward him in panic.

'Oh, Mr O'Flaherty! I beg you, could you not give me a job here below? Washing dishes or something?'

O'Flaherty was busy pulling bottles from racks, his back to her. He didn't seem to hear her. She stood imploring him to his back, helpless.

'What? No, you're serving supper. Up you go now, and set out the cutlery.'

In a fury of helpless embarrassment, she ran up the stone steps again, through the hall and into the Blue Room, where the supper was being laid out.

There were piles of plates to arrange and cutlery to set out for the guests. As she hurried round the tables, all the guests crowded to the windows to see the fireworks. It had got very hot by this time, with the fires, the dancing and all the candles, and the long windows had been thrown open for a few minutes to let in some air.

There was a mighty *whoosh* and she saw over their heads a sky rocket shooting into the air. 'Aaah!' went up from everyone, quite involuntarily. She couldn't help herself crying out with the others, drawn to the magic of the firework display.

The guests were seated round the long tables. The underbutler was giving Bríd orders. She had a bottle of wine and must fill the glasses. It was a long, slender, green bottle. She had already seen Lord Harry; he was sitting with that girl, that Miss Richardson. Bríd's feet were lead, her limbs had no strength. Why was she here in this hell? She felt such a tall, angular, awkward fool. But there was no way out. The bottle was in her hand, she was leaning in past the guests as they talked and laughed and gesticulated to each other. She was drawing nearer to him.

He had seen her, and was looking at her again. He must be used to her in her parlour maid's costume by this time, she thought. But he kept glancing at her as he talked to his companion. Miss Richardson was talking loud and fast, full of high spirits. She was wearing a beautiful pink and white gown, and there were flowers in her hair. She looked vivacious and her eyes flashed. Bríd saw it all.

Why had Mr O'Flaherty put her here? She felt sick. She looked round the elegant room, bright, with candles, noise and laughter, and in her head she heard nothing but a scream of silence.

She was behind him.

'Wine, sir?'

It was a croak, barely a whisper. But he'd heard her. He looked round, into her face. For a moment she couldn't resist his look, and was staring close into his eyes. Yes, that was him. She recognised

40

every feature, everything she had studied as he had lain unconscious on her pillow. She pulled her eyes away.

'Thank you.'

It was a fresh bottle. Full. She leaned forward, holding out the bottle across the table towards his glass. Her hand was shaking as she tipped the bottle. The wine came out with unexpected force, past the glass and across the gleaming table cloth. Wine everywhere. She seemed to go to pieces.

'Oh, Lord!'

She looked round. What could she –? She lifted the corner of her long, starched apron, screwing it up, and leaned over. But Lord Harry was already there with his napkin, dabbing at the puddle of wine on the table.

'It's nothing. Please don't worry.'

Miss Richardson was staring at her.

Bríd couldn't stand any more. She set down the bottle on the table by his side and hurried out of the room. Almost blind, she raced down the stone back stairs into the kitchens. Nothing mattered any more. If she could only get out! She could feel herself undoing her apron as she ran. In the maids' room were her clothes where she'd left them over a chair. The room was empty. She threw off the starchy maid's costume, pulled on her own things, fumbling with the laces of her boots, snatching her blue cloak, and was running through the kitchen and out into the night.

Chapter Six

Never again would he see her in maid's clothes. Never would she go into service. Never! Strange that until that evening she had not even thought about it. At first it had been such fun. Fun! Herself in that starched dress – fun? Waves of irritation and shame washed through her. That glance of astonishment he had given her in the middle of the dance – she would never forget it.

She could not sleep. Garrett had been right again. There could never be meeting, friendship or understanding between masters and servants, landlords and tenants. Uncle Patsy pulled his forelock, Aunt Nora bobbed a curtsy, the Gentry smiled, waved, made fatuous remarks and rode on. Better to get rid of them. Better for her. Her humiliation had been complete, she would never forget it until the end of her days, that moment when, as in a nightmare, the wine had shot out of the bottle across the tablecloth. Because she'd been making sheep's eyes at the young master. She was mad. Mad!

What was she to say to Patsy and Nora in the morning? What did it matter? She had a little money saved up in a drawer. She could present them with a shilling. They'd never know.

But they would know. Molly would ask where she'd gone. The story would get out. She'd spilled wine on the table and then fled in disgrace. Shameful. Ridiculous.

She turned in bed, staring up into the darkness, thinking how Garrett would smile when he heard. He would look into her eyes, understand her – and despise her.

Because what was most shameful, most ridiculous of all, was that the young master had kissed her, had told her she was beautiful, and she in the depth of her folly allowed herself to believe him, though she would not admit it to herself at first. It had pleased her to see him and hear him, and she had accepted his attentions. Most shameful, most ridiculous. Then he had seen her in her maid's clothes, and she

42

had seen him as he had seen her, and then later, she had spilled the wine, and had seen him watching her, and that young lady looking at her as if she had grossly intruded where she had no place to be.

She could not sleep. What was she going to do? Marry Garrett? Maybe go away, go into service on another farm? A lot of girls did it. She'd have to make up her mind sooner or later. Garrett wanted an answer. So did Nora.

She remembered the house, the lights, the gaiety, the elegance, the chandeliers. It had been wonderful, a revelation. It had been food for her soul; she had expanded into it, felt at home there. But a fool's paradise, she knew; no place for her, never would be.

She slept late. At last she dragged herself from her bed, feeling low. She showed her shilling. Patsy was kind, wanted to hear about the ball, about the gentry and who was there. He seemed to know about them all: what they were doing, what they owned. She was forced to recount everything, making it sound like glamour, fun and excitement. As she satisfied him, she ran the parallel story through her mind: the humiliation, the confusion and shame, the misery.

They sat round the table, the three of them, eating porridge. Nora was pleased Bríd had earned some money. She might be able to do it again. Always useful, always came in handy. Good to get in with the castle. Bríd dreaded the thought. Do it again? Go there again? She never could. Never wanted to see it or the family, or have anything to do with them again. She prayed she might be left in peace, never to be troubled or tormented like that again.

Later she went out with Uncle Patsy and helped to bring turnips in for the cows. Life was back to normal.

That afternoon there was a knock at the door. She opened it. Lord Harry was standing there. Behind him stood a jaunting car with the Countess and another woman in it. Harry's face was expressionless.

'Is Mrs Byrne at home?'

Nora was behind her, wiping her hands on a cloth, bobbing a curtsy. Bríd was dreaming. It couldn't be happening.

'Mrs Byrne. The Countess and I have been calling at a few of the cabins in the village. Seeing after tenants' welfare, how everyone's getting through the winter. The Countess has been kind enough to bring a few things –'

They were coming into the kitchen. Bríd closed the door behind them. Harry was very smart in a long overcoat and leather gloves. The Countess was in a bottle-green coat over a wide grey skirt, and wore a bonnet trimmed with artificial flowers. There was another woman with her. There seemed a gross disparity between their dainty elegance and the rough-cast surroundings, the flagstone floor, the broad hearth and its dull peat fire. Bríd was floundering in her mind to account for this visit, but it was quite simple: charity. And as the woman was unpacking some parcels on the table, Bríd recognised the remains from the last night's supper. The Earl had sent them out to get rid of the leftovers.

And they had chosen to visit this humble home. Nora was curtsying, keeping up the pretence. Bríd felt a burning anger at the impertinence, the arrogance that carried them in here, graciously condescending to the lower orders. She had nothing to say. Nora fussed round to find the best chair for the Countess. They declined a cup of tea. They couldn't stay long, had other visits to make. Bríd understood perfectly.

Lord Harry wouldn't look at her, and she could scarcely bring herself to look at him. It gave her a sudden burning pain in her inside when she caught a glimpse of his profile as he bent over his mother to say something.

Nora was fulsome in her gratitude for the presents of cold meat and the pies. Mr Byrne would enjoy those, she said. She knew how the Earl was concerned for the welfare of his tenants. It did him credit, sure it did. There was many a home in the village where his health would be drunk this night. He was a blessing to the tenantry, a father to his people. She wished him long life. And his son – a credit to his father, she wished him every success in the election, though she had no doubt he would get in. Wasn't he the easy-spoken gentleman entirely? And the young gentleman, Lord Harry here, why, what a soldier he would make, to be sure. She could just see him in his uniform, a dashing young officer, would turn the heads of half the girls in the county.

Nora seemed to have an endless store of this rubbish. Couldn't she see how she humiliated herself, performing like this?

The Countess was getting up. Duty had been done, and they were going. There was a scraping of the chair, and the woman had folded the napkins back in the baskets. The Countess turned towards the door, Nora close in attendance. Harry turned away from them and was looking round the room. He saw the sampler framed on the wall. He crossed to it.

'What a pretty piece of work. Is this yours, Miss Flynn?'

Unthinking, she crossed to him, and saw in his face the most intensely anguished expression.

'Send me word where we may meet,' he breathed, and held the look in her eyes for a second, before he turned back to the door.

44

In that second, she felt the strength drain from her limbs; he had sucked the soul from her body with one glance. She couldn't speak.

The Countess had turned in the doorway and was making anodyne remarks in her vague manner. Harry was beside her, pulling on his gloves, and they were going through the door.

Nora and Bríd stood in the doorway and watched as Harry saw his mother and the other woman safely stowed in the jaunting car, and rugs wrapped round them, then he took the reins. He turned back.

'Well, goodbye, Mrs Byrne, goodbye, Miss Flynn.'

Nora was bobbing a curtsy. Bríd couldn't take her eyes from his face. He showed no expression. He turned and whipped up the mare, and they trotted up the *bohreen*.

She only knew one thing. She would meet him if it was at the end of the earth. All her doubts, her embarrassments, her confusion, all her misgivings, all Garrett's words had vanished in an instant.

She and Nora returned indoors. Nora stopped, looking down at the piece of cold beef and the pies on the table.

'Largesse.'

'What?' Bríd turned towards her.

Nora's face was black. Suddenly she brought her hand down on the table with a blow that made it shake.

'Every crumb of it bought with shame and humiliation.'

Bríd was astonished to see the look on Nora's face. For a moment it drove every thought of Harry from her mind. She stared at Nora. Nora was silent for a moment, staring down at the table. Then she seemed to take a grip on herself. She fetched a plate from the dresser and placed the meat and pies on it.

'Well, no matter. 'Tis only a little of our own returned to us. Have you nothing to do, girl?'

She looked angrily at Bríd.

Bríd was shaken momentarily.

'Are the chickens to be fed or not?'

Without saying anything, Bríd went out into the darkening afternoon.

She never could understand Nora. But she did understand the bitterness with which she had accepted the Countess's charity. And the strength of Nora's feeling made Bríd feel horribly guilty as she thought of what she planned.

Because she would see Harry again if it killed her. It was one certain thing in her mind. Nothing would hinder her, not Nora, not Garrett, not the thought of what people would say if they heard, not jeers or scorn or poisonous tattle.

Her first thought then was – where? When? And how would she send him word?

As she scattered grain among the squawking and clucking chickens in the little barn behind the cabin, she began to see clearly the objections, problems and dangers. Wasn't she supposed to be walking out with Garrett? He wanted to marry her, it was understood through all the village. And if she was taking a little time to make up her mind, that was allowable in a young woman. Garrett was a good match, she had better not forget it. True, he was a man of intense convictions, but there was nothing wrong with that – in fact, it was thoroughly honourable, and if he went on at length about the wrongs they all laboured under, well, she agreed with everything he said.

If she was going to meet another man while still ostensibly walking out with Garrett, it had to be in deadly secret. But as she sifted through the possibilities, she realised she would have to take Molly into her confidence. She needed her friend as confidante, ally, alibi. Molly could write. So could Bríd, but her handwriting was a scrawl, she could never let him see it. Molly must write the message, that was clear.

Discovery was not the only danger. What was she thinking of, to meet the Earl's son in secret? It could only lead to one thing, couldn't it? It was the oldest story – the village girl and the fine gentleman, a tumble in the hay, and then the baby. Her lover riding off on his fine horse, and she repenting at leisure, her chance of a good marriage gone for ever. Maybe some old fellow with half his teeth gone, some old miser with his money locked in a tin box, that would be her portion. Who else would take a girl with a baby at the breast? She would be damaged goods.

For a moment a cold shudder ran through her as she thought of this.

And could she trust him? He seemed to descend upon her from a great height, unexpectedly, tell her she was beautiful or kiss her, then be whisked off again. He came and went in ways that were inexplicable to her. How could he want to see her, after what had happened last night? After she had splashed the wine all over the table? And dressed up in all that starch? She didn't understand.

She only knew one thing. That when she saw him, when she looked at his face, she felt the strength go from her, felt her will ebb away, could think of nothing but him.

Chapter Seven

'Now, Larry.'

Bríd took him by the arm. He was an old fellow, a bit weak in the head, but he could remember instructions and he was devoted to Bríd.

'You're to watch out for his lordship. Wait around by the stables. And wait till he's alone.'

She undid a button of her dress and took a letter from her bosom.

'This is for Lord Harry.' She looked intently into his face. 'Can you remember now?'

The old man stared mesmerised into her face.

'Trust me, Miss Bríd. I'll see his lordship gets it. And mum's the word. Never fear.' With an exaggerated gesture, he put his finger to his lips and gave her a slow wink.

'There'll be a penny for you when you return.'

She watched him as he hurried off up the lane, a shambling wreck, destroyed by drink long since.

She looked across at Molly, who had been listening. Molly looked worried.

The letter had been very simple. She would wait for him by the Fairy Ring that afternoon or, if it was raining, tomorrow afternoon, and so on.

Harry saw two girls appear over the rim of the hill, and for a moment he was thrown; then he saw that one of them was Bríd. They came up to him.

'Lord Harry, this is my friend Molly. She has come to keep me company.'

Harry hadn't expected this, but he did his best to be polite. However, Bríd and Molly were in charge of the situation.

'What a lovely horse, Lord Harry! Isn't she a darling? Wouldn't you maybe let me hold her bridle?' said Molly, and soon Harry found himself alone with Bríd and they were strolling along a path across the field. Molly remained by the standing stones with Mignonette.

'Will she –?'

Bríd looked at him for a moment, and spoke in a gentle and reassuring way that made him relax at once.

'Sure, won't Molly take care of your mare, Harry?'

'Bríd . . .' He paused. 'I love your name. I know it sounds silly, but I say it over and over to myself. It's unusual –'

'What's unusual about it? It's very usual indeed. Wasn't St Bríd the companion of St Patrick himself?'

'Oh, God, Bríd, I'm glad you came.'

Speechlessness came on him. All sorts of thoughts crowded into his mind, but none of them could find expression on his tongue. But then she took hold of his hand and in a surge of joy he raised hers to his lips and kissed it reverently.

'I've thought of nothing but you since – since I first saw you. Everywhere I've been, you know, anywhere at all, I seemed to see you and hear your voice.'

They stared into each other's eyes. Bríd swallowed and, with an effort, turned away. They walked on for a while in silence, but she still held his hand.

They came through a copse of trees to a small river, running over polished white stones, and stood looking down into its clear, eddying depths.

'This is where Milligan once caught Uncle Patsy with a salmon – just down there, where the river is shallow. Often the fish can't get over the stones when there's been a dry winter, and they lie among them, struggling to get up the river, and helpless there on the stones.'

'I suppose you must know every inch of these woods and fields, these streams and hedgerows. You must have played here when you were little.'

There was silence. Then Harry remembered.

'But I forgot. Mr and Mrs Byrne aren't your parents.'

'No, they're not my own parents.'

'Are you from this part then?'

'Oh, sure. Haven't I always lived in the village? But my mother died when I was three.'

'How did she die?'

''Twas in childbirth. He would have been my little brother, but God took them both. Then my father died when I was eleven, and left me to Uncle Patsy and Aunt Nora to take care of, them having no children of their own, God have mercy.'

Later, they were walking back through the trees; Harry could see the hill before them, and soon they would be back among the standing stones. He turned to Bríd.

'Bríd, shall we meet again?'

'If you like.'

She looked into his face.

Gently their lips touched – but then she drew away with a bewitching smile.

'No more now, Master Harry.'

'Bríd –'

'You're such a powerful man, I'm quite in awe of you.'

'Bríd – I say, when shall we meet again?'

He caught her hand. She looked at him.

'Thursday maybe.'

'Thursday it is. But I say, Bríd, do you have to bring Miss Molly with you?'

'And would you have me come on my own, Lord Harry? What would the village say to see me walking off up the hill all by myself?'

'The village?'

She sighed.

''Tis little you know of Ireland, that's sure. Don't you know the whole village itself will want to know every step I take? And if they thought I was walking out with yourself from the big house –'

'Well, what if they did?'

'Oh, 'twould never do.'

'Why?'

She shook her head slowly.

'It could only mean one thing, don't you see?'

'No, I don't see.'

'Then I can't explain at all,' she said quietly and took his hand, and they continued walking up the hill.

Molly was leaning with her back to one of the great stones, still holding the bridle as Mignonette cropped at the grass.

'I want to give Miss Molly something for her trouble, but I'm afraid she wouldn't accept money. What could I give her?'

'Harry, you don't have to give her anything at all. Sure, isn't she my friend? And wouldn't I do as much for her?'

A pale and watery sun looked down on them as they stood together looking down across the lake, dotted with little tree-covered islands. It was a mild winter afternoon.

'But still, a gift, you know. Perhaps something, I don't know, something for her trousseau. Isn't that what you girls have?'

49

'And how would she explain it to her mother – did you ever think of that? "How do you like my silk gown, Mother? Lord Harry gave it to me."'

Harry was silent.

'So I could never give you anything either?'

'No more you could.'

She wanted to know everything about him. She wanted to know most of all about that Miss Richardson. But that would have to wait. She started with his childhood.

'I went to Harrow. It's a school outside London. I wasn't much good at school, actually, not much of a scholar, better at games. I love cricket. And riding. Hunting most of all. That's why I love coming over here. I'm never so happy as when I'm on a horse.'

He paused and looked away across the rain-sodden fields, across the little copses, the lanes, towards the distant Curlew Mountains.

'Do you know what I love most? It's that time when dusk is falling on a crisp winter's evening, when we're returning from the hunt and the riders are all straggling along the road. I'm walking Mignonette, tired, silent, at peace after a tearing good ride, and I look across the fields as the thick, tangled hedges sink into a purple gloom, and there's a delicate, gauzy mist, ghostlike, across the meadows, when the sun has set and the western sky darkens into night. I've often thought how capital it would be if one were a painter and could capture that magical and mysterious atmosphere.'

'You're a poet, Master Harry,' she said, looking at him with a smile.

'You'd better not let my father hear you say that.'

'Why?'

'I don't think he'd approve. He's a bit of a tartar.'

'Are you afraid of him?'

'That's not a very fair question. I respect him, you know.' He paused, embarrassed by her question. 'Anyway, as I was saying, I only wanted to be with horses, so I thought I'd try and get into the cavalry. Father got me into Sandhurst.'

She couldn't wait any longer. 'Harry . . .'

She paused.

'Yes?'

'When you were with us, after your fall, there was a young lady came to visit you –'

'Miss Richardson.'

'Yes.'

'What of her?'

'Nothing.'

He looked at her, then laughed. 'Brid, I do believe you're jealous. I've known her since I was a child.'

She pulled her hand away from his and looked away. 'Whenever I see you, she's with you. You were dancing with her.'

'You don't know Stella.'

She felt a slight pang as he mentioned her Christian name.

'She'd no sooner arrived than she'd put me down for the first three dances. I didn't have much choice.' He laughed. 'Perhaps she's sweet on me.'

'Perhaps you're sweet on her.'

He took her by her arms. 'Are you mad? I think of no one but you. When I first wake up I think of you, and when I'm falling asleep. It's only you. I love you, Brid.'

'When did you first know you loved me?'

'When did you first know you loved me?'

'No, you tell me first.'

They were standing close together with his greatcoat over their shoulders. They were at the edge of a copse, looking out across the fields. Harry began.

'It was when you spilled the wine.'

She looked at him horrified.

'Never!'

'It's true,' he said quietly. 'I watched you. Been watching you all the time. You looked so – so dignified in all that starch, as if you weren't a housemaid at all but, I don't know, a great actress in costume, tall and proud. But I could see you were hating every minute of it. All those strange people, everything new to you. I knew you'd never poured a bottle of wine in your life.'

He looked at her full of sympathy.

'I could see everything you were thinking. How wretched you felt. Then when you leaned over me and looked at me, it tore my heart out. And then you shot the wine all over the table. It honestly didn't matter tuppence. Servants do it all the time. But I could see how mortified you were, I felt your distress, and my heart went right to you. I loved you at that moment.'

She reached across and kissed him in silence.

'When did you know you loved me?'

'Oh,' she sighed, 'it was simple. I just loved you the moment I first saw you. You were lying unconscious on the table, with a terrible bruise on your head. And Nora said your neck might be broken. I was so afraid. Then later they put you into my bed, and after they had all gone, I came in and looked at you again while you were still unconscious. I looked down at you, and you were so – I can't explain – you were just so precious, I wanted to hold and touch and kiss every part of you, watch you for ever, be part of you for ever. I can't explain. I just knew.'

'Bríd, why do you call it a fairy ring?'
  'Do you not know about the fairies?'
  'I'm afraid not. Do you?'
  'Sure, doesn't everyone? The fairies are the good people. Aren't they there all the time, all around us, watching us? The Fairy Ring is where they come at night and dance. And the fairy fiddler sits on the highest stone, you see, and plays for them.'
  'So you wouldn't come here at night?'
  'No one, no one at all, would come to the Fairy Ring at night, not even Uncle Patsy, him that's often out at night. He'd pass by at a long distance, sure. You'll sometimes maybe hear their music, far off, but don't you go near.'
  'Are the fairies good people?'
  'They are – if you are good to them. They'll leave you alone so long as you cause them no harm, and maybe leave out a bit and a sup for them at night, and take care of your house and keep it neat and clean, the way they know you're good people and mean no harm at all. And sometimes, if a little old woman should call and ask for a bit of meal and salt, for to make a few scones, well, then be sure and give it her, for she's surely one of them.'
  'And what happens if you're not good to them?'
  Bríd thought for a while.
  'There was Liam O'Conor in the village, him that's drunk all times, and lives in a terrible way, and shows no respect at all. His ass went lame.'
  'But Bríd, how can you be sure that was the fairies' doing?'
  'No doubt of it at all. 'Twas a fine ass, that cost him one pound four shillings at Boyle Fair not a year since. There was no cause for it to sicken, only Liam that is a bachelor man, and lives alone and has no one to care for him or watch over him, and has maybe no one will teach him such things, went out last November and cut down that old thorn tree in his field that was a holy tree to the fairies, though all the village told him, and since that time had no luck at all. And his ass lame that was a good strong ass before.'
  Harry didn't know what to say to this.
  'And there was the woman over in Balintober, her baby boy was stolen by the fairies.'

'Was it?'

'Baby boys is what they want, all times. Isn't that why we dress them in girl's clothes till they're grown a way? You must be careful not to let them out of your sight while they're small. You must watch them night and day and be sure to lock your door safe at night. Sometimes, you know, you can hear the fairies pass at night; when you lie in bed, you'll hear the beat of their wings.'

'Really, have you heard them?'

'I have. Many times.'

They stared away across the lake and the little islands, each lost in thought, only holding hands and feeling all the time an ebbing and flowing between them of feelings they could not easily describe.

'Harry, tell me about London. It must be a grand place, I'm thinking. All the fine ladies and gentlemen, all the fine shops and the theatres and palaces and the carriages in the park.'

'Yes, I should say. Well, you should see Piccadilly or Regent Street. There's so many people you can hardly get along the pavement. The streets are so crowded with carriages and drays and carts and vans, they're sometimes blocked solid. Can't move.'

'And the fine shops?'

'Well, there are some very elegant shops, I must say, the most beautiful things – for the ladies, I mean, bonnets and gowns, and shoes and ribbons, that sort of thing.'

'I'd love to see it.'

'I'd love to take you there.'

'Would you?'

'I'd love nothing more in the whole world.'

'And I'd love nothing more in the whole world.'

She paused.

'And the ladies and gentlemen in their fine carriages in the park . . .'

'Oh yes, we go riding in the park. Mother has her carriage, and sometimes I go with her too on a Sunday morning.'

'Do you?'

'Yes, I used to, when I was home from Sandhurst.'

'Do you have your own house in London?'

'Of course we do.' Harry laughed. 'In King Street, St James's. Family's always been there, since, oh, I don't know when, since the family began, I should think. Very old house, a bit dark. I like it over here better, myself.'

'Do you?'

'Oh, yes. It's cleaner, more open, life's easier, I can ride all the time. Sometimes I think I'm only happy when I'm riding.'

He looked at her.

'I used to think that, I mean. Now there's you . . .'

He looked into her eyes. They kissed gently, barely brushing their lips together.

'Now there's you, everything's different.'

'Yes.'

She stared into his eyes and then slowly pulled herself away and around, looking out again at the lake below them.

'And would you rather be here than in London?'

'I would.'

'Oh, but I should love to see London. I should so love to see it. Tell me something else, about the – I don't know, the palaces and the theatres . . .'

'Well, we're not far from Buckingham Palace. Sometimes I go for a walk in St James's Park. I saw the Queen drive by not so long ago, she's all in mourning still. Not far from us is St James's Palace, that's older than Buckingham Palace, and then there's Marlborough House, where the Prince and Princess of Wales live.'

'It must be grand. And the fine theatres and the opera house?'

'Yes, the opera house. I only went there once. You should see the press of carriages, the ladies in their fine dresses and diamonds, and everything a blaze of lights – chandeliers and candles everywhere. It's as light as day. And then in the opera all the singers and dancers so beautifully dressed.'

'I should love to see it.'

Another afternoon they climbed a hill to a strange old stone construction: one great flat stone, nearly ten feet across, lying upon two upright stones. Harry had never seen anything like it.

'It's a giant's grave,' said Bríd.

Harry was no longer surprised at anything Bríd said.

'I wonder who he was,' he said.

'Oh, I don't know, but they say that hereabouts Oisin landed when he returned from Tir na n'Og.'

'What was that?'

'Tir na n'Og, that's the land of everlasting youth, where the people never grow old but stay always young and beautiful, and sport and play all day long, and never have any kind of work to do.'

'And who was Oisin?'

'He was a prince – the son of Finn McCool, many years ago. He was out hunting one day, they say, and met this beautiful girl in a long white gown, with beautiful long blonde hair and a golden band round her hair, and she was leading a beautiful white horse, and she

54

said, "How would you like to marry me, and come with me to the land of Tir na n'Og, and never grow old, but always feasting and hunting and all kinds of sport and play?"

'And Oisin said he would – naturally, wouldn't you? – so they mounted on the horse together and it carried them away over the land until they came to the sea, and then they flew up through the air, away till they came to this beautiful land, where the sun was shining and there was all kinds of flowers and beautiful trees, and everywhere young people, you know, enjoying themselves at all kinds of pastimes. So they stayed there and were married and happy together all day long, until one day, when they'd been there maybe three weeks, Oisin said to Niam, that was his wife, he was getting homesick for his own people; he was very happy, of course, living with her, but only would it not be possible to pay a little visit home, to see how they were? Niam said of course and gave him her white horse, only she said while he was home in Ireland he must on no account get off the horse and touch the ground.

'So Oisin mounted on the horse and set off and came to Ireland, but as he rode over it he couldn't recognise anything at all. Everywhere he went was different, and he got very confused, not being able to find his way anywhere or see anyone he knew. At last he saw some men in a field trying to move a boulder. But they weren't like any men he'd ever seen. They were small, contemptible, shrivelled little men, with no strength in them at all. And they couldn't move the boulder.

'Well, Oisin stopped by them to ask where the Hill of Allen was, and where was Finn McCool and the Fianna. And these men were very puzzled indeed, and said they'd heard of Finn McCool, but sure hadn't he been dead three hundred years now? Then Oisin was even more mystified.

'But as he watched he saw they would never move the boulder, because they were small and weak, but to him it would be nothing at all, so he thought he'd just lend a hand, and he leaned down from his horse and just gave it a flick of his wrist and it turned over. But as he leaned over, the saddle girth of his horse snapped. He fell to the ground, and the moment he touched the ground, sure wasn't he transformed into an old, old man, with white hair and a long white beard, so old and weak he couldn't even stand, only lay there on the ground. And then he realised that the time that seemed so short in the land of youth, only three weeks, was really three hundred years here in Ireland. They took him to St Patrick and he told him the whole story.'

Her voice, low and musical, sank into silence.

'They were so happy together that three hundred years passed as if it were no more than three weeks. Oh, Bríd, I could listen to you for ever.'

Later that afternoon they walked back to the Fairy Ring, their arms round each other, exchanging kisses.

The election came and went. Uncle Patsy voted for Lord Leighton, and he was duly elected Member for Roscommon. Garrett continued to call; he and Bríd walked out together, and she was amazed to hear herself talking to Garrett for all the world as if Harry did not exist. She felt guilty and confused when she was alone. She was unable to make sense of the situation, could not see how it would end. It was if Harry and Garrett inhabited two worlds so utterly removed from one another that there was no way they could ever be made to meet. She didn't dare imagine Harry would ask her to marry him, it was out of the question. Equally out of the question was the idea that she could ever love anyone else. How it was all to end she couldn't think. She knew it was madness, and might easily – must certainly – wreck her life, but she could not act any other way. It had to be.

One afternoon it suddenly began to rain, and they took shelter in a quaint little stone building with a thatched roof, which seemed to grow out of the earth in the corner of a field by a wood. The stones were round and white, worn smooth with time, and the thatch was a great mass of old, half-rotted straw, settled down to a comfortable shape. The hut was half-full of hay, and as they stood in the doorway, which had no door to it, and looked up at the darkening sky, Harry thought they could light a fire in one end of the hut where a space under the eaves would supply a kind of chimney. Gathering straw and some turves of peat he found, he built a fire. The rain continued to fall, so they sat in the straw while their fire crackled and burned in a merry cheerful way.

The world outside seemed remote, and their world reduced to this little warm room, the fire before them and the sky lowering outside.

Harry turned to Bríd and, without speaking, they lay in the straw beneath his greatcoat and made love to one another, and knew they pledged themselves to each other for all eternity. Beyond the door the rain pattered down in the darkening afternoon, and there before them the little fire, reduced from its crackling, glowed like a comfortable winking eye, as gusts of air from the door caused it to glow brighter for a moment and then to die down again.

Afterwards Harry could only lie beside her, leaning on one elbow, and look into her face.

56

'I shall love you all my life.'

There were tears in her eyes as he spoke.

'Oh, Harry, my darling,' She threw her arms round his neck and held him tightly. 'Oh, my love!'

The rain had set in, and they walked back to where Molly was waiting patiently in the rain. Harry's greatcoat was round Bríd's shoulders. He went with them right to the top of the *bohreen* before he could tear himself away, and tears were pouring down Bríd's cheeks as they parted. They no longer thought to hide their love, and Molly, though standing a little apart, could feel the strength of the passion between them as they kissed. Then she and Bríd stumbled down the *bohreen* in the muddy, rutted tracks. Outside the door of the cottage, Bríd must stop and, still in the rain, breathe deeply, wiping her face and pulling back bedraggled strands of hair. Before going in, she took Molly's hand and pressed it silently in gratitude.

Chapter Eight

'So all your afternoon walks with Molly, just an excuse to meet your fancy man, eh?'

It was the following afternoon. Bríd had been down into the village to see Molly. By the time she returned, it was getting dark and had come on to rain.

Nora was confronting her across the room. Patsy was there too. Bríd was too surprised to speak.

'Don't lie Bríd. I know all about it. All the time you were walking out with Garrett, you've been seeing Lord Harry in secret. You've been deceiving me, my girl. By God, you're a fool! What did you think would ever come of it, eh? He'll take his pleasure, and you'll be ruined.'

She crossed to her, and looked into her face.

'He hasn't seduced you, has he?'

Bríd looked at Nora straight. Suddenly Nora took her by the arms and shook her.

'Answer me!'

'Isn't what I do my own affair, Aunt Nora?'

'Your own affair! Answer my question! Has he lain with you?'

Bríd moved away past her to the window.

'No.'

Nora crossed her arms.

'The sooner we get you married to Garrett, the better. You're not fit to be left alone. My God, if he should get wind of it! We'd be the three biggest fools in Ballyglin.'

Bríd, still looking out of the window, interrupted her in a low voice.

'Aunt Nora, how did you know?'

'He came here hunting for you. He's going off to London tomorrow.'

'Tomorrow!'

'He's off, my girl, and 'twould be best for you if you forgot all about him.'

Bríd turned. 'Tomorrow?' she repeated, as if unable to make sense of it. 'Did he leave no message for me?'

Patsy looked questioningly at Nora, and there was an awkward pause. 'He said he was leaving tomorrow, and sends his kind regards.'

'Kind regards?' said Bríd incredulously. 'Was there nothing else, no other message?'

There was a slight pause.

Bríd suddenly burst out, across the room, 'Did he say nothing else? Nothing at all?'

Patsy could not bear to see her anguish. He went to Bríd but she evaded him. She seemed to have grown, to have become strong and hard.

'Don't lie to me, Aunt Nora. Did he say nothing else?'

'Lie?'

Bríd scorched them with her rage and anguish.

'Was there nothing else? No message?'

Patsy turned helplessly to Nora, then looked again to Bríd. She felt a wild, reckless violence within her.

'Aunt Nora, are you telling me on your oath that he came here this day and left me no other message?'

Nora looked at her for a moment, then, without speaking, she crossed to the fire and placed a piece of turf on it.

'He sent his love,' said Patsy timidly.

Nora turned angrily.

'Love! What talk is that of love? Don't talk daft to the girl. He's gone, my girl, and you had better understand that.'

Bríd could barely take in what she had heard. Harry was going and there was no farewell, no letter, nothing? Everything between them, all their meetings, all their talking together, and most of all the afternoon in the little hut, all gone, all lost, and nothing left to her? She had given him everything she had, and he was gone, and had left her nothing?

Her head was a whirl; her throat felt swollen, as if she would choke. She pulled on her cloak and went out of the door. It was still raining and nearly dark. She didn't care.

It was not possible Harry should go off like that. It was a trick, and Aunt Nora had set it up to separate them. But how did she know about Harry? If Harry had come to the cabin? Why should he come? She was supposed to be meeting him on Friday. What reason could he have for coming, if not to say goodbye because he had been suddenly called away?

She became more and more afraid. It seemed to be true.

She had to know. She was in agony. She must know now, and that meant a message to Harry now, tonight. It was nearly dark. Everyone was indoors. She walked quickly down into the village. The cabins huddled darkly on either side in the gathering gloom. Rain was falling steadily. No matter.

Larry must help her. She had no time to write a letter. He must take a message by word – better still, she would go with him. Now. Yes. Larry would say something – 'There's a person to see Lord Harry', something like that – and she would be outside. Then at least she would know. He wouldn't mind her coming to him. It must be.

She knocked. It was an old cabin, half tumbledown, little better than a cowshed.

'Larry?'

There was no one there.

Where could he be?

Mrs Carruthers's Stores and Bar. It must be.

But what a time to go! Oh, God, if there were others there, what would they think?

She hurried along. It was still raining.

It was nearly dark. She opened the door.

It was even darker inside. A candle. Four of five men sitting on a bench, a smell of tobacco and stale beer.

'Larry?'

She was in the doorway, didn't want to go in too far.

'Miss Bríd?' He shuffled across to her.

'Larry, get your coat, there's an urgent message you must run this minute.'

'Now, Miss Bríd?'

'This minute. 'Tis most urgent.' She sounded strict.

In a few minutes they were hurrying up the *bohreen* together. They passed Patsy's cabin and carried on. Both knew the path in the darkness.

'Where are we going, Miss Bríd?'

'Don't ask questions, Larry. Only hurry.'

It was nearly an hour before they drew near to Castle Leighton. They were drenched to the skin.

Above them was the shape of the house, and here, nearby, the stables.

'Now, Larry,' said Bríd, 'listen carefully. You must go to the kitchens. Enquire after Lord Harry, and then say there's a person – person,

60

mind – has a most urgent message for him, must be delivered to himself in person. Have you got that?'

'Oh yes, Miss Bríd.'

'In you go now. I'll wait for you here.'

He disappeared in the darkness, and she stood in the gateway of the stables, sheltering from the rain.

At least she would soon know. Harry would be able to clear up the confusion.

As she waited, she cooled a little. What was she doing here? She could have waited till the morning. Sent a letter by Larry. Why had she panicked like this? She began to curse herself for her folly. What had those men in Mrs Carruthers' bar thought? What would they be telling their friends tomorrow? A most urgent message? Could she trust Larry to keep quiet? Doubts crowded upon her.

There was a sound. It was Larry.

'What did he say?'

'Lord Harry's gone to England, Miss Bríd. He's gone to join the army.'

It was true.

She was hoarse. 'Gone? When?'

'This evening, Miss Bríd.'

She couldn't think.

'What else did they say?'

'Nothing.'

Was it possible? How could it be? He had come to the cabin, it was true, but then – she couldn't think. She felt dead.

They turned back towards Ballyglin.

It was the longest walk of her life. Every thought she had ever had about him, every aspect of their time together, everything they had ever said to each other, she rehearsed again and again in her mind, over and over, feeling more and more tired, more drained.

They came to the cabin at last.

'Thank you, Larry. I'll give you something in the morning, I've nothing on me.'

'I'm sorry 'twas all in vain, Miss Bríd. Good night to you.'

He went off in the darkness.

Tired and empty, Bríd went towards the door of the cabin.

At that moment a figure emerged from under the eaves, hidden in the darkness, and seized her strongly by the wrist.

'Garrett?'

'Don't move, you slut, only harken to me.'

He spoke in a strong, level voice, but quietly and intensely. She was astonished.

'Let go of me!'

She had no strength to move.

'You whore! Do you think I haven't known what's been going on?'

'What do you mean?'

She couldn't struggle; she was paralysed with guilt and fear.

'Harken to me now. I know everything, see? Everything. Did you think you could steal off to see his lordship, you could let him kiss you, hold you? Have you no shame, girl? God, you, who know how I loved you and respected you, the most beautiful girl in the village –'

'You don't love me, Garrett!'

'God knows I loved you, you whore, and love you still!'

Bríd looked round wildly. They were right outside the cabin door, and Patsy and Nora must be within a few feet of them. She was soaked to the skin.

Garrett still held her tightly.

'You were seen with him. I know everything.'

Bríd looked into his face. She felt dizzy. Her mind raced round and round, unable to seize on anything.

'Harken to me, Bríd. You deserve a whipping. You're a whore and you know it, and I know it and so does Molly. And so will everyone in this village tomorrow unless you promise me now here one thing.'

'What thing?'

'Promise to marry me, Bríd.'

'Marry?' She breathed the word.

'Be my wife, which you should have been by rights long since, and 'twill be a secret between us for ever.'

'No!'

'Bríd, you have nothing. Tomorrow you will be a branded whore, the butt of the village. Who will speak to you? Who will acknowledge you? You will be that slut Bríd Flynn who went with his lordship from the castle.'

'Why should you want to marry me, if I'm a whore?'

'You know me by now, Bríd. I want you for my wife. Let that suffice.'

She stared into his face, dim in the darkness and the rain.

'You want me, thinking I'm a whore?'

She could not understand.

His eyes seemed to burn at her.

'Bríd, I've wanted you since I first saw you. Since you were a child. Don't ask more. Promise me now you'll marry me.'

'No!'

He tightened his grip with sudden force. Pain shot through her.

'Marry me!' he hissed at her, his face a few inches away.

'No!'

'Bríd, I swear, if you don't say this minute you'll be my wife, I'll ruin you. There'll be no living in Ballyglin for you from this out.'

As she cooled, a jab of fear ran through her.

'Give me time to think.'

'No. Tell me now you'll marry me.'

'I'll tell you tomorrow. Let me go in, Garrett, I'm soaked through.'

'Now. Say it now!'

Fear was in her. He was right. Her mind was cool, she could think, and everything he said was true. There was no choice. Where was Harry? Off to London. And never even said goodbye. He had tricked her, betrayed her. How could she ever go pleading to him to help her? As if he would ever marry her! With Garrett before her she saw everything clearly. What was there left her? To be alone in the village, mocked, jeered at?

At last the words came, twisted out of her.

'Very well, I'll marry you.'

The grip on her wrist slackened.

'You'll not regret it. I'm sorry I hurt you.'

She was rubbing her wrist.

'Don't say anything to them yet,' he said.

She turned towards the door.

He took her arm again.

'Mind, that's a promise. We'll be wed quickly. I'll see Father Geoghegan in the morning. Good night, my dear.'

He turned away quickly in the darkness.

Bríd remained outside the door, the hair plastered round her face, rain running down her neck, staring in the darkness, seeing nothing.

And where was Harry? There in the hut hadn't they plighted their troth, sworn to be true for ever? Wasn't it true?

But could she remind him of it? Him that had gone off to England, to his regiment? Him, who had left without saying goodbye, without a note, without anything?

She felt cold, deeply cold, heavy, stupid.

She had given her word. That was the fact. Father Geoghegan would be round to see her in the morning. Uncle Patsy and Aunt Nora would be told. Where could she run? Nowhere. There never was, never would be, anywhere for her but here, in Ballyglin.

She drew a deep, shuddering breath, wiped her arm across her wet face, and opened the door.

The next morning Father Geoghegan called. Although a young man, he had the dried-up seminarist's look of a man who had spent too much time in libraries turning over old books, growing short-sighted with study, a man unused to relaxing, self-conscious and stiff.

Bríd felt a pang of terror as she saw him. He came in and nodded to Nora. She didn't like him, but gave a grudging acknowledgement.

'A happy day for you all, Mrs Byrne,' said the priest.

'What do you mean?' said Nora gruffly, as she ladled meal from the meal tub on to the table, where she was about to make bread.

'Your niece's wedding, of course,' he said somewhat surprised.

Nora looked at Bríd. 'When was this settled?'

'Last night,' said Bríd with a sort of suicidal misery.

'Is this true?'

Nora looked hard into Bríd's face. Bríd tried with difficulty to meet her stern look.

'It's true, Aunt Nora,' she said at last with all the dignity she could find in her shrivelled soul.

Nora unexpectedly took her in her arms and held her tight. Bríd could not remember Nora ever having hugged her before.

''Tis glad I am for you then, Bríd. He's a good man, never fear, and will be a fine husband to you, and a good father to your children.'

'I know it, Aunt Nora,' said Bríd quietly.

'Have you told your uncle?'

'Not yet.'

'Well, run out and tell him this minute. Isn't this the best bit of news in years? Oh, it's glad I am for you.'

Bríd went out to find Patsy.

Garrett had wasted no time. She looked up at the bare branches against the rain-washed sky, the clouds high above. She couldn't believe it. He'd taken her over. He had an absolute power over her. And he was a man who would use it, to the last ounce.

She wanted to scream. What could she do?

As Bríd went to bed that night, she thought she would kill herself. There seemed no other way out. It was impossible to sleep, and she lay the night through, staring into the darkness, remembering the afternoon in the hut when she had given herself to Harry, not thinking of the future, not thinking of Father Geoghegan, not thinking of anything, not thinking at all, only alive there in his arms, yielding, giving herself as she knew she never would give herself again, as long as she might live.

She was the fool after all, just as it seemed she must be. Ruined. Oh, if she married Garrett now, probably no one would ever be the wiser if there was a child. A child – oh, God, better to kill herself now.

64

Chapter Nine

Her first thought was, I'll never marry Garrett. I'll go round and tell him so now. The cowardly villain, to use violence against me. How could I ever be happy with such a man?

She lay in bed, staring at the ceiling. It was dawn. Another damp, misty morning.

What folly! She was going to marry Garrett; that was the reality. It was time to put away her childhood. Time to become a real adult, a married woman with responsibilities, a farm, Garrett's mother and, soon enough, children.

Maybe Harry's child.

But he had gone away. No word, no letter. Left her for ever. A wave of despair swept over her. Was there any way she could just forget? Put Harry away from her and face the future, if not cheerfully, at least without blank despair?

Suppose he wrote to her? What would she reply? Dear Harry, thank you for your letter, by the way I'm marrying Garrett Doyle in three weeks?

Write to her? When he had gone away, never seen her, never spoken to her, never left any message?

Blank despair. She rolled over, staring out of the little window, up at a patch of blue, just visible.

She was suddenly restless. She got out of bed, dressed and went out of the house. Everything was still in the early morning. Across from her, the hedges, the thorn trees were all still, with pearls of dew along them. The wintry grass was dewy. Away down to her left ran the *bohreen* to the village. Again the despair. This was it – home. For ever. What was it then that Harry meant to her? Behind him she had glimpsed that wider world. For a moment she had foolishly allowed herself to believe that he could carry her through to – what? She had never dared to imagine he would ask her to marry him. Yet being with him, she had felt herself closer to a world of possibilities.

Folly. And wasn't it rather shameful after all? Being Garrett's wife had more dignity than mooning after the Earl's son. Better as it was.

In a fit of impatience with herself, she walked up to the byre and looked in at the cows. They set up a mooing when she opened the door. They were hungry. She went over to the clamp, took up the spade and began to heave the turf away from the stacked turnips beneath, and then to take them up up two at a time and carry them over to the byre. They were cold, and her hands became almost numb. What of that? This was real at least. Her reality.

"Tis all arranged, Bríd. Father Geoghegan will be calling the banns this Sunday. And we'll be married on Saturday three weeks. And we're going into Boyle to have you measured for your wedding dress.'

Garrett was very cheerful. They were sitting round the table and drinking tea. He'd been very attentive to Nora too, helping her lift a pot from the fire. He was dressed well, in his smart corduroy jacket and the red scarf.

What was there to say? She had better go. She had no say in the matter anyway.

'Thank you, Garrett.'

Nora was quite frisky. She suddenly turned and pinched Garrett's cheek.

'Oh, Garrett, I'm that pleased, I can't tell you. I couldn't ask for a finer husband for Bríd.'

Suddenly it was too much. Bríd got up and walked out of the door. If she had stayed a moment longer, she'd have been in tears.

After a second Garrett came out behind her. She did not turn.

'I'll never make you happy, Garrett.'

He was unexpectedly gentle.

'You're all I want, Bríd. You're going to be my wife, and I won't let you go.'

'It's just your pride. You want me because I'm good-looking.'

'I want you because I love you,' he said. He was still behind her.

She turned sharply and almost hissed at him, in a quiet, vehement voice, 'You don't love me! You don't know me! You know nothing about me!'

He became very hard. 'Bríd, I've said it before. I know my mind. I want you, and by God I'll have you. Be quiet now, and come indoors. And hark to me, Bríd,' he took her arm, 'no more displays of temper when we're married. I'll not have you disgrace me before my friends.'

She saw the force in his eyes.

*

A week went by in a daze. She felt like a condemned woman waiting for the day of her execution. She went round in a dream of unreality. It wasn't really happening to her. Soon she would wake and it would be all a dream. But it wasn't a dream.

Then one morning Molly came to see her, and as they walked together down the *bohreen*, Molly took from her shawl a letter and handed it to Bríd.

'Liam brought it from the castle.'

It was from England. Harry had sent it via a groom; Liam was Molly's brother. There was fear and accusation in Molly's eyes. Bríd stared at the envelope. It wasn't real. It was real. It was from Harry. She could hardly bring herself to open the letter, tore it open slowly, carefully.

Her eyes were scarcely capable of taking it in.

I'm sorry I couldn't see you before I left. I hope you got my note safely.

Bríd looked up quickly. There had been a note.

I hated having to rush away so quickly. You can't imagine how I felt. My cornetcy had come up, and father insisted on my going over to England straight away. There was nothing I could do about it. You can't imagine how I felt when I came over to Ballyglin and you weren't there. I was in despair. I had no time to wait, so I had to write you a note. It was agony having to write a note there and then in front of Mr and Mrs Byrne. I'd no idea what they were thinking. I was frantic. I prayed they'd give it to you unopened. I was so afraid they would read it that I couldn't say any of the things I wanted to.

Well, I'm here now, a cornet of Lancers. You should see me in my uniform. It is dark green. The trousers are cut very tight with a wide gold stripe down the side. I wear polished black top boots. The tunic is also very tight, and has gold frogging across the chest and at the tail of the back. It has silver buttons. I have a great bearskin busby with a white cockade at the side. It is rather heavy and has taken quite a lot of practice to keep on. At first, if I was suddenly to turn my head, it would come down over my eyes, which made the other fellows laugh. I've mastered it now. Then, of course, I have a long cavalry sabre.

I am the new man here so I have not yet made friends with any of the other fellows. I find them all rather stand-offish after you Irish; you are all so easy-going, so friendly and open. Coming back, I'd forgotten how cool and correct we English are and it's not

67

so easy to get to know the people here as it would be in Ireland. They are determined to enjoy themselves here in London, however, and are in and out at all hours.

I think of you all the time. Honestly, I don't think I can go on alone without you. I am utterly wretched that I had to leave without being able to talk to you and make any arrangements, or settle anything between us.

I don't know what you want, or intend, and what would have happened if we had had time to talk it over. I beg you to write to me as soon as possible, and let me know that you are well, and what you are thinking. I have no idea when I'll be free to come over to Ireland again.

Goodbye, my darling. Never forget I love you.

She blessed him for those last words. She read the letter through three times. She could hear Harry's voice in it, but he sounded so distant, at the end of a long tunnel, in another world, an elegant cavalry officer with his sabre and his tall bearskin helmet.

But Aunt Nora – she must have Harry's note. Unless she had destroyed it. Bríd felt hot with rage as she thought how Nora had betrayed her. Never, never, never would Bríd forgive her.

She looked at the letter again. Harry loved her.

And now she was betrothed to Garrett.

She dictated a letter to Molly.

Life without you is insupportable to me now. I can hardly believe there was a time when I did not know you, only I remember that time, which was really not so long ago, as if it was some remote age, another time, not ours, and I was another Bríd, not yours. That other Bríd was in a daydream, asleep, just marking time till she should be wakened, and now I am awakened to life, and so short too, and already you have gone, I feel cold and dead. I walk through life like a ghost. Aunt Nora is rather strict with me, though I believe she loves me right enough, and Uncle Patsy is gentle and kind. He always was and never changes.

My dearest darling, the most terrible thing has happened. I can hardly bear to say it, even in a letter. Aunt Nora destroyed the note you left me. I shall never forgive her for this as long as I live. When you went away I had no message from you, nothing at all. I thought you had left me for ever. You will never know what despair I was in.

My darling, they have forced me to promise to marry Garrett

Doyle. He is a farmer here in the village. But I shall never marry him. I will kill myself first.

Oh, Harry, why did you go away and leave me? Will I ever see you again? I think of you all the time. You are in my mind from the moment I wake up until I fall asleep at night. When I think of you in London and me here married to Garrett Doyle, I think I must go mad. I know I will kill myself.

My darling, if only I could see you, only for a moment, perhaps I could bear everything. It is so terrible to be alone. Sometimes I wonder if it would have been better never to have known you, but then I curse myself for saying such a thing.

Oh, God, Harry, what else can I say?

I have your letter, which Molly gave me, God bless her, she is my true friend, I shall keep it in my breast and read it every night before I sleep.

God bless you, my darling,

Your own,

Bríd

On Saturday Garrett took her into Boyle in his jaunting car. She sat beside him as they bowled through the lanes, and saw herself already as a prosperous farmer's wife going in to market, a respectable woman, a woman of some consequence in the village – Mrs Doyle. And when they went into the stores in Boyle, the shopkeepers came round from behind the counter, with 'Good day, Mr Doyle, and what can we do for you, Mr Doyle?'

They went into a haberdasher's. Garrett chose her a nice shawl, an expensive one. He was no niggard of his money. It had to be the best for his bride. She stood there in the shop as he turned over the shawls on the counter. 'Try that one on' and 'try that one on'. She was powerless in his hands.

There was death in her heart.

She would kill herself. How? She would drown herself. Stab herself. Throw herself off the church tower. On the day of her wedding, she would be found, by the church door, in her wedding dress. Dead.

Her wedding dress. They went into a little house in a side street. There was a woman, a seamstress. Bríd stood like a tailor's dummy while she was measured. Once it was made, once Bríd put it on, it would be very bad luck to break off the marriage.

Oh, God, it was all madness!

Why didn't Harry come and take her away?

A week later there was another letter from Harry. Molly brought it up from the village. Together the two friends went out and walked up on the hill among the great standing stones, while all around them the silence was broken only by the sound of a lark in the sunny morning. It was a mild day, and a watery sun looked down on the landscape still sodden from the winter rains. In the silence while Molly stared away at the distant Curlew Mountains, Bríd opened her letter.

As she read, she caught her breath. Molly looked across to her. Bríd clutched the letter to her breast and looked at Molly.

'He wants me to go over to London.'

She paused.

'He wants me to go and live there. To be near him.'

Molly stared.

'Live there? Will you break off your marriage? Leave Garrett? Leave Uncle Patsy and Aunt Nora?'

Molly couldn't take it in.

'Live there? Will you go?'

Bríd clutched Molly by the arms.

'Molly, I'll go! I'll go if it's to the world's end!'

'But Bríd –'

It was the only thing to do. In a flash, everything was wiped clear, all problems, dangers and difficulties swept away. Molly trembled.

'Bríd, you wouldn't go, I mean, you wouldn't go to *live* with him, now would you?'

'Molly, you don't understand, we're to be married!'

'Married! When?'

'Oh, I don't know. Harry has to make the arrangements. He has to tell his mother and father –'

'And what'll they say, do you suppose? "You'll be marrying a poor Irish colleen, a Catholic, without a penny to bless herself with?" And him a fine gentleman, an earl's son? Bríd, you've taken leave of your senses, I believe. Him a lord, and marry the likes of you, from an Irish cabin? With never a spare petticoat to your name? It'll never be.'

'He wants me to go and be with him.'

'He wants you for his fancy woman, Bríd, his whore! You, a fine fresh girl, oh, sure he wants you. But what of when he tires of you, did you think of that? What claim will you have on him? Bríd, he'll never marry you. It can't be.'

Bríd was in tears of vexation.

'That's all untrue. Harry loves me. We swore our love to all eternity. I know he loves me. He wants me to go over, and we'll be married in London. Molly, oh, he's the gentleman entirely – a kinder, lovelier man never drew the breath of life. A truer, gooder, more gentle man never was. Harry to leave me? It never could be, I'd swear. I know him, Molly, I do, I do! But then, Molly, to see London, only think! To see London! And Molly, think what's to become of me here – to be married to Garrett Doyle. I'd die, I swear it.'

Molly was filled with fear.

'But Bríd, you've promised.'

'He made me promise, otherwise he'd tell that I was seeing Harry. He forced me. It was no true promise. Oh, Molly, I'll never marry Garrett Doyle!'

Molly was silent for a moment. Bríd waited, hoping for some encouragement.

'But to go away, and leave your uncle and aunt! I mean, to go all that way to London and never be sure he'll marry you. He never will marry you, Bríd, I know it.'

Bríd was cast down by Molly's pessimism.

'You're my friend, why do you talk like that? Why say such things? Don't you know I love him above all things in the world? Molly, I'd die for him. If he wants me to come, I'll go through anything to be with him. Anything. I will.'

Molly was appalled by Bríd's vehemence. At last she spoke, quietly. 'You must at least think it over. Give yourself a bit of time, anyway. Maybe you'll see it different.'

'Time? What time? Won't I be married to Garrett in less than two weeks?'

'Will you tell Garrett?'

Bríd's heart froze.

'I couldn't. He'd tear me limb from limb.'

'So you'll just run away?'

Bríd bit her lip and stared at the ground. 'I will so.'

Now Molly clutched Bríd.

'Oh, Bríd, 'tis a long journey. Will he come and fetch you? Or is it you will go all that way alone? And you a poor girl was never out of the County Roscommon in your life, save once when you went to Ballinasloe Fair.'

Bríd looked down again at Harry's letter. She thought for a moment.

'I'll go. He says if I agree he'll send a banknote to pay for the journey. Molly, I'll go. I must go. There's nothing for me here, don't you see?'

They walked slowly down into the village, each thinking her own thoughts.

But the more Bríd thought, the more Molly's arguments seemed true, and her fears mounted. Harry was a Protestant. Would he wish her to give up her faith? She'd heard of mixed marriages, it was true, but still – it would be a terrible sin to give up her faith.

Would Harry give up his? She could hardly imagine it. All Molly's words returned to her. Him, an earl's son, marry her? Could it be true? That evening she sat very silent by the fire, trying to collect her thoughts.

Then Nora said, 'Garrett called. You're to go into Boyle Saturday for a fitting of your wedding dress.'

It was a terrible bad omen to be fitted for a wedding dress. To have it made, to put it on. It would mean a lifetime of bad luck to have her wedding dress made, fitted, worn, and then to run away without telling Garrett.

The following morning she sent a letter to Harry. She had to force Molly to write it. Molly was frightened. She knew it was a sin Bríd was committing, and she was aiding and abetting her in the sin. Bríd vowed she would make a pilgrimage to St Ronan's well to pray for forgiveness for her sin.

Chapter Ten

When Molly brought her a letter and when she found inside it a Bank of England note for twenty pounds, however, her fears began again. To hold in her hands the unfamiliar banknote was to contemplate her journey as a reality, not a dream.

The following day she and Molly set out on their journey to the holy well of St Ronan. Part of the way they travelled on the Boyle-to-Roscommon car, a stagecoach or omnibus supposed to carry seven, but on this occasion holding thirteen. The girls sat on the back, listening to the uproarious laughing and joking and drinking of the passengers on the roof. The last part of the journey was on foot.

At the holy well there was a shrine of the blessed Virgin and beside her, kneeling, the figure of St Ronan with his hands raised in prayer. Both of the figures were bedecked with posies and garlands of wild flowers.

Bríd knelt and prayed to the blessed Virgin. She did not know at first how to voice her prayer. Father Geoghegan would say it was a sin to go to Harry, would say she had sinned already in giving herself to him, but how could it be a sin to go the man she loved? Were they not to be married? And was it a sin not to want to marry Garrett Doyle? Was it a sin to leave Uncle Patsy and Aunt Nora? They would be relieved to have her off their hands. Her mind was full of confused thoughts. In the end she prayed to be forgiven any sins she might have committed unknowingly. Then in her fullness of heart she prayed the Virgin to watch over Harry and guard him, and to bring her safely on her journey to him.

Before leaving, she and Molly washed their faces in water from the holy well, which was said to make you more beautiful.

That evening she sent a letter to Harry saying she was coming on Friday.

*

73

Very, very early in the morning of Friday she arose, dressed and went into the kitchen. The fire still smouldered and gave a soft light, though it was dark outside. Next door Nora and Patsy were asleep. Molly had lent Bríd a little bag to carry some things in – a change of clothes was all she had, and a hairbrush. She would have to walk five miles to the railway station. She had found out the time of the train to Dublin. She held her best shoes in her hand; she would carry them till she was on the train, and then put them on.

She stood in the room, looking round in the dim light of the fire. She couldn't believe she was leaving. Although she was now going, it didn't seem real, it was a dream; the only life she had ever known was in this room.

She left on the table a letter she had written for Nora and Patsy and started for the door. She looked round. Her harp was in the corner. On an impulse she crossed and took it up. It must go with her. Was there nothing she could cover it with? An old blanket from the back of Uncle Patsy's rocking chair would serve.

Silently, in an agony of slowness, Bríd lifted the latch and opened the door. The cool morning air met her face as she closed the door again behind her. It was dark, but dawn would come soon. Aunt Nora might wake in another hour or less. But once Bríd was on the train they could not come after her. Holding the harp under one arm and her little bag in the other, and wrapped in her big blue cloak, Bríd set out to walk to the station.

It was half past four in the morning when the train pulled into the Euston Square Station in London. She was in a daze of tiredness and every bone in her body ached. All the way from Holyhead she had sat on a wooden bench in a third-class compartment. At last the train drew into the great shed, echoing with the noise of steam. People stirred themselves in the dim light, gathering their things together, and she looked about her out of the dirty window. London! Would Harry be here to meet her? As the train slowed to a stop, doors sprang open, people spilled out on the platform, and, taking her little bag in her hand, stiff and dizzy with tiredness, she got out too. People hurried past her. Where should she go? Where would Harry be?

She followed the people along the platform. The station was enormous, high, vaulted, echoing with the noise of steam hissing.

He was there. Relief flooded into her, life came back to her, she rushed to him, and he swept her into his arms, swung her round and then kissed her, and she knew straight away she had done the right thing, and everything was as it should be. He was about to carry her off to a cab when she said she had her harp in the guard's van. They got her harp, and Harry laughed almost in tears to think she had carried it with her all that way.

Everywhere around them people pushed and jostled past, but Harry got them to a big black carriage, a cab, and then they were inside together, and the cab was rolling and rattling out of the station into the strange streets.

In the cab Bríd told him all about her journey, overexcited in her tiredness, pouring out her experiences, the difficulties she'd had. There was the trouble to change the Bank of England note, she'd had to do that in a bank in town, and the man gave her such a strange look, as if she might have stolen it. She didn't tell Harry that she'd had to invent an excuse, leave Garrett in a corn factor's while she hurried round to the bank. And then in the train men had looked at her as if she was running away. Running away! And she a grown girl, and free to travel where she pleased. In Dublin she had got lost and couldn't find her way from the station to the steam packet at Kingstown, but anyway she found it in the end.

Harry interrupted to ask why she hadn't taken a cab from the station. Oh, she couldn't take a cab and be spending all his money. She fished into her bag and brought out what there was left of it. He laughed, kissed her and told her to spend it all, it was hers anyway. Then she'd got on the ship and the crossing was simply terrible with the wind roaring a great storm, and enormous waves, and the ship near standing on end, and people being sick everywhere. She had felt she wanted to die; she sat on the deck, for the smell inside was just terrible, and she thought it would never end.

At last the ship came into the harbour, the waves died down and it was calm. She had thought she'd never stand on dry land again. And then she had struggled to get a seat on the train, everyone pushing and fighting, but a man who looked kind enough got her a seat next to him, and took care of her harp in the guard's van, and talked to her and asked her who she was and where she was going, and said he knew somewhere she could stay which was good and very cheap. She said she was being met by her fiancé and he had already arranged something, but the man said he knew London very well, had lived there all his life, and would get her something better, but she said no thank you, and later when she tried to sleep he put his arm round her, and she didn't know what to do. When she asked him very politely to take his arm away, he got bad-tempered, but luckily a couple sitting opposite stared at him very hard and at last he got out at a station and she didn't see him again.

All the time she talked, his face was there in the dim light; they kissed, she could kiss him as much as she liked, and she knew she had done the right thing, even for this, these few minutes, and whatever might happen afterwards, she didn't care at all.

Then the cab stopped, and they got out in a silent street, just as dawn was breaking. There was a row of houses on either side of the street, three storeys, the bottom one half buried in the ground, and in front of them railings, and a few steps up to the door. He led her up to a door, carrying her harp, opened the door with a key he had, and led her in through the darkness, up some stairs and into a room.

It was a pleasant, medium-sized room with a carpet, a sofa and some armchairs, a real fireplace and even gaslight. Harry lit the gas. There were pictures on the wall.

'Do you like it? It's yours, until we can get married.'

She couldn't believe it. Her own room.

'There's more. Come on.'

He led her through a door into another room, a bedroom.

'There's another room as well, sort of a box room. Except you haven't got any boxes. Yet.' He laughed.

She put her arms round his neck. She could feel tears springing into her eyes.

'Harry, I don't know what to say. I've never seen anything so beautiful.'

They kissed.

'Now I expect you're exhausted. I've told Mrs O'Rourke to bring you some tea late morning. She's the landlady; she lives in the basement. She's Irish like you. You'll like her. She'll do for you.'

He looked down.

'I – I told her you were my cousin, over for a while. I couldn't – you know . . .'

For a moment she didn't understand.

'Why didn't you say we were to be married?'

'It would have been a bit tricky, to be frank. Not very easy to explain. It's easier this way. It means I can come and go and no questions asked. Don't worry. Everything's taken care of. And it's all yours.'

Bríd didn't understand, but she was suddenly too tired to think, so soon afterwards, Harry left her and walked back to his barracks.

Bríd explored the rooms after he had gone. She examined everything; the furniture, the pattern of the wallpaper, the gaslight and the bed. She looked under the bed and found a large china pot. She had never seen one before, they had no need of anything like it in Ballyglin, but she could see now she was living in a big city all sorts of things would be different.

At last, when it was quite light, she undressed and got into bed.

She couldn't sleep. Her journey ran over and over through her mind. The movement of the ship came back to her, and then the train, the faces of the other people half asleep, the smell of the coal smoke and the steam. And then the cab journey and now being here in this strange bed, on these lovely crisp sheets and the soft mattress. In a daze of tiredness, she at last nodded off.

She woke. It was broad daylight.

A plump, grey-haired woman of sixty, with a rosy-cheeked apple of a face, a large bosom and a white apron, was looking down at her.

'Welcome to London, my dear.'

She was an Irishwoman. Bríd felt immediately at home.

'I've brought you a cup of tea.'

It stood on a bedside table. Mrs O'Rourke brought up a chair.

'Well now, your cousin told me you was pretty, but he didn't say the half of it.'

Bríd pulled herself up a little and took the cup of tea.

'My name is Bríd Flynn.'

'And I'm the widow O'Rourke.'

'Oh, I'm sorry –'

'You needn't be. 'Tis a few years now since he was taken. O'Rourke was always accident-prone. It was only his own fault if he worked in a sawmill.'

Bríd was awake. 'Sawmill?'

'Aye, here, round the corner. When he sawed off his own finger, I told him, "O'Rourke, 'tis time you found another job." Then they got a new big saw, drove by steam. As soon as he told me, I didn't like the sound of it. I warned him a hundred times, "Take care of the steam saw, 'twill catch you unawares." Sure enough, it wasn't long before there was a knock at the door, and a boy, puffing and panting, "Oh, Mrs O'Rourke, will you come, there's been an accident!" I ran all the way and found him there, on the ground with them all standing round, gawping like a lot of dead fish. "Oh, Mrs O'Rourke," says they, "'twas the new saw!" They brought him home here, but it was only a matter of time. He was never a well man again. He just sank and sank, and then that was that.'

Bríd sipped her tea.

'Oh, Mrs O'Rourke, I'm sorry.'

'You needn't be, Miss Flynn –'

'Please call me Bríd.'

'When will your boxes be coming?'

Bríd froze. Boxes? She had nothing.

'My cousin is taking care of that, Mrs O'Rourke.'

'He's a proper gentleman, your cousin, I'd say. Looks very elegant in his regimentals. Interesting, him being so English, should have a cousin from Ireland.'

She gave Bríd a sharp look, and Bríd felt suddenly on her guard.

''Twould be another branch of the family, Mrs O'Rourke. We don't see so much of each other as a rule.'

Mrs O'Rourke relaxed and smiled.

'Now let tell you a few things. You have the whole top floor of the house to yourself. I live in the basement so I shan't interfere in the slightest. You can take your meals in your sitting room. Let me know any special requests you might have, and what sort of time you like to eat. If you want to take a bath, you must give me notice so I can boil up the water.'

A bath! Bríd's head swam. Could there be so much luxury in the world?

'As a matter of fact, Mrs O'Rourke, I'd like a bath now – soon, that is, if you don't mind. I want to wash away all that long journey. You've no idea how smutty it is on the train.'

In a little while, Mrs O'Rourke staggered up the stairs with a tin bath and placed it before the sitting-room fire, and then came up and down from the basement with cans of water. Bríd insisted on helping her. In the daylight she suddenly felt self-conscious in her dull old rusty-red dress.

When Mrs O'Rourke left her alone, she took her clothes off, and, for the first time in her life, stepped into the hot water and washed herself all over. Of course she had washed at home, kept herself neat and clean. But here, to stand in the bath of hot water, in front of the fire, and squeeze the sponge down herself was quite delicious.

Harry called during the afternoon and found her refreshed, settled into her rooms and highly pleased with everything, and on the best of terms with the widow.

'I told her you were my cousin. Oh, Harry, I hate not being able to say freely we are to be married.'

'I know, and so do I.'

There was an awkward silence between them. Harry looked away. He seemed embarrassed.

'We must buy you some clothes,' he said suddenly, 'this afternoon. Now! Come on!'

She took her cloak and they went out into the street. Harry looked so glamorous, so lovely as she took his arm, she immediately forgot the awkwardness. It was a bright afternoon. She looked round, taking everything in: the long, low row of houses, built of brick but nearly black with soot, the masses of chimneypots on the roofs, the paved sidewalks. They turned into a wider street, and there were all kinds of carts and carriages, and a constant clattering of iron wheels and horses' hooves.

Harry hailed a cab, a high, fast, smart cab, quite unlike the one they had ridden in last night. It was a hansom cab, the best sort, he said, and with the horse trotting before them and the houses flashing past, Bríd forgot everything, forgot Ballyglin, forgot Garrett, felt only the excitement of rushing along through the streets.

Here in the daylight she was getting her first impression of London. The palatial buildings had so many chimneypots and so many windows – a girl was leaning from one of them, shaking a rug, and she wondered at the vast gulf between that girl's life and her own. There was an incessant push and jostle of vehicles around them. Then they were trotting through the park, the trees on the verge of bursting into leaf. Nursemaids were pushing perambulators, and a troop of redcoats marched along in the distance. It was altogether a different class of society here; these people were living in a style Bríd hadn't even imagined. London must surely be the richest city in the world, even if it was also the dirtiest.

They got out, and Harry paid the man. She noticed how the man nodded and touched his cap to Harry, and Harry seemed so grand, so elegant, quite at home.

The street was now very crowded.

'Piccadilly Circus,' said Harry. 'We'll go up Regent Street first. Scores of shops to choose from.'

They set off walking up Regent Street, looking in the shop windows. Bríd felt in tremendous high spirits and took in everything, pointing to the carriages of the gentry and the clothes of the fashionable ladies. Everyone seemed so beautifully dressed, the ladies all in great crinoline dresses which swept around them, and the most lovely colours, and such pretty bonnets, too, in all shapes and sizes. Her eyes were everywhere, taking it all in.

When they went in to buy some clothes for her, Bríd couldn't at first believe it, and made him tell her several times.

'You can have anything you like, Bríd. Anything.'

Young girls came forward to attend them, and bobbed and curtsied to Harry. It seemed strange to hear their accents, and she didn't always make out clearly what they said. At first, too, she thought they must look down on her in her Irish clothes, which seemed dowdy and strange compared to theirs. But the sight of such lovely things to try on carried her away; she forgot the girls and only wanted to put on

79

pretty things so she could please Harry. He liked everything and let her run mad, trying anything against herself and standing before the looking glass. Soon there were clothes strewn everywhere, some of them quite unsuitable, made for old dowagers or little girls. She didn't care. It was all wonderful. She would never forget this afternoon as long as she lived, and she owed it all to him. She kept wanting to kiss him, and he became embarrassed.

'Not in front of the shop girls, Bríd,' he whispered.

She laughed. 'Who cares about them, Harry, my darling?'

She ran her hand over the silks, the velvets, the satins, the crisp cottons, the piqués, the lace, the fine wool, speechless with delight and admiration. She tried on a crinoline dress, and when she beheld herself in the looking glass, the great skirt spread around her, she could scarce believe it – she, Bríd Flynn, a fine lady.

Sometimes in the looking glass Harry would catch a twisted smile of contempt on the face of a shop girl, but he didn't mind. How could they help being jealous of his Bríd? His benevolence was infinite, he forgave them everything. Bríd would ask him what he liked – he didn't mind, he liked everything, and besides he'd never been asked to choose a lady's clothes in his life. But in the end, giggling together, holding things up against her, looking at her in the looking glass, they began to sort out her wardrobe. They bought some ready-to-wear clothes as well as all the accessories she needed, and he went and stared out of the window for a while as she chose underwear and stockings. Bríd had never worn underwear in her life. As she held the fine cotton and lace petticoats, the silk drawers, the stockings, it was almost more than she could bear. She felt like a princess in a fairy tale.

In the end they had armfuls of packages and boxes: shoes, hats, scarves, as well as skirts, blouses, woollens, coats, light dresses, heavy dresses, evening dresses, morning dresses, and pins, brushes and ornaments. Other garments were left behind to be altered and delivered later. Harry never parted with a penny. Bills would arrive in due course at the barracks.

That afternoon back in Flood Street, Bríd paraded her new clothes before Harry as they had tea by the fire. She put on a fine muslin dress, white with a pale-mauve anemone design, so light, so flouncy as she walked and turned. Harry sat by the fire with a teacup in his hand, speechless with admiration. When she threw herself into his arms, showering him with kisses of gratitude, he found the crisp freshness of her clothes next to her skin overpoweringly arousing and in a flurry of lace and petticoats they fell on to the bed and made love. Staring at her afterwards, staring, staring, trying in vain to comprehend her, to come to terms with her mystery, the wonderful impossible mystery of her, he would have given anything, risked anything, faced anything for her.

Chapter Eleven

'Sing for me, Bríd.'

She jumped up and fetched the harp from the corner. He was sitting in an armchair by the fire. The curtains were drawn, and the fire was clinking cheerfully in the grate. It was very cosy.

She set herself before him and spent a moment tuning the harp. There in her hands again, it was a link with home, and a wave of sadness came over her. She looked down.

'What is it?'

She looked up at him and dismissed the thought.

'What shall I sing?'

'You decide. You sang for me once before, the most beautiful thing I ever heard.'

She ran her fingers across the strings, and began to sing.

Again, as he remembered it from what seemed so long ago, he heard that unearthly, that strangely beautiful sound. He couldn't explain it, couldn't understand it, just felt himself mesmerised.

Bríd never understood it either. Where the song came from, where the inspiration came from, she had no idea. It was as if she were visited by some strange spirit which filled her, took her over, directed and controlled her as she sang. Yet she never felt so truly herself as in those moments when she was singing.

'I could listen for ever,' he said at last. 'What do the words mean?'

'Oh, 'tis an old song, the lament of a young girl for her false lover.'

'False lover? I say, couldn't you think of something more cheerful to sing about?'

They laughed. Then there was a silence for a moment, as they both thought of what lay ahead.

'Harry –'

'Yes, I know. Bríd, let me explain. Believe me, it's not been easy. You see, when we met, I'd just come out of Sandhurst. Passed out, as we say. Father promised to buy me a commission in a cavalry regiment. Edward came down from Oxford last summer, and had been looking about hoping to get a seat in Parliament. Then, just before Christmas old Mr Shaunessy, the Member for Roscommon, died, and it was too good an opportunity to miss, so the family rushed over to Ireland to put Edward up in the by-election. We were all dashing about frantically to get him in. So Father didn't have much time for me, as you can imagine. That's when you and I met. When you saved my life.'

He looked at her for a moment.

'Of course, Edward got in, and next thing was, Father had written to Colonel Lyttleton of the the 27th Lancers, here in Chelsea, and I had my cornetcy. It happened very quickly.

'It was something I'd been looking forward to for ages: getting into the cavalry. But when I left Ireland and came here – the barracks is only ten minutes' walk from here, we'll walk round tomorrow and I'll show you – anyway, when I came here, I can't tell you, I felt dreadfully low. Seemed to have made a complete mess of it all. You see, I could only think of you, saw you in my mind all the time, everywhere I went, it was you.'

Bríd took his hand. She felt her heart swelling.

'It'll work out in the end, my darling, only for a little while it's going to be tricky. The thing is, just at the very moment I meet you, I've entered the Lancers. I'm just a young subaltern, and of course none of us fellows are married. It isn't done. Getting married would mean resigning my commission. And just after I've joined. Difficult.'

He was silent for a moment.

'When I got your letter, I became frantic – the thought of you marrying someone else. Who is this Garrett?'

Bríd was awkward.

'He's a farmer. Lives near us. I've known him since I was little, in the village, you know. He came to Uncle Patsy and Aunt Nora – oh, Harry don't ask me about it. I'd die rather than marry him.'

'And I won't let you, my darling. You don't have to explain.'

He paused.

'When I received your letter, I could only think of saving you from this Garrett. But I can see now it won't be easy. There's the regiment. Then there's Father. You don't know him, Bríd, but he's a pretty ferocious old cove, and I'm not yet of age, so I can't marry without his permission. That means I'm going to have to handle him very carefully. What I mean is, you're not to worry, because we're going to be together. Only it's going to take longer than I thought. I've got to decide just what to do.'

Bríd went to him and knelt by his chair. She couldn't bear to see him so unhappy.

'Harry, I'll bless you for ever for saving me and bringing me here. You've been so good to me, taking these rooms and buying clothes for me, I'll never be able to repay you. It makes me wretched to think of all the troubles you've got on my account. And I trust you, my darling, I do.'

She sat by him and looked into the fire.

'But you've got to tell your father about me. That's only fair, isn't it? Otherwise, what will I be? A sort of – I don't know – a sort of nobody, won't I?'

'You don't have to worry about that, I swear. But it will take a little time.'

He took her hands, and she could see the anxiety in his eyes.

'Oh, Harry, my darling, be happy! Don't I love you? I won't be any trouble to you at all. Honest, I'd rather go back to Ballyglin than think of you miserable.'

He became more cheerful.

'We'll have lots of fun! We'll do everything together! There's so much to do here – so many things to see. You'll be amazed!'

After he had gone, Bríd was left alone in the room, and as the fire sank low, she sat thinking over everything he had said. A terrible silence seemed to sit in the room, and loneliness oppressed her.

She had run away, left Uncle Patsy and Aunt Nora, betrayed Garrett, thrown away her honesty and respectability for ever, committed a terrible sin, and now here, in this strange, big city, found her position by no means regular, nor as simple as she had imagined. She was here in these rooms on false terms, pretending to be what she was not. And Harry had made it clear to her that he had considerable difficulties to overcome before they could be married.

Suppose she were to have a baby? A cold wave of fear swept through her. She had given herself to him foolishly, not thinking of the consequences. Girls were usually very careful. In the village they had all seen the fate of those who who did not guard their chastity with iron fists. What had she been thinking of?

She had not a penny in the world.

Why had she come? She tried to think back. What was it that had driven her? She stared into the fire. She loved Harry, oh yes, she loved him, loved him now this minute, as she had never loved another. Would always love him.

But there was something else. If she thought very hard, she could see it. It was an ambition. To get out of the village, to see the great world. That too had helped to bring her all this way to London, to this strange room, alone.

She must write to Aunt Nora to let her know she was safe. What must she think?

She asked Mrs O'Rourke for some paper and a pen and ink, and then for a long time sat staring at the blank sheet on the table, as the gas hissed and the fire clinked in the grate. Sat staring, trying to compose her thoughts.

She couldn't tell them everything, couldn't even tell them the truth. Still she must tell them she was safe at least, and that they mustn't worry.

Finally, grimacing at her own handwriting, large and ungainly on the page, she composed a letter. She was well and safe, and had some very pleasant rooms of her own. Nora would be very impressed. She was terribly sorry to cause them all distress, sorry to disappoint Garrett. She hoped he would understand. She would never have made him happy as a wife, she knew. She and Harry were planning to be married, and she would write again, when she had further news for them.

She wondered whether to give her address. Then something in her revolted. Why not? She had nothing to hide. Suppose one of them came over to find her – Garrett maybe – what then? They couldn't force her. She wasn't ashamed. She would see it through.

In this spirit of defiance, she at last went to bed.

Before she did so, she opened the wardrobe and looked at her new clothes again. They were packed close into the wardrobe, so many new things. She ran her hand over the stuffs, pulled things out to look at. So elegant, so lovely.

She woke the following morning feeling more cheerful. Things would work out somehow, everything would come right. Meanwhile there was London to explore, and they would be together.

Harry called for her in the afternoon. Dressed in her new clothes, she set off arm in arm with him. She wanted to look a real lady, so she put on a crinoline and over it a fine wool dress and a great shawl. At first it felt strange, having this great cage swinging round her as she walked, but she had seen herself in the looking glass and thought she looked extremely elegant.

The area where she lived was Chelsea, a suburb of London down by the river, with narrow streets, little shops and workshops and small factories, and, on the river, the sawmill where Mr O'Rourke had come to grief. It was a pleasant, out-of-the-way little place, quiet, where ordinary working people lived, and soon Bríd would come to feel at home there. She enjoyed walking down to the river and along the riverbank, watching the red sails of wherries and barges drift silently by.

They came to a great open space surrounded by high railings, and beyond them long, elegant buildings. She saw some soldiers on horseback, looking smart and dashing.

'The barracks.'

She didn't know what to say. It looked very impressive.

'I haven't seen you in your uniform, Harry.'

'No more you have.'

'Won't you wear it for me sometime?'

'Tomorrow.'

But then, even as he said it, she was thinking, will he give it up for me, all this? Him a gentleman, an officer, give it up to marry me?

The next day he did come to Flood Street in his uniform, clanking up the stairs in his spurs and sabre, and showed off to her. He looked so delicious she could have eaten him, and she couldn't resist starting to undress him. They fell on the bed then and there, half undressed, and made love furiously, and she thought nothing could be more perfect.

Later she had doubts again. So much trouble, his father purchasing his commission, all the uniform made – and wasn't it something he had looked forward to so long? Was he to give it all up for her? Who had nothing? Had nothing to give him but her beauty and her love?

But it had been his idea. He had written to her. Sent her the money, brought her over. He loved her, she knew. It would work out, though she wasn't clear how.

Chapter Twelve

In the days that followed, Harry took Bríd all over London. He took her walking in the park and was so proud of her beauty. In Ireland they had always been alone together, but here among the crowds in the streets and parks, he noticed how men looked at her, and he felt light as air, to have such a beautiful woman on his arm.

He took her to the top of St Paul's Cathedral to admire the view; he took her to the zoo; he took her to Buckingham Palace to see the changing of the guard. Bríd loved everything. Every spare minute Harry could get away from the barracks, he was with her.

He took her to a West End hotel for tea one afternoon. Bríd looked ravishing in a high-necked gown of fine, figured silk a cool brown, which set off her own strong colour. Harry, looking across at her as they sat in the spacious foyer of the hotel, among the tall columns, the potted ferns and the delicate French furniture, was conscious of the attention she drew from other men, embarrassed almost, as if he weren't quite sure how to handle anything so gorgeous, as if he were holding some rare and priceless object in his hands, and terrified that he might let go and shatter it.

Bríd didn't know this. She didn't feel fragile. She was a big, strong girl who knew how good she looked, and was exhilarated by the sense of her own beauty and the attention she drew, the knowledge that heads turned as she passed. It gave her a feeling of strength and vitality. She knew these elegant clothes suited her, and she knew how to move in them so as to set them and herself off to their best advantage.

She didn't know what to do with the cutlery, though, or how to cut the cake, use a tea strainer or spread a napkin on her knee, and she could see the mixture of delight and apprehension in Harry's face as he began to teach her these trivialities of polite society. She was keen to learn, but couldn't take it very seriously. They doubled up with laughter like schoolgirls when she dropped a plateful of bread and butter face down on the carpet.

As they were picking up the bread and butter and attempting to clean off the wool threads, an elderly lady passed them on her way out, and with her were a young lady and two young men. Bríd recognised one of them as Harry's brother Edward. As Harry straightened up, the old lady saw him and her face lit up. She turned towards them.

At that moment Edward saw them too, and Bríd saw a look of astonishment on his face which quickly turned to granite. His eyes glazed, he leaned over the old lady and whispered something, and then simply turned and steered her out of the door. The other young people with them followed, though, as they were going out of the door, the young lady turned again and looked at them with curiosity.

Harry was on his feet looking after them.

'Well, I'll be blowed . . .'

She looked up at him.

'What is it?'

'Hang on a moment.'

He started for the door, but as he reached it, Edward returned, and he and Harry stood talking for a moment. Edward went out again, and Harry came slowly back to Bríd and sat in silence staring at the carpet.

'Damn them all,' he muttered.

She saw he was angry. Suddenly she was frightened. 'Harry, won't you tell me?'

He was trying to regain his composure with an agonising effort.

'It's nothing.'

'Harry, what is it? That was Edward, wasn't it?'

'With the dowager Lady Shalford. Old family friend. Known her since I was a child. She's supposed to have dandled me on her knee. Edward recognised you.'

Bríd was becoming annoyed.

'Well, there's no law says I can't sit here if I choose. Why didn't he say hello?'

'That's just it. You – you haven't been introduced, and so on . . . ' His voice trailed off.

Bríd was angry. 'You mean I'm not respectable?'

'In a manner of speaking.'

'Why don't you make me respectable, Harry?'

He was silent. She stared at him.

'Poor Harry, I've landed you in it, haven't I? Do you wish I'd never come?'

He turned sharply. 'No! Never, never! Bríd, you're the one thing in my life – my guiding star.'

'Be cheerful. I love you, Harry, and everything will be for the best, I know it.'

He seemed relieved, smiled at her and cheered up. She thought, Why am I cheering him up? It's him should be reassuring me.

For the rest of the afternoon, there was a shadow over their fun. Bríd now knew deep in herself that she was stronger than Harry, but she was out of her depth. Still, she was determined that no amount of social etiquette or polite society was going to come between them.

About a week after she had arrived, Mrs O'Rourke brought Bríd a letter. It was from Aunt Nora. Bríd had to force herself to read it. Nora was appalled by what she had done and Uncle Patsy had taken it very hard. The whole village had talked of nothing else since she had gone. Garrett alternated between violent rage and terrible despair. Bríd had cut herself off from her family and could never be acknowledged again. She had committed a terrible sin; not merely run away to live with a man out of wedlock, but a Protestant to boot. Nora and Patsy could scarcely show their faces in the village. It was a most terrible disgrace, and nothing Bríd could do would ever make it up to them.

Bríd sat over the letter all the morning in misery.

One afternoon they were in the park and on an impulse took a boat out on the Serpentine. It was a lovely day of early spring, hot, the trees just out in fresh green, and a heavenly feel in the air. Harry was in a pale-grey suit with a straw hat on the back of his head, and Bríd was in a white cotton dress with a large check weave, trimmed with emerald-green satin ribbon and looped up to show broderie anglaise petticoats and striped cotton socks. She wore a wide so-called Amazon hat.

Harry pulled easily at the oars and they drifted across the lake, relaxed, silent, enjoying the glorious weather and the freshness and novelty of the water slipping past them, only a few inches away. The lake was crowded, and along the bank people sat enjoying the unaccustomed warmth.

Harry rested a moment on his oars, looking at Bríd lying back in the stern with the rudder ropes over her shoulders and her face in shadow. She smiled at him. Then she sat up.

'Let me row.'

He made a face. 'If you like.'

They changed places.

There were a number of other boats out on the water, and one nearby was severely overcrowded. There seemed about eight young men in it, unable to decide who should be rowing. Fierce arguments raged, shrieks of laughter, the boat heaved and rocked, and for a moment Bríd thought they were going to turn over. They were having a jolly time, Bríd thought, watching them over Harry's shoulder. She rather wished Harry and she were having so much fun.

The heaving mass of young men drifted nearer. None of them was steering, nor rowing much either. Then, as they disputed the oars for the umpteenth time, standing up and rocking the boat in the most dangerous fashion, one of them, nearly falling in the water, lurched across with an oar, splashing the water violently and sending up a great sheet of water that came down all over Harry.

He started up angrily. 'What the devil!'

Bríd burst into laughter. Without thinking, she stood up in the boat, taking up her own oar, and returned the compliment. A shower of water descended on the rival boat. A roar went up.

'By Jove, it's war!'

Several of the young men were on their feet, the boat was rocking alarmingly, oars were swung through the air, and cascades of water were shooting up all around them.

'Come on, Harry,' shouted Bríd, who was almost choking with laughter and swinging her oar as hard as she could.

As Harry turned to see where the water had come from, his face froze.

'Wrenshaw! Langstone!'

The rival boat sent up a great shout.

'Leighton! You sly dog! So that's where you've been sloping off to! And by Jove, what a stunner!'

'Come on, Harry, teach them a lesson!' shouted Bríd.

'What an Amazon! Come on, you fellows, don't disappoint the lady!'

Harry turned to Bríd, but she hadn't noticed any of this, and was busily attacking the others with all her might and laughing uncontrollably.

The young men opposite her were splashing as hard as she was, and their boat seemed incapable of staying upright a moment longer as they lurched about in it.

It turned over. With shrieks and roars they were all floundering in the water, clawing for the boat, gasping, and shooting water everywhere.

Bríd sat down, almost weeping with laughter. Harry was watching them all with an irritated expression.

'Try and turn their boat up,' she shouted at him. Leaning out of theirs at a dangerous angle, she reached for the boat in her delicate lace gloves, pulled it towards them and tried to turn it upright.

It was too difficult. She sat back, panting and laughing, her clothes soaking with water.

'Oh, Harry!'

'Come on, Leighton, take us aboard, can't you?'

'Harry, help get them in.'

They were all crowding round the boat and trying to climb over the side.

In a chaos of heaving and rocking and water splashing everywhere, they were pulling them up and into the boat until it seemed about to sink in its turn. When they were packed from edge to edge, puffing, soaked to the skin, one of them turned to Harry and said,

'I say, Leighton, aren't you going to introduce us?'

'Bríd,' said Harry gravely, 'allow me to introduce Major Sir John Wrenshaw of the 27th Lancers, Cornet William Langstone of the ditto, Captain Thomas Graves of the ditto . . .'

With a straight face he went through them all.

'Gentlemen, permit me to introduce Miss Bríd Flynn of County Roscommon, Ireland.'

'Charmed, Miss Flynn,' they chorused.

Bríd had never had so much fun in her life. They were such jolly dogs.

'Harry! They must all get dry, then come back to Flood Street and have tea!'

Universal acclaim. The boat was steered to shore; the bedraggled young men clambered ashore and hailed some cabs.

Harry tried to take Bríd to one side. 'We can't invite all these fellows round –'

Bríd was hardly in a mood to hear him. 'Why ever not?'

He looked at her. She was pretty well soaked to the skin, her hair was plastered round her face and her hat hanging down her back, but her eyes were shining and she was exhilarated.

'Well, you're a single girl, and alone –'

'Oh, Harry, who cares?' She turned to the the others. 'You fellows go off and change and we'll all meet round in Flood Street. Harry will show you the way.'

Harry gave up trying to point out to Bríd that it simply was not done for a single girl to entertain half a dozen officers alone in her rooms; Bríd seemed in such high spirits.

'Oh, Harry, I haven't enjoyed myself so much in ages!'

Back in Flood Street, she changed and dashed down into the basement to tell Mrs O'Rourke to bring up a tray.

'Harry's friends are coming to tea!'

Mrs O'Rourke raised an eyebrow slightly but said nothing.

Soon two cabs drew up outside the house and Harry and his fellow officers came bounding up the stairs and into her sitting room.

Mrs O'Rourke brought up the tea, and they were all sitting round Bríd, plying her with questions. Although she could see that Harry was not very happy with this invasion, it was such a relief to have company round her, lively young men to chat to her and admire her, after what had seemed an eternity of loneliness in her room, watching out every day for Harry to come. She was careful, though, to cover Harry's tracks for him. She was his cousin, over in London on a visit.

'Your first visit to London, Miss Flynn?'

'It is.'

'And how do you like it?'

'Grand! Sure, I've never enjoyed myself so much in all my life, and the sights we've seen! You'd never believe it. Harry's taken me everywhere. We was at the theatre last night.'

'What did you see?'

'*Lady Audley's Secret.*'

'Ah. And what was her secret?'

Bríd laughed. 'Oh, you'll have to go and find out for yourself. I love the theatre. There was the most lovely girl I ever saw in the play last night –'

'Not half as beautiful as you, I'll wager.'

'Sir John –'

Sir John Wrenshaw was older than Harry and had a more adult and reassuring manner; he seemed more solid. He was attentive too, flattered her and didn't ask any embarrassing questions about home. She was surprised to find that Harry seemed to have told him almost everything about her and Ballyglin. It could have been awkward, but he didn't find it so, and his manner put her at ease. He seemed a man to trust.

John Wrenshaw was thinking that Leighton had had a nerve to bring her over and install her here; when he'd made the suggestion that night under the elms, he hardly thought Leighton would have acted on it. And he was in for some heavy weather when he introduced her to his father. Looking at Bríd, though, he rather thought it would be worth it. Almost too good for a little shaver like Harry Leighton, really.

*

92

Later, after they had gone, Bríd was despondent.

"'Tis all very well for you, Harry. You can go go about wherever you like; I'm starved for company. It's mean of you, so it is, not to have introduced me before. If it hadn't been for that accidental meeting on the Serpentine, I would never have got to know your friends.'

Harry was silent. He was angry at the way Bríd had grandly invited everyone back to Flood Street. Now it would be all round the regiment that Harry Leighton was keeping a little Irish girl down in Chelsea. And if word got back to his father . . . fortunately the family were still in Ireland.

'Bríd, you still don't seem to realise that there are certain conventions, which have to be observed. I can't introduce you to fellows until we become engaged.'

'In other words, never.'

'Trust me, I beg you. I will tell Father. It's just a question of finding the right moment.'

'Molly said you'd never marry me.'

'You don't know my father. He's got to be handled carefully.'

'You're afraid of him. Afraid he'll not approve of me.'

'Oh, don't talk like that. Only give me time.'

'Sure, I can see it's hard for you. You an earl's son, to marry a poor girl like me.'

'Bríd, we shall be married, I swear it. Otherwise why would I bring you over here? It'll just take time, that's all.'

One evening they went to a music hall. Bríd loved it. As they sat listening to a young girl of about Bríd's age, he leaned over and whispered, 'She can't sing half as well as you.' Later, as they were returning to Flood Street, he suddenly had an idea.

'Would you like to have singing lessons? Why don't you?'

She would refuse him nothing, so he made enquiries and found a Maestro Pertinelli who was a coach at the opera and gave lessons to young ladies.

One afternoon Bríd took the omnibus up to Piccadilly, and then set off into the confusing mass of little streets called Soho. It was a poor neighbourhood, although close to the elegance of Regent Street. The streets were narrow, and she had to pick her way among dung heaps outside livery stables, market stalls heaped with fresh vegetables and fruit, and vendors and hawkers offering anything from broadside ballads to patent medicine. Chickens darted past her. Windows were open, for it had become warm, and lines of washing stretched across the road. Some children were playing a

93

game in the road and shouting at each other in a foreign language. There were little workshops and many restaurants with strange names.

She arrived in Dean Street. Signor Pertinelli had rooms above one of these restaurants, which she soon found were all Italian, and the language she heard too was Italian. In the front room overlooking the street, there was a grand piano and a lot of sheet music scattered on a table. Maestro Pertinelli was slender, probably about sixty, his thinning hair greased down with pomatum. His eyes were sunken and seemed to glitter, which gave him a sinister appearance, and he had a thin moustache. A small man, shabby, insignificant-looking.

Bríd stood in the middle of the room as he looked her up and down. She felt cheerful, blithe. She didn't really care about singing lessons. She was here to please Harry.

He was polite to her, and spoke with a foreign accent. 'Would you like to sing me something first? Something you like? Something what gives you pleasure.'

Bríd didn't mind. She knew she had a good voice and was happy to show it off to this funny little man. She decided to sing him something in Irish – that would fool him.

Despite all her high spirits, at the moment she opened her mouth, a quite different thought entered her mind. I'll show him, I'll sing the very best I can.

She composed herself and folded her hands. Standing in the middle of the room, without any fear, she sang as simply and sweetly as she knew how.

She felt the strange power arising incomprehensibly from within her. The power which was hers, which thrilled her as she felt herself in command of it.

The little man was sitting on a chair between the two windows looking down into Dean Street, so that, as Bríd sang, he was in shadow. When she had finished, there was silence, and she suddenly felt afraid. Perhaps she wasn't as good as she thought. Perhaps he thought her arrogant and conceited.

Then he said, quietly and thoughtfully, as if he were meditating to himself, 'You have a great gift. One day you will be a wonderful singer – and a wonderful actress.'

Bríd was flattered, but the words meant little to her.

'Oh no, I'm going to be married to Harry. Me on the stage! Sure, I'd be ashamed of myself in front of all them people!'

Still she was flattered and for a moment saw herself as she had seen the young girl at the music hall, looking so pretty and singing with an orchestra to accompany her, and all the people clapping her. She was happy to start the lessons.

Maestro Pertinelli soon made her realise there was a whole world to the art of singing, which she had never been aware of. He was never so flattering again for a very long time, and from being an insignificant little man who had praised her, he turned into a tyrant. He was the first man who seemed quite unconscious of her beauty, regarding her simply as the vessel which held the voice, and he expected her from the first to take the same disciplined interest in it that he did. The still, soft-spoken man with the glittering eyes exerted an impersonal power over her, held her with its force until she began to be in awe of him, afraid of him.

The first thing he did was to make her go into the room next door and take off her stays.

'No woman can sing with those things on! How can you open your ribcage?'

She had to stand with her fingertips on her lower ribs, at the back, breathe deeply and feel the ribs expand.

Then he would press his fist against her stomach and shout, 'Tighter! Harder! Press! You're not pressing! You got to sing from here, right down here, from the diaphragm. *Dio mio!* Now –' ludicrously changing to a gentle, mellifluous tone – 'let you voice float. Float!'

Holding her fingertips against her ribcag and screwing up her stomach muscles for all she was worth, and trying to sing smoothly at the same time, Bríd had never felt more awkward in her life. Thank God Harry was not there to see her! As her lessons progressed, however, the deep breathing became second nature to her.

Although these lessons were sometimes embarrassing and made her feel awkward, she was glad to go. Besides her love of music, it was something for her to do, something to look forward to in the desert of emptiness between Harry's visits.

Another time, he made her stare down her own throat in a mirror.

'Lift the soft palate! The part at the back! No, no, *cara mia.* Not the tongue! The soft palate. Now look in my mouth'. She had to stare down his throat. 'Look – see? The soft palate. You must open the throat . . .'

At last, when she was frantic and the perspiration was dripping down her face, he would relent.

'Have a rest. You want a drink of water? That's the hardest thing, to lift the soft palate, to really open the throat.'

On the mantelpiece of the maestro's room were two plaster busts. One day she asked him who they were.

'Bellini and Verdi. This one –' pointing to the head of a young man – 'Vincenzo Bellini. *Poverino*. He died so young, but what music! One day you will sing it. Eh, listen!'

He found some music on the table, set it on the piano and sat down and began to play. Then he began to sing. He had no singing voice at all, his voice cracked. Besides, he was trying to imitate a woman's voice. It was ridiculous, but Bríd could hear through it the limpid melody.

Casta Diva, che inargenti
Queste sacre antiche piante,
A noi volgi il bel sembiante
Senza nube e senza vel.

When he had finished, they sat for a moment in silence.

'That's wonderful,' Bríd said softly.

He turned on the piano stool and looked at her benevolently.

'The pure bel canto. You want to try it?'

'Me? Oh, maestro . . .'

'You try – you got a better voice than me.'

She stood behind him at the piano and he played the opening bars, then she came in, hesitantly, feeling her way along the line of the melody.

Afterwards he gave her the sheet of music.

'Take it home with you. Practice it over to yourself.'

Chapter Thirteen

'Member of Parliament murdered!'

It was a newspaper boy on the street corner shouting, as Bríd walked quickly along with her music sheets under her arm.

'Lord Leighton murdered! Fenian outrage!'

She looked up, then quickly bought a copy of the newspaper. Lord Leighton murdered in Ireland, while on his way home after addressing a meeting in Athlone. Dragged from his trap and stabbed on a country road. His servant also murdered. Thought to be the work of Fenians – Irish rebels fighting to throw off British rule.

The world swam round. Harry's brother, brutally murdered! Where was Harry now? She must see him immediately, give him her comfort. She hurried on, turned into Flood Street, and was soon running up the stairs into her rooms.

Mrs O'Rourke shouted up to her.

'Bríd! There's a telegram for you!'

She came up into the sitting room and placed it in Bríd's hands.

'Edward murdered by Fenians. Have gone to Ireland. Harry.'

Bríd sat heavily on a chair. Mrs O'Rourke looked at her with apprehension.

'What's the matter, dear?'

The telegram was on the table.

'Oh, that terrible murder! What's the world coming to – is it some friend of Lord Harry?'

Bríd could hardly say it. 'His brother.'

'Bríd, you never say so! Oh, them Fenians! What'll it ever come to with murder and bombing and all sorts? His brother – oh, the Lord!'

Bríd was in a daze. Edward murdered and Harry gone. Oh, the poor man! Now what could she do, except wait and read the newspapers? Would he send her news? She was helpless.

A horrible thought struck her. Had Garrett been involved? When

Edward went over to speak at the meeting, had Garrett taken this opportunity to strike at the family? Would Garrett do such a thing? He might. There was something in his character, she knew, a hard, implacable quality. Could he have done such a thing in revenge for her seduction, as he saw it, by Harry?

She decided to write Harry a letter. That at least would reach him. She sat down at the table, placed the paper before her, opened the bottle of ink, took up the pen. Oh, God, her handwriting! What would he think? It was always Molly who had written before. Well, no matter, it was too important. As if he would notice such a thing.

My Dearest Darling,
I have heard of your terrible news. Oh my darling, I do sympathise with you in your hour of sorrow. It is a terrible thing. I feel for you, I wish I was with you to hold you and comfort you. Please send me word soon, I am dying here without you. I think of you in your terrible sorrow and can do nothing to comfort you. Please come soon to
    your
      Bríd

The letter was posted off. There was nothing else she could do. One day she walked past the family house in King Street, St James's. Harry had taken her past before. It was a tall, gloomy old house, red brick, black with soot. They'd stood outside, staring up at the windows. 'My room is at the back,' he'd said. 'Looks out at a brick wall.' It was a joke.

She stood outside now. The blinds were drawn. Could she go in and ask for news? What would she say?

Sometimes the door would open and servants would come in or out. She felt horribly excluded.

She bought all the newspapers. No news. Investigations were proceeding, but still no news. Then there was a small paragraph. The funeral had taken place at the Church of Ireland parish church in the village of Ballyglin, County Roscommon. Lord Leighton had been buried among the tombs of the earls of Elphin, his ancestors. The heir to the title was his younger brother, now Lord Leighton – that was Harry. Bríd stood in the street, holding the newspaper, thinking. This must change everything, surely?

But how? She had not the faintest idea how these things were arranged.

A week passed. She couldn't sleep properly, and had nightmares in which Garrett was struggling with Harry. Garrett was stronger and more violent; Harry had no chance, and was being forced down and down. Garrett was surely going to kill him, while she stood by and was powerless to help. Some inexplicable force held her back. She saw the implacable will of Garrett, she saw the sweet and gentle Harry slowly being forced down and she could do nothing. At last she would wake up, sweating with terror and find dawn breaking. Out of the window, she could see the pale-pink sky across the rooftops. She would lean on one elbow in bed, breathing fast, frightened and unable to think of anything.

There was no message from Harry.

She was having giddy spells, too, in the morning soon after getting up. It was the nightmares and the lack of sleep. She would feel nauseous, sometimes couldn't eat anything, while at others she was ravenously hungry and sometimes craved the strangest things, things she had never eaten, never thought of eating.

The horrible uncertainty of her position, the days going by with no word from Harry, the almost nightmarish unreality of her situation, sitting alone in this room, far from Ireland, from everyone she knew, and not knowing what was to become of her – this was making her ill. She began to think she would have to go to a doctor. She had no one to talk to.

It was a lovely afternoon of summer, and she was sitting at the open window, looking down into the street. It eased her loneliness watching the carts of tradesmen go by – bakers, chimney sweeps, rag-and-bone men – and neighbours coming and going from their doors. Mrs O'Rourke was scrubbing the doorstep. She smiled up at Bríd, and Bríd smiled down at her. Comforting to watch the world go about its business.

A poor woman came down the street, leading a child. The child was howling and pulling at her mother, and Bríd watched her idly as they came nearer. She noticed the woman was expecting a child, was far gone, in fact. She looked tired and careworn, and the child was pulling and fretting, and Bríd felt sorry for the woman that she would soon have another to care for.

At that moment the thought hit her like a thunderbolt. She too was expecting a child. She must be. She hadn't been to a doctor, but she didn't need to. The symptoms were clear. It all made sense.

She got up from her chair and walked round the room. How could she have been so stupid? Of course. She walked up and down the room possessed by a freezing fear. She was expecting. It was so obvious. She thought, I've got to speak to Harry. As soon as he comes back from Ireland. We've got to be married as soon as possible. Nothing else matters. As soon as possible.

Every day she was looking out for him.

Surely he must come soon. Surely he must?

One afternoon she was in her sitting room. It was a warm day and the windows were open. There was a knock at the door below. She was alert at once. At last, at last he was coming. She jumped up and was about to rush down and open the door when she heard Mrs O'Rourke going to answer it. She waited, her heart beating. Mrs O'Rourke was talking to somebody. It wasn't Harry. She sank back on to a chair. Not him. Some tradesman.

They were still talking, then the door closed and there was a tread on the stair. She was puzzled.

The door opened and Mrs O'Rourke was there.

'Gentleman to see you, Bríd.'

She stood aside, and a middle-aged man, dressed in a black frock coat and holding a black silk top hat in his hand, came into the room. He was slightly shorter than Bríd, with a round face, a high colour, and Prince Albert mutton-chop whiskers and moustache. He had rather prominent eyes, which gave him a fierce expression. She knew who he was.

'Miss Flynn? I am the Earl of Elphin.'

He spoke brusquely, with a slight drawl in his voice.

She drew herself up, tall and dignified before him.

'I won't stay long,' he went on, without waiting for her to say anything. 'I've come to talk to you about my son, Lord Leighton.'

'Harry.'

He looked around the room for a moment.

'Is he paying for this?'

'What?'

'How long have you been here?'

'Lord Elphin, please come to the point.'

'Miss Flynn, it'll never do, you know. Did you really think you could catch him?'

'I beg your pardon?'

'Don't play the innocent. It was a damn silly game. What did you think a younger son is worth, anyway? Harry would have had to make his own way in the world. As it is –' He paused. 'As it is, he's now the heir to the title.'

'Your son Edward. I read about it. It was dreadful. I'm sorry for you.'

He looked away, faltering. 'It was a terrible blow. His mother . . .' He paused, then looked back at her. 'Now Harry is the heir.'

'Where is Harry?'

'Where you can't get at him.'

Bríd was taken aback at his change of tone. He had become strong again, aggressive. Bríd reacted.

'Where is he? Why can't he speak for himself?'

'Never mind about that. I'm here, and I'm speaking.'

'Not to me, Lord Elphin. Please go.'

'Hark'ee, Miss Flynn. Harry is the heir to the title. I'll be frank with you. We haven't a penny, any of us. Family's practically bankrupt. Every foot of land is mortgaged. When Harry told me he'd borrowed a thousand pounds of the Jews, I couldn't believe it.

'There's only one thing that can rescue us now and that's if Harry makes a good marriage. So I'd better tell you straight away that he's engaged to Miss Stella Richardson. Can't announce it publicly yet. Family's in mourning.'

Bríd could hear nothing. It was as if there were a great scream in her ears. She knew only one thing: she had to speak to Harry. She had to, or die.

'Where is he?'

'I won't tell you.'

'I'll find out.'

'You won't.'

'I'll find him. We love each other and we've pledged ourselves for ever.'

'You're clever, Miss Flynn, I can see that. But you'll find out I'm a damn sight cleverer. It would be best if you went home.'

'I'm expecting a baby.'

He looked at her and his expression changed to contempt.

'Up to every trick.'

He opened a wallet and took out several banknotes. He looked at them for a moment as if calculating and then placed them on the table. He then took out some coins and laid them on the notes.

'I think that should get you home and help to buy you a husband.'

She stood before him.

'Where is Harry? I will speak to him.'

'You won't speak to him, I'm afraid. Don't try to come to our town house. You won't be admitted, and in any case he isn't there.'

'I'll find him, Lord Elphin. I don't believe a word you say. He loves me, I know he does.'

'You tricked him for a while, I grant. But he's engaged to Miss Richardson. It'll be announced in the papers when we're out of mourning.'

'Oh, God!'

She sat heavily on a chair.

'Go home, Miss Flynn. Go back to your family. It's best.'

She tore round at him.

'You blackguard! What have you done to Harry? You haven't thought of his happiness, have you?'

'Happiness? Are you mad? The entire family's about to sink! What does his happiness matter? What does one person's happiness matter when an entire family is at stake? You've had your holiday, now go home. This is serious.'

He turned towards the door. Bríd sat, leaning over the table. She turned to him again as he was in the doorway.

'You scoundrel! I'll never forgive you. I'd kill you if I could. Where is Harry?'

Elphin stood in the doorway looking down at her for a moment.

'Good afternoon, Miss Flynn.'

He put his hat on his head and went out. A moment later, she heard the front door close.

It couldn't be true. It was a foul trick. Harry – they could never force him to marry that girl. She knew him. It was impossible.

What could she do?

She'd go to King Street. They'd never let her in. He wasn't there anyway.

Write a letter? It would never reach him.

She couldn't believe it. She would scream.

The Earl of Elphin, that vile, loathsome blackguard was obsessed with his family. Ready to ruin Harry's happiness for his own pride. How could a father treat his son this way? She would scream.

She had to find Harry. That was all. If only she could find him, all would be well.

Sir John Wrenshaw. He was Harry's friend. Send a message through him. She stood up. It was her only chance. Find Wrenshaw. Send a letter. She was in a fever of impatience.

She took a large paisley shawl, threw it round her shoulders, put on her bonnet and went out.

This was highly irregular, as they would say in the cavalry. No matter.

She walked quickly through the streets. A message. Just tell Harry to come to her. It was urgent. No more than that.

The long railings, the barrack blocks. It was the most pleasant summer afternoon, but she felt none of it. Only a hideous weakness in her body, a coldness, but also a clear certainty in her mind.

The gates. A soldier on duty. What must he think? Some whore? No matter.

'I must speak to Sir John Wrenshaw. It's extremely urgent.'

She was standing at the gates. The soldier had a slightly amused smile. He was going to make the most of this. She saw what was going through his mind. But then they had to move to one side as a carriage came down the road and was about to turn in at the gate. Distracted, she looked up, and saw Harry in the carriage.

'Harry!'

His head shot out of the window. In an instant he was out of the carriage. He turned to the man on the box.

'Go up to my room. It's all packed up.'

The man touched his hat with his whip and the carriage continued across the parade ground.

Harry came quickly across to where she stood transfixed.

He was here. Relief swam through her. All was well. She threw her arms about his neck, and for a moment he held her tight. Then he drew her along, and they walked away from the gate along the street by the high railings.

'Harry, you're here! I'm so thankful! It's been a nightmare – your father –'

'I know, I know. Oh, Bríd, you can't imagine what's been going on. It's been frightful. Think of it – Edward murdered! The family was shattered. I still can't believe it.' He paused. 'Then, after the funeral, Father and I had a long talk. I'm now the heir. He spelled it all out. I'll have to give up the cavalry. Got to start thinking about the estates, the property and everything. Father insists I marry money –'

They stopped.

'Then it's true.'

Harry was desperate.

'He says we're practically broke. Everything's mortgaged. I'm under age anyway and couldn't marry without his consent. Then there's all the money I borrowed to bring you over. You can't imagine what a time I've had.'

'Then it's true.' She couldn't take in his words.

'Fact is, I've been living in a dream world. Edward being murdered has woken me up. It could never have been. I mean, you a Catholic, and me an Anglican.'

She was thinking, Dream world? But I'm not in a dream world. I'm right here, wide awake, and he's getting ready to drop me like a hot potato.

'Harry –'

'It's out of the question, our marrying.' He became enthusiastic. 'But that needn't mean we have to part! We can go on as we are. I was

103

coming to see you to talk about it. Very tricky at home, as you can imagine, and it needed some thinking out.'

'Go on as we are? You're getting married!'

He looked away. 'I thought somehow there could still be room in the world for us together. You here in Chelsea, and me coming to see you.'

'Harry, I can't stand it. You want to keep me as a mistress, even when you're married to someone else?'

He looked wretched. Bríd felt giddy, as if everything was collapsing. Harry a traitor. It was not possible.

'You're the one I love. But what can I do?'

'Marry me,' she said, with icy authority.

For a second they looked each other full in the eye. At last he broke away.

'I can't,' he whispered.

She was thinking, What about my baby? His child? What shall I tell him? He looked wretched. Tell him? That would change everything, wouldn't it? That would make him think again.

It didn't come. She wouldn't say it. If he was preparing to leave her, so be it. He should never know. She felt heavy, leaden. She turned away. There were no tears in her eyes. She felt a million times stronger than him. She would carry on. She would survive.

Part II
1865–70

Chapter Fourteen

A wild, stormy day, the sea very high. A little fishing boat just coming into the harbour, sails billowing. Above the blue sky, gulls turning in the wind over the mast. The sailors at the ropes. The jetty, the lighthouse, bright red. People watching anxiously. Women, they must be the wives. Behind, half visible, the harbour. The old Dutch houses, chimneys, smoke blown by the wind. The quayside. A dog barking.

Roses. Anemones. Violets. Irises. Geraniums. Then roses again. Intertwined, anemones, violets, irises, geraniums again, and so on, up to the ceiling. Endlessly repeated. Roses, anemones, violets, irises, geraniums, roses, anemones . . .

White porcelain, there was a little flower on it. What was it? Pink, a rose. Key in the lock, never used it. Door, brown, streaked, painted, uneven stain.

Her eyes wandered up to the gas mantle, flickering, hissing gently. Green, white, greenish-white, with a little orange at the very edge, just a slight orange flush.

Then she was looking at the wallpaper again: roses, anemones, violets . . . Her eyes were dry with weeping. She had no more tears to weep. She was dry, shrivelled, finished.

For the thousandth time her mind ran back through the afternoon. But even then it got lost in the wallpaper, the little picture on the wall of the fishing boats, the gas hissing . . .

A distant bell rang. Two o'clock. Slowly her mind engaged. She was cold, stiff, she could hardly move from the sofa. She had been there, it seemed, for ever. The gas was hissing. The windows were still open, and it was cold in the room. She must have been asleep. She shuddered. Her face was dry and tight, her body weak and lethargic. She was stiff and tired. She felt stupid and old.

She pulled herself up with difficulty, threw down her shawl and

107

went into her bedroom. Cold, aching in every fibre, her head aching, her bones aching, her eyes . . . Slowly she pulled at her laces, her buttons, her fingers clumsy, slowly she pulled off her boots. Naked in the dark, silent room, she dragged her nightdress over her head, drew back the covers and got into the cold bed.

A shaft of fear struck her. Oh, God, she was alone. In the darkness she lay, staring up, unseeing, seized by a gripping, freezing feeling. Alone. She could never return to Ireland. And what would Mrs O'Rourke say if – when – she found out? Would she throw her out? Where would she go? She would be lost. Who was there, in all the thousands of people here in this great city, this teeming mass of strangers, to whom she could turn? She was alone. A crawling sensation of terror ran over her skin. She started up in the darkness. How could he be so cruel? She would have died for him. Why didn't he listen to her? She depended on him entirely, she had lived for him, had thrown everything away, left all behind, to come here and be with him.

She slept uneasily, fitfully. She would wake with a start in the dark room. Where am I? Oh, she sighed, turned her head on the pillow, and then remembered, oh, it was true. Her mind struggled to understand, as she lay staring up into the darkness.

Her mind drifted away; she slept, had a dream. They were there together, it was afternoon, on the hill looking down over the lake, the little islands tree-covered, the sun mild, watery. He was holding her, looking into her eyes. They kissed. She was safe. A warm, deep feeling of peace stole through her body, and she wanted him, wanted him close, tight, holding her, tight, she felt his face against hers, his lips, warm, safe . . .

She woke. It was morning and someone was knocking. She started. She heard Mrs O'Rourke.

'Bríd? Bríd! Bríd!'

The dream was over. Her head turned on the pillow, her hair dishevelled.

'Bríd? Bríd!'

The door of the sitting room opened.

'Bríd dear, are you there? Bríd?'

Mrs O'Rourke was looking in.

'You're not ill, are you, dear?'

Bríd could not look at her. Mrs O'Rourke came to the end of the bed.

'Let me look at you. Dear, whatever is the matter? You look terrible. Are you feverish? Bríd, for heaven's sake tell me, dear.'

Bríd could not look at her.

'Bríd dear, you must tell me what's the matter. Shall I fetch the doctor?'

Bríd shook her head, rolling on the pillow. Mrs O'Rourke clasped her hands in her apron.

'Oh, holy mother of Jesus, I don't know, I've never seen you like it. Oh, Jesus, Mary and Joseph, you must tell me, you must. I can't have you lying there, you poor, poor thing, and you such a merry, light-hearted creature. Will you have some breakfast? You must be half-starved, you had nothing last night. I'll bring you up some breakfast this minute.'

She hurried away downstairs. Bríd turned her head to the wall.

Roses, anemones, violets, irises, geraniums . . . Her heart would break. She began to weep again, her exhausted body shivering. Her head ached, her bones ached . . .

Mrs O'Rourke came in with a tray of breakfast; clearing things off a side table, she brought it up to Bríd in bed.

'Now, Bríd, I've made you a little bit of breakfast. You must eat it, dear, you had no supper last night. You'll get run down, Bríd dear. For heaven's sake, eat it'll cheer you up.'

Roses, anemones . . .

'I'll just leave it here. Oh, dear, at least have a cup of tea, don't just lie there staring at the wall – you frighten me. Won't you have a cup of tea? Well, are you ill? Shall I go for the doctor?'

Bríd didn't move; at last Mrs O'Rourke went away.

Again she drifted into a shallow sleep. She remembered the first time she saw him – in his red coat, his muddy boots, so pale, so beautiful, so helpless, unconscious on the table, would he ever wake up? She had loved him at once.

The sun had moved round, the shadows changed. She was here, in this bed. The sun was shining, it shone in here in the morning, it was moving round, though. What time was it? It didn't matter. Time, food, clothes, it didn't matter, roses, anemones, irises, violets . . . She drifted into sleep again.

It was darker, nearly night. The tray had gone. Mrs O'Rourke must have come while she was asleep. The room was dim, fear seized her. What was she going to do? Alone in this desert of strangers, where could she go? Who would help her?

It was dark. She had no idea of the time. Suddenly Bríd was seized by a restlessness. She must move; she must go out and walk. She dressed hurriedly, and threw over her shoulders the cloak Harry had bought her, an elegant dark-blue mantle with fur trimming. Clumsily her fingers tied the cord, and she went out into the street.

The cold air in her face stimulated her; she breathed deeply and began to walk. It didn't matter where. The houses loomed down at her in rows, dimly lit by gaslight. The street was deserted, her footsteps sounded hollow on the pavement. She turned into a wider street. A cab rattled by. She walked on. A policeman saw her from the other side of the street. He shone his bullseye at her but she didn't notice, only walked. She heard the heels of her boots tapping on the hollow pavements, left, right, tap, tap, tap.

The regular motion calmed her and she felt more tranquil. It was good to walk, just to walk.

She was under trees, tall trees, and the light of the streetlamps was broken and deflected through the branches. Behind them, the houses, white in the gaslight, looked blindly down.

She was in the park, and there was the lake. The bushes seemed grotesque and disproportionate, shadowy in the half-light from the street. Ducks slept, their heads under their wings.

Now there were lights again, it was brighter and there was more traffic; cabs and broughams clattered past her, and people were everywhere about her; men in top hats and satin-lined cloaks, smoking cigars; girls, finely dressed in beautiful gowns, satin and silk, the prettiest straw bonnets with pink ribbons. She pushed her way through, but everywhere around her was noise, people, crowds, girls, beautiful girls, noise, men in top hats, noise.

She crashed to the pavement in a dead faint.

She was lying on the pavement, looking up. A circle of faces looking down at her. She tried to move but couldn't.

'Now, now, dearie, take it easy, you just stay there a moment. You fainted. Don't crowd round, everybody, let the poor girl breathe. Haven't you ever seen anybody faint before? Come on, back off. Don't worry, dearie, we'll take care of you, you fainted, that's all.'

She was weak as a rush, couldn't lift her arm, let alone her head; empty, cleaned out, finished.

'We'll get her inside somewhere. Oh, she's a pretty girl, we'll take her into Kate's.'

Hands lifted her, arms around her, under her; she was carried inside.

It was bright and warm and she was sitting on a padded red velvet seat by the wall. It was some sort of restaurant or club. Around her were lights, chandeliers, looking glasses on the walls, gilt chairs and tables, and crowds of people, men in evening dress, lovely girls . . .

'What happened?' She had a throbbing headache, and the light hurt her eyes.

A girl was fussing over her.

'You fainted, dearie. Don't you worry, Bella's gone to get you a

110

drink. Here, let me loosen your mantle. Nice one too. You do look pale – been overdoing it, have you?'

Another girl pushed through the crowd with a tray and three tall glasses of some hot drink.

'Oh, Bella, you good, kind girl! Here, take a sip of this, a nice hot brandy punch, this'll do you good; it's cold out tonight. Bella, you are an angel! Here's to us.'

They had placed the long, hot glass in her hands, and Bríd took a sip. The hot drink seared down through her; she spluttered, choked, breathed, tears came to her eyes. Then came the warmth, the strength. She looked round. Where was she? And who were these kind souls who had brought her in?

'You're in Kate's, of course. Never heard of Kate Hamilton's? You are green – never mind. That's done you good – you've got a bit of colour in your cheeks. You passed out like a light, dearie, just keeled over like a log. You don't seem to have hurt yourself, though.'

'You are so kind. I don't know how to thank you.'

'Irish are you?'

Two girls of her own age were sitting with her at a little marbletop table. They were ornately dressed in pretty little bonnets, their cloaks thrown back to show off low-cut silk dresses with tight waists and flounced skirts. They were drinking the same steaming, invigorating drink she had, clasping the glass with both hands.

'You're very kind,' Bríd said weakly. 'Really, I don't know how I came to be here. I was out walking.'

The girls sipped at their drinks. The girl opposite looked over the top of her glass at her with a shrewd glance.

'Weren't we all? You new to the game?'

'Pardon?'

'How long have you been gay?'

'I don't understand . . .'

'A pretty girl like you ain't in the Haymarket at midnight for the good of your health, I take it. You don't have to be stuck up with us, dearie.' She adopted a tolerant, world-weary tone. 'You was a governess too, I expect, which your innocence was took advantage of, and you was brought down to a life of shame through no fault of your own.'

The two girls caught each other's eye and broke into laughter.

Bríd went pale.

'She looks hungry. Tell you what, Bella, I'm a bit peckish myself; what about pies all round, eh? Got to keep our little strengths up.'

The girl beside her signalled to a waiter and gave their order.

Bríd watched the waiter weave his way expertly through the chattering crowd and the cloud of cigar smoke.

111

'You've been so kind, I don't know what to say. I've walked so far. What is this place?'

The two girls looked at each other and laughed again.

'What does it look like? A night house, ain't it? We come here most nights around midnight. All the swells come here from the Argyll or after the opera. We meet all our friends here, don't we, Bella?'

Bríd, more awake now, at last understood.

Through the noise and crowd that swirled about them, the waiter reappeared, balancing three plates and carrying knives and forks, salt and pepper stands, and bottles of relish. With brisk efficiency he set them all down in front of the three girls, clattering the plates and the bottles on the marble table.

'Thanks, Freddie, you're a love. Here you are, dearie. What's your name, by the way? I'm Fanny and that's Bella.'

Bríd looked down. 'My name is Bríd.'

The two girls tucked into the meat pies with enthusiasm. Bríd, watching them, took a mouthful of the hot food herself. She felt as if she had eaten nothing for a week.

'And we'll have three more brandy punches, Freddy.'

Bríd's curiosity about these girls grew. They were so beautifully dressed; were they really on the streets?

'Listen dear, a word to the wise – in this business, you've got to be well dressed. Nothing but the best, ain't that so, Bella? I spend a fortune on clothes, new bonnet every week.' Her attention was distracted by something across the room. 'Bella, there's that old marquess of yours; don't look now, I'll tell you when to look round. He's coming over here. Don't look round.'

A cadaverous, elderly man in evening dress and a silk hat was coming towards them. Bella looked up briefly.

'What are you doing out at this time of night, you naughty old dog?'

But he was looking at Bríd. 'Bella! Thank God, I've been looking for you all evening.'

He had long dundreary whiskers and, as he pulled up a chair and sat at the table with them, Bríd saw they they had been dyed a violet colour.

'Been having the most unspeakable time. My man walked out on me today. Inherited a public house, if you please, snapped his fingers at me this morning and walked out. Had to send round to some confounded agency for another fellow; useless, have to find everything myself. Worn to a shadow. So I said to myself, I'll just pop down to old Ma Hamilton's and see if I can't find my little friends Bella and Fanny. What about a drop of something bubbly? Waiter, let's have a bottle of bubbly here. Now Bella, who's your pretty little friend, eh?'

Bríd looked at him. Who was this old roué, leering at her with an impertinent stare? Bella gave her a sharp look, but Fanny said,

'This is Bríd. She's new to London, your lordship.'

'New to London, eh?'

Bella cut in decisively. 'She wouldn't interest you, Dolly.'

The marquess turned plaintively to her. 'Bella, my sweet, I called last Tuesday, and you weren't at home.'

'I've told you you a thousand times, Dolly, never come knocking without telling me. It would have saved you a wasted journey.' She went on eating for a moment. 'I was in the park, riding, as it happened. I do love riding, I love to feel the fresh air in my face and a strong, spirited horse under me, doing a brisk canter by the lake.'

The Marquess giggled.

'My sentiments exactly, Bella. What better of an afternoon than a brisk ride with a strong, spirited creature under me? Getting my leg over a fine mettlesome filly to put her through her paces; nothing I like better, what?'

As he spoke he gave a leer at Bríd. Bella gave him a slap on the wrist.

'You dirty old thing! Dolly, you should be ashamed in front of my friend Bríd. They're not used to that kind of talk in Ireland, you know.'

Bríd had no idea what they were talking about, but she resented the inquisitive, proprietorial look the Marquess had given her as he sat down.

Soon after, Bella and the Marquess got up and went off.

'Feeling stronger now, Bríd?'

'Fanny, you must think me very innocent not knowing about Kate Hamilton's and everything, but I should like to know . . . I mean, well . . .' She paused, looking down. 'Don't you mind, you know, I mean – that disgusting old man?'

'Mind? Dolly? Are you serious?' She laughed. 'At his age it's all talk anyway.' She finished eating and wiped her mouth; looking at Bríd, she suddenly became serious. 'Rather be in service? Rather be a housemaid? Up at five in the morning, on the go from morning till night, yes ma'am, no ma'am, upstairs, downstairs, one afternoon off a month, and eight pound a year wages? And just you answer back once, *once*, mind, and you're out with no character. Catch me!' She sniffed, and looked round the room for a moment. 'No, this is the life. Mind you, I could pack it in any time I chose. I've had offers, so's Bella – that dirty old marquess, I reckon she could have him – but I likes my freedom. I've got money, I've got my own place, I've got my regulars, I goes to the opera, I goes in the park riding, I've got all the clothes I want; look at them boots, made to measure.' She lifted her leg, and Bríd saw the beautiful, soft green leather boot on her foot. 'Twenty-five shillings – you won't get them for being a good girl.' She adjusted a pale-violet glove she was wearing, and gave a self-satisfied sigh. 'I expect I'll settle down and get married in the end. Either that or the other thing – too much of this stuff.'

She emptied her champagne glass.

'Well then, but Fanny, how did you begin? I mean, what led you into it?'

Fanny stared into her glass for a moment.

'I'm not from London actually. I was brought up in Dorking. My pa's a butcher. It was very dull, and I was bored, and then I met this fellow and we decided to run away to London and live together. He tempted me, and to be honest I didn't need much tempting, I was so eager to get away from home. Anyway, we came to London, and he had a job, I don't know, in a paint factory or something. We enjoyed life, spent all our money, went out to theatres, restaurants, always having a good time. That's all I wanted, to enjoy myself. Well, then I found I was expecting. 'Course I told him, but he was furious. He shouted at me, and I'd hoped he would be pleased. After that everything went cold between us, and one day he says to me, it'll never work, we weren't right for each other, and he puts twenty pounds on the table and walks out. I cry my eyes out, then I count the money. I'm not going home, says I to myself, and that's flat.

'Well, the baby comes, a little darling, I was so pleased. But money was running low. I didn't know what I was going to do. Then the baby fell ill, he was terribly sick, cried all the time, really screeching, it would tear my heart out, blue it was. I was terrified. I took him to the hospital. Meningitis, they said, very little hope. I went mad. I raved. I couldn't believe it, my little darling. He died. I had to organise the funeral, my last money gone. His tiny coffin, I tell you I was mad, out of my mind.

'Then one day I thought, fine, I don't care anyway, I'll enjoy myself. What does it matter? I deserve it after what I've suffered. I wanted money, I wanted clothes, I wanted pleasure. And I've got them. I'm happy with my life. And no man will ever tell me what to do, believe me.'

There was a pause for a moment, and silence between them. Bríd held the look in Fanny's eye, the hard, defiant stare, then, embarrassed, she looked away over the crowds of people at the other tables, laughing and joking, shouting across at each other, calling to waiters, the clouds of cigar smoke, and the waiters hurrying from table to table. Fanny became brisk and cheerful again.

'There's few as well off as me. And I'm free. My own woman. That's what counts in life.'

She waved across the room. A heavy-set man, his hair gleaming with pomatum, joined them.

'Just coming, Georgie. You ready? Listen, Bríd, I've got to go. Look after yourself, won't you? You'll do well, pretty girl like you – only don't let them get you down, know what I mean? Cheerio now. Come on, Georgie.'

Bríd watched her go, then slowly tied up the ribbon of her bonnet and stood up to leave. She was making her way through the crowd when a man leered into her face from one side, a cigar in his hand.

'Hullo, my dear, I don't believe I've had the pleasure.'

He pulled at her arm and lurched against her. He was drunk.

'I'm sure you've time for a chat, my dear. Come and have a drink.'

She placed her hand against his chest and thrust him away with a force that made him stumble backwards. Pushing her way through the crowd, she made her way into the street.

She had to get home. She walked quickly through the streets. The Haymarket was still crowded; men and women thronged about her. The cafés were still open, brightly lit. She had to get home. A cab? She had no money on her. Still, she hailed a cab, and as the hansom rattled through the dark streets down into Chelsea, she saw Fanny's face in her mind and heard her story again.

Could it happen to her? Could she become like that? What should she do? How was she to keep her baby? Would any man marry her with a child? The thoughts turned over and over in her mind; she felt as if she were at the helm of some small boat in heavy seas – could she keep upright? Could she keep afloat? Or would she go under?

When she reached the house, she ran indoors to fetch some money for the cab. There on the table was the money Lord Elphin had thrown down. She paid off the cab.

She came in, untied her cloak and went to bed. She was tired to death.

115

Chapter Fifteen

The following morning Bríd woke late, but as soon as she opened her eyes, a restless energy seized her. She had to face what was to come; she had to make decisions. When Mrs O'Rourke brought her breakfast, Bríd put on a cheerful face. Mrs O'Rourke was pleased at that, but Bríd didn't want to tell her anything until her own thoughts were clearer. After she had eaten some eggs and toast and drunk two cups of coffee, and Mrs O'Rourke had cleared away the tray, Bríd took out the money Lord Elphin had left, and counted it on the table. It amounted to fifteen pounds. It would have made a handsome dowry in Ballyglin. But who would take her with a baby?

Still, she could live on it for a long time, if necessary. She could have the baby – but then what? And where was she to bring him up? She stared out of the window, down into the street. There was no question of going back to the village. She must stay in London. What would happen when the money ran out? She thought again of Fanny, and Kate Hamilton's, and those men and their insolent looks, the looks that said, 'We've got the money that can buy you', the way they stared into her face.

Never, never, never, never would she allow such a man to touch her. For a moment in blind panic, as the thoughts crowded in her brain, she stared wildly round the room. Then she caught sight of the money on the table, and, thinking of Fanny and her twenty pounds, she vowed to herself, never!

She must be careful with the money until she could see her way forward. Think carefully, plan ahead. She would have to cut down on all her expenses. Her singing – she thought of Maestro Pertinelli. Today was the day for her singing lesson.

There could be no place in her future life for singing lessons. It had been a luxury, part of that life of make-believe she had lived with

116

Harry. That would have to end. She would go and tell the Maestro now.

She took courage. She dressed in a light, flowery dress of white muslin, printed with blue anemones over a wide crinoline skirt, and with puffed sleeves. She picked out her big Amazon hat. It was a bright, sunny morning, and she determined to put a brave face on her new world. As she looked in her mirror to put up her hair, she was astonished to find so little mark of sorrow on her face. She brushed her hair, remembering how she had loved to see herself in her looking glass; this morning she found her beauty unchanged, yet she could never again take pride or pleasure in it. She looked on her face as the face of another.

She was just walking out of the door when her eyes fell on her little Irish harp. She set it on a stool and ran her hands over the strings for a moment. But what good was it to her now? She would give it to Pertinelli as a pledge of friendship, a keepsake to remind him of her.

She carried it on the omnibus to Piccadilly and walked up into Soho, picking her way through the street markets, the stalls of fruit, the butchers' stalls, the girls with their flower baskets. All around her, there was life and energy, shouting and laughter. Once she could have felt part of that, and laughed in sympathy. Today she held herself tight together. She had business in hand, decisions to make.

She stopped at the door beside the Italian restaurant. She could hear the voice of another girl above her, a young, immature voice, running up and down scales in time with a piano.

Bríd was early. She waited in the street while above her, the voice went on. Unconsciously Bríd's ear corrected her, wincing at the girl's lack of feeling for the music.

The singing stopped and a few minutes later, a girl of fifteen or sixteen came out in a hurry, some sheets of music carelessly clutched in one gloved hand, and tore off down the street. Bríd went up the narrow stairs and into the Maestro's music room.

He was staring down in to the street. As he heard Bríd come in, he turned and looked at her, hunching his shoulders in a characteristically Italian shrug.

'These young girls! *Dio mio*, why do their mothers send them to me? Why do they pay me? You think they want to learn? You think they interested in music? Stupid music-hall songs is all they think of. Is a waste of time. I come here to this filthy, ugly city, where I never see the sun, where the food is terrible, it rains all the time, I think I teach beautiful music, and they only want stupid music-hall songs.'

117

Looking down on the table where the scores lay in profusion, he seemed old, defeated. At last he looked up again and smiled.

'*Ma, come tu sei bella stamattina!* Bríd, such a pretty dress! You more beautiful than ever. Your husband, he will be a lucky man.'

His eye fell on the harp.

'What's this?'

Bríd pulled off her shawl and carefully let it fall over the back of a chair.

'It's a gift. Maestro Pertinelli, I have something to tell you. I won't be having any more lessons. I want you to have my harp to . . . remind you.'

He stared at her.

She looked down, feeling her strength, her calm, oozing away.

'The fact is, well, I don't quite know how . . . You see, Maestro, my circumstances are changed. That is –'

She sat down heavily on a chair.

There was silence. The Maestro waited for her to find the words.

'Well, there it is. From now on I won't be able to afford it, that's all.'

Still the Maestro said nothing. She could feel his gaze on her as she sat looking down at the old carpet. At last she looked up into his face. In a moment something, a fleeting look of sympathy in his eye, unlocked her tongue.

'Well, if you must know, Maestro, I'm not getting married after all, and I'm going to need all the money I have, and 'tis as simple as that.'

The old man was silent. A natural delicacy made him loath to pry into her private affairs, and he could not meet her eye for a moment.

'Of course I understand you have other things, no doubt important –'

He suddenly pulled up another chair, almost knee to knee, and began to speak rapidly in a low voice.

'But Bríd, you got talent, you are a singer, you could have a career. Believe me. There's not a woman in a thousand got what you got. They come in here every day, up those stairs, they got no talent, it's painful for me to listen to them. But you, you got talent. And more than that, you got a love for music.'

Bríd sat listening in a mood of impatience. All his grand talk of being a singer didn't mean much to a woman who was soon going to be a mother.

''Tis very kind of you, Maestro –'

He continued, holding her attention with his low voice.

'Bríd, you know the holy Bible, eh? You're a good Catholic girl, eh? You remember the parable of the talents? The master, he gives a talent to each of three servants. The first servant he goes, he makes money, he comes back with ten talents. The second servant, he goes away, he does business, he come back with five talents. But the third servant, what did he do? He buried his talent in the ground. He buried it, Bríd. And what did his master say when he comes back? To the first servant, to the second servant, he says, well done, you good servant, and he rewards them.'

His voice sank lower.

'But what does he say to the third servant, eh? He says, you bad servant, you waste my talent I give you, you do nothing with it. And he punish him. Bríd, what's it mean, eh? It means, God gives you a talent, and it's your duty, Bríd, not your pleasure, to use it the best you can.'

There was silence between them. His words had sunk into her heart. Yet how could she tell him? He talked of duties. She had a greater one before her.

'Maestro, everything you say is true, don't I know it. Only there's reasons, please don't ask me, there is reasons.'

He was the only man with whom she had ever been able to talk about singing, the only man in London apart from Harry with whom she had any intimacy, and she did not want to let it pass. She wanted to go on talking, yet hesitated for fear of what she might say.

Disturbed, she sat looking down at her hands on her knees. She could not bring herself to look up into the Maestro's face. He continued to stare intently at her, however, willing her to look at him until at last, under the force of his will, she looked up. His eyes glittered.

'What's the matter, Bríd? You're troubled.'

Her self-possession broke, and she looked wildly up and about the room, looking at it for the last time.

'Well, if you must know, Maestro, I'm going to have a baby.'

There was silence. This time it was his eyes that fell from her gaze.

'And you're – you're alone, eh?'

'Yes.'

There was another silence, and then he raised his eyes and looked into hers again, and his gaze had softened.

'Bríd, I'm sorry. I'm really sorry. Is difficult for you, I see.'

'You don't blame me?'

'It's not for me to blame you.'

She reached out her hand and took his.

'Bríd, if ever you think of singing, you think of me. I help you. And maybe, you have a baby, you still be a singer, eh? Why not? What

119

else will you do? A baby is not the end of everything. You think every girl who has a baby just disappears, or what? They carry on, they work in the theatre, in the opera house. They carry on, Bríd. You wait there, I'll make a cup of coffee. We talk.'

He set a kettle over the fire and they waited for it to boil.

'I been in a lot of theatres, opera houses, concert halls. You think I never seen any babies? What you think? Life goes on. These girls, they don't care, they go on, they got to make money.'

They sat on his old plush chairs and sipped the bitter Italian coffee as he tried to make her see beyond the fact of her baby to a future life, but she could not see it. There was the baby, that was as far as she could see. There had to be a hearth and a home for it. A theatre was no place to bring up a baby.

When she rose to go, refusing all the Maestro's offers and pleas, his last words to her, as she stood in the doorway at the head of the stairs, were:

'I'll keep your harp on loan, Bríd. I'll hold it till you come back for it. That's all. You come back for it, Bríd.'

She went down into the street. She knew she would never return for her harp.

She walked back down into Chelsea. The sky was blue with little white clouds, cotton wool, high up. Although the sun was warm, the wind was still rather cool.

Mrs O'Rourke brought her up some lunch. Seeing Bríd looking more composed and cheerful, she sat down at the table with her as she ate.

She had often sat with her at her meals, and her kindliness and motherly warmth had encouraged Bríd to confide in her; she had told her much of her story, and talked about Ballyglin and her childhood. Mrs O'Rourke had been interested and friendly.

Bríd looked across at the comfortable, cheery woman, her white curls peeping from under her mobcap, her elbow resting on the table.

'Sure I'm glad to see you looking better, my dear. I thought you was dying yesterday, I was that worried. Won't you tell me about it, Bríd dear?'

Bríd dropped her eyes and went on eating as she thought for a moment what to tell Mrs O'Rourke. What would she say if she knew about Harry? Mrs O'Rourke went on in a lighter vein, looking out of the window.

'There, but men is such vain, flighty creatures. You never know where you are with them. No doubt all will come right.'

She gave Bríd a big, motherly smile.

'When you get to my age, my dear, you will understand. Women was made to suffer. Of course, 'tis no business of mine, my dear, only I look on you as a daughter, Bríd. Is something the matter between you and Lord Harry?'

Looking up, Bríd was surprised to see a shrewd, suspicious gleam in the old woman's eye. She had been on the brink of telling her everything, but that look stopped her.

And yet, how she needed to talk! She was dying for the want of a friendly face and a sympathetic ear. The moment passed, but Mrs O'Rourke had changed again.

'No doubt 'twas the death of his brother. That terrible murder. Poor man! Och, where is the world going?' She clasped her hands together in her apron. ''Tis the times we live in! Murder! Thieving! Raping, and all sorts! I wonder, isn't it a judgement on us for our wicked ways?'

Bríd was confused by the old woman's abrupt changes of direction. What was she aiming at?

'Wicked ways, Mrs O'Rourke? Lord Leighton wasn't wicked. 'Twas the men who killed him was wicked.'

'If you had only heard Father Donnelly on Sunday preach his sermon on the wickedness of the world. It was so true, oh, it was so true! Men have strayed from the true faith, Bríd, and there'll be no peace in the world till the lost sheep are back in the fold. Ah, you should hear Father Donnelly preach, Bríd, 'tis an opening to the soul to hear him.'

She reached her hand across to Bríd.

'We'll go together to Mass this evening, my dear, and make our confessions. 'Twill ease our hearts.'

Again that look in her face. Bríd wondered if she knew something. Had she been listening that afternoon; had she heard everything Lord Elphin had said?

Bríd thought she would go to church that evening and confess her sins. Would Father Donnelly help her? She desperately needed help from someone. She had no idea how she was going to prepare for the birth of the child, or how she was going to cope with it after it came. It all still seemed a long way off, but she felt a growing sense of approaching catastrophe. She had to make some arrangements, and soon.

However, before she could go to confession, at about four o'clock she had a visitor. Mrs O'Rourke knocked on the door, looked in and whispered,

'There's a gentleman to see you, Bríd.'

A moment later the door opened and Sir John Wrenshaw walked in. He was tall and slim in a regimental uniform, which Bríd recognised immediately as the same as Harry's: the dark-green jacket with gold frogging, and the tight trousers with the wide gold stripe down the side. His moustache was trim, his clothes fitted him immaculately; even when relaxed, he had an air of military alertness and precision. He stood in the doorway, smiling at Bríd, his head slightly to one side. Bríd rose quickly, surprised and flustered, smoothing down her skirt.

Mrs O'Rourke bent her head over a card in her hand and read with difficulty, 'Major Sir John Wrenshaw.' A little in awe of this august personage, she retired and pulled the door to behind her.

'Good afternoon, Miss Flynn.'

He bent over her and offered his hand; he seemed perfectly at home.

'Sir John.'

What did he want? For a second she was pleased to see him; he had flattered her that afternoon he had come to visit with Harry and they had got on well together. Then another, less pleasant thought intruded.

'Have you come from Lord Henry?'

'No,' he said airily, looking round the room. 'In fact, I called by mere chance. Happened to be strolling through this part of Chelsea, and thought I'd look in and see how you were. Nice set of rooms you have. Are you comfortable here?'

'I see.' She turned away from him. 'Am I some kind of an exhibit in the zoo now? Has Lord Henry told all his brother officers to come and see his tame Irish girl? Well, Sir John, take a good look.'

'Pardon me, Miss Flynn, you seem upset about something.'

'Did you come here to mock me? Listen, Sir John, or whatever you're called, you can carry a message to Lord Henry Leighton. You can tell him he behaved like a blackguard, and I wouldn't speak to him again if he came up those stairs on his knees.'

On the edge of tears she turned away towards the window.

Wrenshaw said nothing for a moment, as he digested her words. This was going to be interesting; clearly he had walked into more than he bargained for. What fresh revelations were in store, he wondered? He was glad he had come.

'I assure you I was merely strolling past,' he said lightly. 'I haven't bought any message, and, with respect, I don't particularly want to carry any back. If there is some misunderstanding –'

'Misunderstanding! That's good. Oh yes, there's a misunderstanding. Lord Leighton misunderstood me if he thinks I'll speak to him after –'

'Miss Flynn, I beg you. I am an innocent party, and I really don't –'

'What did you come here for then?'

He was nonplussed for a moment.

'I don't know. To see how you were, I suppose. Look, if there's been some difficulty, I'm sure it can be patched up.'

'He found me wanting. So be it. Let him go; 'tis all one to me, I can shift for myself. I shouldn't have told you.'

'I'm glad you did, all the same. What are you going to do?'

'What do you care?'

He studied her closely, his arms crossed on his chest.

'Well, it looks as if you're in need of some help. I understand you're very angry, but there's no need to take it out on me. I suggest you give me a cup of tea and we talk it over. You've obviously got important decisions to make.'

Whatever she said, Wrenshaw maintained an imperturbable calm. She looked at him, then suddenly relaxed.

'Very well.'

She went down to the kitchen to order tea. Wrenshaw looked round the room. It was a woman's room, with pretty wallpaper, flowery curtains, and a little print of fishing boats.

'Mrs O'Rourke will bring us some tea in just a minute. Take a seat.'

Wrenshaw threw himself into an armchair.

'Terrible business about the murder. Leighton was very cut up. He still hasn't come back to the barracks. I went round to see him at his family's place.'

Bríd's thoughts changed. Harry and his brother. She shouldn't blame him if he had been so cruel to her; after his brother's death, he must have been so disturbed.

'I think he was.'

'You must have been terribly shocked too.'

'Yes,' she said softly after another moment of silence.

'I never actually met him myself. Did you?'

She nodded. Soon afterwards Mrs O'Rourke came in with a tray of tea and a cake. Bríd stirred herself.

'This is Mrs O'Rourke, the truest friend I have in London; Sir John is a friend of Lord Henry, Mrs O'Rourke.'

'Your servant, sir. A friend of Lord Harry's? We haven't seen him in a day or two. I was wondering what was become of him. Is he well?'

When she had gone out, there was silence. Bríd fiddled with the teacups. Seeing Wrenshaw in his uniform brought back everything she had determined to forget, all her memories of Harry, all their times together, rushing back, flooding her with feelings. All her strength, all her anger were leaving her. She felt tears in her eyes, felt herself crumbling. She cursed her weakness. She put the teapot down abruptly, rose and crossed to the window.

'You must excuse me. It was just . . . seeing your uniform . . .'

She leaned against the crossbar of the window, her head on her arm, weeping. Wrenshaw could not resist getting up, taking her by the shoulders and holding her against him, with her head on his shoulder. She sobbed uncontrollably, and he felt her body against him shaken by a passion it could not control. He had no words to say but he was excited by her grief and her vulnerability. He could feel her body through its thin muslin dress, he could feel her softness, the closeness of her; at the same time the uncontrollable shaking, the sense that she was possessed by a force which she could not control, set him at a distance, made him a spectator of her grief.

Gradually her passion subsided. She withdrew from him, dabbing at her eyes with her pretty little handkerchief. He offered her his own large one. She thanked him, her voice muffled, looking down, and went for a moment into the next room, He could hear her pouring water into a bowl, and the sound of her washing her face. Wrenshaw sat in the armchair, looking at the table with its tea tray.

Bríd came back into the room and sat opposite him again.

'I don't know what you must think. Let me give you your tea, it will be cold by now.'

She could not bring her eyes to meet his for a while. It was only after she had poured the tea and was handing it to him that she slowly and shyly looked into his face. She was pale, her eyes a little swollen, but still, in spite of all, she was radiantly beautiful. Wrenshaw was more puzzled than ever. What had possessed that little beggar to make this lovely girl so wretched?

'So –' He looked at her across a cup of tea. 'You've been left in the lurch?'

Bríd gave a deep, shuddering sigh, then drew herself upright. She looked into his eye.

'Don't take any notice of that, Sir John. I'll be able to manage somehow.'

He ignored the defensive note in her voice, and looked steadily at her.

'A beautiful girl like you is going to need a protector.'

She tried to laugh, but it came out forced and hollow.

'I'm a big girl now, Sir John, I think I can protect myself.'

'In London? What do you plan to do?' He spoke carefully, with a quiet authority. 'Consider the avenues open to you, Miss Flynn. You could go into service. Or you could get a job in a tavern as a barmaid. Or you could work in a shop. Or you could go on the streets. Or –' he paused and sipped his tea – 'you could find a wealthy man, with taste and discrimination, a man who knows the ways of the world, to protect you. I take it you have no intention of going back to wherever it was you came from?'

'I come from County Roscommon in Ireland,' she said quickly, while digesting the various possibilities Wrenshaw had laid before her. He ignored her interruption.

'You now have, if I may put it bluntly, a past. Even if you were to go back to your native woods and pastures where, no doubt, your schoolmates are still dwelling in virgin innocence, you would have some difficulty in explaining –'

'Please don't go on,' she interrupted, 'I have no intention of returning to Ballyglin.'

His voice flowed on, unaffected by her interruption.

'More to the point, you would have difficulty in finding a husband. Even if you were to persuade some blameless young man to take you, you would be plagued for the rest of your life with the fear of being found out. You have fallen, and sooner or later, you would be found out, Miss Flynn, it always happens. You have been marked for life.'

He paused, set his teacup down on the table between them, and looked up into her face again.

'Now. It may be that what I have said fills you with despondency. You may have been living in hopes of somehow sticking the pieces of your life together again; in hopes of pretending this unfortunate episode had never happened. Abandon such hopes. The past is behind you. It has happened, and cannot be unmade. Do not, however, abandon *all* hope. All is not in fact lost. Do you regard yourself as lost, Miss Flynn?'

'That's my affair. I'm waiting to hear the end of this speech.'

'You are a woman of spirit.' He smiled. 'I wager you do not consider yourself lost. A woman like you, Miss Flynn, is one in a thousand; you are a free spirit. You have the mind of a man in a woman's body.'

'I'm not sure that I am flattered.'

'You are flattered. It is the highest praise of which I am capable. You have lost something that the world esteems: your innocence. Do not grieve for it. Do not wish it back. It is something no man of sense would give a farthing for. It is part of the monstrous deception which

125

is practised upon the weaker sex. You have strength, character, wit and intelligence, Miss Flynn; these are the true virtues.'

Bríd could not help being flattered in spite of herself.

'And where is all this tending, may I ask?'

'A woman with beauty, wit and good health can do anything she wants in this city. But with this proviso. It is a man's world, Miss Flynn; we are the lords of Creation. You must have a man. Mind, I don't say a husband. A protector.'

She waited for him to continue, but he was silent, looking carefully into her eyes.

'I see.'

She looked at him squarely and unblinking.

'And are you offering yourself in this capacity?'

'That depends, doesn't it? We scarcely know each other. I was speaking at large. Naturally such things take time to develop. You wouldn't want to rush too precipitately into a liaison. Neither would I.'

'And what would be the first step in such a liaison, do you suppose?'

'The first step would consist of my taking you out to dinner, Miss Flynn; I'm feeling rather hungry. I suggest you change that gown for something a little warmer.'

It was an expensive restaurant, the food and the wine were good, and on the way back to Flood Street he kissed her in the cab. Desperate as was her condition, however, she did not intend that Wrenshaw should buy her with one dinner. She pushed him off.

Chapter Sixteen

It couldn't go on like this for long.

Every morning when she washed herself she looked down at her belly, the reality of her situation. She ran her hands over the swelling: her baby. That was what decided everything, had changed everything. A little creature destined to come into the world and dictate her life to her for many years to come. As she stood naked before the looking glass, she felt cold at the prospect. The swelling was small yet; her clothes easily swamped it. But time was passing, and she would have to make decisions soon.

What would Mrs O'Rourke say? And what would Wrenshaw say? And what would Mrs O'Rourke say about Wrenshaw? And about Harry not coming? Perhaps she had better move? How? But then Mrs O'Rourke was a friend; she would be true. Mrs O'Rourke knew the world, she had suffered too. Bríd knew she would be able to rely on Mrs O'Rourke's strength and good spirit. There was a bond of sympathy between the two women.

Wrenshaw was calling that afternoon. He liked her, Bríd knew; he was spending money on her, taking her to expensive restaurants. So far he had been content to kiss her in a cab; soon he was going to want more. It wouldn't do; she would have to be open with him. What would he say when he knew she was expecting a child? In any case, child or no child, was she to be Wrenshaw's kept woman? She didn't love him. How could she? That part of her heart was locked up for ever, and the label on the key was marked Harry.

She had stored her money for safety in a Chinese vase on the mantelpiece. Now she took out the money, spread it on the table and counted it yet again. Fifteen pounds: this was what stood between her and absolute ruin. As she stared at the money, inanimate on the table, she thought what a strange thing it was: metal, paper, marks, symbols. The Queen's head, the words 'one pound' or 'five pounds'.

These marks and words, these signs, were her bulwark in the world against disaster.

She replaced her money in the Chinese vase. Unable to settle, she wandered through the rooms. Opening her wardrobe, she looked at the rack of beautiful clothes Harry had bought her. She remembered how he had first admired her in them; her pleasure in them had been doubled by his admiration. She closed the door. How could she ever take pleasure like that again? By being Wrenshaw's kept woman?

Yet she needed him. He was right. In this man's world, she needed a man to shield her from insult and abuse. She decided to tell Wrenshaw everything.

Wrenshaw came that afternoon; he wanted to take her out in the park. He was elegantly yet negligently dressed, as always when not in uniform. He was a vain man, she had already seen that. No doubt there was a valet at home to brush his clothes, a man to polish his shining boots, women to press his linen.

Vain or not, she had to confide in him.

'John –'

'Yes?' He was holding her, kissing her face, her neck, running his hands through her hair.

'There's something I haven't told you.'

'What?'

'It's not easy. I know you're my friend.'

'What is it?'

She pulled away from him and crossed to the window, looking out.

'Can't you guess?'

'Apparently not.'

'Try and guess.'

'My dear, I really can't. What is it? You are beginning to alarm me.'

She still could not bring herself to look at him. Staring out of the window, she spoke softly.

'You'll hate me, despise me.'

'What on earth do you mean?'

Very quietly she said, 'I'm going to have a baby.'

There was a long silence.

'I see,' he said at last. 'Why didn't you tell me this before?'

'Do you think it's easy? You said I was a fallen woman. Are you surprised?'

'Does Leighton know?'

'No.'

'And you won't tell him?'

'Can you ask that question? I'll never tell him in a thousand years.'

'Have you any money?'

'A little,' she said quietly, searching his face. He was thinking.

'How much?'

'A little.'

'How long could you live on it?'

'A few months if I'm careful.'

He thought for a moment, looking at her seriously.

'How long have you been with child?'

'I'm not exactly sure. Three or four months.'

'You're a fool to have let it come to this. Still, there's no helping that. We shall have to make arrangements.'

She was immensely relieved. 'I knew you would know what to do.'

'You'll have to book yourself into a lying-in hospital.' He rubbed his chin. 'There are plenty of them. And preferably where they don't ask questions. They can be decidedly stuffy if they don't see a ring on your finger, some of them. I think there's one in Marylebone that will accept you.'

'Oh, good! How much will I have to pay?'

'I don't know offhand. Several pounds at least.'

'I can manage that. And then – I wonder whether Mrs O'Rourke will let me bring the baby back here. I'll have to ask her soon.'

'Bring back the baby?'

Bríd was thinking fast. 'Yes. Lord, there'll be such preparations to make. I haven't begun to think.'

'You don't intend to *keep* the child?'

'What?' She didn't take in the import of his words.

'The baby will go to an orphanage. Obviously.'

She looked at him.

He went on, 'What on earth would you do with a baby?'

'I don't know. I thought –'

'A single girl with a baby? You'd be an outcast, a pariah! It's utter ruin. You might as well throw yourself into the river.'

She turned pale.

'No. The baby goes to an orphanange. Girls do it all the time.'

Some deep and quite unexpected instinct surfaced at this moment. No one was going to take her child from her. She looked away, and said softly,

'I'm not any girl. I don't think you have any heart at all.'

'Heart? What has that got to do with it? I took you for a woman of character, I said nothing about heart. That's just part of the iniquitous web that binds women to subjection. Be free! Have the courage to be independent of the traps laid for you.'

'Free? I thought you said I had to have a "protector"?'

'I didn't say anything about a baby. If the baby goes to the orphanage, things can go on as they are.'

'A fine protector you're turning out to be, Sir John. No protection at all! And little you know of me. You think I'd give up my baby?'

'Bríd, the world is full of women ruined by childbirth; ground down, exhausted, worn out, sucked dry by children. Stay free! Be your own woman. Didn't I say that at the first?'

She felt herself becoming angry.

'That's all words. And it's very convenient talk for you, isn't it? Very easy, and no responsibility. But I have the responsibility in me now, and no one will take it from me. No one one will take my child from me.'

He looked at her pityingly, dismissively. 'On your own head be it.'

'That's all you have to say?'

He turned to the door. 'I'll let you have the address of the lying-in hospital.'

It took her a little while to realise that John Wrenshaw had walked out on her. She could not accept at first that he could have had so little feeling for her. What had he wanted? Just a companion in his pleasures; nothing more, no love, no comradeship or warmth. She was well rid of him. It seemed that she had for a moment been deceived by his ease in the world, where all doors opened to him, where doormen had bowed to him, cabs had stopped for him, where everything ran on oiled wheels.

All that day she walked about the streets of Chelsea. It was summer and doors were open; children played in the street, girls with skipping ropes, or leaping along the pavement at hopscotch. At the corner a man sold fish from a barrow and was attended with concentration by a dozen stray cats.

She looked in at the gate of a wheelwright's shop. Two men with long tongs were holding the iron rim of a wheel, red-hot from the forge, and were fitting it over a new wheel, bright new wood. There was a violent hissing, black smoke, and the strong smell of burning as they hammered the rim into place.

She walked along the Cheyne Walk, beneath the trees, and watched the red-sailed wherries making fast to the wharf. A tug-boat came swiftly down with the flood tide, black smoke billowing from its tall smoke stack.

Everywhere the world going about its business, everyone in his allotted place, at home. Only she was not at home, and had no allotted place.

Wrenshaw had been right. A single girl with a child. She looked down at the river, running swiftly with the tide. So many women had been taken from the river; it was in the newspapers every day; no one took any notice. Another woman, another corpse in the morgue. They were hardly ever traced. Another mystery, but to her no mystery at all. She looked into the swift water. No mystery at all.

She turned and walked quickly back up through the narrow streets, and back to Flood Street. She had to make preparations; she ought to start making things for the baby. That would be a useful thing to do, and she must tell Mrs O'Rourke too. She must tell her now. She tried to think hard what Mrs O'Rourke would say; the old lady had been a true friend to her, had confided in her. Would she help her now in her hour of need?

It was midafternoon when she returned to Flood Street. The house was quiet as she went down into the basement and looked into the kitchen. Mrs O'Rourke was asleep in a carver chair by the window; from the area window a shaft of sunlight fell at a sharp angle across the old lady. It was hot in here; winter or summer, Mrs O'Rourke kept the range alight. Above it hung a rack of drying clothes.

Bríd stood uncertain in the door for a moment. As she came into the kitchen, Mrs O'Rourke stirred in her chair, and her eyes opened.

'Bríd, dear,' she said drowsily.

The young girl came uncertainly towards her and rested a hand on the wide table.

'Mrs O'Rourke, I've been wanting to have a talk with you.'

She paused. Mrs O'Rourke was more awake.

'That's nice, dear. Sit down. Well. 'Tis a long time since we've seen Lord Harry. Is he away with his regiment?'

For a moment Bríd thought this would be a wonderful opportunity to make up a plausible story about Harry's disappearance. But Mrs O'Rourke was her only friend; she longed to confide in her, to tell her the truth.

'Mrs O'Rourke, I – that's just it. I have to tell you. You see, well, Lord Harry is not my cousin.'

Mrs O'Rourke stared at at her. 'What are you saying, Bríd?'

'We was to have been married. We was! I came here to be near him. But he's gone away. I don't know where. He didn't tell me.'

Mrs O'Rourke sat up. 'Bríd, you lied to me.'

'Honestly, Mrs O'Rourke, what else could we do? Harry being under age, he couldn't marry without his father's permission, and we had to wait till he was twenty-one, but then . . .'

She couldn't go on. The old woman supplied the rest.

'And now he's gone.'

'Yes.'

'Bríd, I'm sorry.'

'You don't blame me?'

'Women was made to suffer, Bríd. Wasn't it ever so?'

Bríd felt a wave of relief; she had known Mrs O'Rourke would sympathise.

'So, Lord Harry is gone. What are you going to do now? Will your family have you back?'

'Mrs O'Rourke, you are the only friend I have in London. I have to tell you something else. There's more. Oh, God, I hope you'll understand. I'm going to have a baby.'

'A baby! The saints preserve us! Well! A baby!'

'Yes – '

'But, what are you going to do?'

'Mrs O'Rourke, that's what I've come to ask you.'

'Well, you can't stay here, dear.'

Bríd was silent for a moment.

'I had hoped, maybe –'

'Oh no, Bríd, this is a respectable house. You can't stay here. Your rent is paid until the end of the month, then you'll have to go.'

'Yes . . .'

'Well, dear, what are the neighbours going to say when they see you carrying a baby in and out of the house? They'll think you're a whore, Bríd, and you with no husband, and no ring to your finger. And what'll they say to me, eh? That I've been keeping a whorehouse, so to say, with soldiers coming and going all the time.'

She got up from her chair, crossed to the range, opened it, raking inside for a moment, and then pushed the little door shut with her foot. With the poker still in her hand, she turned and looked down at Bríd, seated at the table.

'My, what a fool I've been! Here's me thinking you were such a little innocent with your cousin so grand and lordly, and your Sir John this and your Lord Harry that, and all the time you were just a little whore, and now you must pay for it. Well! You'll not stay here, my girl. First of the month, and out you go!'

Bríd sat in the gloomy church, waiting for the confessional to become free. There was a faint odour of stale incense, and somewhere away out of sight, the sound of two cleaners talking was distorted among the echoing chapels and vaults of the big church. She pulled her mantle round her. The priest was her last resort.

She was still smarting from her interview with Mrs O'Rourke that afternoon; nothing had quite prepared her for the way the old lady

132

had turned against her. It had hurt Bríd far more than Wrenshaw's defection.

She drew a deep breath. She wished now that she had come to Mass more often; if only she were known to Father Donnelly. Why had she never offered to be of assistance? Surely there were ways she could have helped about the church? Well, it was too late now; and it was no use pretending she was very religious, because she was not, and that was that. She had come here occasionally with Mrs O'Rourke. But while Harry was around, she had had other things on her mind.

She was alone in the world. Alone in this great city. Walking here this afternoon, the sheer vast scale of everything had come to her as it had never done before, and for the first time fear had entered her very marrow. She was alone; a horrid crawling fear made her clamp her jaws, stare fixedly before her and will herself to walk on, because otherwise she might have run out screaming into the road among the traffic to hurl herself beneath the hooves that clattered past.

Now too she held herself tightly, looked at the feet of the woman in the confessional before her, hearing the low buzz of conversation within, thinking, praying that when it came to her turn the priest would have something helpful to say, and wouldn't call her names.

The woman rose and walked hurriedly out past Bríd. She went forward, crossing herself, and knelt in the woman's place. This was going to be a long story.

'I have sinned deeply, Father'

'Of what nature was your sin?'

His voice seemed tired, remote. He was not threatening, only weary. Strangely, even in the midst of her trouble, she had time to feel sorry for him.

'I was in love with a man, and . . .'

'Yes? Go on.'

'Father, we was to have been married, I swear! Only, we was both under age and couldn't marry without his father's permission, and I knew he would never give it, so we had to wait until he was twenty-one; only – well, something happened, I don't understand how. I did nothing, I swear, but . . . he went away and I never saw him again. And now . . .'

'Go on.'

'Father, I – I gave myself to him.'

She heard the priest give a long sigh. She thought, I have to tell him everything, otherwise he won't help me. Although how the sad, ghostlike presence behind the grill was going to help her, she couldn't see.

'Is this all?' he said softly.

'No, Father.'

'Well?'

'I'm expecting a child. I can't ask the father – I know he wouldn't help me, and I wouldn't ask him anyway, not after what happened. So don't suggest it, Father. But Father, I don't know what to do.'

She waited. The wraithlike voice wafted through the grill. 'Do you repent of your sin, daughter?'

'Oh yes, Father,' she replied quickly.

'Do you repent of the sin or are you only sorry at the outcome?'

'I repent, Father, sincerely.'

'Do you understand what I say? You must repent of the act itself, daughter, not merely that you have been deserted by your lover.'

'Father, I do repent, honest.'

And yet she wasn't sure whether this was quite true. How could she repent of her love for Harry, the only true beacon, the lodestone, the centre of gravity of her life? She was sorry that he had left her, but that hadn't been her fault.

'Very well.'

He prescribed a lengthy penance, and it seemed as though the interview was at end. She spoke quickly.

'Father, please don't close the shutter. I need to ask you. You see, now that I'm going to have a baby, I must leave my lodging, and I don't know where to go. I was hoping that you . . .'

Her voice faltered.

'Are you quite alone in London, my child?'

'Yes, Father.'

'How old are you?'

'Eighteen.'

Again, the ghostly sigh emanated from the grill.

'I see. Do you have any means of support?'

'What? Oh yes, Father, I do have a little money.'

There was a long silence, and Bríd's nerves were stretched taut as she waited for the priest to speak.

'Come and see me on Friday. Come to the presbytery. I may be able to help you. Now you may go. *Ego te absolvo peccatis tuis. Pax tecum.*'

Chapter Seventeen

Bríd opened the wardrobe and looked at the clothes she and Harry had chosen together; her lovely cream woollen dress, her black and brown velvet gown that looked so elegant and set off her figure so well, the summer muslin dresses, her silk dresses, her coats, her mantles. She looked at her bonnets, too, with their pretty ribbons and the artificial flowers woven round them, and at her shawls with their paisley patterns in rich scarlet and gold, her walking boots, her pretty shoes, her silk stockings.

She decided to sell them. She bundled them together and carried them down into the King's Road. There were plenty of pawnbrokers' shops there and it didn't taken her long to find one. She felt wretched as she watched the man pull them about on his counter in such an offhand way, and offer her prices that were not a fifth of what they had cost. Her mind was made up, however; the clothes went and she took the money.

On the Friday she returned to the church and found the priest's residence at one side. She had never looked very hard at Father Donnelly during Mass, and remembered him only by the terrible sadness which seemed to hang over the confessional box as she had knelt at it. She knocked with some trepidation, and a housekeeper showed her into an office which faced out over a dank and dying garden. The priest was out but the housekeeper would send a girl to find him.

When he did come in, she was surprised to find him younger than she had expected; was this the man so burdened by the cares of the world? But it was he; she recognised his voice immediately. She reminded him who she was. He did not smile but, shoulders bowed, he rummaged among the papers on his desk, picked up a letter and studied it for a moment. He looked up seriously into her face.

'I have written on your behalf to the Convent of the Good Shepherd in Fulham. The Sisters maintain an Asylum for Female

135

Penitents.' He sat behind his desk, folded his hands among the papers before him and looked at her wearily. 'Ignorant girls for the most part, who have fallen and seek with a contrite heart to be raised again. You will stay at the convent until your confinement. The sisters will arrange a foster home for the child, and thereafter it is to be hoped you will be placed with a respectable Catholic family as housemaid. Such is the reputation of the Sisters that their recommendation is usually sufficient. I hope you may come to deserve their approbation. You will, of course, be expected to pay for your board.'

Three days later, numb in mind and heavy in body, Bríd left Flood Street. Mrs O'Rourke had relented of her hard words, softened towards Bríd again, and said she was sorry to see her go. Although she did not change her mind, she shed a tear as she kissed Bríd goodbye. Bríd did not weep; she had done all the weeping she intended to do for one lifetime.

She carried a bag in which she had carefully rolled up the two dresses she had not sold. She might be destined to be a housemaid, but some instinct had prompted her to save these gowns, favourites of hers which she felt had once, in what now seemed a previous existence, become her prettily, and might one day, who knew in what circumstances, be of use again. They were a kind of talisman of hope which she carried with her, together with a little leather purse containing twenty-eight pounds, all that stood between her and disaster. As she sat in the omnibus bumping and rattling on its way into Fulham, staring unseeing at the nursemaid sitting opposite her, she prayed that it would be enough.

The Convent of the Good Shepherd was a large Gothic building near the centre of Fulham. A high wall separated it from the street. As she pulled at the bell, Bríd felt as if she were ringing for admission to a prison.

The door was opened by a nun in a black habit, who addressed her sharply in a marked French accent. Bríd found out later that the convent was a French foundation and the nuns were a mixture of French, English and Irish. She followed the nun silently across a garden in which several pregnant girls were hoeing up weeds, into the house and up several flights to the Mother Superior's office. A girl, hugely pregnant, was scrubbing the steps, and Bríd supposed glumly that before long she too would be allotted her share of household duties. The air was full of stale cooking smells, which made her queasy, and a gloomy silence hung over the house, broken only by distant footsteps echoing along corridors.

She lied about her money, terrified that they might try to take it all

136

from her; but to her relief the amount the Mother Superior required was no more than five pounds. The Mother Superior was indeed a very superior woman, French, extremely dignified, positively aristo-cratic in her manner, and exercising, it seemed, an iron rule. She was a busy woman and after a few minutes Bríd was led out again and taken up to a dormitory, a long bare room, uncarpeted, with ten iron bedsteads ranged on either side of the room between dormer win-dows. Each bed had a curtain that might be drawn round it but these were, when Bríd first entered, drawn back. The nun, thin-mouthed and sallow-skinned, briefly indicated Bríd's bed.

That evening she attended Mass in the high chapel, and it was the oddest sensation to find herself in the midst of pregnant girls, before, behind, on either side, row upon row; it didn't seem possible so much breeding could be concentrated in one place. It was as if she were in the midst of a herd of cows, bloated, bovine, all waiting, expectant. They were her own age or younger still, and, glancing along the row on either side of her as she sang the hymn, she was struck by their clear, unmarked faces. So young, so innocent, so pregnant: their swollen bellies a comment, like an irreverent snigger, on the rapt expression in their faces as they sang. Cynical for a moment, she thought sin had never been so much in fashion.

Above them the nun's choir sang exquisitely, and Bríd's spirit re-sponded in spite of all her troubles. For that short time she gloried in the music, was uplifted and restored by it, so that when she came to take the host she felt a rush of dedication, as if she would like to put her follies and sins behind her and begin life afresh. Afterwards, even as this enthusiasm faded, she tried to hold on to the sense of dedication she had briefly felt.

In the refectory they sat on benches along deal tables and the nuns administered a simple supper of bread and hot milk. The girls ate in silence, and Bríd looked shyly about her, trying to guess what stories the other girls must have to tell: every one fallen; every one of them in disgrace. Where did they come from? Were they rich or poor? It was impossible to tell. They wore a blue smock over their dresses, and ribbons or jewellery were strictly forbidden. As these thoughts drifted through her mind, the silence was abruptly broken.

'You wicked, wicked girl!'

Looking across, Bríd saw the nun who had opened the door to her that morning. She was bending over a girl at the table further along, who was cowering beneath her rebuke.

'No, really, Sœur Ursule! It was only an accident! I swear! I do, I do!'

'You do this deliberately and then you lie to me! I know you!'

The thin-faced nun was attacking the girl before her with the utmost vehemence, her face red with rage, while the young girl on the bench was hunched, averting her face.

'You shall report to Reverend Mother tomorrow morning.'

'No, I beg you!' The girl buried her face in her hands.

A girl on the opposite side of the table interrupted them.

'Really, it wasn't her fault, Sœur Ursule. The jug was hot, and she picked it up without thinking –'

'Be silent! Silence all of you! Tomorrow morning, to Reverend Mother!'

The nun walked quickly away, and Bríd again caught a glimpse of her face, contorted with rage. Looking back, she saw now that a jug of milk had been spilled; two other girls were busy mopping up the table. She sat in silence digesting this strange eruption, and the violent emotions which it had unleashed. The girl was hunched over weeping into her hands, and two girls on either side were leaning across her, trying to console her.

Soon afterwards they went upstairs to the dormitory. It was late summer and, being under the roof, the room was hot. She drew the curtain round her bed while she changed into her nightdress. It felt stifling to be surrounded by the other girls, all of them in various degrees of pregnancy, all of them waddling with the peculiar walk of the expectant, all of them with that bovine milky look; for a moment she wasn't sure she would be able to stand it. Peeping from behind her curtain, she noticed near her the girl who had been attacked so vehemently by the nun, and was able to look at her. She was a slender, fine-boned girl, blonde and delicate-featured. She seemed gentle and nervous, and Bríd could not imagine how she might have offended anyone, still less a nun. Neither could she imagine how such a genteel-looking girl could have fallen from grace; such a fragile girl scarcely seemed to have the vigour to be sinful, or the strength to bear a child.

The following morning they rose early for Mass; when they were in place, the Mother Superior swept in past them to take her place. It being a Sunday, the priest preached them a sermon on the Magdalen; the girls shrank lower and lower in their pews as he expounded mercilessly the sins of self-indulgence, of yielding to carnal temptation, and contrasted the virtues of purity, self-denial, repentance and a life of service, which was what they all had to look forward to; a life of self-abnegation to wash away the stain of sin.

Later, upstairs in the morning room, the girls sat in a circle and worked on their baby clothes, presided over by a mild, elderly nun, Sister Agnes. Talking was permitted here, and one girl told Bríd that the sermon she had heard that morning was a familiar one, and she could expect to hear it, in all its variations, many more times before she left.

During the morning, the door opened and the blonde girl came in, looking pale and subdued. Bríd felt sorry for her. The other girls asked her what the Mother Superior had said, but the nun interrupted and told them to find some other topic of conversation, so the girl was left alone.

After dinner in the early afternoon they went out into the garden for recreation. As they walked among the dismal flowerbeds, decaying now as autumn came on, Bríd found herself addressed by a big, round-faced, merry girl, Irish like herself. Her name was Maisie; she linked arms with Bríd readily, and as they walked together she asked about Bríd's past, and how she had come to be here. Bríd gave her a simplified version, and then Maisie, who didn't seem in the slightest ashamed or remorseful, told her story. She seemed to have taken it in her stride, as if it had been intended by the Lord in his scheme of things. Not far away they saw the blonde girl, and Bríd asked Maisie why the sharp-faced nun had been so unkind to her.

'That Sœur Ursule!' Maisie exclaimed. 'She has a wicked tongue on her. She should never have been a nun, if the truth was told. They say she was forced into it by her hoity-toity French family. You can see she hasn't the vocation.'

'But why was she so cruel to that sweet girl?'

'Bertha? She's jealous! She's jealous of her that Bertha has to bear a child, and she never will. That's the truth of it, if you ask me.'

'I don't understand why she should have picked on her.'

'She's of gentle birth, Bríd. Most of us here are simple folk, from poor families. Bertha is different. I don't know why her family sent her here. Poor creature! She bears it hard.'

'Does she?'

'Dreadful hard. I hear her weeping in bed at night. Her family was that cruel to her, they say. 'Tis different for us, somehow. She never expected to be here. Neither did we.' She laughed. 'Still, somehow we can bear it.'

Bríd became more and more intrigued by the sad Bertha, and would have liked to have spoken to her, but the girl carried about an aura of loneliness, of being set apart from the others, so that Bríd didn't like to approach her.

A few days later, however, she was assigned to cleaning duties, and when she arrived at the stairs with her mop and bucket, she found herself beside Bertha. The pale girl did not seem inclined to open a conversation, and for some time the two girls mopped their way down

139

the stairs in silence. Then Bertha stopped, resting on her mop handle, and Bríd thought she might have something to say, but as she looked up she saw that Bertha was white-faced and looking exhausted. Bríd threw down her own mop, took Bertha's from her and made her sit on the step.

'You shouldn't be doing this heavy work.'

'Oh, I beg you, don't say anything! I've been in so much trouble! I beg you! I'll be fine, I will!'

She tried to rise, but Bríd held her down.

'No. I'll go and tell the nun. I'm sure they'll excuse you from cleaning duties.'

The girl became quite frantic.

'No! You must not! They'll send me away. They say I'm a troublemaker, and I've been warned.'

'Troublemaker?' Bríd was astounded. 'Who says?'

'Oh, well, it doesn't matter. Only, I beg you, say nothing. I can cope, really, I swear it, only give me a moment to recover myself.'

'You're not fit for the work. You'd not have the strength for it, even if you weren't . . . in this condition. I'll tell Reverend Mother.'

Bríd still didn't grasp the extent of the girl's anguish.

'On no account!' She tried to rise, but again Bríd held her down. The girl burst into tears, clasping her face in her hands. Bríd was at a loss. She couldn't understand why the girl should be in such distress, nor why the nun seemed to have such a terrible dislike for her.

'Oh, well.' She hesitated. 'It's really not so bad.'

'It's as bad as ever it can be,' came the girl's muffled voice.

'Listen.' Bríd took command. 'I don't care what the nun says, you're in no state to mop stairs, or to do anything except lie on a bed. You stay there and don't move.'

She took up her mop and set to work; she was a big, strong girl and had plenty of strength for domestic work. As she worked her way down, she looked up at Bertha on the steps above her and smiled. The girl smiled wanly back.

'Don't move, do you hear? You've got a little one to think of, you know.'

The smile was wiped off the girl's face in an instant.

'Cheer up, my dear, you'll come through.'

'Will I?'

'Sure.'

Bríd mopped on. Somewhere above them a door opened and steps clattered down towards them. Sœur Ursule appeared on the landing above. Bríd saw her, and continued unconcernedly mopping the step.

Sœur Ursule rattled down on Bertha.

'Little miss is too delicate, I suppose? You are content that others should work for you, eh?'

Bertha leaped to her feet. 'Oh –'

'I might have known, you lazy, wicked girl, that you never do any work, that you allow others to work for you –'

Bríd intervened. 'Bertha is unwell, Sister, and should be resting, not working here.'

'Hold your tongue!'

'She is not strong enough for this work!'

'You are in charge, are you? Reverend Mother has set you in authority here, has she? Be silent!' She turned to Bertha. 'You have been warned many, many times by Reverend Mother. If you continue in wilful disobedience, you will be returned to your family.'

Bertha became frantic. 'Really, Sœur Ursule, I just came over a little faint, I promise. But I'm fine now!'

She was reaching for her mop, which still lay on the step, but Bríd took it before she could.

'She'll do no cleaning this day.'

Sœur Ursule turned her full wrath against Bríd, but Bríd spoke again, in a gentler tone.

'I'll do her work for her, Sister, I can easily do it. Then she can rest.'

'You will do as you are told! How dare you interfere? Each girl must do her share of duties.' She came closer to Bríd. 'There are many girls who would like to be here – thousands. London is full of girls who would like to be here. We have no room for ungrateful girls who do not know their duty. If you speak again I shall report you to Reverend Mother, and you will be sent away. We shall find another to take your place like that!' She snapped her fingers in Bríd's face and swept past them and on down the stairs.

Even as the nun had been speaking, Bríd had been studying her face. She was a young woman, as Maisie had said. She might have been attractive once, perhaps not so long ago, but a blight had settled on her, withering her, fading the colour in her cheeks, making her lips thin and hard. She was a bitter woman, Bríd thought.

That evening, as she sat among the girls in the refectory with her bread and milk, Bríd watched Sœur Ursule walking up and down between the benches. The woman was a menace; Bríd decided she must be stopped before Bertha became really ill. In her concern for the pale girl bending silently over her bowl of milk, Bríd for a moment forgot her own worries.

She could not go to the Reverend Mother. If she were made to leave – no, that was impossible. She was helpless, that was the fact.

141

And anyway, was it really her responsibility? Didn't she have enough worries of her own? Why had she become so concerned about a girl who was a complete stranger to her, and with whom she had exchanged barely half a dozen sentences?

It didn't matter. She was strong enough; she would make her way, somehow or other, whereas Bertha . . . Bríd wondered whether the girl were destined to leave the convent alive. Would she have the strength to give birth?

She thought of writing a letter to the Mother Superior anonymously, but rejected it. Her skill at letter writing was not equal to the task, and in any case, she doubted whether the Mother Superior would take any notice of an anonymous letter. Bríd was at a loss. She must bite her lip and bear all in patience. This was the theme of the sermons they heard in chapel, after all; was not a woman's lot to suffer, to bear sorrows with Christian fortitude and, in their case especially, meekly to expiate their sins?

Bríd was ready meekly to expiate her own sin, but to watch Sœur Ursule's cruelty was another matter; she was not ready to bear that with resignation. Sœur Ursule had to be stopped, at least until Bertha should have had her baby and have departed the convent. Mad ideas ran through Bríd's head. How was Sœur Ursule to be incapacitated for a few months? Drop a flowerpot on her head? Polish the stairs so that the nun would slip downstairs and crack her skull? Put bleach in her coffee? She looked again across the table towards Bertha, and at that moment the pale girl caught her eye and smiled. Bríd smiled back, a flash of friendship between them, and she vowed Sœur Ursule should torment her no longer, and Bertha should have her child safely.

As they walked upstairs after supper, Bertha took her hand.

'Bríd,' she said quietly to her, 'I've never been able to thank you for the way you stood up to Sœur Ursule for me. It was very brave of you.' She looked up into Bríd's face with an expression almost of adoration.

Bríd said nothing for a moment, looking down into that fragile face.

'I wish I could have done more,' she said briefly.

'Oh, no! It was so, so brave! If Reverend Mother knew you had answered back to Sœur Ursule . . .'

The consequences seemed too awful to utter.

That night as Bríd lay in bed, and after the desultory chat in the darkness had gradually subsided as the girls dropped into sleep one by one, she saw her curtain move, and in a moment Bertha's face was close beside her.

'Bríd,' she whispered almost in her ear, 'you'll think me awfully forward but would you ... would you mind if I got in with you, just for a few minutes? Sometimes I feel so dreadfully alone.'

Bríd made room for the slender girl and drew her arm round the girl's shoulder as she snuggled against her.

'You were so good to me,' Bertha whispered. 'I shall never forget it.'

Bríd said nothing, and they both stared up into the darkness. After a few moments Bertha went on softly.

'You don't mind if I talk, do you? It's such a relief to find a friend at last. Sometimes I've thought I should go mad here.' She paused. 'My father is a doctor. Without wishing to boast, I should say the most fashionable doctor in York. We know all the best families in the county; Papa is very busy making himself agreeable to all the aristocracy and land-owning families. I should think he spends as much time riding to hounds as attending to his patients – during the hunting season, anyway. Of course Papa and Mama wanted to see me married well, but you see, though we are accepted in all the best houses, Papa doesn't actually own a great deal of property, so I shouldn't have a large dowry, – you understand, don't you? There was no possibility of my making a really brilliant match, though Mama hoped for something respectable at least.'

Bríd thought she understood all too well. Bertha went on in a whisper.

'It's such a shameful story; you're the first girl I've ever told – I never liked to talk to any of the others. Well, there was a man, of course, his father is a duke. Papa got to know him when he treated the Duchess for something, so we were invited to one of those routs when the whole county seems to have been invited. Alfred – this man – asked me to dance with him and, of course, we danced again. And then, can you imagine, he asked Papa's permission to call. My sisters teased me to death about it; I never believed he could really be serious, a lord, you know, but he was just such a poppet, the dearest, sweetest man in the world, I thought, and so upright and noble and everything, the soul of honour, I swear.'

Bríd could hear the tears in her voice. Bertha paused for a moment as she wiped them away with a corner of the sheet.

'How foolish of me! I should be hardened by now, I really should. Well, Mama was wild about him too; she said it would be the making of us – allied to a duke! She was at me night and day to encourage him. Honestly, Bríd, I didn't need any encouragement, I thought he was the loveliest man I had ever met. Having Mama behind me though, sometimes made things awkward – she was always popping in when we would be sitting together, always leaning over him trying to curry favour with him. I told her not to do it, but it didn't make any difference. So one day Alfred – it does sound strange speaking his name again like this, I swear I haven't uttered it in months – he made a suggestion that was, well, wrong. You see, his family have a house in York, and it's often locked up for months at a time when they're in the country, and he suggested that, since my mama was such an ogre and for ever pestering us, that we should, well, meet in this house. It would be so easy, and no one need ever know, and then it would be so cosy to be together. Of course I knew it was fearfully wrong, and if ever Papa got to know I should be in terrible trouble . . .'

She paused again; it was as if she needed Bríd to goad her into a full confession.

'And you agreed?'

'Oh, Bríd, do you blame me? I was besotted with him, I could refuse him nothing. Of course I went with him. You can imagine what happened. Me! I always thought myself so innocent, so proper; I was astonished at myself, at both of us. Bríd, we simply got carried away; I did things I had never dreamed of, that I didn't know could be done. And afterwards, we stared at each other, amazed at ourselves and each other. We were so shaken, we tottered out of the house. It was almost laughable in a way, except that it wasn't funny. Of course Alfred said we should be married, and he would speak to his papa.'

She stopped again.

'Go on,' Bríd said softly.

Bertha's manner grew sombre; clearly she was approaching the unpleasant part of her story.

'A week went by, and I heard nothing from Alfred. Then Papa called me to his study. He was very grim. At first he could hardly say anything, he was so black. Finally he said he had a letter from the Duke. There was no possibility of a marriage between me and his son; he said I had inveigled Alfred and led him astray, and other vile accusations, all untrue, and there was to be no more contact between our families. Then he demanded to know what I had done to offend the Duke. I could only stammer that I had done nothing and then burst into floods of tears. He shouted at me that I must have done something, what had I done, over and over again, and I couldn't think of anything to say, only cry and swear I was innocent. Finally he sent me to my room. I think he was more angry about losing the Duke's friendship than anything.

'You can guess the rest. A few weeks went by and I realised that I was, well, expecting. Oh, Lord, the terror! Never, as long as I live, shall I feel such terror as I did that day. I couldn't hide it long – I've got two sisters, and they quickly guessed, then Mama found out, and the whole family knew except Papa. We held conferences to work out how to tell him. At last Mama broke the news to him. Bríd, I hope I never see such a day again. I thought he would murder me. He said if anyone ever found out it would be the ruin of the family; all his work, a lifetime building up the practice, all destroyed by my folly. We were all brought into his study, even Mama, forced to go down on our knees and swear a solemn oath on the Bible not to tell a living soul. Then he sent the others out, became very practical, and said arrangements had to be made quickly, and the next thing was that it was given out that I was to go to Switzerland to learn French and be educated and so on. All my schoolfriends were green with envy, and all the time I was thinking, If only you knew. Of course I didn't go to Switzerland. When we got to London, we took a closed cab here.'

She paused.

'Papa says that after the child is born it is to be placed with a poor family he knows. Then I am to go home and try to pretend nothing has happened.'

The tears had returned.

'Pretend nothing has happened! Oh, Lord!'

She sobbed silently on Bríd's shoulder for some minutes while Bríd thought over what she had said.

Chapter Eighteen

'Bríd, Reverend Mother wants to speak to you.'

A girl had come into the day-room where they sat at their needle-work. Bríd set down her needle. This had to be Sœur Ursule's doing – she must have complained to the Mother Superior about the way Bríd had answered back to her on the stairs.

'Will you excuse me, Sister Agnes?'

'Of course, dear.' The old lady smiled in her ineffectual way.

Bríd went down to the Reverend Mother's door and knocked. This was it: they were going to throw her out. She had not learned her lesson, had not become sufficiently self-abased, contrite and repentant.

'Bríd Flynn.'

The Reverend Mother was holding *The Times* in her hand. It looked odd, as if she were like anyone else, relaxing with the newspaper.

But the Reverend Mother never relaxed; she was sitting, as ever, bolt upright. She now ran her eye down the column of the paper, folded it over and then handed it across her desk to Bríd, pointing to an item.

It was the front page, covered with personal advertisements. Bríd took it, and found the place.

> Bríd Flynn. If anyone having information as to the whereabouts of this lady would communicate it, they will be well rewarded. Write in confidence to Box 97.

Bríd looked up. Then she looked down again and read it through.

'What does it mean, Reverend Mother – Box 97?'

'You should write to *The Times* and mention the box number. The letter will be forwarded to whoever inserted the advertisement.'

Bríd could think of no one who would seek to communicate with her – unless it was Harry? She was thrown into a terrible agitation. She didn't really want him to see her in the convent, and now so great with child. She looked at the Reverend Mother.

'What should I do?'

'That is up to you. Do you wish anyone to know where you are?'

Of course Bríd had to answer the advertisement, and with much difficulty, crossing out and rewriting, she at last composed a short letter and it was despatched.

She could think of nothing else; waking or sleeping, the advertisement dominated her. What if Harry's family had had a miraculous change of heart? Then she would roll over in bed and think how impossible it was, how it never could be. Someone else must have placed the advertisement – Garrett? No, she would bite her lip, lying in the darkness, no, that was not likely. So the thoughts revolved in her head, and all the time a terrible suspense.

One afternoon as they sat at their needles, Bríd happened to look out of the window and was amazed to see Bertha digging the garden. She turned to the nun who was supervising them.

'Sister! Bertha is digging in the garden! That can't be right. She's never strong enough for that work!'

The urgency in her voice drove the kindly old lady to the window.

'To be sure, dear,' she murmured uncertainly. 'Well, I don't know . . .'

The other girls, glad of an interruption crowded to the window. They stared down in silence at the solitary girl in the garden below them, digging, turning over the thin soil, and bending to pull up weeds. Bríd was angry.

'Sister Agnes! Bertha is not fit for heavy work. You know she isn't!'

'I'm sure Reverend Mother knows best, Bríd. It's not for us to question her wisdom.'

'I don't believe Reverend Mother knows anything about it, Sister Agnes. She would never permit such a thing.'

As she spoke, she noticed Bertha had stopped and was leaning on her spade.

'Look at her! She hasn't the strength for the work. You can see for yourself! Oh, Sister Agnes, won't you speak to Reverend Mother? Won't you? For Bertha's sake?'

'Well, dear,' the old lady wavered, 'I don't know. Perhaps, if I can catch her alone. She has so many things to think about, so many duties . . .'

Her voice tailed away.

Bríd knew she would do nothing. She turned again to the window and looked down at the frail figure alone in the garden. A violent spurt of anger ran through her; she felt she could murder that spiteful French nun, and before she could think she was out of the room and stumbling down the stairs. She would speak to the Mother Superior if it cost her her place. She would not wait a second longer.

In a heat of fury she knocked at the door, standing in the half-light of the landing, breathing heavily. She knocked again, still not thinking, only full of rage. And then she heard a voice, mocking, evil and with a French accent.

'You know it is forbidden to speak to Reverend Mother direct! What do you want?'

Bríd swung round to see Sœur Ursule crossing towards her.

'What do I want? I want to tell her about you, about your cruelty to Bertha! How could you send her out to dig in the garden? You know her condition!'

'You are insolent! I shall speak to Reverend Mother about you. You have become a bad influence here, you bring disruption and cause dissatisfaction. I shall be very pleased if you will go!'

'I don't care what you do about me. I shall speak to Reverend Mother, and I shall tell her all about you!'

'You shall not! I shall see to that! As for Bertha, I shall decide what is good for her. Now return to your work.'

She glared into Bríd's face, and in an instant, Bríd's anger snapped. She seized the nun by the wrist in a rigid grip and forced her several steps backwards so that she struck the wall and was for a moment breathless.

'You may get rid of me,' Bríd hissed into her face as she pressed her to the wall, 'but I swear before God you'll be in the infirmary for months after!'

The nun was speechless. Bríd broke away from her.

'And I'm bringing Bertha in from the garden now.'

Without looking back, she went down the stairs as fast as she could and out into the garden. For a moment she couldn't see Bertha, and thought she had already come in, but then in a cold shock she saw that the girl was lying on the ground among the plants. She ran to her.

Bertha's face was contorted and she could not speak. For a moment Bríd was paralysed. Bertha on the ground in pain – was her time come? Bríd had no idea.

'One second, dearest, I'll fetch help.'

She ran back to the open door and saw one of the Irish nuns, Sister Teresa.

'Sister, for God's sake, it's Bertha – her time is come! She's in the garden – come quickly!'

Some of the girls were also coming downstairs; they had seen Bertha from the window as she fell. They all gathered round the poor girl and tried to raise her.

'If we help you dear, will you be able to walk?'

'She'll never be able to walk. We'll have to carry her. And for heaven's sake, be quick.'

Willing hands outstretched, they supported the feeble girl, thin and light as she was, up the interminable stairs and into the infirmary.

She was helped into bed, and already a girl had gone for the physician.

The Mother Superior came in, followed by some of the other nuns. Seeing Sœur Ursule among them, Bríd looked heavily at her, but the nun would not return her gaze. The girls stood round as the Mother Superior questioned the chief nursing sister, then all the girls were ordered briskly out of the room. As she left, Bríd caught a last brief glimpse of Bertha, her face still twisted with pain.

The girls trooped back to the morning room and tried to take up their needles, but work was impossible. The thought of Bertha above them hung in the room like an ominous cloud.

Before Mass, Bríd went up and knocked on the door of the infirmary. It was opened by a nursing sister, who informed her that Bertha's labour had begun.

As she returned, Bríd tried to compute Bertha's time; although she was not sure of her dates, she was certain that the birth was not due for another six weeks at least. She had begun her labour prematurely. In her anxiety for Bertha, Bríd felt a wave of anger run through her against the nun who had heaped such heavy work on her.

It was long before they slept that night. The girls whispered to each other in the darkness; as each of them thought of Bertha up in the infirmary enduring her labour, they thought also of themselves and how they too would soon be there, how the grimace of pain which they had seen on Bertha's face would soon be on their own.

Before Mass in the morning, Bríd went up to the infirmary. Bertha had had her child – a girl, still-born. Bertha herself was alive, though very weak. Bríd was not permitted to go in.

'Well, when can I see her? I must see her soon!'

'That's for Sister Francesca to decide.'

After breakfast Bríd returned to the infirmary.

'You must let me see Bertha! You must!'

The nun wavered, looked over her shoulder, and then nodded briefly.

'She's awake now. Not long, mind!'

Bríd approached the bed carefully, treading gently. Bertha was lying on her back, her face dead white, her eyes sunken, her cheeks hollow. Bríd had never seen anyone look so close to death. Her eyes were open, however.

'Bertha,' she whispered.

The girl moved her head slightly to see Bríd and for a moment said nothing. At last, barely audible, a croak in her voice, she said,

'My baby is dead.'

The look in her eyes was so awful that Bríd had to turn away. There was silence until Bríd gradually brought herself to look into Bertha's face again. Her expression had not changed.

'Oh, Bertha, I'm so sorry! I'm so, so sorry.'

'My baby, Bríd. I don't know . . . I don't know what to do.'

'Oh, my dearest!'

She took Bertha's hand, which had been lying on the coverlet, and held it between her own.

'Bertha, dearest, you must rest, you must get well again. Do you understand? You must get well again.'

Bertha had not heard her.

'My baby – dead . . .'

Sister Francesca came into the room and crossed quickly to where Bríd was bending over the bed.

'You cannot remain here – surely you see how weak she is? Out you go, straight away.'

Unflustered, Bríd turned to the nun and led her away to the door.

'Sister, I beg you to tell me – will she live? I couldn't bear it . . .'

'It's too soon to say. The physician is coming this morning to examine her. We must all hope and pray.'

That morning, as the girls sat at their needles, a heavy silence hung over them. Sometimes one of them would look up timidly at another, exchange an apprehensive look and then return to her work. Sometimes a remark, brief and aimless, would break the silence. The thought of Bertha above them was in every mind, oppressing them all. Was this how it would be for them? Would their own child live? Bríd's thoughts were muddled. She knew Sœur Ursule was responsible for this, and she was resolute that the Reverend Mother should know all. But the anxiety for Bertha which weighed on them all subdued her too; what did Ursule matter when Bertha might be taken from them at any moment?

Bertha died. The news was broken at about seven that evening after Mass.

Bríd was too full to think. Bertha was dead and she had never had the chance even to say farewell. That sweet, gentle girl was gone. It simply was not right that Bertha should be taken from the world so young. Bríd felt anger at the father who had consigned her to this place, anger at the man who had led her into her undoing, anger and frustration that there was nowhere any tangible redress. Sœur Ursule – what did she matter? If it had not been her, it might have been someone else. And besides, what could Bríd do? Attack her as she had threatened in her anger? Absurd.

The girls sat in their rows in dead silence as the news was announced; no one looked at another, each staring up towards the Mother Superior, each, like Bríd, trying to grasp the appalling fact of death.

A requiem Mass was sung the next day. Before it began, the girls were allowed to see Bertha in her coffin, dressed in white like a bride, still, cold, her face relaxed in death, as if all her pain and unhappiness had been relieved by a greater power. The spirit had withdrawn from the flesh. A strange shudder ran through Bríd as she gazed on the calm face there in the coffin, so awful, so final.

Bertha was buried in the nuns' graveyard. All the girls attended. Afterwards Maisie whispered to Bríd that this was by the family's wish. She linked arms with Bríd as they walked back into the house afterwards.

'Can you imagine, Bríd? Not come to your own child's funeral? They say 'twill be given out that she died in Switzerland. They simply wanted her forgotten. And 'tis my belief that her father gave orders for her to have such heavy work to do. Why else would the nuns do it?'

Bríd was incredulous.

Maisie went on, 'Why else would Sœur Ursule have been allowed to torment her?'

Thinking over the way she had seen Bertha driven and humiliated, Bríd still could not believe that it had been by some malicious design. Ursule was a tormented, unhappy woman who had vented her spite on Bertha; next, it would be somebody else.

The dreary weeks passed. Bríd was summoned once more to the Reverend Mother's office.

'This arrived for you.'

It was a small packet. Bríd turned it over and over in her hands, wondering at the handwriting – Harry's. She was almost afraid to open it.

'Excuse me, Reverend Mother.'

She carried it up to the dormitory, empty at that hour, sat on her bed, and then began carefully to unwrap the packet. Inside the brown paper was tissue paper, and as she carefully unfolded it she at last disclosed a small gold locket with a thin gold chain, and a letter. She looked down at them in her hands, timidly, reverently, and at last unfolded the letter.

My only darling,
I am writing these words, knowing it is the last time that I shall ever be able to address you. It is almost too painful to do it, to have to think so carefully of each word, knowing you will hold this paper and read every word I have written.

My darling, I did not write before because I have been ill, and then, when I was strong enough, I wrote to Flood Street, and when my letter was returned unopened, I was in despair.

I do not know where to begin. I thought I should die when I had to leave you; my life is utterly meaningless, but I must struggle on; my duty requires it. I have thought and thought what I could do, and there was never any way out. I know the course I must follow, and I will follow it even it kills me. I have decided to leave England for a while – I am leaving tomorrow. It will be best, I think; I could not bear to be here in London and know you were somewhere near, only a few streets away perhaps, and never be able to see you and speak to you.

My darling, I do not know what you must think. Oh, if only I could have seen you once more before I go, but it cannot be. I have sent you a locket – will you accept it from me, as a reminder? Think of me sometimes, wherever you may be, as I will never cease to think of you, and pray for you as long as my life will last.

Harry

Harry ill. It was the strain, it was his family, his father forcing him, making him think only of his hateful family. It wasn't Harry, she knew he loved her, she had always known it, only it was that overbearing, vile tyrant who had forced him to break with her. She turned the locket over and over in her hands; it was of beautiful workmanship, chased in delicate patterns.

When at last she was able to regain control of herself, she carefully wrapped the locket and the letter back in the tissue paper, and put them into the pocket of her smock. They should never be separated from her.

He was leaving England. No, he had already left. She could not even write to thank him. He would not even know she had his locket

152

and the letter. Once she left the convent, she would wear the locket for the rest of her life.

The letter helped Bríd through what remained of her time at the convent. Her child would be born soon; in a few weeks she would be walking through the convent gate into the street, out into the world again. And in her arms – a child. Her child. It was still impossible for her to grasp this reality, so swiftly approaching.

One afternoon she was summoned to the Reverend Mother.

'It is customary for deserving girls to be placed as housemaids in respectable Catholic families. I hope you will strive to deserve this opportunity. Your needlework leaves much to be desired, I am informed. Still, you are strong, and if you can curb your temper, you may do well.'

Bríd had nothing to say to this.

'Your child will be placed with foster parents. It is fortunate that there are many childless couples who are willing to take in a stranger's child.'

'No.'

It broke quite involuntarily from her lips.

'I beg your pardon?'

'I beg *your* pardon, Reverend Mother, but I will not give up my child.'

The aristocratic nun looked up at her for a long moment.

'You have other arrangements?'

'I – that is, I don't know yet, but I will find something –'

The Reverend Mother was severe.

'You are a foolish and ignorant girl. Have you any money? Will your family accept you back? Who will care for your child? What respectable employer will accept you with a child born out of wedlock? It will be the grossest irresponsibility to your child.'

This thought struck Bríd forcibly. She had a responsibility to her child. What was she to do? She had not even begun to think it out, and here was the Reverend Mother setting out her options with brutal clarity. It was the scene with Wrenshaw again: a single girl with a child? An outcast! A pariah! Muddled and confused, she stuttered.

'I will think of something, Reverend Mother, only I need a little time. Just let me think!'

But she could not think. She grew heavier as the days passed; the child was now moving within her, she could feel it; her time was close, and still she could not think it out. She could not go back to Ireland – take a baby back to Ballyglin? Impossible. Get work in London? As

153

what? No respectable household would take her. Go on the streets? Never!

It was one day in Mass that the answer came to her, and it was so simple, so obvious when it came. Of course the Maestro had been right. She must become a singer. He had always had faith in her, had pressed her, cajoled her, told her the parable of the talents. She remembered so well the last interview she had had in Dean Street, the little man leaning forward, gazing earnestly into her face.

Even as she stood among the other girls singing the hymn and heard her own voice lifted with theirs, feeling, as she always did, released and uplifted by it, she knew it was the right thing to do.

But how was she to keep her baby? This was the thought that kept her awake, the thought that went round and round in her mind as she lay in bed, feeling the weight of her child shifting within her, the heavy consciousness that birth must be soon. A decision must be made soon.

There was perhaps one other possibility. Write to Aunt Nora and ask her if she could think of some way of caring for the child for a few months, just until she got started. She was very hazy in her mind, but Nora was clever and understood the world – she might have a suggestion, an idea that had escaped Bríd so far. Perhaps a relative, a cousin, would care for the child. Bríd could send money of course, and it would just be for a short while – that was the main thing.

Her time came. For ten hours she lay in the infirmary, enduring her pains, screaming, straining, cursing and then, in extraordinary relief, bathed in sweat, lying and staring at the bundle beside her pillow, her little boy, her little miracle, the prize which suddenly had wiped her account clean, had made up to her for everything, had justified everything, and was there, his face red, his tiny fists opening and closing. Sister Francesca leaned over him, playing delightedly with his little fingers.

Bríd thought of Harry, and was glad she had a little piece of him that she could fold in her arms. Looking down at her son as he sucked greedily at her breast that first time, feeling his little will tugging at her, so many strange thoughts ran through her mind, so many memories of Harry. She wondered again where he was now. He had been wiped so swiftly out of her life, yet she knew now that there was a part of her, in her innermost self, where he would remain as long as life itself.

It seemed incredible, but Sœur Ursule came into the infirmary, quickly, as if she were on some errand of importance, looking round as if for someone in authority. As if by an afterthought, seeing Bríd in her bed with the baby beside her, she came over, almost grudgingly and yet wanting to, and at last looked down with rapt attention at the baby. For a fleeting moment, Bríd saw an expression of anguish on her face that she would never have believed; she felt a burst of pity for the unhappy woman, and reached for her hand. For a moment only Ursule allowed her to see the suffering before reining herself in, drawing a deep breath and breaking away.

Three days later the baby was christened in the chapel and Bríd gave him the name Matthew.

In ten days she would have to leave. She made up her mind and wrote a letter to Nora. It was a difficult letter to write, and she tried many versions; at last, she simply asked Nora to meet her in Dublin. She did not even mention the boy, in case Nora might refuse to speak to her.

In reply, Nora sent a brief note that Bríd should appoint a place where they should meet, and she would come. No more than that.

On a cold February day, her bag in one hand and her baby clutched to her with her other, Bríd left the convent. Many of the girls who had been there when she first came had left before her, and others had come since. Bríd had conflicting feelings. She was leaving Bertha there for ever, in the cold ground. She knew she would never forget her. Life had been too hard for her. It was better not to think too much after all, but just to get on with it.

On the morning Bríd left she fastened Harry's locket round her neck, under her dress.

She took the train to Holyhead, and in the late afternoon was standing at the prow of the mail packet as it approached Kingstown. In her ears was the throbbing of the engines and the threshing of the paddles. Away to the west, in the declining sun, the Wicklow Mountains were white with frost and far off to the right the mass of Howth Head crouched like a lion. As the ship came into the harbour and she saw the spire of the church and the row of villas nestling there so comfortably, she felt a sudden gladness to be returning to Ireland; she felt she was coming home, in however ambiguous circumstances. Home.

Yet she had no home here any more. She was coming as a stranger, and must pretend to be one. That evening in Dublin she found a respectable boarding house not far from Sackville Street, gave a false name, a ring now flashing on her finger, and told the landlady that she was recently widowed, her soldier husband having died in India. ''Twas the cholera that took him.'

The landlady accepted her story without comment, and a week's rent in advance.

Bríd wrote again to Nora, giving her address, and settled down to wait for an answer. It came quickly, and two days later Nora and Patsy came up to Dublin.

It was early afternoon. Bríd had requested the use of the sitting room for their meeting, and now sat rocking the baby absent-mindedly in her arms as she waited. She looked down at Matt – his name had somehow abbreviated itself – staring into his little face, full of fears, trying to guess Nora's reaction when she walked through the door. Would she turn and walk straight out again? It was going to be a terrible shock for them both. How could she ensure that they would stay long enough for her to get her story out?

Chapter Nineteen

The moment had come. She heard the knock at the front door, she heard the landlady go to answer it, she heard Nora's voice, the steps in the hall. Then the door opened.

Nora stood in the doorway, Patsy looking over her shoulder, smiling. Nora did not smile. In one instant she had taken in the situation. Bríd was standing in the centre of the room, tall, noble, filled with trepidation, the baby in her arms.

They came into the room.

'Shut the door,' Nora said briefly over her shoulder. Patsy, obviously nervous, quickly closed the door.

Nora stopped in the room. The two women faced each other without speaking.

'I had an idea,' Nora said quietly, still unsmiling, making no movement towards Bríd. Patsy behind her was waiting for Nora to set the tone of the interview.

Nora loosened her bonnet, set it on the table and peeled off her gloves. Bríd, relieved to see her again, yet afraid to make a move, said, 'Aunt Nora, I couldn't tell you before. I was afraid you might not have come.'

'This is a sad day, Bríd.'

'Aunt Nora, I know it. I beg you, don't scold me!'

Patsy unexpectedly came forward and took the baby from Bríd into his arms, looking down into his little face. He smiled up at Bríd.

'He's a darling little fellow.'

Bríd was about to speak, but Nora cut in harshly to Patsy,

'Hold your tongue – you're a fool.' She sat at a chair at the table, looking up at Bríd. 'And what of the father? What of Lord Harry Leighton?'

'He went away, Aunt Nora. He's to marry another. Honest, it wasn't my fault!'

'Wasn't your fault? Wasn't your fault for running after him to London?'

Bríd was silent, looking shamefacedly at Nora while she awaited her verdict.

'Well, it's done now. You're a great fool, but it's no use to cry over what's past. What are you going to do?'

Patsy broke in, the baby still in his arms.

'Nora, my darling, we're barely inside the door. First of all we're going to give Bríd a kiss, then we're going to ask her for a cup of tea. We'll make ourselves comfortable, then we'll talk. Bríd, my darling, we've missed you badly.'

The baby still in one arm, he took Bríd in his other and squeezed her to him for a moment, then kissed her on the cheek.

Nora stood up and silently took Bríd in her arms and held her a moment. Bríd was on the verge of tears.

'I'll ask the landlady to give us some tea.'

Tea was brought, poured, served, cups handed round, but still conversation was difficult, each skirting round the main theme which was to come.

Bríd looked down into her teacup.

'Is Molly well?' she said faintly.

'Molly? Aye, she's well enough.'

'And Garrett?' she said even more faintly.

'Garrett?' Nora was grim. 'After you left, he went nearly out of his mind; his mother came to see me one day and told me he was that near to taking his life, she was afraid for him. He wouldn't talk to anyone, and there was no coming near him. And then, last summer, he went away, no one knows where, and there's been no word of him.'

Bríd still could not bring herself to look at Nora. Patsy was rocking the bundle in his arms, looking down into the little face asleep.

'Aunt Nora, I feel so ashamed to have brought this on you –'

'Ashamed! You have the face to talk to me of shame? Have you any idea what we've been through in the village? The pointing, the whispering, the tales, the gossip, the rumours, and us never able to deny a word of it? And Father Geoghegan in the pulpit, reading a sermon on you for a fallen woman, a disgrace to the village, and saying you was a lesson to all women to avoid the snares of the world, and how chastity was a jewel, and a pure woman a beacon in the home to guide her family, and a deal more of the same, and the women turning and looking at Patsy and me till we was ready to sink through the floor, and saying, "Oh, how we feel for you, Mrs Byrne,

158

in your hour of disgrace", the lying bitches. And you talk to me of shame?'

Bríd sat listening with a white face, and Patsy was still looking down at the baby. There was a stunned silence as the two women stared into each other's faces.

Nora drew a sigh of resignation. 'But, as I said, what's done is done, and there's no use in crying over it. You'd best tell us what you plan to do.'

'Aunt Nora . . .' It was difficult for her to get started; Nora seemed implacable. 'I know I can never return to Ballyglin. So, you see, well, while I was in London, I had singing lessons, and this music teacher, he said I stood a chance of making a living at it –'

'Singing? What kind of a living is that?'

'Well, it seemed since I have, well, quite a good voice, it would be worth a try. I mean, it'd be better than going into service, wouldn't it?'

'Would it?'

'So what I wanted to ask you, Aunt Nora – and Uncle Patsy – was this: can you think of some way I could have Matt looked after for a few months, till I got started? It would be impossible if I was caring for Matt all the time.'

There was no reply. Patsy was looking at Nora. At last Nora spoke.

'Cared for.' She said it as a statement, not a question.

'Just temporarily. A few months, till I got started.'

'You want me and Patsy to take your child?'

'I don't know . . . Do you have any ideas?'

'You want me and Patsy to take your baby back to Ballyglin?'

Nora was dragging the answers from her into a harsh and unforgiving light. 'Have you any idea what I'm supposed to say in the village when I produce the child?'

Bríd was silent. Nora had no intention of helping her. Bríd was to be made to carry the burden of her sin alone. It was understandable; Nora had never liked her much, she reflected.

Nora rose, walked to the window and looked out. The other two waited, and at last Nora returned again and looked down at Bríd, sitting at the table.

'There's only one way I'll take your child to Ballyglin. And that's for ever. I'll take him, and Patsy and I will bring him up as an orphan. He'll be well looked after, he'll be able to hold his head up, and he'll have the farm to take on after Patsy's gone.'

Bríd could not follow this. Something was missing from the equation.

'Orphan?'

'We shall tell him his parents are dead.'

Patsy was staring at her open-mouthed. Bríd could not believe her. 'No!'

'No? What do you mean? You'd rather the boy was brought up in disgrace? The son of a whore? You'd rather that? What have you to offer him? A singer? What kind of a life is that?'

'No! Aunt Nora – give up my child? No!'

'You're selfish and you always were! Who are you thinking of – yourself or the boy? Is he to have a respectable, secure life? What else can you offer? A life in the music hall – or on the streets?'

'No!'

Bríd burst into tears and flung her head on her arms on the table.

Nora was implacable.

'As you please, but it would be best for the boy.'

'No, no, no!' Bríd's voice was muffled.

Patsy was too stunned even to move. Still holding the boy, he looked between the two women. Nora looked down unmoved on Bríd's head as she sobbed into her arms.

'I thought just for a few months . . .'

Nora said nothing. Slowly Bríd looked up at her. At last Nora went on quietly,

'If it got out that he was your bastard, it would ruin him. You are disgraced, fallen. It must be for ever; this is the only way.'

'And believe that I am dead?'

'It's best.'

Bríd looked towards Patsy. 'For ever? Uncle Patsy, must I?'

Patsy was helpless. 'Well, Bríd, what Nora says is true –'

'Oh, God! I'd rather die!'

'Whether you're alive or dead, the child must be provided for! That's what matters! It's no good sobbing and wringing your hands; you've brought this upon yourself, and you must pay for it! Do you want to provide properly for the child or not? That's the question!' Nora was leaning over the girl at the table, blazing, pitiless.

'Yes, I do want to. But there must be some way –'

'There's no way. He must believe himself to be an orphan. Patsy and I can make up some story to satisfy him – and the village. He'll have respectability; he'll hold his head up before the world. Isn't that what you want? If anyone asks, we'll give out you're dead or disappeared. No one will ever know. No one will connect him with you.'

The floor was heaving beneath her feet. She must wake up soon – it couldn't be real. But it was real. In Patsy's arms the boy was still asleep.

Suddenly she collapsed; as weak as a rush, she could scarcely speak.

'Aunt Nora, just give me a little time to think.'

There was nothing to think over. Everything Nora said was true. It was best for the boy. It was best for the boy. The words burned into her brain. Oh, God, better to be in her grave like Bertha – but it was best for the boy.

The following afternoon, in a daze, Bríd went with Nora and Patsy to an attorney and signed a document. She agreed never to return to Ballyglin, never to make any contact with Nora or Patsy save through the attorney. She was to send as much money as she could to contribute to Matt's education. She was in a dream, in a nightmare, could not believe it was happening. Why not simply take the boy back to London? Surely anything was better than this – than to be torn in half?

Nora's logic was implacable: it was better for the boy. That afternoon Bríd went with them to Amiens Street Station, saw them on to the train. Her eyes filmed with tears, she heard the hooting of the engine, the whooshing of steam, clasped Uncle Patsy a last time in her arms, kissed Aunt Nora, saw for a moment, a last moment, the little morsel in the bundle, his little face, his little hands, then the train was pulling out of the station in clouds of steam. A roaring noise in her ears drowned her thoughts, and unable to think or understand, she knew only that she had done a very bad thing, and every mistake, every error, every sin she had ever committed was as nothing to this great sin, and that she would regret it every day of her life; it was burned into her soul, branded on her as a mark of infamy, a thousand times worse than any sin she had committed. Conceiving the child, begetting him, was nothing compared with this.

161

Chapter Twenty

At four thirty in the morning her train drew into the Euston Square Station. Aching, tired, her eyes sore, numb and disoriented, she stumbled along the platform among the other passengers. There was no one to meet her this time. In the chill, damp air of early morning she emerged into Euston Road, her bag with the two gowns in it in her hand, missing the weight of her child, yet curiously unable to feel any more.

Standing in Amiens Street Station, crossing Dublin to the packet boat, and even on the train from Holyhead, she had been seized by wild urges to return, go to Ballyglin, snatch her child back. But every time she had beaten back the feeling, had tightened her grip on herself by a blind act of will. There were to be no more feelings.

She set off down to Soho in the half-light, and as the carts of market gardeners were rumbling through the streets towards the markets, and working people were beginning to make their way to work, she arrived again in Dean Street. As she looked up at the blank windows of the houses in the dim light, it seemed better to wait until the Maestro might be awake, so she returned to a coffee stall she had passed at the street corner.

The coffee stall was a modest box on wheels with a counter at one side where a man sold cups of coffee and bacon sandwiches. It was lit by an acetylene lamp which hissed gently and threw a green glow on to the faces of the few people who stood around – two carpenters with their bags of tools at their feet and folded paper caps on their heads; two servant girls together, clutching hot cups between their hands to warm them, staring vacantly in silence, still half asleep; and a policeman. The light strengthened imperceptibly. The day dawned.

Bríd had a cup of coffee. Her feet were cold and she looked down at the boots she wore; a present from Harry, elegant once, now grey with dust, broken and frayed. The coffee warmed her and she looked at the others, silent, immobile figures in the dawn, and wondered who they were and where they were going.

By seven o'clock she had grown so cold she could wait no longer and she walked down to the Maestro's door again. She stood uncertain for a while, praying he would not be angry at being woken so early. She looked up at the blind windows. The street was deserted, the shops and restaurants closed. She stamped her feet from the cold, and at last, plucking up courage, reached up and rapped on the door.

There was a long wait, so long that Bríd began to fear he might be there no longer, but then at last she heard footsteps shuffling down the stairs, and the door opened. It was Maestro Pertinelli in his dressing gown, his hair dishevelled.

'Yes?' He stared at her. 'Bríd?'

'Maestro, I'm so sorry to be waking you at this hour. Oh, God, will you forgive me, but sure, the train got in at half past four, and I had nowhere else to go.'

He was still staring at her in amazement, then shivered in the cold air.

'Come in.'

He turned and began shuffling back up the stairs in his carpet slippers. Bríd followed, uncertain of herself, unsure again of all the reasons for being here.

They went into the front room, with its grand piano and the table covered with sheet music. In the corner stood her little harp.

'Now, Bríd, I don't understand. Where did you come from at this hour?'

'Maestro, I've just come from Ireland. It's what you said: I want to be a singer.'

'Wait, I go and get dressed. You have any breakfast?'

'I just had a cup of coffee down the road.'

'Well, you be a good girl, you light the fire and put on the kettle. Make me a cup of coffee while I get dressed. Then we have a talk.'

She took off her bonnet and cloak, knelt before the fire and began to clear out the ashes. When she had lit the fire, she set the kettle over it.

The Maestro came in. He took her shoulders in his hands, looked at her for a moment, and kissed her on the forehead.

'You still lovely as ever, Bríd,' he said. 'And you have a little baby?'

She stared down at her hands, dusty from lighting the fire.

'I did have a baby, Maestro,' she said, in a low voice, 'a boy.'

'And what did you call him?'

'Oh, er – Matthew.' She did not want to speak about him.

'And you did not bring him?'

'He's with my aunt and uncle.' She felt impatient. 'It's no good talking about it. I couldn't bring him, and that's flat. Is there somewhere I can wash my hands?'

'In my bedroom, Bríd, there is some water in the jug.' He pursued her, talking as they went. 'I understand. We got to find you some work. Where you going to stay?'

'I haven't got anywhere. I only arrived this morning.'

She washed her hands. Pertinelli handed her a towel. She looked round his bedroom, with an unmade bed, at the back of the building. He watched her gaze.

'This is a very small apartment, Bríd, I only got one bedroom. Very difficult. I got my pupils, if they see you here, they maybe get the wrong idea. Then their mamas get fright and take them away.'

'Oh, Maestro, I didn't mean –'

'I will ask around. We can find you a room somewhere near here. Now, what clothes you got?'

They returned to his front room, where the fire had now caught and the kettle was coming to the boil.

'I saved a couple of gowns.'

'Let me see.'

Bríd opened her small bag, and took out the two gowns she had not sold. One was in a rich orange and gold pattern and the other was the cream woollen dress.

'What you got for the evening?'

'I haven't anything. I sold all the other clothes I had.'

'You must have a black dress for the concert platform. How much money you got?'

'Not much. I had to go to Dublin and back, and pay for lodgings. I have to find work as soon as possible.'

'You got to have a black dress. One at least. You got a little money. That's good, because you're not ready for the concert platform or the opera yet. You need to rehearse a while before you're ready to sing in public. We're going to stun the critics, Bríd, eh, but we got to get it exactly right.'

He rubbed his hands in satisfaction at the thought. Bríd turned to the kettle, which was now boiling, and began to make coffee from a tin which stood on a tray with a coffee pot by the fire.

'Maestro, you know, I was thinking, maybe, rather than concerts, I could get a job in the music halls . . .'

Pertinelli was silent. She had her back to him as she poured water into the coffee pot, but she heard the mixture of hurt and surprise in his voice when he spoke.

'Music halls? Bríd, you are a serious musician, an artist. You go on

164

the music halls, they ruin you, ruin your talent, you degrade your art. You want to sing comic songs?'

She turned to him, speaking quickly, trying to smother his objections.

'It's not all comic songs, Maestro. Harry and me used to go. They have good singers. You don't understand, I've got to get some money. I can't afford to wait, and train for the opera, and then maybe hope in the end to succeed. I haven't the time.'

She turned again to the coffee pot, stirred the coffee and poured him a cup. She turned to hold it out to him, but he was looking at her with reproach.

'Bríd, in this business you start the way you mean to go on. You can't be a serious singer if you go on the music halls. That's entertainment, not art. Art is difficult, it takes a long time, it takes all your dedication. You got talent, you could be a great singer, maybe a great actress too. But what's the music hall? Just common, low entertainment, where the people drink and smoke and talk, and maybe they listen if you're lucky.'

She pressed the coffee cup on him, speaking urgently.

'But it could be a beginning, don't you see? And I could find a job more easily. I have to get work.'

He walked about the room for a moment, not touching his coffee.

'I seen it before. I seen it many times. These young girls, they got talent, but they're not ready to wait, not ready to work, they want success and make money. A few years go by, they're all used up, finished, and another one comes along, takes their place. That's not art, Bríd. Art is more than that, more than a pretty young girl and a sweet voice. Art is dedication, you give your soul, your everything . . .'

She saw the hardness in him, heard it in his voice, but she too hardened.

'I'm ready to work, Maestro, but I can't wait. Sure, can't I be studying with you while I work in the evenings, why not? You'd see whether I've got dedication. But you must help me, you know so much and I just don't know a thing. You've got to help me get started.'

He stared out of the window, sipping his coffee. She waited for his verdict. He shrugged his shoulders.

'I'll help you if I can.'

Suddenly she was very tired, and he let her rest on his bed. She slept until the afternoon. Her sleep was uneven, and she dreamed she was back at Amiens Street Station, and the train was pulling out, it was too late to call it back, and Matt was being taken from her for ever.

She was running down the platform, but the train was going faster and faster, and Matt was receding, getting smaller and smaller . . . She woke with a start, and from the next room the sound of singing mixed with her own still present, vivid dream.

Later the Maestro knocked on the door.

'You want something to eat? We go downstairs for some dinner, eh? And Bríd, I found you a room.'

She sat up quickly.

'Come. I'll explain.'

On the ground floor was Calvi's Italian restaurant, and it was crowded when they went in. The restaurant had windows on to the street, with lace curtains, and just inside the door there was a hat stand covered with coats, and with umbrellas clustered round the bottom. Maestro Pertinelli was a friend of the proprietor and all the staff, and he introduced Calvi to her.

He was stout, middle-aged, with a bald head and the dark, sunken eyes of a man who works too hard and never sees the daylight. He said there was a room at the top of the house which she could share with his niece, Isabella. It was just a room, he insisted; there was nothing else, no kitchen. She would have to take her meals down here, and whenever she wanted to wash she'd have to come down for hot water. The rent was one shilling and three pence a week.

After they had finished their dinner, which the Maestro insisted on paying for in honour of her arrival, Isabella came to their table. She was the ugliest girl Bríd had ever met. She was about Bríd's own age, shorter than Bríd, sturdy, with a square face and dark hair with a hairline which seemed to start immediately above her eyebrows, a pug nose and a wide mouth. She worked in the restaurant kitchen.

When she was introduced, she smiled. Bríd saw she had the sweetest and mildest expression and the most beautiful eyes, and hated herself for making such a hasty judgement.

'You have to thank Isabella,' Pertinelli said, 'she offered you the room.'

The ugly girl held out her hand. 'Come. I show you.'

Bríd followed the girl up four floors to the attic, into a room with a sloping ceiling and a low window which looked down into little gardens where the sun never penetrated, and where later Bríd was surprised to see pigs and chickens rooting and nosing in rubbish heaps.

The room was bare. There was no carpet on the floorboards, and two iron bedsteads stood at right angles along the walls. There was a small table under the window with a basin on it, and on the windowsill a broken piece of looking glass. On the wall was pinned a crude paper print of the Virgin Mary.

Isabella turned and smiled at her. 'That's your bed.'

She went out and returned in a moment with an armful of bedding and, as Bríd watched, she quickly and skilfully made up one of the beds. The other was already made up and covered with a plain, grey blanket. Isabella smiled beautifully at her again.

'You're tired. You rest. I'm going down – plenty of work to do.'

She laughed merrily. Bríd heard her boots clattering down the stairs.

Silently she looked round the room, then hung her bonnet and cloak on a hook behind the door and took her boots off. Pulling the blanket over her, she lay down on the bed.

Chapter Twenty-One

When Nora and Patsy returned to Ballyglin with a baby, the news quickly went round the village. Nora told anyone who asked that the child was the son of Patsy's nephew who had died in a cholera epidemic in Dublin, and such was her character that no one was inclined to comment to her face.

It was the greatest day of Nora's life. God had inexplicably, unjustly, withheld children from her, but now at this late hour a miracle had been vouchsafed them. A little baby was in the house, hers to care for and rear. This had not been in her mind when she had spoken to Bríd. Nora was an honourable woman, and everything she had said that afternoon had been true. It was not until they were back in the cottage that the reality dawned on her, that she had now at last a child of her own. Nothing and no one should take him from her.

Molly came up the *bohreen* to see them a few days after they returned. As soon as she saw the baby in the cradle by the fire, she could not resist bending over to admire it. She recognised the child immediately as Bríd's and Harry's. Molly had mixed feelings; she knew Bríd had done wrong and had paid a price, how great she could only guess; and she felt sorry for her old school chum. On the other hand, she could not repress a certain glow of satisfaction that Bríd had paid for her folly. It consoled her for the fear she had felt in the face of Bríd's boldness in running away.

She and Nora drank a cup of tea together; after a few random remarks, Molly came to the point.

'I wonder whatever became of Bríd now?'

Nora was stonefaced.

'Who knows? She's gone, that's all I know. And wherever she may be, she's made her bed and she must lie in it.'

'Liam says that Lord Harry's left the army and gone to India.'

'What's that to me?'

Molly looked into her teacup.

'Oh, nothing. Only, knowing Bríd was sweet on Lord Harry –'

'I know nothing of the sort.'

Molly was not inclined to continue.

'And Molly Kennedy –' Nora looked hard into her eyes – 'you know nothing of the sort either. Whatever Bríd has done or is doing, she's nothing to either you or me. You understand?'

'Oh yes, Mrs Byrne.'

Bríd was standing outside the Oxford Music Hall in her orange and gold dress, covered by her cloak. The morning traffic in Oxford Street clattered and rumbled past. The music hall was a new building, tall with a classical façade, columns rising above the doors, and at the top two towers, with the name OXFORD in enormous letters between them.

Bríd had been here before, with Harry. For a moment she felt a wince of pain at the memory of the two of them together and the excitement she had felt being with him. As they came out afterwards he had said, 'She doesn't sing half as well as you, Bríd,' and she had imagined herself on the stage in a beautiful gown, all the people clapping her, and how wonderful it would be. But then, holding Harry's arm, it seemed that nothing could compare with being with him; being married to him was all she could hope for or desire.

She looked up. Where should she begin? How was she to get in? Whom could she ask?

The front door was open. She went inside to the box office, and waited as a couple in front of her were buying tickets. At last she was looking through the narrow opening to a man sitting inside.

'Please, sir, would it be possible to see the manager? Would there be a vacancy just now?'

'I beg your pardon?'

His mystification increased her embarrassment.

'I'm sorry to be troubling you, sir, but would there be a vacancy now for a singer?'

She was aware of a man standing behind her.

'This is the box office. If you want to see the manager, ask at the stage door.'

'Oh, thank you, sir. Sorry to have troubled you, sir.'

She moved away, confused, and the man behind her moved forward to the little opening.

But where was the stage door? Vexed and irritated with herself, she waited for what seemed an eternity while the man spoke at the opening, and at last as he moved away she darted forward again.

'I'm so sorry to be troubling you, sir, but please can you tell me where would be the stage door now?'

'Turn right out of the door and follow the wall round to the back.'

A narrow alley ran down one side of the building between two high brick walls. It was dirty, there were rain puddles, and she had to pick her way between beer crates and a rubbish heap. There were tall wood and canvas frames leaning against the wall, which must be stage scenery. As she came round to the back, there was only one small door, with no sign over it or any indication of what it might be. There was no one about.

She knocked at the door, then noticed that it was not locked, so she pulled it open and looked inside. A corridor with white-painted brick walls was dimly lit by one gas lamp. Close by, in a little room, she saw an elderly man wearing a bowler hat, sitting reading a newspaper. She looked at the man, uncertain what to do, but he took no notice of her. At last she gave a little cough. Casually he looked up as he turned a page of his newspaper.

'Well, young lady, and what can I do for you?'

'Please, sir, I'm looking for work singing. Would there be a vacancy just now?'

The man laid down his newspaper and swivelled round in his chair. He took a long look at the tall, dark-eyed young woman who stood before him in the doorway, looking down at him with a mixture of fear and dignity, reserve and expectation. He stroked his spade beard for a moment as he looked her up and down.

'Well, now, let's see. Had any experience, have you?'

'I used to sing a lot at home, sir.'

'Ah, yes, at home. Ever been on the stage before?'

'No, sir.'

'Never mind, you've got to start somewhere, eh? Let's have a look at you. Take off that cloak.'

Nervously, Bríd undid the ribbon of her cloak and slipped it off to show her gown. It had a low neckline and was stiffly boned over a tight corset which pinched her waist in, above a flouncing skirt over a crinoline.

She looked superb. The man looked her up and down in silence for a moment, leaning back in his chair and crossing one leg over the other.

'Not bad, not bad. Turn round.'

His eyes took in her bare shoulders and her thick dark hair, taken up behind her head.

'Yes,' he said slowly, 'you've got possibilities, I should say. What's your legs like?'

Bríd looked down at him, not understanding what he meant.

'What's your legs like? Show us your legs,' he said in a matter-of-fact tone.

Reluctantly Bríd lifted the hem of her dress a little.

'Go on. Higher.'

She lifted the hem a little higher.

'You've got to have good legs if you want a job here. Go on, let's have a good look. Higher.'

Vexed and uncertain, she lifted her dress higher still.

'No, no, much higher than that. Go on, lift it right up.'

She had lifted her hem right above her knees, almost to her stocking tops. She could feel her face warm with embarrassment.

At that moment the stage door opened with a crash and a young man wearing a broad check suit came in. She dropped her skirt and turned quickly towards him. He stopped as he saw her, looked at her for a moment, then turned to the man in the chair.

'What's this, Jimmy? Up to your tricks again?'

The man leaped up.

'Morning, Mr Winston, sir. No post this morning, sir.'

The young man was looking at Bríd, who had been quickly pulling her cloak over her naked shoulders. He glared at the stage doorkeeper again.

'You ought to be ashamed of yourself, you old reprobate. Has he been getting you to sing for him, young lady?'

'No, sir,' said Bríd quietly.

'Only a bit of fun, Mr Winston,' said the doorkeeper in a jocular tone.

'Who did you want to see?' the young man went on in a friendly tone.

'Please, sir, I was only asking whether there wasn't maybe a vacancy for a singer just now.'

'You're a singer? Well, you'd have to write in to Tommy Maxwell. He's the manager.'

'Write?'

'Yes. Usual thing. Tell him what you've done and ask for an audition.'

'An audition?'

He looked at her hard for a moment. 'Are you new to this?'

She looked down at the floor and bit her lip. 'I am,' she said softly.

'Well, don't worry, they're always looking for new faces. Write in all the same and ask him to see you. He's bound to.'

'Oh, write in? Thank you, sir.'

'Don't thank me, really. I'm sorry if this old villain has been embarrassing you.'

He turned to the doorkeeper.

'You should be ashamed of yourself, you dirty old man!'

The old man writhed. 'No offence, sir, we was only having a bit of fun, young lady, wasn't we?'

Bríd moved towards the door, turned and said, 'Thank you again, sir', and went out again into the alley and the light of day.

She was in despair. That disgusting old man was nothing at all, nobody, just the doorman. How could she have been such a fool as to mistake him? And then to let him humiliate her; she could feel tears of vexation start in her eyes as she made her way quickly down the damp alley and into the roar and noise of Oxford Street. There was comfort in the anonymity of being part of the crowd that flowed up and down, hurrying and jostling past her. She stood at the kerb staring blindly at the carts and drays, the broughams and hansoms, the carriages and omnibuses that clattered ceaselessly past.

And that was not the worst. That young man had been kind, but when he said 'write' her heart had sunk. She had written three letters in her life and it had very nearly killed her. It was impossible she should write a letter to the manager. Impossible.

She was walking idly along Oxford Street, and it was not long before she found herself standing outside another music hall. She stood looking up at the posters. So many names – surely there was room for hers too? She decided to make another try. She made her way down the side of the building to the stage door. Again, there was a stage doorkeeper in his little office.

'Excuse me for troubling you, sir, but would it be possible to maybe get an audition as a singer now?'

This doorkeeper gave her the same advice as the young man. She should write a letter.

She was out on the street again.

Later that morning she was in Drury Lane outside the Middlesex Music Hall. This was the fifth. She remembered coming here with Harry once too, but her memories were becoming blunted. She had to find a job, that was all.

The stage doorkeeper was an energetic man with a round, red face. He had a thin friend with him who smoked a clay pipe.

At first he told her what the others had said, but as she was turning to go, he called her back.

'You new to the business?'

'Yes, sir,' she said quietly, looking at him with all her dignity.

'He won't take you on till you've had some experience, young lady.'

'She wants to try down the Grapes,' said the other man, taking his pipe from his mouth for a moment. The stage doorkeeper looked round at him and then turned to Bríd again.

'Now that's a very good idea. You go along to the Grapes. Plenty of singing there, every night. Just suit a young girl like you.'

'That's very kind of you, sir. Where would that be now?'

'Ten minutes from here. Goswell Road. The Grapes. Just ask to see the manager.'

He came out of the door on to the pavement with her and pointed. Full of gratitude, Bríd hurried away quickly down the street as he directed. She knew she had only to keep trying, and something would come up. This was her chance. She walked quickly, excited, her mind full of hopes, building pictures of a future career. She would be a singer, she would earn money. She could even send money home to Ireland as she had promised.

She was standing looking up at a tall new building in red brick with large, ornate etched-glass windows: the Grapes. It wasn't a music hall, only a pub. That man had deceived her. All her strength and hope emptied out of her. What did it matter to him, anyway? Weren't there dozens of girls coming through his door every day?

She stood wearily on the pavement, trying to collect her thoughts. What next? Five music halls she had tried and every one had turned her away. Hungry and tired, she was about to go home when she saw for the first time a notice in the window:

CAVE OF HARMONY!
ENTERTAINMENT EVERY NIGHT!
A FEAST of DRAMATIC and MUSICAL RECITATION
Performed NIGHTLY for the
DELECTATION of our PATRONS!
ADMITTANCE SIXPENCE
in EXCHANGE for REFRESHMENTS!

She stared up at the notice. Was this what the man meant? It must be. Singing. It was only a pub, still . . . she had to ask. She pushed open the door and went in.

173

Chapter Twenty-Two

It was late morning, and the bar was fairly empty. It was a spacious room with etched mirrors on every wall, embossed ceilings supported on cast-iron columns and, behind the bar, enormous barrels with BRANDY, SHERRY, WHISKY written across them in gold lettering. The floorboards were scattered with fresh sawdust.

Along the bar two men were talking to the barmaid. Bríd waited, trying to catch her eye. The girl was engrossed with the two men. She laughed. Then she looked up and saw Bríd. She excused herself and came casually along the bar.

'What can I get you?'

'I'd like to speak to the manager, please.'

The girl turned to an opening in a glass partition which led to another bar.

'Mr Wordsworth! Girl to see you!'

A tall, solid man with bulging eyes, heavy side whiskers and an impatient manner came through the partition. He was in shirtsleeves and a waistcoat.

'What can I do for you?'

Bríd swallowed. She didn't like to be overheard by the two customers who had turned and were watching her, but she had to get a job here or forget the whole thing. She spoke in a low, urgent tone.

'If you please, sir, I'm looking for work singing. I was recommended to you.'

'Recommended? Who by?'

'A gentleman at the Middlesex Music Hall.'

'Oh, yes? What can you do?'

'Well, sir, I've had singing lessons, and I was recommended to try and get work as a singer, you see.'

'Any experience?'

Bríd looked down. 'Not actually, sir, not on the actual stage, no. But I've been trained by –'

'What can you sing?'

'Oh, I know plenty of songs, sir, Irish, English and Italian –'

'Hmm.' He looked at her for a moment. 'Come through.'

He led her through a door at one end and into a rectangular hall filled with chairs and tables. At the near end to the right was a platform with a piano on it. Above the platform was a large inscription: CAVE OF HARMONY. There was a stale smell of tobacco and food that almost made her retch.

'Up you go, then. Let's hear you.'

In the dim light from the windows, where the curtains were half drawn, Bríd made her way up on the platform. The emptiness of the hall was emphasised by the distant noise of the traffic outside. As she took off her cloak, her mind was racing.

There was a song she had rehearsed with the Maestro which she had once heard a *serio* sing at the Oxford in Italian; it was from Gluck's *Orfeo*. She thought it would impress him, and it suited her voice. This was her chance, and she had to show herself off to her best. She stood alone in the middle of the platform, in the gloom, looking down to where Mr Wordsworth sat among the empty chairs and tables, and sang.

In the stillness of the room, her voice flowed, soft, strange and low, different from any other voice the man had heard. He watched her as she stood, her arms by her side, as the voice rose from within her.

As she finished, her voice subsiding, drawing at last into silence, the man continued to look at her without speaking. A few minutes earlier he had been in the cellar connecting a new beer barrel; he was a man who ran a musical entertainment for working men and their wives. He had never heard anything quite like this before. It was a voice of strange power and intensity. The problem was whether he could use it in his show.

'Do you know anything in English?'

All her fears and uncertainties returned to Bríd. Why had she sung in Italian? Was it wrong?

'Irish, aren't you? What about something Irish? "Danny Boy"?'

She knew some of the words of 'Danny Boy', though she had never rehearsed it.

When she had finished there was a long silence. Bríd looked down through the gloom at the man, standing among the tables. Would he say anything? What did he think? She was about to say something when he spoke at last.

'That'll do. Come back in the bar.'

She followed him back, drawing her cloak over her shoulders. He leaned over the bar and shouted to someone behind the glass partition.

'Nell! Nell! What did Bessie say to you? Is she coming in next week?'

'No,' came back a woman's voice, 'she's got to go down to her uncle's in Camberwell that was took sick.'

He turned to Bríd and looked her up and down again.

'I tell you what, young lady, I need a barmaid. I'll pay you four shillings a week and your dinner. Then, in a week or two, if there's a spot, I'll give you a chance to sing in the Cave of Harmony. If you're any good, I'll give you a permanent spot, sixteen shillings a week. Have you got any sheet music for the pianist?'

Bríd was in a daze. She told him she would get her sheet music.

'Start tomorrow, eight in the morning.'

She was in the street again. She stood at the pavement's edge, in a trance. She had a job. He would give her a chance to sing. She was on the bottom rung, she had a start. She set off back to Soho, hurrying, in a daze of joy and excitement. Her first morning. She couldn't believe her luck.

In the restaurant she took Isabella, who was busy among the lunch-time clients, to one side, holding her tightly by her arms as she looked into her face and poured out her news. Then she rushed up to the Maestro's room. He listened gravely.

'So they no like Gluck? They want "Danny Boy"? I understand. No, no, Bríd, I understand well.'

She was about to speak, but he went on.

'I know you in a difficult position, you need money, and maybe you get on quicker this way. So I help you. Like you say, maybe you sing good music later, eh? Tomorrow we work out music for you to rehearse –'

'That's going to be difficult, Maestro. You see, they haven't actually given me the singing engagement yet. I'll be working as a barmaid for the moment, till there's a spot for me.'

He was incredulous.

'A barmaid?'

'Yes. But then he'll give me a spot.'

'Bríd – you leave your little boy in Ireland to come to London and be a barmaid?'

She was angry that he couldn't see how important it was.

'It's a chance, that's the point. I'll do anything, if it'll give me a chance to sing. Anything.'

That night Bríd hung her golden dress on a hook on the wall as she undressed for bed, and gazed at it as she brushed her hair. That dress was her passport to the theatre. That was her singing dress, it would bring her to the job she wanted more than anything in the world.

Isabella was already in bed and watched her as she brushed and brushed, unthinking, her eyes on the dress.

'You got lovely hair, Bríd,' she said at last.

'Thank you.'

'You brush it every night?'

'Oh, yes,' said Bríd dreamily.

'You very beautiful.'

Bríd stopped and looked at her. Then she sat on the edge of Isabella's bed. Isabella had the blanket drawn up to her chin, and her gentle eyes looked up into Bríd's.

'Isabella, I shall never forget that you gave me a bed in your room. All my life I shall never forget it.'

She bent down and kissed Isabella on the cheek.

By the time Bríd had been working four days at the Grapes, she felt she had been there all her life. It had swallowed her up. She no longer saw daylight. She arrived at eight in the morning when it opened, got home after midnight and fell exhausted into bed. On her second day she was so tired that Mr Wordsworth let her sleep for an hour in the afternoon on a pile of sacks in the storeroom, because trade was slack. None of the other girls seemed to get tired and Bríd thought they must have got used to it.

As soon as she arrived on the first morning, she had to clear the tables in the Cave of Harmony. The room was cold, but thick with tobacco smoke from the previous night, and the tables were still covered with all the plates and glasses left when the entertainment finished around midnight.

She opened the curtains and threw up the window, trying to clear the air. It took an hour for three girls to clear the tables and carry everything to the kitchen. There were a number of girls working there, all around Bríd's age or younger, but she didn't get to know them well, for they were always changing. Some came in late, some left early, each seemed to have her own arrangements. There was one girl, Maggy, whom she became friends with. Maggy lived nearby, a real Londoner, and at first Bríd did not always understand everything she said. Maggy taught her about the drinks, what 'half and half' was, or 'a draught of satin', or how to make 'shrub', and when she worked behind the bar Bríd had difficulty with the prices and was always rushing along to Maggy to ask how much a schooner of sherry was, or a gin and bitters.

In the evening at seven she became a waitress in the Cave of

Harmony. The curtains were drawn, the fires were lit, the great rings of gaslight which hung from the ceiling were lit, and as the room filled it became very hot. By nine it was packed. Working people of all sorts, men and women, children too, a constant noise of chatter and laughter, the clatter of plates and glasses on the tables, the scraping of chairs on the floor, shouting to waitresses who hurried continuously between the tables.

For the first few nights, Bríd found it exhausting. She had trouble remembering what people had ordered. The waitresses wrote up the orders in the kitchen on a blackboard in chalk, and as the cooks served up the dishes the orders were wiped off again. Whenever she rushed in and saw the line of plates balanced on a narrow ledge, ready to be taken, her mind would go blank. Which were hers? Chops, beefsteaks, pies, joints, the menu was not complicated, but the orders went up and were cleared so fast, the plates were placed on the ledge and taken so quickly, Bríd's head spun.

She had trouble too with the money, and would stand at a table where four young men were sitting, their little pipes in their mouths, their hats on the back of their heads, as they fired their orders at her, chops, pies, porter, ale, whisky, her mind struggled to remember it all and reckon it up. By the time she reached home and dragged herself up to the room in the attic, she was dizzy with tiredness.

For the first few days she hardly had time or energy to notice the show going on above her on the platform. But as she grew more familiar with her work and less tired, she began to turn her attention to it in odd moments. The first thing she noticed as she moved among the tables was that the people's attention veered toward the platform and away again according to how they liked the performer. Their attention would not hold a second beyond their interest and she saw with dismay how most of the time they were talking to each other and took no notice of the performers at all. Was this how they would greet her?

There was one performer whom they always applauded loudly. He was a young man, slim, with humorous eyes and a cheeky grin, who fearlessly took hold of the audience. He talked to them, bantered with them, noticed individuals, addressed them, sometimes by name, and was effortlessly in command.

He sang a comic song with piano accompaniment called 'Alice, Where Art Thou?'

> 'My Alice is a nobby gal
> As gentle as you please
> And for a rorty sort of bloke

178

She's just the very cheese
And as I mean to wed her soon
I've sweared a solemn swore
If e'er I gets hold of that toff
I'll dislocate his jaw!'

His name was Phil Courage.

Another man, tall and thin, with a sombre, worried look, performed a Lancashire clog dance which made a deafening noise on the boards of the platform until Bríd feared he would rap so hard one night he would crash right through.

Another sight she had never seen was a young woman dressed as a man, in evening dress, with top hat and cane, and smoking a cigar. Bríd couldn't help smiling to think what Aunt Nora would make of her.

After ten days Mr Wordsworth had not offered her the chance to get up and sing and Bríd began to worry that he was never going to. One morning, when things were quiet, she asked him about it, and he told her in a casual, offhand way that she would get her chance. He would fit her in when there was a spot free. She was left vexed and irritated and feeling he was cheating her and suddenly frightened that she would spend the rest of her life as a waitress and never have her chance.

Two days later, while she was clearing tables in the empty Cave of Harmony, he told her she could go on that night. He was walking off, but she ran and stopped him.

'Mr Wordsworth. I can't wait at table as well as sing! You must give me the evening off to get ready.'

'Get ready? What are you talking about?'

'I have to run through my songs, and change my dress. I can't just get up at a moment's notice. And where shall I change my clothes?'

The performers arrived in costume ready prepared, with a cloak thrown over them.

Mr Wordsworth looked at her as if she were making a tiresome nuisance of herself.

'I can't let you off. Who else can I get? I'm short of staff as it is. You can change in the storeroom.'

'Well, I have to go back home to get my dress, and my music.'

Reluctantly he agreed to this.

That evening at six, Bríd hurried home in near panic. She had not yet had a chance to rehearse her songs with the pianist. Mr Wordsworth told her she could have a practice run-through before the customers came in at seven o'clock.

179

Full of excitement, she knocked on the Maestro's door.

'It's tonight, Maestro! I'm going on! I'm going back now to rehearse with the pianist!'

He took her hands, and she looked down into his face, old, tired, careworn.

'I'll think of you tonight, Bríd.'

She ran up to her room and put on her golden dress, then looked at herself as well as she could in the piece of broken looking glass. She arranged the dress round her bosom, anxiously thinking that she would be soon showing herself off to audience, inviting their approval – or criticism. Then she took up her brush and began to brush her hair, staring at her own reflection.

She was still beautiful; it surprised her to see it. She felt she had been through so much, worked so hard, come home exhausted so many nights that there could be nothing left of her looks. Yet there was still a lustre in her dark eyes and a peach bloom in her cheeks. The face that had so bewitched Harry was changing subtly, her beauty had matured into something stately, silent, noble. She was still only eighteen.

In her orange and gold dress and wrapped in her cloak, she returned to the Grapes. Customers had not yet come into the Cave of Harmony, but the pianist was there and she had time to run through the songs quickly with him. The chairman was already in his place, too; he sat at a table just below the platform and waitresses had instructions to keep his glass full of brandy punch. His job was to introduce the performers and he had a little gavel to beat on the table as he did so. He told her she would be on early in the evening, before Sally Beauman. He also told her she would have to change her name: he would introduce her as Bridget Flynn.

Many performers worked several pubs every night, and arrived only a few minutes before they were due on the stage. Bríd had noticed Phil Courage walk in, throw off his overcoat and, after a moment's chat, be called to the platform by the chairman. As soon as he finished, he was off again.

Customers were coming in. Bríd put on her cloak again and went out into the street. People hurried past her on the pavement as she stood looking up in the darkness of the night sky. The acrid smell of coal smoke hung in the chill air.

She could not concentrate on anything. Observing the people coming in that evening, she had suddenly had the appalling realisation that soon they would be watching her. She would be up on the platform that night. Every person who paid their sixpence to go in to the Cave of Harmony would watch her.

What madness had possessed her? Why had she come all this way, left her darling little boy, left Uncle Patsy, and Aunt Nora, left the village, to come here and stand up in front of all these strangers? Why? A wave of stomach cramps seized her, making her almost retch. All through her limbs ran a strange fizzing, as if her blood were on fire; her throat was dry, her hands constantly sweating no matter how often she wiped them.

She didn't have to be here. Why couldn't she just walk away? Tell Mr Wordsworth she felt unwell and would be unable to sing tonight. That would be simplest, then just walk away, never be seen again, just disappear. For ever. Just disappear.

The church bell chimed seven. This was it! She wiped her hands again and went in. The Cave was nearly full. Why had so many people come tonight? Why didn't they stay away? She made her way through the tables, smiling vaguely at the girls as they hurried past her. Maggy said, 'Good luck, Bríd'. She bent over the chairman and he whispered she would be on the act after next.

181

Chapter Twenty-Three

Bríd sat on a chair in the corner beneath the platform, behind the pianist. She slipped the cloak from her shoulders on to the chair behind her, and waited. Her heart was beating wildly, her head buzzing, her limbs felt like jelly; she didn't think she'd be able to stand. She couldn't lay her hand on her knee without it shaking. She had not the courage to look at the people sitting at the tables, talking, clattering plates and glasses, moving about constantly. She sat looking at the floor.

The chairman was on his feet.

'Thank you, Gus Elton, for a droll display of mirthful, tongue-twisting hilarity! Ever welcome at the Cave of Harmony, Gus! And now, ladies and gentlemen, pray silence! It is our proud custom here to offer a helping hand to young artistes making their start in the business, and tonight the Cave of Harmony welcomes a young colleen from the Emerald Isle who I am sure is going to delight and enchant us all. Pray silence, one and all, for the Lily of Killarney, Miss Bridget Flynn!'

Even as she stepped up on the platform, Bríd was thinking, Sure, I'm not from Killarney at all! What does he mean?

The pianist had already struck into the opening bars of 'Danny Boy'. Bríd arrived in the centre of the platform and for the first time took in the whole of the audience. Everyone in the hall seemed to be staring at her. Plates were ignored, glasses forgotten, everyone was waiting for her, expectant. Bríd stared back at the audience, struck dumb. So many people, how could she satisfy them all?

The pianist arrived at her entry, and, as if pushed from behind, she felt herself launched into her song. But where was her voice? It sounded faint, far away, it barely reached beyond the edge of the stage. How could she be heard? She seemed to have no strength, her

182

will paralysed. She had no resources to confront so many people, to win them to her.

Some unconscious power supplied the words to her, and behind her terror and confusion, she heard all the time the piano beating out the tune.

In a dream she realised she had come to the end of the song. There was a thin scattering of applause. A tiny voice from within her said, 'Thank you, ladies and gentlemen. I should like to continue with that lovely air "Come Back to Erin".'

The pianist, like a machine, beat out the opening bars and again she was singing. And now she could see the very thing she had always dreaded: the people were turning away, they weren't listening, the plates and glasses were moving, the talk was beginning again. Feeling she was drowning, she searched round for something to cling to. Then she saw one man was listening. He smiled at her, and in relief she directed her song to him, returning his smile. A gush of gratitude poured from her to him. He gave her strength. She blessed him.

The song ended. There was slight applause. Before she could think, the chairman was on his feet.

'Miss Bridget Flynn! A lovely young colleen from ould Erin's isle! Thank you! And now, ladies and gentlemen, that ever popular young lady, the sweetheart of the Cave, the idol of the halls, Miss Sally Beauman!'

As the audience roared its welcome, a girl had bounded up the steps past Bríd and launched straight into a comic song. Before the end of the first verse, the whole room was rocking with laughter. In a daze Bríd fastened her cloak and took up her bonnet, and, nodding to the chairman, made her way out into the street.

She had barely gone in, and here she was out again. All that lifetime of agony, that utter humiliation, had been but a few minutes.

She turned along the pavement heading for Soho. What madness, what lunacy had driven her, had made her think she could be a singer, a public entertainer? A few minutes had shown her with brutal honesty the scope of the task. That Sally Beauman, that Phil Courage, that travesty girl, all of them, they were professional, they had experience. They knew the art of holding people's attention. She would never forget the utter confusion which had overwhelmed her as she beheld there the great sea of faces looking up, expecting to see what they had paid for. She had nothing to offer them. She was the most ignorant, unskilful girl ever to come all the way from Ireland to London to find a job.

Tears were in her eyes. She scarcely saw where she walked, her legs carrying her mechanically forward. God, what humiliation! Again and again, like a nightmare, the memory returned. Where could she go? Where hide? She stumbled on mechanically, seeing nothing, bumping into people, walking, wiping the tears from her eyes. Hideous, black humiliation. She shuddered, wanting to shake it off; could she ever speak to anyone again? Restless, she reached Dean Street, but was unable to go in. She must walk on, on, through these hateful streets, along the hard, unyielding pavements.

In the darkness she felt herself cooling, and at last she was weary. She returned slowly to Dean Street and climbed the stairs to the attic room.

It was dark, empty. Too tired to go down for a candle, she took off her dress in the darkness, her practised fingers finding their way down her back, undoing the hooks and eyes, undoing the laces. The gown fell to the floor about her; she pulled at the strings of her corset, flinging it down, and pulling her shift over her head, for a moment naked in the darkness, reached for her nightdress. She pulled the pins from her hair, felt it falling about her shoulders, and without brushing it, fell into her little bed and pulled the cold sheet over her, trying to shut out her memory, and immmediately fell asleep.

The following morning she was back at work in the Cave, clearing plates from the tables, polishing, sweeping, tidying, oblivious now of the stink of stale food and tobacco smoke. No one mentioned her singing. She could not bear to think of it herself, and all that morning she trembled lest anyone should speak of it. No one did. Then she understood: they were being kind to her, tactful. During the day a gloom settled on her, deeper and deeper as the realisation came to her of what had happened. This was the end. She had had her chance. Her dream, so long guarded, hoarded so long in her fantasy, had been dragged out into the harsh glare of reality and brutally smashed before her face. Be a singer? What a joke. No; a waitress, a barmaid, that was her role. Long hours, low pay; that was her lot in life.

Mr Wordsworth asked her where she had disappeared to after her spot. He had needed her that night as a waitress. She had not the courage to mention her singing; he didn't comment on it, but he was very annoyed she hadn't carried on as a waitress afterwards.

Her work continued as before, as if she had never had the temerity to get up on the stage at all. Days flowed into days, her routine established; she became expert at remembering steaks and pies, reckoning up orders of ale and whisky. She scarcely noticed the stage any more.

Then one afternoon, perhaps a fortnight after her disastrous debut, Mr Wordsworth stopped her.

'I'm putting you on again tomorrow night. For a week. Sixteen shillings, like I said.'

Bríd could not understand him.

'To sing?'

She stared into his face, which was a picture of utter indifference.

'Sally Beauman's going off to the Grecian, and I can't get a replacement in time.'

He was turning to go.

'Mr Wordsworth –'

He looked back impatiently.

'Mr Wordsworth . . .'

Her mind was a blank.

'To sing? You mean – I mean – I was, I mean, satisfactory, then?'

He seemed vaguely surprised.

'What? Oh, yes. Only sing *louder* next time.'

He was about to go, but turned again.

'Tell you what, I'll get Phil Courage to hear you through tomorrow afternoon. Give you a few tips.'

He had gone.

Bríd looked after him as he disappeared into the back room, and then turned slowly, unseeing, where she stood. To sing again. What did it mean? To get up there again? To go through that again? The memory of the humiliation returned. Sing again? All the faces? She could never do it. She was about to run after him, to tell him it was impossible. But then – perhaps she hadn't been so bad, not as bad as she thought, at least. And then, it wasn't only for her, not for herself at all. Sixteen shillings: she could send money home. As a waitress it was impossible, but as a singer . . . A kind of desperate hardness grew in her. She would have to try again.

The following afternoon Phil Courage came into the Grapes while Bríd was behind the bar. She didn't recognise him for a second; he was dressed in a smart frock coat with a velvet collar and a bowler hat. She was surprised to find he recognised her. He came over to the bar and leaned on it with an easy smile, his hat pushed back on his head.

'Miss Bridget Flynn, I believe?'

'Yes.'

She couldn't help smiling. There was such an open, friendly feeling about him; he made her feel at ease at once.

'Mr Wordsworth said you might come –'

185

'And give you a few hints, eh? In the vocal art.'

Bríd quickly turned to Maggy. 'Will you take over?'

Together she and Courage went into the Cave.

'Now, Bridget, Mr Wordsworth tells me you only need a little thawing-out to make a first-rate singer.'

Bríd was stupefied.

'He said that? A first-rate singer?'

Courage looked surprised. 'Why not?'

'Oh – nothing.'

'What shall we start with, eh? What's your favourite song?'

It was a relief to have this affable man so kind to her. She looked into his blue eyes for a moment.

'Any comic songs?'

'I don't think I'd be any good at comic songs, Mr Courage.'

'Call me Phil.'

'Well, then, Phil, perhaps "Danny Boy" or "The Meeting of the Waters"? "Come Back to Erin"?'

'Very good. Let's run through "Come Back to Erin".'

He sat at the piano and ran through the introduction. His light-hearted manner and cheery blue eyes had lifted her spirits. She wanted to sing well for him. So without any caution or reserve she launched into the song. He fitted his accompaniment effortlessly to her singing.

'Very good, Biddy, very good, lovely voice, most musical. What's the problem?'

'Oh, Mr Courage – Phil – when I sang before, I can't tell you, I just froze with fright. Sure, I'd never been on a stage in my life. All the people, to see them there, it just shut me up. I could hardly bring myself to open my mouth.'

He looked up at her for a moment.

'Are you sure you really want to be a singer?'

Her resolution hardened.

'I'd do anything to get it right.'

He sat on the piano stool for a moment regarding her.

'You mustn't be afraid of the audience. They're your friends, not your judges. They're ordinary people like us, and they only want to be entertained. It's very simple.'

'Simple for you.'

'You'll be a success. You've got it in you, I can see it.'

He looked hard at her, seriously.

'And I'll tell you something else, in case no one else has. You're a stunner. Not a girl in a thousand has your looks. You've only got to stand there, and people would pay to look at you. What do they come here for, if it isn't to look at a pretty girl? Let them look at you, smile at them, tease them, they'll love it.'

'I couldn't tease them, Phil. I'm no good at that.'

'I don't mean comic songs. But when you sing, you know, smile at 'em, entice 'em, draw 'em on, make 'em think they're privileged to be sitting there listening to you. You're in charge, Biddy. It's your stage.'

Bríd tried to resist the pressure of his will.

'It's easy for you to say that, Phil. I've watched you. You can wind them round your little finger.'

'So will you. You'll see. You have beauty, and beauty is power – use it.'

In the face of her fear and uncertainty, Phil Courage was opening a way of hope, of possibilities. With all her trepidation, she had an irresistible vision of a way forward. She had to take it.

'It's worth sticking at till you get it right. There's plenty of work, and it's well paid. If you make a go of it here, I'll introduce you to some of the music halls I work. There's all the work you could want.'

She sang for him again. His talk and his airy confidence had lifted and strengthened her. Despite her fears, she was almost ready to believe in herself.

As he was going, he said, 'I'll watch you tonight. If there's anything else I can think of, we'll have another session tomorrow.'

After he had gone, Bríd was elated. Plenty of work, he had said. That was it. Let the audience be what it might, she would fight her way through. Plenty of work – those words had unlocked her ambition. She wanted that work, and she would get it.

That evening in the attic she dressed with special care. She pulled her bodice down as far as she dared to show off her bosom to its best advantage; she put her hair up with special care; and then, peering into the broken looking glass, she put carmine on her lips. She had never done it before, but she noticed all the girls in the Cave wore it. Tonight nothing was to to be left to chance.

Throughout her preparations Isabella helped her and fed her words of encouragement. She did up the hooks and eyes at the back of the golden dress. In all her nervousness and uncertainty Bríd found time to envy Isabella, whose life seemed ordered to a simpler plan. She was going to marry her cousin from the next village. Why hadn't Bríd done so? Why make the disastrous mistake of falling in love with the landlord's son? And now she was here, alone, to try and earn a living as a singer, to survive in a strange and unreal world.

As she sat behind the pianist waiting to go up on the platform, her

187

nervousness returned as strong as ever. She was constantly wiping the palms of her hands and she could feel her heart beating as fiercely as before. Gus Elton was up above, singing a comic song, and he looked as comfortable as if he lived there. The people responded to him immediately. She looked at their faces, happy and relaxed. Why couldn't it be like that for her too? Why was she sitting here in such agony? She wiped her hands again on her handkerchief.

She looked up and Phil Courage was standing there, smiling down at her. He bent over her and whispered, 'You're beautiful, never forget. Be the queen of the stage.'

'Can I?'

'You can. You will.'

Then she was on the stage, and again the sea of faces was turned up towards her, that great weight of expectation. How could they be her friends? She couldn't understand what he meant. She had no time to think, however, because the pianist was beating out the bars and she was into her song. Entice them? Tease them? That was not her way. Let them come to her, very good. And at that moment some inner sense of her own dignity rose within her, lifted her, unlocked her voice so that she felt it flowing free. She had the most unusual feeling, as if she were flying.

Suddenly she knew she had them. A sense of her power filled her, relaxed and calmed her. She was in charge. And towards the end of the last verse she allowed her voice to diminish, bringing out the pathos, and she had the thrilling feeling that they were leaning towards her, straining to hear her. She was flying on an exultant feeling of power, cool, in charge, and she was able to bring her voice up again at the end on a long ringing note that she could feel hitting the back wall.

The applause deafened her. Helplessly she smiled, dropped a deep curtsy, smiled, unable to help herself. They were clapping her. She had them.

After her second song she came down from the platform in ecstasy. She had done it; she had the power, she was safe, she could make it work for her. And as Phil Courage stood there before her, she threw her arms round his neck and kissed him, delirious with excitement.

Already another performer was on the platform behind her. For a moment she clung to Phil, whispering over and over, 'I did it, I did it. Oh, Phil, I did it. Oh, God, I can't believe it.'

She sat down at the side of the platform behind the pianist. Phil was beside her. Waves of pleasure and relief swamped through her, her cheeks were burning, her brain alive with electric impulses.

Phil whispered in her ear, 'After my turn I'll take you round to the Wellington and then we'll get some supper.'

Still glowing with success, she watched him do his song and thought how clever he was, how talented. Then they were in a cab and soon he was leading her through a stage door, just like the stage doors she had seen before, with the white-painted brick walls, and she was just walking in as if she belonged there, as if it were hers. Phil waved cheerily to the doorkeeper, who greeted him and smiled at her, and then they were going upstairs and into a small room with a fire burning.

'Things are a little more comfortable here at the Wellington, Biddy. Make yourself at home. Now let me see: ten past ten. I should be on in exactly seven minutes' time.'

At that very moment there was a knock at the door and a boy looked in and said, 'Your call, Mr Courage.'

Phil raised his eyebrows in a comical expression. 'The precision of a well-oiled machine.'

'Do you give two performances like this every night?'

'I give three. The Grapes comes second. And there's fellows do four a night. Why not? The money's there if you want it. Now excuse me and I'll see you in a few minutes.'

He looked at himself in a long mirror, in his costermonger's costume, and adjusted his neckerchief before he went out. Bríd sat back in her chair and looked round the small room. It was shabby, but warm and cosy. A fire burned in the grate, and some theatrical costumes hung on a rail along the opposite wall. There was a long dressing table fixed to the wall, with a looking glass above it, and as she sat there she couldn't help looking at herself.

Her colour was heightened. She seemed quite pink in the cheeks; her lips were red and her eyes flashed. She thought she had never looked more beautiful. Her bosom was heaving, almost pressing out of the dress. She sat staring into the looking glass, and the memory of her own songs returned to her. She had triumphed. The elation still tingled in her veins.

The door opened and Phil came in again. He too was glowing, his eyes bright.

'Gave it to 'em tonight!'

Without thinking she leaped up and, for the second time that evening, threw her arms round his neck and kissed him. He slammed the door shut behind him and took hold of her tightly, kissing her all over her face, down her neck and over her bosom as her arms held him tightly. She wanted him, needed to hold him. He

189

could feel the strength of her desire as she clung to him, intensely aroused.

But even as they kissed and clung passionately to each other, and she could feel his hands moving over and under her clothes, a deep, primitive fear took hold, and she pulled herself away, still holding and kissing, but yet pushing away his hands. They were both flushed, looking into each other's faces, feeling a shock of recognition.

Chapter Twenty-Four

They were in a restaurant. It was midnight, but the place was crowded, people pressing about her on all sides. Waiters holding her chair, taking her cloak, Phil looking funny and nice, looking through the menu, holding a spoon to his eye as if it were a lorgnette, then quizzing the waiter and ordering oysters and white wine, and then steak pie. The wine flew to her head, she was ravenously hungry, she loved the oysters. Phil made her laugh with his Ceremony of the Oyster, raising it to the level of a sacred rite: 'The Raising Aloft of the Oyster,' he intoned, 'the Offering to the Deity, the Sanctification of the Oyster, the Blessing of the Oyster, the Sign of Celestial Approval. The Oyster finds favour in the Sight of Heaven; the Transubstantiation of the Oyster, and at last the Consummation, I should say, the Consumption of the Oyster' and, raising it on high, he slid it down his his throat.

It was scandalous, blasphemous, but it unlocked something in her, reducing her to tears of laughter.

They ate the pie, drank the wine, had coffee, and all the time Phil talked. She was entranced, couldn't believe it was happening to her. He talked of her, of her prospects, her chances. Told her of all the jobs he'd done, all the different managements, all the different halls, which were the good ones, which were the ones to avoid.

'When you've had more experience, I'll introduce you to George Thompson. He runs the Wellington. In the meantime we're going to work on your act. Smooth off a few rough edges.'

The smile was wiped off her face.

'Don't worry. You've got what it takes, Biddy, I could tell. And you're going to do well. But we've got to bring up that professional finish.'

His infectious smile cheered her again.

'And he pays well. What are you getting at the Grapes?'

'Sixteen shillings a week.'

'He'll pay twenty-five at least. More, if you do a panto for him.'

'A panto?'

'Why not? Next Christmas, maybe. Just the thing.'

Her mind was in a whirl.

'A pantomime? But isn't that, well, acting?'

'Acting, singing, everything. You can do it. Easy.'

He told her of his childhood in London.

'Lambeth, that's south of the river – "the transpontine suburbs".' He mimicked a lordly accent. 'My dad wanted me to be apprenticed to a gas-fitter – no, don't laugh, it's a good trade, plenty of work, and I started when I was fourteen. Trouble was I was already a slave of the footlights, a denizen of the pit, Biddy, I couldn't keep away, every hall in London, I knew 'em before I was twelve. I knew the songs, had my favourite singers, I'd go anywhere in London to hear some of 'em, walk miles. And at friendlies in the pub I was on my feet ready to give a song – I knew all the words, you bet. Well, when I was seventeen, I took matters into my own hands. There was one singer – still is, for that matter – called Tommy Trotter, I thought he was the best. I modelled myself on him, I copied his voice, and the way he sang. If Tommy Trotter leaned on a word to get a laugh, so did I. So one night I went round to the stage door and asked to see him. 'He's gone,' they said. 'Gone home?' I says. 'No, he's gone over to the Grecian.' That's how I found out performers do more than one hall a night. So the next night I came back early, and waited for him outside the stage door. At half past nine he comes rushing out, there's a cab waiting. 'Mr Trotter,' says I. 'Haven't got time now!' he shouts, leaps into the cab, and he's gone! Well, I thought, the Grecian it is. I ran all the way, two and a half miles. I get to the Grecian. 'Mr Trotter?' I ask. 'He's gone!' they say. 'Oh Lord, where to this time?' The Middlesex. I run all the way. But this time, I caught him. 'You again?' he says, 'you must be keen. Come and have pies.' So we went round the corner to a café and he told me everything, how to write to managements, who to write to – just like I've been telling you. And that did it. I went home and sat down to write. Got my first engagement at Liverpool.'

He paused. Bríd had been laughing during Phil's comic recitation. Everything he said was funny. It was as if he never stopped performing.

'That's it. After that there was no turning back. I broke the news to my dear white-haired old mother; she wept, I wept, the cat wept, and off I went. Good-bye to the gas-pipe, the solder and the blow-lamp. And for ten years I haven't stopped. If there's a hall I haven't played,

I don't know of it. Big ones, small ones, palatial ones, rabbit hutches; and the audiences – crowned heads, toffs and their ladies, riff-raff, it's as if I've entertained the whole world. It's a wonderful life. I never get tired of it. And so far, touch wood, they haven't got tired of me.'

It was after one o'clock when Phil walked back with her to Dean Street, and she kissed him good night on the steps.

'Won't you call me Bríd? That's my real name.'

'I've never met anyone like you,' he said. 'You looked like a queen up there tonight.'

'Ssssh, Phil. Good night now. You've been a true friend.'

As he was walking away down the street, she called after him, 'Did you mean that about Mr Thompson, Phil?'

'All in good time!'

'And you'll help me, won't you?'

'Never fear, sweet maid! Trust in your uncle Phil and he shall provide!'

Bríd smiled. Phil was such a kind soul, undemanding, modest, generous. He didn't preach to her or make demands on her. And with him as a friend she knew she had a chance of getting a foot in the door of the theatre.

She was very tired. She went to bed and fell asleep.

Her week of singing at the Grapes finished and she was once more waiting at table. But Phil came round and they worked together an hour here and an hour there, whenever they could. She heard that there was another pub nearby, the Marquis of Granby, which did the same kind of thing, and she got work there too, so that throughout the summer she worked in them both, singing or waiting at table, as opportunity offered. Phil was always with her, encouraging and coaching her, and gradually she was conscious of herself relaxing and becoming more assured before an audience.

She was intensely grateful to Phil, for she could never have done it without him. She loved him in a way, and often felt a powerful urge to thank him in the most appropriate way a woman can. Sometimes they would find themselves kissing with a frantic intensity, but then, always there was within her, deep, immoveable, a fear, a bar. With difficulty, reluctantly, she would find herself pushing him off, embarrassed, awkward, and making fumbling excuses.

That part of her was closed, and she had no idea whether it would ever be free again.

Phil was away on tour for two months during the summer. When he got back near the end of August, he heard her through her songs again, and at last pronounced that the time had come.

The next evening he told her he had left a message for Mr Thompson; he hadn't been able to speak to him personally. Thompson was a very busy man, and it wasn't always easy to catch him.

She only had another week at the Grapes, and if Thompson didn't come, her only chance so far might pass by. She pestered Phil every night.

'I'll make him come, Bríd, if I have to drag him here by naked force.'

On the fifth night Bríd arrived at the Grapes, and there was a message from Phil. Thompson was coming.

George Thompson was not yet forty, of medium height and beginning to put on weight, with a moustache, dark hair flecked with grey, and an urbane, confident manner. Many of the regulars of the Cave of Harmony turned their heads to look at this 'swell', in evening dress under a long fur coat, and holding a gold-topped cane as he sat at a table. Bríd soon spotted him as she waited behind the pianist to go on.

Phil had told her about him. George Thompson had started life as a performer, but when he came into a legacy at twenty-five, he took a lease on the Wellington, a music hall in the Waterloo Road, and set himself up as a manager. After five years he rebuilt the Wellington from the ground up and it now held one thousand five hundred spectators. The interior had been constructed using cast-iron columns painted to look like Italian marble. The seats and the carpets were of the best, and everywhere was gilt, red plush, pale pastel shades, mouldings, coats of arms, statues, medallions. Behind the scenes the stage now had every mechanical device known to the theatre. His Christmas pantomimes were famous, and employed all the scenic and lighting effects and tricks that could be fitted into the story and many that couldn't. Harlequins leaped from star traps, fairies descended in celestial chariots, scenes dissolved from a sultan's harem to a London street, a forest to a seashore, ships were wrecked, and heroes voyaged to the moon. Nothing was impossible.

Soon after she had sung, Phil arrived and introduced her to Thompson. Bríd was a little surprised at Phil's tone with Thompson, deferential and eager to please. But soon Phil went up to do his piece, and afterwards went off, and Bríd was left alone with Thompson. It was difficult to talk much with the show going on before them, and the chatter all around. Bríd could feel Thompson was sizing her up.

'I've got my carriage outside, Miss Flynn. Can I drop you anywhere?'

'Do you know, Mr Thompson, I was thinking of going over to see the show at the Wellington.'

To her surprise she found herself taking a rather cool attitude. It was the sight of Phil being deferential that had done it.

'Very good! We'll go together.'

They went out to his carriage, a black square brougham with a man on the box. Thompson helped her into the dark interior and as she sat back on the leather seat and felt the carriage begin to move, he began to speak at once.

'Courage has been at me all week to come and see you, Miss Flynn. He told me he'd found my next star. Was he right?'

There was something about his tone, and about Phil's manner towards him, that provoked her.

'I don't know if I'll be yours, Mr Thompson, but I intend to be a star, yes.'

'You have a long way to go, you realise that?'

'I don't care how far I have to go.'

'It's a lot of work, and there's no certainty you'll ever come to anything in the end.'

'Mr Thompson, since you have been kind enough to give me your time, I'll be straight with you. I have no choice in this matter. I *must* succeed. Others depend on me. Whatever it takes, I've got it. Be sure of that.'

She spoke with a low level voice. He was silent for a moment.

'I liked you very much, Miss Flynn. You have an interesting voice. Unusual. And you look very good on stage. Lots of presence. I think you could do well. In fact I think I can use you.'

Bríd was glad of the darkness in the carriage. She could feel her heart beating.

'There's only a few minor things. That dress – get rid of it. You want something more theatrical, and with more of an Irish tinge to it. Go along to Morris Angel and see what they can do for you. The other thing is, I suggest you widen your repertoire a bit. Sentimental ballads definitely your line. Do you know "Last Rose of Summer" or "By Killarney's Lakes and Fells" or "The Harp that once in Tara's Halls"?'

'Oh yes, Mr Thompson,' she lied.

'How much longer are you playing the Grapes?'

'Till next week.'

'You haven't got an agent, I suppose? How can I contact you?'

'Calvi's restaurant in Dean Street.'

'Good. Well, you have a look at the show tonight, and see if you think you could fit in. You can have my box.'

The carriage arrived outside a large new theatre, with an imposing portico of classical columns. He took her arm and led her up the steps. A doorman saluted him smartly and held open the door. In the spacious foyer, brightly lit by enormous gas candelabra, Thompson nodded to a girl who came over to him.

'This is Miss Flynn. Show her to my box.'

He turned to Bríd and took her hand. 'We'll talk soon.'

Bríd was led through carpeted corridors, elegantly decorated with striped wallpaper and shown through a little door. She found herself in darkness, in a box overlooking the stage. The show was in progress, and as she peered out she saw the great auditorium was full of people, their faces lit by an eerie light reflected from the stage. Below, the pit was crowded, and rows of staring faces rose up to the gallery receding into the darkness. A feeling of tense concentration was almost palpable in the air.

Below her an orchestra was playing a refined and delicate piece. The stage was brilliantly lit with elaborate scenery showing a woodland glade and a distant view of countryside stretching away. Some fifty dancers were going through a complicated routine which looked like rustic revels. Young men, handsome and athletic, performed with light-footed, beautiful young girls in flimsy muslin dresses, cut low across the shoulders and reaching barely past the knee. As good as naked, Aunt Nora would have said.

Bríd thought it enchanting: the bright lights, the lovely colours, the elegant and graceful dancers, the music. She sat with her arm on the padded balustrade and drank in the scene.

She wondered where Phil would be, and whether he had done his spot. They had made no arrangements to meet.

The dance finished, the curtain came down, and at one side of the stage, the chairman stood up.

'Thank you, ladies and gentlemen. A most lovely interpretation by our corps de ballet. And now, before I introduce our next artiste I must warn those of a nervous disposition that what follows is not for delicate stomachs. During what we are about to witness, ladies have fainted and grown men have wept! Your special attention then for one of the great artistes of our era, a legend in his own lifetime. Ladies and gentlemen, pray silence for Mr W. G. Ross in his celebrated rendition of "Sam Hall"!'

A black curtain had fallen near the front of the stage, and from one side a small man emerged carrying an ordinary kitchen chair. He was dressed in old working clothes, wore a black peaked cap on the back of his head, and his face had a coarse, grimy aspect. He placed the chair in the centre of the stage, with its back to the audience and sat astride it, fixing them with a baleful scowl. The orchestra meanwhile had been sawing out a gloomy and repetitive tune, and Bríd

196

was mystified by this strange apparition with its sombre accompaniment coming after the light-hearted dance.

Then he began to sing, or rather he uttered his words in something between speech and singing, sometimes following the dreary tune, sometimes barking at the audience, sometimes growling, sometimes whispering, sometimes defiant, sometimes with an expression of dread. 'Sam Hall' was the story of a man on his way to be hanged, sitting in the cart as it rumbled on its way to Tyburn. The condemned man, execrated, loathed and detested by the crowd, turns their hatred back on them, spits on them, pouring out his rage, even as the audience can see in his face the rising terror as he approaches the gallows.

> 'My name it is Sam Hall, chimney sweep,
> My name it is Sam Hall, chimney sweep,
> My name it is Sam Hall,
> I have robbed both great and small,
> And now I pays for all,
> Damn your eyes!'

Every verse came to an end with 'Damn your eyes!' and Bríd felt a chill as he growled, cursed, hurled the words into the audience. The little man on the stage was the picture of human degradation, despair and terror, hidden by the force of will beneath a mask of defiance and bravado.

During this uncanny song the audience shrank from his gaze. Shrivelled before the power of his hoarse-throated curses, they could feel in their own bones his terror. Bríd prayed he wouldn't turn his fear-haunted eyes up towards her.

At last it was over and he was gone, in a storm of applause. Bríd relaxed and sat, quite unable to think for a minute, stunned by the force of Ross's performance.

On her way home she stopped on Waterloo Bridge and leaned on the parapet, looking down in the darkness at the water and the shapes of the spars and rigging of the ships moored below her in the darkness. Even at this time of night, and it was nearly midnight, she could hear shouts and movement among the ships and the warehouses along the riverside. Her head was still full of Ross's performance. It had been the most astonishing thing she had ever seen. That was acting, that was what it was about. She could still feel the chill she had felt, sitting in her comfortable seat in the safety of the box, afraid, absurdly, lest she might somehow catch his eye.

Looking down at the water rushing beneath her in the darkness,

Bríd made a solemn vow to herself. She would work towards that vision of power she had seen. Whatever it was, and she could not herself define it, she would aim towards that, she would give up all else, only to be like Ross, to remember his power, his single dedication. If people would say in after time 'she was as good as Ross,' she would ask no more.

In that moment of exaltation she thought of Matt. It should be for him. She would work for him, sweeping all else aside to provide for him. She prayed Thompson would take her on. Resting her elbows on the parapet, she prayed for Thompson to give her that job. Then, feeling a great surge of energy, she set off, walking fast over the bridge and through the night streets, and so home to her bed.

A few days later Phil had a message for her from Thompson. He wanted to see her the following morning in his office at eleven.

Chapter Twenty-Five

Thompson was down to earth.

'I'm rehearsing a new show. I'm going to put you in the first half, singing your Irish songs; then you'll come on again in the second half in a burlesque scene; you'll also be a high priestess in an Egyptian spectacle; and I want you to learn some new songs for a song and dance routine based on the war in America. Black face, coon songs. You'll be in the grand finale as well. I'll keep you busy. Three pounds a week. Interested?'

Bríd couldn't speak.

'I'm also writing a new pantomime for Christmas. There might be something for you in that.'

She walked back to the Grapes and gave notice to Mr Wordsworth she would be finishing at the end of October. He had extended her engagement so she continued to sing every night at the Grapes while she rehearsed at the Wellington during the day.

She went to the theatrical costumier and bought an 'Irish colleen' costume. She didn't recognise anything very Irish about it, but she was assured it was what Irish colleens wore, on the London stage at least. It was a pretty dress: the skirt was short, just below the knee, and of a vivid emerald green, with a charming laced bodice, and low décolletage trimmed with lace. She wore white stockings and red shoes – the most expensive item in the ensemble – a little white apron and at the back a short cloak. It looked very theatrical, she thought, as she looked at herself in the mirror, if not very Irish. But what did that matter? If it was what they wanted, she would wear it. She was glad Aunt Nora could not see it, though. She knew what she would have called her for exposing her bosom in such an indecent fashion, and wearing a skirt so short no respectable woman would be seen in it. She didn't have the money to buy it outright, but they gave her credit when she told them she was appearing at the Wellington.

So far she had sent no money home to Ireland at all. It was now early October and she had been eight months in London. Every night she prayed for her son. Sometimes she dreamed of him, strange, horribly muddled dreams that he had grown up, except that somehow he was still a baby, and came to her, reproached her for abandoning him. In the morning, as the dim light of dawn showed through the rag that was stretched across their window, and Isabella was already on her feet, dressing herself, Bríd would wake, seized with a furious restlessness, as if to drive the dream from her mind. She concentrated on her plans for the day, the week and the month ahead, filled with an anxiety to control her life, control her thoughts; in an agony that if she failed now, that huge terrible act, that sin, that error, that folly she had committed in Dublin would have been in vain. And if that were to be the case, what force in creation could stop her throwing herself into the Thames? How many times had she stood on Waterloo Bridge since the night she had seen W. G. Ross, looking down into the dark waters below as if they invited her? So simple, so simple.

By day her life was now tightly ordered. There was a musical director at the Wellington who coached her in her songs. He was a gentle, patient man, Jewish, quite unlike the Maestro, knew exactly what he wanted and how she should present herself and the song. He made it easy for her, so that she quickly got into the spirit of the theatre. She would have an orchestra to accompany her too, the thought of which made her rather apprehensive.

Bríd now dreaded going back to Dean Street, for she had had a painful and bitter quarrel with the Maestro. How it could have happened she did not foresee, yet afterwards it seemed inevitable. It first arose because the show included a burlesque of a favourite opera of the time called *La Sonnambula* (The Sleepwalker) by Bellini, under the title *Harlequin Sleepwalker, or Stark mad in White Satin.*

Early during the rehearsals, Bríd had come back to Dean Street with a manuscript copy of her part in this short play, and without thinking asked Pertinelli to help her with it, and hear her through it. In her excitement she did not think of the bust of Bellini on the mantlepiece. Pertinelli took the manuscript from her and looked through it. He did not say anything, but sat at the piano, and Bríd looked over his shoulder, as he played through the piano part.

He stopped, got up and went over to the table, looked through some musical scores, and came back with a leatherbound volume, and set it on the piano. It was the full piano score of *La Sonnambula.*

'That's easier,' he said, without expression.

Bríd took her sheets of manuscript, and stood facing him as he played the introductory notes. She began to sing the melody, infusing into it some of the burlesque and comic exaggeration they had been rehearsing that morning. After a while, Pertinelli stopped. Bríd was puzzled.

'Bríd, I can't go on with this.'

'Why not?'

'It's a disgrace, an insult to this music. Bellini is a supreme musician, these are some of the most beautiful melodies ever composed, and you make mockery of them. I can't do it.'

He paused a moment.

'And Bríd, *cara*, I'm very disappointed you doing this, this burlesque – making fun of this beautiful music for ignorant people, for an easy laugh. How can your musical instinct let you do this? You prostitute your art.'

'Prostitute!'

'You know very well –'

'I do not know anything of the kind! And it is certainly not prostituting my art, as you call it.'

'Bríd, you got a very special quality, you got talent, I recognise it when I first hear you. And I take you, I help you, so I can help your art. But now instead, you go to this music hall, it's not what I thought.'

'Maestro Pertinelli, I'm very grateful to you for what you've done, but I've got to earn a living. It's so easy for you to talk about art, as if we were in some consecrated temple, but we're not, we're in the world, and the world likes burlesque –'

'Well, I don't like burlesque! What did I say to you years ago, before you go back to Ireland? You got talent, but you also got a duty to use it for the very best. Now, instead of that, you sing this comic song, you make this beautiful music sound ridiculous. I'm ashamed of you –'

'Ashamed! Well, thank you! I must say, that's good! Here you are, you're in two rooms over an Italian restaurant, and after a lifetime, what have you got? One pupil, practically – me! This is what your devotion to art has brought you, Maestro Pertinelli, a shabby little flat in Soho, an old piano and a few volumes of operas. Because you can't accept that out there are the people on whom you depend, the public, and they must have what they want. What's the use of you holding up some beacon of art, when no one's interested? So please don't feel ashamed of me, because I've got a job to do, I'm making money, and I'm paying you for lessons, and paying your rent.'

Bríd rushed out of the room, down into the street, and set off walking fast and had walked nearly to Waterloo Bridge before she slowed down. Even after she had cooled off, however, she could not bring herself to forgive him for what he had said. Prostitute her art – he was attacking her very livelihood. She had to be working, he couldn't grasp that, he wanted her to dedicate herself as if she were a nun. She wasn't a nun. She lived in the world, and had to make her way, by whatever means might be offered. She was still simmering with fury at his obstinacy and blindness when she arrived at the theatre.

Now when she arrived home at night, usually around half past twelve, she would trudge wearily up the stairs, past his door, silent, in the cold and dark, get to her room, undress in the dark and climb into her cold bed. And in the morning, she would get up around ten, go down to the French patisserie along the street for a cup of coffee and a brioche, and then spend a couple of hours taking things to the laundry or running little errands for herself before going back to the theatre. She had almost no life outside the theatre. Except for Isabella, she knew no one now in London outside the theatre.

She was particularly depressed because a voice inside her was nagging her all the time that Pertinelli was right. There was more to it, and better things than a south London music hall. Deep inside herself she knew she still had a long road ahead of her.

When the variety show opened, Bríd moved into her dressing room with two girls of about her own age, Madge and Ria (short for Maria). It was a small room with a coal fire alight, and was crowded with costumes hanging on a rail and clothes thrown everywhere, over the backs of chairs, behind the door, and on a wicker skip that stood at one side. There was a dressing table running along the wall with a long looking glass over it and the room was brightly lit with gas lights over the looking glass. When Bríd arrived with her Irish colleen costume, Madge and Ria were naked except for white shifts, and sitting at the looking glass putting their make-up on. Bríd had bought herself some theatrical make-up that morning, and had it with her in a bag.

Outside it was already dark, for it was now mid-November, but it was bright and warm in the dressing room, and made cosy by the profusion of coats, gowns, stockings, hats and underwear strewn everywhere. Bríd set her things down on the dressing table and changed into her colleen costume. Madge helped her into it, doing up the hooks and eyes at the back. She and Ria both admired her costume, and thought it 'very Irish'.

Bríd watched them as they put on their make-up. She was in some difficulty. She had never worn make-up in her life, and knew no one who did. Madge and Ria, however, were past masters of the art, and busily making themselves up.

Bríd stared into the looking glass at herself and with an uncertain hand began to apply rouge to her cheek. The effect was of a bright-red blob on her face. She wiped it off with an old towel and started again, trying to be more delicate, and managed to tone it down and blend the edges. It still looked absurd. But she persevered, and tried to blacken her eyebrows with a charcoal pencil. She looked like a doll. Her heart sinking further, she tried her hand with mascara on her eyelashes, leaving black marks all over her cheeks and nose. In a fit of rage she snatched up her towel and tried to wipe it all off her face. They could take her just as she was. She threw the towel down on the table.

'Made a pig's ear of it, Bríd?' said Madge. 'Just let me finish and I'll give you a hand.'

Bríd sat in silence, simmering in vexation, as she stared at her own face. In half an hour she was going on. Fifteen hundred people were waiting to see her, and she didn't have the faintest idea what she was doing. She was an absolute beginner. She couldn't even do her own make-up. The lunacy of the situation rushed over her, she burst into tears and buried her face in her arms on the table.

'There, there, Bríd, it ain't that bad. Just nerves. Come on, I'll give you a hand. Just nerves, dear. Dry your eyes, you'll be fine. Now come on, sit up, back straight. Ria, got any of that witch hazel? Good for puffy eyes. Now then, let's see, got any grease paint? Let's put that on first, shall we? Some of the good old five and nine. Have to put this on, dear, because the colour of the gaslight is rather green, ever noticed? You'd look as if you'd been dead a week otherwise. This'll make you look nice and warm under the lights. Now just a touch of rouge in the cheeks, nicely blended, not too much, don't want to look like Pantaloon. That's good. Now, let's see, a little kohl on the eyebrows – actually you've got strong eyebrows anyway, very nice, too. And the eyes, most important, plenty of mascara, just use a little spit, that's easiest, and go gently, brushing outwards, see? Got to bring out the eyes, your most important asset – that and your tits. Now just powder it all down, and last but not least, carmine on your lips. There, lover-ly! Ain't she a treat, Ria?'

Bríd stared at herself in the looking glass. She looked grotesque, her face distorted, ridiculous. But Madge and Ria looked just the same.

There was a knock on the door.

'Five minutes, please!'

Bríd was shaken into life.

203

'Thanks, Madge, I'll never forget it.'

She adjusted her hair and set on her head the jaunty little cap that completed her Irish colleen costume.

'Ria, just do me up, dear.'

Ria helped Madge into her costume, and did the hooks and eyes up at the back of the bodice.

'You're putting on weight, dear,' she said, 'any more of them cream cakes and you won't get into this dress.'

'Don't remind me.'

Madge and Ria were billed as 'the Sisters Dacre' though they weren't sisters. They sang duets and danced. Madge was younger than Bríd, seventeen, petite, blonde, with a sharp cockney sense of humour and a lightning wit. Both she and Ria had been in the theatre since they were children. Madge's father was a carpenter in a theatre in east London and she had gone on the stage as a child dancer at the age of eleven. Ria's parents had abandoned her when she was seven and she had been brought up by a foster-father who, she said, tried to interfere with her, so she ran away and for a while had danced on the street for pennies, until like Madge she had got a job as a dancer in a theatre. She had mousy hair and a sallow complexion, with bony cheeks and hollow eyes. Offstage she seemed ill, consumptive, and had a guarded, wary manner, hard and off-hand. On stage, she was another person altogether, pert and winsome, and young men in the audience found her irresistible.

Madge and Ria seemed to Bríd very hardened to the world and took a cynical and opportunistic attitude to life. They had strings of admirers who called for them after the show, but they felt they owed nobody anything. They regarded men as fools to be exploited for whatever they could get out of them, and they would shriek with laughter as they sat recounting their exploits to each other and drinking port, of which they got through a good deal. There were always several bottles opened on the dressing table. They regarded it as normal that if a man took them out to supper after the show they should go to bed with him (though more usually it was a brief scuffle in a cab).

They believed they understood male lust, they knew what men wanted; they didn't resent it or expect anything different, but they believed it gave them the right to get everything they could in exchange for their favours. None of it meant a thing, and they described their adventures in the grossest physical details with coarse laughter, which at first shocked Bríd and made her feel an ignorant simpleton.

'Overture and beginners, please.'

Bríd's heart jumped. The other two got up.

'Well, girls, best of luck.'

'Best of luck, Bríd. Now, just a glass of port for my throat.'

Madge and Ria went out, and Bríd sat alone for a moment, but she couldn't keep still so she went out and walked up and down the corridor. Singers, dancers and other performers rushed past her. There was a full-length looking glass at the end of the corridor, and she stood before it, adjusting her dress, pulling and pushing at her bust to get the fit right, pulling her stockings up for the fifteenth time, setting, resetting, and setting again her little cap. She stared at her strange painted face.

It was the Grapes all over again. All her experience gone for nothing. There, out front, all the people waiting for her, expecting her. Oh, God, what could she do, where could she go? Why did it have to be tonight? Why couldn't she just slip out on the street, mingle with the people, disappear?

She was at the side of the stage, in the darkness. She was next on. Out on the stage was a young man juggling with Indian clubs. He was wearing a lion's skin and a star-spangled belt over pink tights. Now he was lifting heavy weights with his teeth. He invited any man in the audience on to the stage for a simple trial of strength, and a young fellow was pushed blushing on to the stage by his friends. Bright red, he grinned foolishly at the audience. He failed the trial of strength, and the strong man concluded his act by holding the young man upside down over the orchestra with one hand to great applause. As the band struck up he ran off stage; for a moment he was beside Bríd, breathing hard, his face glistening with sweat, and then he was on again to take his bow.

The chairman was introducing her, and without quite knowing how, she found her legs had carried her to the centre of the stage. The orchestra was playing her introduction. But this time, she found herself bathed in a sea of light. Everywhere light was in her eyes, dazzling her, flooding her, warm, life-giving, and through it she was only dimly aware of the audience, safely cordoned behind the orchestra. Instead of the intimidating sea of faces, there was only this warm, safe light. This was her space, and she felt all the dread, the stomach-gripping nerves translated into energy that lifted and gave her wings. So as the orchestra came to her cue and she could dimly see the conductor's baton raised, she heard her voice flowing into the void, filling the theatre, and thought she could do anything.

Chapter Twenty-Six

Afterwards the dressing room was full of young gentlemen in evening dress and silk hats who knew Madge and Ria and seemed to worship them. Madge and Ria, quite unimpressed, sat in their shifts, drank port and kept up a stream of badinage and sarcastic wit. Phil came in too and was full of praise for all three of them. He kissed them all, and for a moment Bríd wondered how well he knew the others, and felt a shaft of jealousy through her. Then he was kissing her and telling her she was the most beautiful girl in the show and sang like an angel, and she relaxed and despised herself for her jealousy.

George Thompson threw a party on stage. Staff came in from the pub over the road and set up tables, and George presided over the food and drink like the Ghost of Christmas Present. Bríd was starving hungry. She and Phil drank glass after glass of champagne until her head was ringing, and everything was wonderful, everyone was beautiful, she loved them all, so talented, she enjoyed their acts, their songs, their dancing and their clever stunts. The whole world was glowing with hope and possibilities and optimism.

'He's offered me the Emperor of Morocco.'

Phil didn't seem very pleased. They were leaning on the parapet of Waterloo Bridge.

'I should have had Idle Jack, but he's already promised it to Alf Merriwether.'

Bríd didn't know what to say. What was the difference between Idle Jack and the Emperor of Morocco? She knew nothing about pantomime.

'Isn't it a very good part?'

'It's nothing. A cough and a spit. And I've played Idle Jack before, in Sunderland. It's my part. Alf's quite good in his way. Still –'

He looked away, irritated.

'What did you say?'

'Oh, I told him what to do with his Emperor of Morocco. Can you imagine? Me? Oh no, no thank you, I said.'

She squeezed his arm.

'Quite right, Phil, there must be thousands of other managements eager to have you.'

'There are. Don't you worry. I'll probably get a tour.'

'A tour?'

'That's where the money is, Bríd – entertaining the heathen provincials. Raking in the lovely doubloons.'

She didn't like the idea of Phil going away; he had been a good friend to her here. But he was easily hurt, she could see, and Thompson had humiliated him with his offer. She did her best to cheer him up.

'I expect they're crying out for you, Phil; I can hear them in their thousands calling, "Phil Courage, where are you? We need you!"'

Phil laughed and hugged her. She saw how easily he cheered up again.

When Phil had gone off and she was walking back to Dean Street, she thought, What about me? He hasn't said anything to me about it. There has been a lot of talk backstage about the pantomime. If he doesn't give me a part I'll be out of work in three weeks.

That night Thompson came into the dressing room.

'Let's see your legs, Bríd.'

As she drew up the hem of her Irish colleen dress, Bríd couldn't help remembering the stage doorkeeper at the Oxford who had humiliated her. Here it didn't seem to matter. Had she changed? Had she lost her modesty? Was she becoming hardened?

'What was that about?' Ria said after he had gone.

'He wants your body,' Madge said as she went on with her make-up.

Bríd said nothing. She still did not know how to respond to this kind of talk. She adjusted her little cap in the looking glass.

'He's been through most of the girls in this building at one time or another,' Madge went on.

'He's not going through me,' said Bríd.

'Want to bet?' said Madge. 'He hasn't offered you anything in the panto yet, has he? Well then. Suppose it comes to the crunch, eh? Drop your drawers if you want to play Fairy Bluebell?'

Madge and Ria laughed.

'Anyway, she can't play Fairy Bluebell, because I am,' said Ria.

'Did you drop your drawers?' asked Madge.

'As a matter of fact, I did. Only not on this occasion.'

'Hope it was a better part,' said Madge.

'What does it matter? He got what he wanted. So did I. Anyway, it didn't last long. What's the fuss?'

Bríd looked at herself in the looking glass. He hadn't offered her anything yet, it was true. Was this going to be her test? Her initiation to the theatre?

That night as she lay in bed, she tried to clear her thoughts. Were there any circumstances, was there any part she would go to bed with Thompson for? How badly did she want to succeed? Was this what she had given away her child for? Was this to be just another kind of whoredom? Yet this was all words. Did she want to be in Thompson's pantomime? That was the question. At last she decided she did, let the cost be what it might.

The following morning Bríd found out what Thompson intended.

'There's a part for you in the panto if you want it. Dick Whittington, four pounds a week. Interested?'

'What part, Mr Thompson?'

'What part? Dick Whittington, of course.'

'Oh.' She paused. 'I must be very stupid. I thought Dick Whittington was a boy.'

'This is pantomime. Where were you brought up?'

'You mean he's a girl?'

Thompson gave her a long-suffering look.

'He's a boy acted by a girl.'

'But why?'

'Bríd, don't ask me, I didn't invent it. Do you want the part?'

'Yes.'

'Dick Whittington?'

Phil leaned across the little table. They were in the pub over the road.

'Bríd, that's wonderful! Mind you, no more than you deserve. I knew you'd strike lucky. Miss Bridget Flynn, star of the Waterloo Road! Return by popular demand! Standing room only! Make way there for Miss Flynn's carriage!'

'But, Phil.' She reached across and grasped his arm. 'What will I have to do?'

'Do, my darling? Just stand there and look beautiful.'

'Be serious. I've never acted before. Why did he give me the part?'

'Don't ask. Just be grateful. It's the chance of lifetime.'

'But why me? There must be thousands of girls in London who

could do it. Anyway, I'm Irish and it sticks out like the Rock of Gibraltar.'

'Well.' Phil thought for a moment. 'He may have wanted a new face. He needs a good singer. And you've probably got good legs.'

'I see. That's why he wanted to see them the other night. What will I have to wear?'

'A delightful little creation that will set you off to perfection, my darling.'

'And show my legs?'

'Of course.'

'Oh, Phil, you will help me, won't you? I'd never heard of panto-mime till I came here, honest. Will you help me and teach me how to do it?'

'I'll do anything you like, my darling.'

'Well, kiss me, I'm going to do it.'

They were arm in arm walking down the Strand.

'Do what?'

'I've swallowed my pride. He's going to get the best Emperor of Morocco in the history of panto.'

'Oh, Phil, you're going to be in it! I'm so pleased!'

She kissed him impetuously on the cheek, her arm round his neck.

'There, it was worth it, just for that. I humbled my proud heart. Mr Thompson, says I, I am a man of the theatre, it's in my blood; I've played every hall from Aberystwyth to Zouthampton, but on this occasion, for reasons which must remain closeted within my bosom, I shall consent to enact the role of the Emperor of Morocco.'

'And you're sure you won't mind not playing Idle Jack?'

'So long as we're together, my darling, I care not a straw.'

Rehearsals started for the pantomime. Thompson had written it, and was very busy rehearsing everyone in their parts, overseeing the making of the scenery, discussing the music and the dancing, as well as running the theatre. One day someone told Bríd there were a hundred and twenty people working in the theatre, and she was as-tounded. There were a lot of children in the show, and among other things, they came on as the rats, and many hours were spent coaching them in their rat dances.

In the story, Dick Whittington was accompanied by his cat, which was played by a twelve-year-old girl called Annie. Annie had played the cat before and had worked up a whole repertoire of catlike behav-iour; she could miaow, arch her back, lick her paws and rub her back against Bríd's leg in a very engaging and comic manner. Offstage she was a tough, half-starved child. She despised Bríd as a fumbling beginner, and Bríd found, after the show had opened, that she was a skilful scene-stealer. While Bríd was playing some dull but necessary love scene with Alice Fitzwarren (played by Madge) in Alderman Fitzwarren's kitchen, Annie was behind her back getting up to side-splitting antics with ladles and saucepans.

Bríd could not understand what the strange laughs were for until, a few days after they had opened, Madge told her. On the next night, as she and Annie were waiting to go on, she took Annie firmly by the ear and whispered that if she didn't stick to the script in future, she might not *have* a future.

Another thing that irritated Bríd was that Annie made references to her Irishness. Bríd was acutely aware that she was in a play about London, and she could hear how her accent stuck out among the cockneys around her. George Thompson didn't mind and that was good enough for her, but it didn't stop Annie making sarcastic remarks behind her back and just within hearing – 'Aah, sure and begorrah, 'tis Dick Whittington himself, bejazus' – and collapsing into a fit of sniggering with the other children.

Because she had to work so closely with Annie, this vindictive spirit in the little girl made Bríd's life very difficult. She was struggling to master her part and her moves, try to get to grips with the spirit of pantomime, which was broad, plain and straightforward, calling for large gestures, a powerful voice and a clear head which could gauge the audience's mood. All this was exhausting for Bríd, and Annie's lack of cooperation made things hard for her.

All the time she was rehearsing Dick Whittington by day, she was on and off stage each evening in the variety show, so she was in the theatre from ten in the morning until after eleven at night, six nights a week.

At the end of the first week of rehearsals she went one morning to a solicitor's in Lincoln's Inn, whose name had been given to her in Dublin, and arranged for ten shillings to be forwarded to Aunt Nora through the Dublin lawyer. It gave her a bleak satisfaction, provided some slight justification for what she was doing, and gave a faint link with what she still in her innermost thoughts regarded as home. Afterwards, as she came out into the busy Strand and set off back to the Waterloo Road, the emotions this little ceremony had stirred up were too much for her, and she could not stop the tears which smarted in her eyes. The worst of it was that no message was permitted. She could send the money, that was all.

Chapter Twenty-Seven

One night in the middle of December, Bríd was walking home. It was nearly midnight, cold and misty. The street lights glimmered through the fog, and she walked quickly to keep warm. There were still quite a number of people about as she reached Trafalgar Square and turned up into Leicester Square, and traffic clattered past her. There was a coffee stall in the corner of Leicester Square, and as she passed it she decided to have a cup of coffee to warm herself for her bed, which would be icy.

She clasped the hot cup between her hands as she sipped from it, looking idly round the square. She was tired and would soon be in bed. The square was crowded with people coming out of the theatres and music halls round it, talking and laughing as they passed her.

Two young women with long velvet cloaks over their wide gowns, and wearing pretty, flower-trimmed bonnets, were standing together drinking coffee and talking in low voices. They were prostitutes, and Bríd moved a little away from them, looking at them, fascinated in spite of herself. She wondered whether she would ever make enough money to buy herself such elegant clothes.

A group of young men in long overcoats over their evening dress, and wearing silk top hats came along, talking loudly, and stopped for coffee. The two girls were alert, looking at each other and angling for an opening. Bríd stood watching, interested; she noticed how quickly one girl had caught the eye of a young man, and suddenly there was conversation going on between them, and the men had clustered round. The girls were young cockneys, bright, hard and funny, and reminded Bríd of Madge and Ria. She felt contempt for them in their trade, until she remembered the night she had fainted in the Haymarket, when she had been befriended and taken in, and blamed herself for her hardness.

As she watched the group talking and laughing, the girls flirting, using all their coquetry on these rich bored young men who had had too much to drink, it dawned on Bríd that these men had no intention of going off with either of them, and the girls were wasting their time but hadn't realised it. Her sense of disgust turned against the men, that they should be making fools of the girls, and it seemed shameful that women should be so dependent on a man's whim.

She finished her coffee and was passing the group on her way, when one of them turned at that moment and was face to face with her.

It was Sir John Wrenshaw.

They both stopped in surprise, and there was a moment of silence as they looked at each other.

'Bríd,' he said at last.

'Sir John.' For a moment she didn't know what to do.

'Bríd, by Jove! After all this time! How are you?'

He looked at her hard, and then round at the other two girls.

'I say, do you girls know each other?

He took Bríd's arm, introducing her into the group.

'Now here's a stroke of luck, you fellows. An old friend.'

The other men were looking her over but the two girls were giving Bríd stony looks.

'You are mistaken,' Bríd began, trying to remove her arm.

'She's a regular corker, Wrenshaw, you sly dog, where did you find her?'

'Never you mind, old fellow, but finders keepers, what? Listen, you fellows, why don't we all make a night of it? Here's an old friend, the prettiest little creature ever to come from the Emerald Isle –'

'You're mistaken,' Bríd repeated, pulling away from him.

'Mistaken, Bríd? About a thing like that?' he said gaily, taking her arm again.

The two girls were looking on icily. The other men had clustered round to inspect Bríd.

'There is a mistake, nevertheless,' she said, forcefully pulling her arm from his and walking away.

He came after her and stopped her. 'Bríd, what's the matter?'

'You have confused me with your friends.'

She began to walk again, quickly. He followed her as the others stared after them. Wrenshaw looked back.

'Hang on a minute, you fellows.'

He turned to her. She was angry and breathing hard. It made her eyes glow. In his conceit and arrogance he had confused her with the two whores. Wrenshaw was looking hard into her eyes. God, she was beautiful, he thought. She'd had a child, hadn't she? She must be on

212

the streets. Why else would she be here? He lowered his voice, trying to control the situation.

'Bríd, it must be over a year since I saw you. How are you getting along?'

She looked at him coldly. At last she spoke, in a low, level voice.

'I am getting along very well, Sir John, thank you. Good night.'

She turned to go again. He walked beside her.

'Won't you join us, Bríd? We can have a jolly time. And I'll make it worth your while.' He gave her a significant look. 'Why turn it down? No need to be proud. Come!' He gently took her arm, as if to turn her again.

'I am on my way home, Sir John. Good night.'

'Come on, Bríd, I understand. You're new to the game. No need to be bashful, I assure you. No one but me will know.'

'You are insolent. Take your hand off me.'

Wrenshaw was puzzled. Bríd was walking away. He turned to the others.

'You fellows carry on without me.'

He caught up with Bríd.

'Well, at least allow me to accompany you. It's midnight. No time for a young lady to be out alone.'

'I am very well used to walking home at night, Sir John, and I don't need a chaperone now.'

She attempted to ignore him.

'Ah, yes, quite, I understand that –'

'Do you?'

'Well, my dear,' he said in a sarcastic tone, 'here we are in Leicester Square at midnight, and you're alone. What's a fellow supposed to think, eh?'

'Sir John –'

'But don't take me amiss, my dear. After all, I understand your predicament, and I should be the last man –'

'Understand my predicament? How dare you talk to me about my predicament? How on earth can you know anything about my predicament?'

'Well, my dear, the last time I saw you . . .'

She had turned and was looking hard at him. She could feel her heart beating, and was breathing quickly.

'Yes? The last time you saw me? Yes?'

He smiled. 'As I remember, you were in what is called an "interesting condition".'

'Yes?' she said forcefully.

'Well . . .' He paused. He was not getting the right response from her.

213

'Yes, Sir John? I was in an "interesting condition", as you call it. And what happened to you when I told you about it? You disappeared like a scalded cat.'

He didn't like her turn of phrase, but he tried to keep cool.

'Well, Bríd, you can't exactly hold me responsible, now can you?'

'No, you weren't responsible. You were as free as the air. I was alone, with no money and expecting a child, but you weren't responsible so you were free to go. After all, you are a gentleman. And no one could expect a gentleman to help a lady in distress.'

Wrenshaw liked this even less.

'I am afraid, Bríd, that a girl in your condition could not have been called a lady.'

She felt contempt for his easy assumption of superiority, as if she were supposed to be grateful for his company.

'Then obviously I am wasting your time. Good night.'

She attempted to walk on, but her high-handed tone needled him. She had got the better of him in a way he couldn't immediately understand, but he would not allow her to get away before he had evened with her. He kept up with her as she walked.

'You know, Bríd, you won't have much success if you take this tone with all your gentlemen.'

'Success?'

'My dear girl, even you have a living to make.'

She stopped again and looked at him.

'Sir John, you may be accustomed to talk to your other friends in that tone, but I will not tolerate it. It may surprise you to know that I am not on the streets, as you have assumed. Now please leave me.'

She turned again and walked away quickly. Wrenshaw was astonished, and was lost for a moment. Then he recovered his wits and went after her. This was fascinating; he had blundered, and the girl was deeply offended. He caught up with her.

'Bríd, I have insulted you. I must apologise. I was so taken by surprise to see you there at such an hour that I jumped to rather an unfortunate conclusion.'

'You behaved like a cad, but that is probably how you behave with all women.'

'By heaven, I must stop you! I tell you I could have no reason to assume any different! When I last saw you, you were with child, and friendless. Now I find you alone in Leicester Square at midnight. What should a fellow think?'

'Whatever he thinks, a gentleman behaves as a gentleman should,' she said quietly, looking into his eyes.

214

Wrenshaw was impressed in spite of himself. She was beautiful. He swore to himself she should not get away.

'I mistook you, I see it now. Let me make some recompense. Come! I expect you're hungry – I am. Why don't we get some supper at one of these little Italian restaurants round here? There's a very good one I know; we can have a few oysters and a bottle of wine and exchange news. I'm eager to know what you've been doing –'

'I'm very tired, I've been working all day, I'm about to go bed, and frankly, if I was starving to death, you're the last man I'd dine with.'

Bríd was astonished that Wrenshaw would not give up. His conceit seemed boundless.

'Well, tell me at least what you're doing. You say you've been working?'

'Yes, working. It's not a term you'll be familiar with, but many of us do it now. It's how we get our bread.'

'Don't be sarcastic with me! I only asked what you were doing. Come, tell me what you're up to.'

'John Wrenshaw, if you don't stop pestering me, I shall call a policeman.'

'I shouldn't do that, Bríd. He'd be more likely to take you in charge than me, wouldn't he? But seriously, we were friends once, don't be so standoffish.'

'You call yourself my friend? After the way you disappeared? Simply vanished?'

'I don't understand. Vanished?'

'Don't pretend you don't know know what I mean. You vanished right enough once you knew I was expecting a baby.'

'But my regiment was posted to Ireland. I wrote to you.'

'I never got any letter.'

She was quieter.

'Of course I wrote to you. Surely you didn't think I would have walked away without even saying goodbye? Or without trying to help in some way?'

Bríd was silent, unsure whether he was lying or not. Perceiving his advantage, Wrenshaw adopted a light-hearted tone.

'That's the trouble with army life, Bríd; one moment you're here, the next moment wafted to some godforsaken spot – no disrespect to your country, but it was the devil of a hole, barracks roof leaked, rained incessantly, roads were mires . . .'

Bríd was not listening. It had just occurred to her he might have news of Harry, how he was, where he was.

'Yes, I dare say it's a muddy old place, after all.'

She turned away and went on walking. He kept up with her.

'Sir John,'

He noticed her change of tone.

'Call me John, Bríd, for heaven's sake.'

'John, in your regiment, do you ever . . .'

She paused and walked on for a moment, looking down at the pavement before her. Then she spoke in a low voice.

'Do you ever hear anything of Lord Leighton now?'

Wrenshaw gave an inward sigh of relief. Now he had her.

'Bríd, I have a proposition to make. Why don't you let me take you to dinner one night and we can have a good long talk about old times, and exchange all our news in comfort?'

She looked up at him. She understood.

'I am not free in the evening.'

'Really?'

'No, I work every night.'

'Well, can't I meet you after you finish? Where do you work?'

'If you must know, I sing at the Wellington.'

'By Jove, Bríd, sing in the music hall? Capital! Let me call for you one night, and we can get some supper and I can tell you all the news.'

At that moment they had reached Calvi's. She turned and looked at him.

'Very well,' she said in a low voice. 'Now you must excuse me. This is where I live, and I am very tired.'

Wrenshaw was very pleased with himself. He smiled down at Bríd in an indulgent way.

'I will detain you no longer, Bríd. *A bientôt.*' He took her hand and kissed it. 'Good night, my dear.'

As he strolled away down the street, Bríd watched him, angry with herself. What moment of weakness had made her yield to him? And why had the memory of Harry come to her so suddenly, brought back that time, so happy and so miserable, that she was trying to put behind her? She had plenty to occupy her, plenty to look forward to. Why did she have to start raking up the past?

That night in the dark room where Isabella was already asleep, Bríd knelt before the paper Madonna and, holding the gold locket in her hands, prayed for Matt, Uncle Patsy and Aunt Nora. Although they were far away and she could never go back to them, still they were in her deepest self her home, her truth. They were why she was here. She was working for her little boy, so that he could grow up in dignity, so that he should look men straight in the eye, and she vowed that not Wrenshaw, not anyone, should come between her and the path she had chosen.

Chapter Twenty-Eight

The next night, when the three girls were in the dressing room changing out of their costumes, taking off their stage make-up and letting their hair down, there was a knock at the door, and the boy put his head in and said, 'Gen'leman to see you, Miss Flynn.' Before she could say anything, the door opened and Wrenshaw stood there in evening dress and fur-trimmed coat, wearing his top hat and with his silver-topped cane negligently over his shoulder.

'Pardon the intrusion, ladies. Capital show! All three beauties, capital singing, lovely dancing. Haven't enjoyed myself so much in years; profoundest compliments.'

Bríd could not return his smile. She was vexed at his easy manner, his assurance, the way he walked into the girls' dressing room when they were barely half dressed; vexed at his good looks, the power that flowed effortlessly from him. She looked round at Madge and Ria.

They were unabashed in their white shifts, and smiling at Wrenshaw.

'Madge, Ria, this is Sir John Wrenshaw. Sir John, Madge, Ria,' she said listlessly.

'Charmed, ladies. Deuced fine show, enjoyed every minute of it. Bríd, I thought we might get a bite of supper tonight, what? I'll wait for you downstairs.'

He was gone.

Madge and Ria looked at Bríd. Madge gave her a long, cool stare.

'You cunning devil. Tsk, tsk.' She shook her head slowly. 'I might have known you had something like that tucked away. Getting your oats on the QT? And a good, pious Catholic girl like you, I'm ashamed of you. What would Father Murphy say if he knew?'

'Who is he, Bríd?' said Ria.

Bríd had turned again to her looking glass and was brushing her hair. She didn't answer for a moment. She was angry with herself for allowing Wrenshaw to stroll in and take over the dressing room without a murmur. She bit her lip.

'He's a man I used to know. I've no idea what brought him round. I haven't the slightest interest in him.'

'"Not the slightest interest"? I should think so!'

They laughed knowingly.

'Shut up, both of you! I tell you he is nothing to me, nothing!' She was near to tears.

'If he means nothing to you, why are you going out with him? Free supper?'

'Nothing is for free,' said Ria.

Bríd went on brushing her hair, trying to soothe herself. 'You can come too, if you like. It makes no difference to me.'

'Come too? *Very* likely.'

'You go along and have a nice supper. Only tell him to hop it if he puts his hand up your skirt.'

They looked at her in the mirror with knowing smiles.

'He could put his hand up my skirt any day of the week,' said Ria, 'so long as he gave me supper first.'

'How did you meet him, Bríd?'

Bríd brushed her hair. 'He's a friend of someone I used to know. He's in the cavalry.'

'A soldier! They're the worst. Here today, gone tomorrow. Be sure to get your money's worth out of him.'

'I'm not interested in him. He's just a nuisance, and he'll get nothing by it.'

'Let 'em know who's boss, eh? Ria, you had that lord hanging round after you, didn't you, but he never got nothing, did he?'

'I told him, the day I see that band of gold, I'm yours and you can do what you like with me. Until then, keep your sticky little fingers to yourself. I think he might come round in the end, if I keep him dangling long enough. The day he proposes, I'll be out of here like a rat up a rope. I might invite you round to tea on the terrace some time. Silver service, bone china, the works. Ooh, wouldn't I make a loverly countess, and wouldn't I give him the run-around!'

Bríd had finished brushing her hair and was pinning it up. She couldn't think why she was going out with an arrogant, supercilious man like Wrenshaw. Only for some crumb of news about Harry, was that it?

Wrenshaw was waiting at the stage door. He offered her his arm and handed her into a cab he had waiting.

'The Pall Mall Restaurant,' he called as he stepped in after her. As

218

the cab swayed into motion, he sat away from her in the other corner, and she saw at first only the glint of his silver-topped cane in the darkness.

There was silence for a while, then he spoke.

'Yes, I enjoyed the show immensely. I thought you were particularly fetching as the Egyptian princess. Such dignity and restraint. You know, I believe you have it in you to become a tragic actress. Really, I could see you up there as Lady Macbeth, Mary Queen of Scots – someone like that. And when you sang "Come Back to Erin", well, the audience went very quiet. I can't remember when an audience was so concentrated. And I'm something of a connoisseur in these things.'

'You were going to tell me about Harry – Lord Leighton,' Bríd said in a low voice.

'All in good time. We were discussing you.'

'I'm grateful for your interest, Sir John –'

'You see, Bríd,' he went on, 'you live too much alone. I can see you have a terrific strain coping with everything by yourself; you're in need of relaxation. So we'll have a nice bite of supper together, and talk everything over fully.'

'Oh. For a moment I thought you were going to apologise for your disgraceful behaviour last night.'

He laughed. 'The wine spoke, I fear, Bríd. A genuine and pardonable mistake. The hour, the place –'

'A mistake. But not pardonable.'

'Oh, I'm sure you will. Not at this moment, perhaps, but when you know me better. You know, you're a little on the starchy side, Bríd. Too much of the Irish Catholic; you need to unwind. You must learn to take life as you find it.'

'You were going to tell me about Lord Leighton.'

'Are you still in love with him?'

'That's my business. What do you know about him?'

Wrenshaw looked out of the window. 'Ah, we have arrived.'

The cab had pulled up outside the brightly lit entrance to the Pall Mall Restaurant. It was thronged with people from the opera and the theatres. Wrenshaw again offered Bríd his arm and the door was opened for them as they went into the brightly lit foyer. Wrenshaw appeared to be known here. Bríd's cloak was taken, making her conscious of the expensive French clothes on the women around her, and their bare shoulders, and embarassed by her own plain dress with its high collar.

The head waiter was guiding them through the restaurant, between tables where elegant men and women were dining beneath large chandeliers, and she caught sight of herself reflected in the large mirrors on the walls. There was a thick carpet on the floor. A pretty French chair was pulled back for her, and she found herself at a secluded table at one side, from which they could survey the scene without being too much in view themselves. There was a subdued, well-bred buzz of conversation.

'An apéritif, madame?'

She looked up, then across at Wrenshaw.

'Glass of sherry, Bríd?'

He was so clearly in control here that it seemed pointless to disagree. She nodded. The waiter handed her an enormous, leatherbound menu. It was in French. For some time they both studied their menus in silence. It could have been in Egyptian hieroglyphics for all it meant to Bríd.

'What do you say to some soup, whitebait, and a chop to follow? One doesn't look for anything too pretentious at this time of night. And a bottle of claret. Show me a bottle of the Montrachet '55. *Bien chambré.*'

He said this last to the waiter beside him, who took the menus away with him.

'Are you going to tell me about Lord Leighton?'

'I take it you haven't heard from him since I saw you last?'

Silence.

'He resigned his commission and went to India. Aide-de-camp to the governor of some hill province, Rawalpindi, I think. It was in the *Pall Mall Gazette*. I'm surprised you didn't see it.'

'Strange as it may sound, I don't read the *Pall Mall Gazette*.'

'You should. Especially in your position. You pick up all sorts of useful information. Matter of fact, I've left the army myself. Sold my commission a few months ago.'

Rawalpindi. It sounded so far away, so foreign. Harry among the natives. She hoped he was safe. She felt no resentment against him. His brother's death had made him very upset. Then his family . . . his father. She could not bring herself to mention the marriage. Had it been postponed? Were they already married? What did it matter now, anyway? It was not his fault.

'You'd do well to put him out of your mind. For good.'

'Mind your own business.'

'It is my business. I'll get no pleasure from taking you out if you're going to want to talk about young Leighton all the time.'

'What makes you think you're going to take me out again?'

'My dear Bríd, of course I am. I told you, you need it. You work too blessed hard. And what else am I going to do now that I'm a free man? I've been hugging myself all day. What a stroke of luck that we should meet again! Thought I'd seen the last of you. Thought you'd gone back to Ireland.'

She studied the thick tablecloth, the heavy silver cutlery, the thick crystal wine glasses.

'I did go back to Ireland.'

'And you had the child?'

'I did.'

Silence.

'Your child is here with you in London?'

'No, I left him with my family in Ireland.'

The sherry came and warmed her.

'A little boy. What did you call him?'

'Matthew.'

'Who is looking after little Matthew while you're over here?'

'My uncle and aunt.'

'Do you miss him?'

She thought of her baby for a moment, and then looked away, pained.

'What do you think?'

He was thoughtful for a moment.

'It must have been quite a sacrifice for you to leave him behind and come back to London to work.'

The food came. As she ate, she could feel herself thawing out towards Wrenshaw, becoming more talkative. The wine was warm, thick and red like blood, and fed life into her veins. The food was good, and she felt stronger, rescued from tiredness and hostility into an atmosphere wider and more generous.

Wrenshaw told her of his exploits in Ireland, and some of the escapades of his fellow officers. The man who carried a sack of potatoes with him in his jaunting car, and used to shy them at the villagers as he drove about; the cricket match they had tried to get up against a local Irish team, and the impossibility of getting the Irish to understand the rules. Some of the stories, though told against her own countrymen, never put them in a disadvantaged light, but brought out their quaint sense of humour. And Wrenshaw came across as a witty and humane man.

As Bríd relaxed, she began to tell him of her own adventures in London, and how she had got her first job at the Grapes.

Later they took a cab to Dean Street. He dismissed the cab and they stood talking in the street for some time outside the door. At last he said he would call for her another evening, and she found her resistance had withered away. He took her hand and kissed it, said,

'*A bientôt*', and strolled away down the street with his cane over his shoulder.

Winter had come on, the days were short, and rehearsals for *Dick Whittington* were in their final days. Bríd had much to learn and practise. Thompson prided himself on the lavishness of his productions and every stage device he could think of was employed in the show. They spent hours rehearsing all the moving scenery, getting quickly out of the way as flats slid into place along grooves cut in the stage, or avoided painted cloths which came plummeting down behind them from the flies overhead. Ria, who came on as Fairy Bluebell, had to appear through a star trap, shot up through the stage like a cannonball.

Thompson was very attentive to Bríd. He'd given the part of Dick to her partly on account of her height and her legs. Her costume as Dick, made specially for her, had her in gold tights with fawn calf-length boots, dark-red velvet shorts with gold edging, a slashed doublet in pale gold and brown with a pretty lace ruff, and a little turned-up hat with a feather. She liked herself in this outfit very much, and would stand admiring herself in the long looking glass, adjusting it, pulling up her tights, pushing and pulling, fussing with her hair and her cap. What Aunt Nora would have made of it, she didn't like to think, but didn't really care any more.

Phil coached her in her words. She had one of the easiest parts in the show, though he didn't say so. As long as she looked right, spoke her words clearly and didn't trip over the scenery, not much more was expected of her. Phil told her the whole thing revolved around her, she was the kingpin. Bríd learned quickly and had a good ear for dialogue, and Thompson was pleased with her.

She was clever enough to realise, however, that many of the other characters required far more acting skill and experience; Barney Coates, for example, a middle-aged man with a rubbery face, who played the cook was the pantomime dame, and came on in a grotesque padded woman's costume with an enormous bosom, striped stockings and big boots, a dirty yellow wig and a large mobcap. He looked as if he hadn't shaved for a week. He had a powerful bass voice and a broad cockney accent, and was really the star of the show.

He worked up a considerable amount of ad-lib business with Alf Merriwether as Idle Jack, much of which took place in the kitchen and involved saucepans and other kitchen implements. Phil would stand beside Bríd as she watched Barney and Alf, and she was conscious of him studying them minutely. All through rehearsals it was the only topic of Phil's conversation. In the end she ran out of things to say. Alf was very good; no doubt Phil would have been very good. What more was there to say? No doubt he had been in many other pantos, and there would be many more – why make a fuss? But Phil could not get over it. He was convinced he would have been better than Alf, and whenever they had any free time, Phil would explain elaborately how he would have done a certain piece of business differently – and better than Alf.

She didn't complain, because Phil had been very helpful to her, but sometimes she was on the verge of telling him to change the subject.

It was always very crowded backstage. The pantomime had a large cast, and there were at least forty stagehands operating the machinery, running flats off and on along grooves in the stage; under the stage, opening and closing traps or shooting actors up through star traps; or up in the flies, lowering and taking out cloths and gauzes and many smaller items of scenery, as well as a host of special items like the Man in the Moon.

The lights were controlled by the gas men. The gas made a subdued hissing noise, which Bríd got used to. Phil had advised her to give the gas men generous beer money. 'You don't want to lose your spot, Bríd,' he said.

223

Chapter Twenty-Nine

'I tried to explain to him.'

'But why?'

'It's always done. It's what everyone does in that scene. He had no call to get so peevish.'

Bríd was cleaning her face in the looking glass. Phil was behind her. He was not looking at her, but walking back and forth in the little dressing room like a caged animal. The other girls had gone to the bar.

'Was that wise?' Bríd said. She was tired of this conversation. They had less than a week to go before the panto opened and the pressure to get everything ready was relentless.

'There was no need for him to take on so. I told him: it's simply a question of doing things properly.'

'Perhaps he has his own way of doing things.'

'Bríd, you don't understand. In panto there are traditional ways of doing things. Alf is deliberately refusing to do it because it's always been done that way.'

'Or because you told him.'

'What do you mean?'

He turned on her quickly. She looked into his face, tired and strained.

'Look, Phil, I'm not Alf Merriwether, so there's no need to take it out on me. What's more, I'm dog tired so can we change the subject?'

'Bríd, this is important!' He swung away impulsively. 'God, I knew I should never have agreed to do the Emperor. It's a step backwards.'

'Phil,' she shouted, 'it's only a play! What does it matter? In a month you'll be on to something else, and it'll all be behind you. Let's change the subject!'

'Only a play? What do you mean? I'm an artist, Bríd, and so are you. Everything matters. Every last little detail matters, the fringe on the hem of your dress matters, the flower in your hair matters. Never say it doesn't matter! I'm just angry with myself, that's all; I can't stand not to see something done exactly as it should be done.'

'You'd better ask Thompson to let you produce it then.'

'Don't you care, for God's sake?'

'Phil, at this moment I couldn't care less, and that's a fact. You'd be very good as Idle Jack, I'm sure. Probably better than Alf Merriwether, for all I know –'

'Probably!'

'Yes, probably. Right now, I'm going to get changed and then go home to bed, if you don't mind, and I'd rather not hear any more about Alf Merriwether tonight, thank you.'

There was a slight knock at the door and, as it opened, a voice saying, 'May I come in?'

Wrenshaw was there in evening dress and silk hat.

'Bríd, I have to confess I came to see you again. This makes the third time. Simply couldn't keep away. I thought we might get a spot of supper together, what do you say? All that singing and dancing has given me an appetite.'

He ignored Phil, who was staring at him.

'John.' She looked uncertainly from him to Phil. 'Phil, allow me to introduce Sir John Wrenshaw. Sir John, this is Phil Courage.'

Wrenshaw looked at Phil as if from a great height.

'Splendid,' he said, rather offhandedly. 'Yes, Bríd, there were all kinds of complimentary things being said about you in the foyer. I was glad you weren't there to hear them; might have turned your head.'

'Excuse me,' Phil began. He looked at Bríd, and spoke with pedantic slowness. 'And may I just enquire who "John" is?'

She sensed all his bitterness and frustration; now there was jealousy as well. At this time of night neither of these men mattered very much to her.

'He's an old friend. Is that right?' She looked at Wrenshaw in the looking glass. He smiled.

'And are you in the habit of entertaining "old friends" in your dressing room in your underwear?'

'You've never complained before.'

'I'm different!'

She swung round and looked at him. Wrenshaw was watching.

'Are you?' she said, looking at him with a level stare.

'I thought I was. But it's obvious I was wrong. Obviously, since any stage-door johnny can stroll in and make himself at home.'

'You presume too much.' She turned back and continued to clean her face.

225

Wrenshaw said, 'Bríd, I'll be at the stage door. I've a cab waiting,' and went out.

Phil swung back to her.

'Well, as it happens, I thought I had some rights I might presume on. I thought we had an understanding –'

'We have no understanding! How dare you?'

Phil was staggered.

'How dare I? Bríd, what have we been doing all these months? Why have I been going through your lines with you? Why have I spent every waking minute with you, helping you, encouraging you, watching over you –'

'Phil, I'm sincerely grateful to you, believe me, but that doesn't give you the right to take me for granted. You don't own me.'

'My God, I've been a fool! I thought you were fond of me and all the time you were just using me.'

'I am fond of you but has it occurred to you that I too have had to listen to your incessant whining and complaining about Alf Merriwether?'

'I only accepted the part of the Emperor to be near you.'

'Phil, I'm grateful! Thank you! Now will you allow me to get dressed and go home to bed?'

'Go off with your swell, you mean.'

'I mean nothing of the sort. I didn't know he was coming.'

'What kind of a fool do you take me for?'

'A very big fool indeed if you won't understand the simple truth.'

'You're a liar, Bríd, you're lying to me –'

Bríd was blind with anger.

'Liar! My God, if that's it, then good night to you, Phil Courage, and I hope I may never see you again.'

'Yes, a liar and a fool that doesn't understand a man's love is worth more than money or station!'

He went quickly out of the door.

She snatched up a brush and began violently brushing her hair. She was angry with Phil, but she wasn't sure whether she was angry with him because he didn't trust her, or because he didn't have the right to take her for granted. Either way every nerve in her jangled.

She had completely forgotten Wrenshaw and was surprised to find him at the stage door with a cab. Since it was half past midnight, and she was asleep on her feet, she couldn't construe a reason for not getting into it.

'He seemed upset about something.'

'I'm going home to bed.'

'Yes. I'll drop you off.'

At first neither spoke as the cab rolled away, clattering over the cobbles in the darkness. She was agitated after the scene with Phil, and could still feel the blood hot in her cheek.

'I've had him breathing down my neck every day for three weeks. He's obsessive. Thank God the panto's opening on Thursday. I'll get some peace.'

'Bríd, can we change the subject? You can't imagine how tedious it is to an outsider. The world is still rolling round, you know, and there are real people still walking about London outside your theatre.'

'That's what I told him. I said, "It's only a play, why get in such a huff?" I think he's slightly mad.'

'Oh, no. He hasn't enough imagination.'

'I didn't ask him to play the Emperor of Morocco. In fact, now I remember, I told him there was plenty of other work about. But he took the job so he could be near me.' She thought. 'Oh, God, I wasn't very kind to him. He's been a real treasure; I don't know how I could have got this far without him. I just wish he wouldn't get so steamed up, that's all. Now he'll go home and brood all night. I know him.'

'Bríd, I don't want to hear another word about your comedian friend, not tonight or any other night. Heavens above, there are limits! I'm very pleased for you, and you were really splendid tonight, but your little friend is after all just a singer in a music hall, and it's time you looked further than that.'

He had taken a more forceful tone.

'What do you mean?'

'You're not going to spend the rest of your life chewing over backstage gossip and flirting with red-nosed comedians. You've come a long way already, and you're going to go a long way yet. Holding hands and simpering behind the scenery. Oh, God!'

'What do you know about it?'

'It's obvious. I bet he told you he's in love with you.'

She was silent. Yes, he did. Phil loved her. She felt a rush of tenderness towards him.

'Do you love him?'

She was silent for a moment.

'Well, do you? You must know.'

The carriage swayed through the dark streets, a street lamp flickering in from time to time. Did she actually love Phil? She was very fond of him.

'You don't.'

She resented his tone, commandeering her, taking her over just as Phil had tried to do.

'Well then, be honest with yourself. Stop wasting energy on him.'

227

'You know nothing about it. He's been very good to me.'

'You don't love him.' Wrenshaw was insistent.

She was silent.

'You know you can do better for yourself.'

'Do I?'

'Yes.'

'You seem to know a lot about it.'

'You forget I know more about you than any other man in London.'

'I forget nothing.'

'You don't like to be taken over, do you? You want to keep your independence. So do I.'

'So?'

'So we're suited, you and I. We're well matched.'

'You'll have to prove it.'

'I intend to.'

Without speaking, he leaned across in the darkness, took hold of her and kissed her forcefully. She did not respond but was inert in his arms.

Afterwards she was silent and then said in a neutral tone, 'That proves nothing.'

'It means I want you. That's a great deal.'

'You want a bit of pleasure, that's all.'

'No, Bríd, I want you, and I mean to have you. You're a woman I can get on with. You know what you want. You're like a man, you've got energy and force. You're not sentimental, you're strong and I believe you want me. You may not know it yet, but you'll come to realise it.'

The cab had stopped. Bríd looked out of the window. They were outside the Criterion Grill in Piccadilly.

'You said you were taking me home.'

'I am. But you must be ravenous. A little supper first is what you need. You'll sleep better.'

'You've done without. So have I. I know about sleeping on the ground and living on rice for weeks. I've frozen in the Himalayas and sweltered in Bombay. Luxury means nothing to me. I can take it or leave it. But it gives me power. For instance, I can confer it on you – if I choose, and if you choose. You can have your comedian friend in the music hall – or you can choose me. Choose style, class, move into a circle where you belong.'

They were sitting over wine in the Criterion. The remains of dinner was spread on the table between them.

228

'And talking of class, why don't you get yourself some decent clothes?'

'Since you're a man and accustomed to think only of yourself, it won't occur to you that every spare penny I make is sent home.'

'My dear girl, I'll buy you some clothes. What's money for?'

She thought, What am I doing here? I have important tasks to get done. I've got to make a success of the pantomime; I've got to build a career. Why am I wasting my time with this man?

'You like elegant clothes, don't you?'

'Is the woman born who doesn't?' she said listlessly.

'We're talking about you. I'd like to help you; I want to lavish a little care and attention on you. You look, shall we say, unprovided for. It's time you spared a little thought for yourself.'

'There'll be time enough for that when I've established myself. At the moment I'm still on the starting line.'

'That's what I mean. My God, you're difficult to talk to. I'm not asking you to go out and spend your hard-earned wages. All I ask, Bríd, is to be allowed to spend a little of my money on you. I'm not asking anything in return, honestly.'

'Honestly?'

'Hand on my heart.'

The following morning there was a note waiting for Bríd at the stage door. It was from Phil:

> I loved you, I offered you my devotion, and you have spurned me. I took you for a better woman.
> Goodbye.
> Philip Courage

Before she could think, or help herself, there were tears of vexation in her eyes. What right had Phil Courage to judge her so? Still in her bonnet and cloak, she stood in the dressing room holding the letter in her hand, and wiping the tears from her eyes. How dare he say that to her? How dare he?

The technical rehearsal of *Dick Whittington* took place on Monday. They worked from eleven in the morning until three the following morning. When Thompson gave everyone a short break at six, Bríd slipped a cloak over her costume, went over the road to the pub for a jug of porter and a plate of meat pies, and the three girls sat round the fire in their costumes and had an impromptu supper.

Christmas Day came two days later and Madge invited Bríd to spend the day with her family. She took a cab out to Bow, and was introduced to Madge's father and mother, her three younger brothers and sisters as well as Madge's grandmother on her mother's side and her uncle, who was first mate on a coal steamer and happened to be home for Christmas. The little house was very crowded, so that when they they sat down to dinner, there was scarcely room round the table. Later in the afternoon they played games, and in the evening had a cold supper.

As she undressed for bed that night, she thought of Uncle Patsy and Aunt Nora and her son, wondering how their Christmas had been. She thought of Phil too; she hadn't been kind to him. If only he hadn't been so hot-headed – there had been nothing between her and Wrenshaw then. Now all had changed, and she had lost him. She bit her lip with vexation.

And where was Wrenshaw? She had heard nothing from him. He'd made no appointment to see her, nothing. For all she knew she might never see him again. Her life, which she had tried hard to organise and control, seemed to have become confused and unsatisfactory. She knew, however, deep within her that it was all a consequence of the one great bad thing she had done. That sense of guilt, the memory of the railway station in Dublin, and the last glimpse of Patsy holding her child, hovered always behind her thoughts.

The following day – Boxing Day – she was back at the theatre early for the last dress rehearsal before the first performance at half past two. As the girls sat in the dressing room, they began to hear distantly the sounds of the audience coming into the theatre, the bubbling of excitement and anticipation. Once again there was the terrible churning in her stomach, the physical agony, the feeling that she was putting herself through an ordeal by fire.

A hundred times she stood before the looking glass tugging at her costume, adjusting her cap, pulling up her tights. There had been no sign of Wrenshaw, no message, but she didn't care. He and all the world had faded to a distant shadow while here the show, the theatre, was the only reality.

She was hurrying down towards the stage when she was startled to find Barney Coates near the stage door alone, in all his pantomime costume, his wig, his red nose. He was bent over, one hand clutching the banister of the stairs, his other hand on his knees.

'Barney! What's the matter?'

He grimaced, an attempt at a smile through a look of agony.

'Don't worry, darling, Stomach cramps. I always get 'em on a first night.'

'Stomach – you're not ill, are you?'

'No, darling, it's nothing. Just leave me alone, I'll be right as rain.' His face contorted again.

'Barney, you look terrible. Sit down a moment, I'll get you a glass of water.'

'It's nothing. Nerves. I've been getting 'em for thirty years now so I know. I'll be fine.'

Bríd was silent. Barney Coates with nerves? It was impossible. She'd seen him out there, with the audience eating out of his hand. He'd dazzled her by his banter, a man afraid of nothing.

'Nerves, Barney? I don't believe you.'

He looked at her with a pained expression and heaved a great sigh.

'Wish I didn't believe it either, but it's true. Anyway, Bríd, best of luck. They're going to love you, I can tell. Oh, God, right now I wish I was dead.'

He bent over again, groaning, and waved her away without speaking.

In the darkness, waiting to go on, Bríd thought of Barney. Annie was beside her, whispering to a friend of hers, giggling over some trivial piece of gossip. Obviously she hadn't a care in the world. How could a twelve-year-old girl have less fear than a man of over fifty who had been on the stage all his life?

Paradoxically, Barney's fear eased Bríd's. If Barney could be nervous, then so could she, and she immediately felt better.

At that moment the curtain went up and the opening scene began; there was a gasp from the audience. To sombre and chilling music they beheld, in some subterranean sewer, King Rat surrounded by hordes of his rat followers, their eyes gleaming red in the gloom.

The scene was short and there was a round of applause as the lights came up. Then, with a whisking of painted cloths from above, a rattling of flats sliding into place, the dingy sewer was transformed to a bright London street. Bríd strode on with Annie at her heels.

DICK: We've tramped all night with aching feet,
　　　　My purse is empty, we've not a crust to eat,
　　　　But still we're here in London, and somehow
　　　　I'm sure we'll make our fortunes and –
CAT:　Miaow!
DICK: Oh, puss, your paws must be so sore,
　　　　We'll pause awhile –

Words, moves and costumes they had dithered and agonised over, had changed and changed again, were now fused together in the heat of the audience's presence, and the tense, crowded atmosphere, the light, the half-awareness of so much attention and expectation, carried her on a wave of controlled excitement.

Before she knew it, the show they had all worked so hard to

prepare was over, the audience were applauding with wild enthusiasm, and she was in the middle of the line, taking bow after bow.
And when, an hour later they began the second performance, she felt
she'd been doing it all her life.

Chapter Thirty

During those weeks over Christmas and into January, Bríd was baptised into the theatrical life. On most days the light was going by three in the afternoon, and as the wind whipped round the building and gusty squalls of rain and yellow-green smoke, acrid and choking, blew down the streets and round corners, Bríd came to feel she was living in the theatre and knew no other home. She was in the Wellington by half past twelve every day and didn't get away until midnight, and her world was confined to the dressing room, bright and warm, the fire clinking in its grate, the smell of powder, the piles of clothes and costumes everywhere, the happy confusion that gave the room its cosy feeling, and the companionship, the jokes, the rumours and gossip; the backbiting and tittle-tattle, the malice and generosity, the taste for excruciating puns. One evening, Bríd had come in with a quart jug of porter and a plate of pies with a cloth over it.

'Ooh! Here's Bríd with pies. What a loverley sur-pies! Bríd, you are the flower of Ireland's womanhood!'

'Let's hope the flower hasn't been plucked.'

'Bríd's a plucky girl, she's been well plucked in her time, ain't you?'

'Well, pluck us a pie then, I'm starving.'

On the first Sunday morning after *Dick Whittington* had opened, Wrenshaw unexpectedly turned up in Dean Street in a cab and proposed taking Bríd down to Brighton for the day. She had been lying in bed, talking to Isabella, and enjoying the first hours of freedom she had had in weeks. There was a shout from downstairs; Bríd threw an old gown round her shoulders and ran down to see what the matter was. The Maestro in his dressing gown, with a disapproving expression, told her there was a man outside asking for her.

'One of your admirers, Bríd,' he said gloomily, and disappeared into his room.

Wrenshaw's arrival took her by surprise, as he had intended it should, and she jumped at his suggestion. Apart from anything else it would be an opportunity to show off some new clothes she had at last bought: a dark-brown wool dress over a crinoline, trimmed with gold braid, a short jacket with a fur collar and a matching muff, shiny new black boots, and a Glengarry hat with a feather in it. She dressed herself with some care for she was nervous about Wrenshaw; he was fastidious where matters of taste and fashion were concerned, and she had heard him pass crushing remarks about the clothes of women they had seen in the streets or restaurants.

As she was dressing and Isabella was helping to tie up the drawstrings, Bríd suddenly thought, Brighton? In all the chit-chat back stage at the Wellington, a trip to Brighton meant only one thing. Did it also mean that to Wrenshaw? Bríd was in a hurry, but the thought lodged in her mind – was this it? Was this what he wanted? Very likely. And what did she want? She would worry about that when it came.

They took the train down. It was nearly empty. Wrenshaw had got them a first-class compartment all to themselves, and as he sprawled on the seat opposite her, a cigar between his teeth, her spirits lifted to be sitting in such spacious surroundings. Spreading her skirt round her as she made herself comfortable, she couldn't help contrasting it with the wooden benches in the third-class compartments of the train from Holyhead. She watched the countryside float by.

When they got to Brighton the sky was full of racing clouds and the sea was high; monstrous rolling waves, grey, white and splendid, crashed on to the beach with a monotonous roar. The seafront was deserted.

They walked by the sea together, barely able to stand up in the wind. Though it was the beginning of January, it was not very cold. Bríd was in heaven. Holding on to Wrenshaw with one arm and her hat with the other, she held her face up to the wind, damp and fresh from the sea, staring and staring out at the sheer magnificent power of the waves. They made their way down across the shingle as near to the waves as they could, so that her mind was filled with the raw might of the sea. It seemed inexplicable that so much power could just waste itself in its futile dash on to the shingle, and then return, pulling back in a harsh grating of pebbles to tumble forwards again, unstoppable, interminable, relentless. She surrendered to its hypnotic force and would have stood there all day, if Wrenshaw hadn't pulled her on.

They turned into the little alleyways that led off the seafront, and strolled up and down, looking into windows sometimes, where they would catch a glimpse of a poor fisherman and his family round the fire. For a moment, seeing them there, Bríd was reminded of home, of the quiet settled family in its humble cottage, and the fire burning cheerily.

Eventually, as darkness fell, the cold began to seep into their bones, and they went to a hotel for dinner. Wrenshaw chose the Albion, the biggest and most splendid hotel on the seafront. Inside it was warm, and her face glowed after her walk. The restaurant was crowded, but waiters, impressed by Wrenshaw's easy superiority and the likelihood of a generous tip, hurried to attend them.

Bríd was hungry; Wrenshaw ordered a large dinner and they had a bottle of wine, and then another. After the exhilaration of the cold day outside, the food and wine gave her strength and relaxed her, as if the pressures of her life had suddenly receded, the theatre was a long way away, and life was spacious and at her command.

She was grateful to Wrenshaw for all this. Looking across at him, in her expansive mood, she thought what a good-looking man he was, so elegant and debonair, and noted the way servants and waiters ran to do his bidding; being with Wrenshaw was to be carried through life on oiled wheels, where doors opened, staff were deferential and obliging, meals were regular and tasty, the wine was good and there was plenty of it.

Time melted away; there seemed no longer any rush. Everything was fine; the pantomime had gone well and she could look forward to the run for the next month without anxiety. It was time to relax; she was entitled to it. She sat in a haze of contentment.

Wrenshaw leaned across and murmured, 'Seems a pity to have to rush back to London tonight, Bríd, don't you think?'

She answered dreamily, 'Hmm? What do you suggest?'

'I suppose I could see if they've any rooms here?'

Since the last thing she wanted was to have to go out into the cold night, take a train all the way back to London, get there at some unearthly hour and then be unable to find a cab, and since she didn't have to be in the theatre until twelve thirty the following morning, it seemed a very good idea to stay the night. She waited while Wrenshaw went off and made enquiries. He returned.

'Just the thing. Place is damn nearly full, but I've taken the imperial suite – best set of rooms in the hotel, two rooms with snug little parlour and a bathroom, and we'll have it all to ourselves. Told 'em you'd like to see it first, of course, before we made any decisions.'

'Of course.'

Whom was she fooling? Still, Bríd went through the motions.

'Well, let's see these rooms.'

She floated up to the first floor, where the manager produced a key and let them in, and hastily lit two candles.

The fires had already been lit, and the parlour was very cosy with the curtains drawn; there were comfortable old armchairs, and pretty gilt mirrors in the walls.

'There are two bedrooms and a bathroom.'

He threw open the door. Bríd looked in. A bathroom. Her head swam.

'It's the only one in the hotel, Bríd. Very latest thing. Just been installed.'

She had seen pictures of these in the *Illustrated London News*. A great white enamel bathtub with brass taps at the end, and thick fleecy towels on a rail. There were no facilities for bathing in Dean Street. She carried a can of hot water up six flights of stairs to wash herself in a bowl in front of the window. After her day in the wind and the sea spray --

Wrenshaw went on, 'And two bedrooms – you can take your pick.'

She looked in at the two bedrooms. One was larger than the other, with a wide double bed in it, already turned down, and a merry fire flickering in the grate, warm and inviting. The other, smaller room, for some reason had no fire. The bed was unmade.

'What do you think? Do you think we can make ourselves comfortable here?'

He smiled his relaxed, easy smile. It was as if all the edges of her existence at this moment were blurring, and she felt herself spreading outwards, and opening up to everything; it was all so easy.

Wrenshaw nodded to the manager, who bowed his way out respectfully, closing the door behind him.

He threw himself into an armchair. Bríd went into the bathroom. She ran her hand over the towels. By some miracle they were heated. This was something she had dreamed of, a great bath where she could stretch out at full length and just soak up the heat.

'I think I'll have a bath,' she said as casually as she could.

'Do,' he called.

She turned on the water. Thunderous jets cascaded into the tub. She undressed in the bathroom, pulling at the strings, the hooks and eyes, the laces, pulling off her boots, her crinoline falling about her, her petticoats thrown over the rail, her little jacket hanging on a hook behind the door. When the tub was full she lowered herself into the water inch by inch, feeling the heat creeping up round her, until she was immersed to her neck.

Never could she remember such sheer bliss. She closed her eyes and melted into the pleasure of the heat.

She opened her eyes.

Wrenshaw was looking down at her. He had taken off his coat and collar and was undoing a cufflink. She looked at him impassively, saying nothing. He ran his eyes over her body.

'By God, you're a woman to die for.'

'Would you die for me?'

'Looking at you this minute, I think I might.'

She laughed. 'Liar.'

'More to the point, I'd die with you.'

He knelt beside her, and brushed his lips very gently over hers.

'I ordered a bottle of champagne. Could you bear it?'

'I think I might.'

He went out. Lying in the water, she wondered why she had not been outraged to find Wrenshaw in the bathroom inspecting her.

He returned with two glasses of champagne. She pulled herself up a little.

'*Sláinte*. Isn't that what you Irish say?'

Bubbles went up her nose. She giggled.

She came into the bedroom wrapped in a towel, her hair flowing round her shoulders, to where he lay in bed waiting for her. Letting the towel drop to the floor, she slipped in beside him.

He had put out the candle and only the fire threw an uncertain light across the room. She heard distantly the surge of the breakers outside and the wind rattling round the building. The room seemed doubly cosy.

As he took her by the waist to draw her to him, she whispered, 'John, you won't – you know?'

'What?'

'I can't afford another Matt, not just now.'

'Have no fear, just leave everything to me.'

Wrenshaw had thrown aside the covers to expose her nakedness, and as she reached up, her arms round his neck, he took her firmly in his arms. They kissed hectically, madly, straining against each other, clutching, gripping, oblivious. She was free at last of the iron discipline that had bound her for so many months, free to satisfy the huge need which had built within her. It was as if she had not felt a man's body, the hard, heavy strength of him, for a hundred years, as if she had almost forgotten what it was like, and how great was her own need. A hunger drove her, pressing up against him, as he, bigger, heavier than she, controlled her, always pressing on her, implacable, demanding. Her body was alive with impulses, electric, caressing, faster and faster, driven by a need that would not let her be.

237

Wrenshaw was everywhere about her, his hands running over her thighs, his lips exploring her breasts, brushing, teasing, her nipples, so that she arched herself to him, wanting him a thousand times more with every moment.

He was running his hands over her back, through her hair, spread over the pillow, and then his lips were running down, over her belly, down the inside of her thighs, and then up again, so that she wanted him in her, but he wouldn't come in her yet. Only touching and caressing lightly, his lips explored her, even there in her secret place and at that she gasped, could not help herself – he had kissed her *there*. Wouldn't he come in her? She was dying, but he *must* come in her.

Filled with a driving restlessness, she made him turn on his back, and now it was her turn, exploring his body, stronger than her own, running her lips across his chest and down across his belly. Taking him into her mouth, wanting to pleasure him, she could tell he liked it, but he wouldn't let her go on, because, roused even more, he had turned her again on her back, and now at last he was entering her, and she moaned, oh, it had been so long, so long, she had almost forgotten, oh but it was intolerable. Her skin seemed flayed with a delirious heat, she could feel the sweat running between their bodies.

He made her sit astride him, and she arched her back, her hair streaming about her shoulders, as he ran his hands over her breasts. It seemed to go on and on and she felt annihilated, as if she would just melt, all self gone, as she seemed to flow out and out into his arms.

But now he was over her and coming into her again. She clutched him tightly as she felt herself losing all control, floating adrift on a current of ecstasy, her head thrown back across the edge of the bed, words tumbling from her lips, oh how she had waited, and how it reminded her of before, and how she remembered, and then unthinking, as she felt him shuddering within her, she cried out, 'Oh, Harry.'

In the morning, she sat up in bed, propped against the pillows, pulling the blankets round her. That name, sacred to her, had come as much of a surprise to her as to him. Afterwards she lay trying to unravel the processes of her mind that had brought her to it. Why, just then, had Harry's name slipped past her lips? Yet, why not – was he not often hovering close behind her thoughts?

Wrenshaw ministered to her; uncomfortably and dimly at first, as he handed her a cup of tea, he began to perceive how far she still was from him. That one word, which had escaped her unawares, had sufficed to put him in his place.

She sat now, looking at him with a sideways look, a half-smile on her lips, saying nothing as she sipped her tea. Outside the sky had cleared, and they could hear the dull roar of the sea.

Wrenshaw noticed the locket on a side table. It usually hung beneath her clothes and he had never seen it before. He reached across and took it in his hand, turning it over and inspecting it.

'A keepsake?'

She said nothing. He looked into her eyes.

'No need to ask who from.'

'No.'

'What's the point? You'll never see him again.'

'Mind your own business.'

'He's getting married, you know.'

Bríd was silent. Wrenshaw shrugged.

'Still, it's a pretty little thing.'

He got up and crossed the room to the window and stared out at the sea.

'You're a strange creature. So strong, so independent – you're not like any woman I know, as if you had broken through all the normal boundaries of existence. Do you remember the night we met in Leicester Square? You were walking through the middle of London alone at midnight – extraordinary. You're afraid of nothing. You earn your own living. You can do anything. And yet, beneath it all you have this sentimental weakness. You can't let him go.'

'He loves me.'

'Not much use if he's marrying someone else.'

'We will find each other again one day.'

'How?'

She was silent.

'Bríd, how?'

She would not look at him. 'I don't know how.' She spoke very quietly, so that Wrenshaw hardly heard her. 'We are fated to be together.'

'Oh, fate! Well, of course, that changes everything. If you are *fated*, then that settles it. Lucky for me that we were fated to go to bed together last night, eh?'

On the way back to London that morning, Bríd wondered what exactly she was doing. She had betrayed the memory of Harry, and in a way she had used Wrenshaw. Her life had divided into an inner and an outer part, and they could never be joined again until she and Harry were united, and how that could be she had no idea.

A few days later they went together to Regent Street into milliners and haberdashers and looked at clothes. Wrenshaw knew what he

239

wanted and she respected his taste. She was content to let him choose, to educate her. She loved herself in fine clothes, loved the feel of newness on her skin, the crispness of fresh cotton, the softness of silk, loved to look at herself in the looking glass and admire her figure; she loved the colours, the patterns, the textures, the feel of fabrics. She would have had them all, but Wrenshaw was more discriminating, approved some and discarded others.

Chapter Thirty-One

One Saturday evening, when *Dick Whittington* had been running for two weeks, and the girls were changing after the show, there was a knock on the door. It was Phil.

Bríd had hardly spoken to him since the night when he and Wrenshaw had met; there had been horrid moments when they would pass each other on the stair, and their eyes would avoid meeting, and during their scene together in Morocco when Dick Whittington's cat got rid of all the rats, they had also avoided looking straight at each other. It made the scene difficult to act, and left her feeling depressed. This evening he seemed sheepish, unsure of himself until he saw that he was welcome; he smiled, pulled himself up and came in.

'Phil, how are you? You don't seem to come up here nowadays.'

'Preserving my strength, girls; plenty of early nights.'

Neither Madge nor Ria knew that Bríd and Phil had had a row. Bríd was pinning up her hair, studying herself in the looking glass, so she had been able to avoid looking Phil in the eye. She had felt guilty seeing that first anxious look when he had put his face round the door, and after welcoming him she had turned again to her reflection.

Phil took a seat as the three girls continued dressing, brushing their hair and tidying their dressing tables.

'Just got a tour fixed up when the run finishes. Second half, top of the bill, first-class dates. I'll be glad to get out on tour, get the smoke of London out of my lungs.'

'Good money, Phil?'

'Can't complain, you know, Madge. Mind you, the real money's in management. I'm thinking of going into management myself. Setting up a tour. It's money for old rope.'

'Will you offer us an engagement then, Phil?'

'You bet. I'll offer you all engagements, girls, and we'll travel round together and make our fortunes.'

241

Phil seemed full of enthusiasm and energy. Bríd felt she must have been mistaken in that first look of his. She was pleased to see him back on the old footing, glad he'd been able to put away all the tension between them. He had a reassuring face, friendly, comforting, cheery and unafraid. You always felt safe when Phil was there. She was sorry she'd shouted at him.

The other girls finished dressing and went home, and Phil and Bríd were left together. The fire was low in the grate, and Bríd turned down the gaslight, for it was hot in the room.

'Do you want a drink?'

There was a bottle of port unfinished. She poured a couple of glasses and they raised them in silence. As soon as Madge and Ria had gone, Phil had become awkward and tongue-tied.

Bríd didn't know what to say.

'It was nice of you to come and have a chat again. Like old times.'

'Seemed silly to hold a grudge, you know; and every time I passed this staircase, I'd think of you up here . . .'

He paused.

He was staring into the fire. She looked down at him. She knew why he had come now, but she was surprised to see him so changed, to have lost all his bounce and sparkle. He hardly seemed the same man.

'I'm glad to see you, Phil. I'm sorry about –'

At that cue his face turned up towards her and he was a man in agony.

'Oh, Bríd, I've been thinking about you night and day since that – that night. The worst night of my life. I can't go anywhere, I can't do anything, but you're there. I see you all the time. Why did you do it? You know how happy we was together. Why, Bríd, why?'

Bríd could feel tears starting into her eyes.

'I can't explain. We were happy together, don't I know it, and if you hadn't come that night, shouting and calling me all kinds of names, we might be so still. I was completely faithful until that moment.'

He stared at her. 'Until that moment? What do you mean?'

'I mean that it was your own fault. You drove me away by your jealousy and stupidity.'

'I drove you away?'

She nodded in silence, looking down.

'Let me make it up to you. I love you, Bríd, don't you see? Let me show you. What shall we do? Anything, anything at all – you say it. Oh, we'll have a grand time, won't we?'

'It's too late.'

'Don't say that, Bríd!'

He leaped up, still in a burst of enthusiasm.

'Don't say it! We'll get married and travel round together – and you can bring over little Matt, and we'll all be together. We'll be such a happy family!'

Bríd was staggered. Married? And with Matt? Could she do it? Break the agreement, go and bring back her son? In a moment she saw it all, a family, security, and a home for Matt. Phil his father.

He looked at her, his glass in his hand.

'Say the word, Bríd, only say the word, and I'll get a special licence on Monday and by God we'll be man and wife!'

His face was lit up, fiery with excitement; she could feel the force of his will. All his goodness, his kindness, his generosity, his honesty and openness were there before her; he would be hers – and a father to Matt. The very thing above all else she needed.

Yet what had she said to Wrenshaw? That she and Harry were fated to be together? It was a thought that she had never uttered before and yet the moment she had said it, she knew she had always known it. It stood like a great rock barring the road to the past. Phil was shut off.

Phil saw her hesitate.

'Say the word, Bríd, only say the word. We could be married this day week!'

'Phil . . .'

He was straining towards her, his face alight with enthusiasm and longing.

'You loved me, I know you did. I remember when we were together, that night you sang at the Grapes – oh, God, you were lovely, Bríd, a fairy you looked and the voice of an angel – and afterwards in the dressing room, when you kissed me, I know you loved me then.'

He seemed pathetic.

'It's different now. We were happy together, and you was very kind to me, sure, will I ever forget it –'

She saw a new thought in his mind.

'It's that stage-door Johnny, isn't it? Isn't it? Bríd, answer me.'

He stood upright above her, as she sat at her looking glass. He was determined.

'I'll find him and thrash him, so I will. Where does he live? Come, give me his address. I'll beat him there in broad daylight on his own steps. Tell me, where does he live?'

'I will not tell you, Phil, and stop shouting! The nightwatchman is locking up, we'll have to go.'

He snatched her arm and pulled her to him with sudden and brutal force.

'Bríd, you'll not leave me so! Damn it, you'll never find a truer man and you're a fool if you don't see it!'

She wrenched herself free, stung and angered by his sudden strong grip.

'Don't touch me! I will not be handled by you or anyone against my will. And I think the less of you for using force against me.'

At this he collapsed as suddenly as he had erupted. He threw himself into the chair again and covered his face. There was a moment's silence. Bríd couldn't tell whether to feel angry with him or sorry for him. She wished she were anywhere but there. She wished she were dead.

She leaned against the mantelpiece staring down into the fire. Tears were in her eyes.

'I think it's most unkind. If you had any consideration . . .' She paused. 'We were happy once, but it's over now, that's all. You'd better forget me.'

Phil sat slumped with his face in his hands.

'Bríd, forgive me. I don't know what I'm doing. I'm sorry I hurt you. I'm sorry to trouble you. Oh, God, I'm so unhappy.'

She could hear him weeping, and his shoulders shook as he sat hunched on the chair. A terrible tenderness for him ran through her and she reached out a hand to his shoulder.

'Phil, don't. Don't. We'll be friends. But don't cry, please, I can't bear it. We can still be friends.'

He looked into the fire. There was a long silence, then he spoke in a deep, terrible, bitter tone.

'We can never be friends. Never. I loved you and you destroyed my love. I will never forgive you.'

He stood up, took his hat, and went quickly out of the door.

Tears forced themselves into her eyes, and she was powerless to stop them. She sat by the fire weeping, seeing nothing, only feeling that nothing was fair and there was no justice and she would never be happy in the world. Maybe she had just thrown away the only chance of happiness she would ever have. What was Harry anyway but a sort of chimera? As for Wrenshaw, he'd never promised her anything. He picked her up and put her down as it suited him. And she had thrown Phil away for that?

But as she thought, sitting with her head resting on her hands, she knew she could have done no different.

On the Monday, Madge and Ria asked about Phil. Bríd didn't want to tell them too much, but their inquisitiveness wormed it out of her slowly, and at last she was forced to admit he had asked her to marry him. To her dismay they were critical of her treatment of Phil.

'He's a heart of gold, Bríd. One of the best. You'll never find a truer man.'

'That Wrenshaw's only a rich swell,' said Madge. 'He's only after one thing. Looks like he's got it, and all.'

Bríd swung angrily round. Madge looked coolly at her.

'He's got what he wants, ain't he? Just so long as you get what *you* want, Bríd.'

Bríd was angry with Madge, and with herself. At least they were honest with their lovers. What did Bríd want from Wrenshaw? She bit her lip angrily, and returned to her make-up.

That evening there was a knock on the door and the boy said, 'Gen'leman to see you, Miss Flynn.' A middle-aged, portly man with a walrus moustache, dressed in a voluminous ulster and holding a bowler hat, came in.

'Saw your show, tonight, Miss Flynn, and enjoyed it very much. Are you represented?'

Bríd was nonplussed.

'Have you got an agent, Bríd?' said Madge.

'No.'

'My card. Albert Johnson, theatrical agent. I'm interested in representing you, Miss Flynn, if it should suit.'

Bríd was thinking.

'My address is on the card. Old Compton Street. Perhaps you'd care to call tomorrow morning and we can have a chat? I see you have a successful career ahead of you.'

After he had gone, Madge said, 'I should go, Bríd. They say he's good.'

The following day Bríd went to Albert Johnson's office and talked to him, and accepted his offer. A few days later she had a letter from him saying that there was a tour going out immediately the pantomime finished and there was a place in it if she wanted it. A concert party were going round the country playing in concert halls, church halls, private drawing rooms, institutes. The tour would take her through to the summer. The money was four pounds a week, the same as she was getting for the pantomime, and she would be able to save out of it and send money home regularly.

One morning in the middle of January she woke and remembered it was Matt's birthday. He was one year old. What did little boys look like at that age? She lay in the cold dawn, the blankets pulled up to her chin, trying to picture her little boy. Was he still a baby? No, he would be a toddler by now. He would be growing quickly, and as every birthday came round he would be bigger. He would learn to talk soon. What would he sound like?

And then she thought, It's almost two years to the day since I met Harry. Was it possible? So much had happened, and only two years ago? She struggled to remember him but could not see his face; yet the sense of him, and of them together, remained as strong as ever. Where was he now? In India, on top of some mountain, she imagined, surrounded by the natives, brown-skinnned in turbans and outlandish clothes, and Harry, slim, noble and brave, the English gentleman, in his green uniform, a pistol in his hand. Was he safe? Was there a danger he might be attacked? She remembered the Great Mutiny in India only a few years before.

She composed her hands holding her locket and, closing her eyes, said a prayer for him, as she lay in bed.

Wrenshaw had gone down into Yorkshire for a week or two, to murder some grouse, as he put it; he was always vague about his movements so she didn't know when he was returning. Since the Brighton episode they had settled into a new pattern of existence, which consisted of his calling for her two or three times a week after the show, taking her to supper and then back to his rooms, where they would make love. She always insisted on returning home afterwards to Dean Street, however; it was not a long walk from the Albany to Soho. Wrenshaw had a manservant who was the soul of discretion. He had come in once when she was in bed with Wrenshaw and had conversed with Wrenshaw as if she were invisible. It was an odd sensation.

Wrenshaw did return however, they did go out to supper, and to his rooms, and did get into bed together, and then, later, when she was dressing herself, she remembered Albert Johnson and the concert party.

He was lying in bed watching her and was suddenly irritated with her. He tried to adopt his usual offhand manner.

'Well, you've had your pleasure, and now you can't wait to get home.'

'You've had your pleasure too, haven't you?'

'God, you're a selfish little madam.'

She looked down at him as she tied petticoat strings with quick, practised fingers.

'If I am, I have you to thank for it.'

'Me?' He was genuinely baffled.

246

'Isn't it what you taught me? Wasn't it your first lesson? Wasn't I supposed to break free of the constraints that bind me, or some such?'

Wrenshaw's vanity had been touched more nearly than he liked. He was afraid she had got completely out of hand. He had the uncomfortable realisation that it was she who was enjoying *him*, employing him for *her* comfort; she who gave nothing, took all, and still managed to hold aloof; an uncomfortable realisation that since the night in Brighton, their positions had become reversed.

She buttoned her jacket and was adjusting her hair in the elegant French looking glass.

'I am going to be out of London for a while when the panto closes.'

He sat up, pulling the bedclothes round him.

'For a while? How long?'

'I've been offered a job. A tour. I couldn't refuse.'

Wrenshaw was silent for a moment, giving this news some weighty consideration. He took a cigar from the box on his bedside table.

'You shouldn't leave London, Bríd, not at this stage. Think of it, aren't you going to get all sorts of offers after *Dick Whittington* here? Won't be much use if you're roaming round the provinces.'

Would she? She had no idea. Albert Johnson had recommended the tour and she had taken his word for it. Anyway it was a question of money. She couldn't afford to wait for something to turn up.

'I have a living to make.'

Wrenshaw was not satisfied. He had lit his cigar; he turned to her again.

'It won't do, Bríd. I can't have you disappearing into the countryside. I want you here. I see little enough of you as it is.'

'I have no choice,' she said briskly.

He shifted, looked round the room, and knocked some of the ash from his cigar.

'Now listen, Bríd, and I'll make a proposition to you. How much are you going to earn on this tour of yours?'

'Four pounds a week.'

'Four. Very well. I'll take a little house for you in Bayswater, I'll hire you a housekeeper and I'll pay you four pounds a week myself. How's that? Then we can be together as much as we wish. And you won't have to work.'

For a moment she was too surprised to think.

'Well, I suppose . . . and then, if anything turned up in London –'

'Oh you wouldn't need to work. We could just be together and enjoy ourselves. Go about, you know, travel. Ever been to Paris?'

247

'Paris?' She couldn't resist a sharp intake of breath. The acme of glamour.

Wrenshaw noticed her reaction and warmed to his theme. He was back in the saddle now.

'I was planning to take you to Paris once your pantomime finished. Spend a month there. There's so much I could show you. Things we could do together. Good God, to think of you working like a horse in some godforsaken provincial music hall! That's not for you, Bríd!'

He laughed, and so strong was his character and his certainty that as he said it she almost believed it too. A great new thought struck her.

'And Matt – I could bring him over too. I could have him here and bring him up!'

Break her agreement – this was the second time she had thought of it. Could she go to Ballyglin and demand her little boy?

There was silence. Wrenshaw had gone cold again. He drew on his cigar and looked up at the ceiling.

'Mmm. Don't think it's such a good idea, you know. London's no place for a little lad. Think about it, Bríd: there he is in Ireland, among the people he knows, playing with his friends in the woods and fields. Wouldn't do to bring him over really, would it? In London? Really? And then, well, he'd get under our feet terribly, wouldn't he?'

'Under our feet? You don't understand mé at all. I earn money to send back to Ireland. That's why I'm here. 'Tis the whole point. Don't you see that? If I did as you said . . . you know, if I, well, accepted your offer, well . . .'

Wrenshaw looked away expressionless and drew on his cigar. He leaned back in bed and said in a light tone, 'Well, Bríd, I don't know what to say. I thought I was making a pretty generous offer, and you seem rather offhand. I get the impression you don't care for me at all.'

He was using her again. Her back stiffened. Feeling the force of his will, her own instinctively rebelled.

''Tis better this way, John. I must make my own way.'

They stared at each other in silence.

'I must go now.'

She fitted on her bonnet and tied up the ribbon.

Why did she tolerate Wrenshaw? Was it right of her to break his bread, to drink his wine, when he knew she would never love him? Sometimes she simply shrugged and told herself that was his concern. Had she become hardened like Madge and Ria? A practiced flirt, getting a good time out of a man, leading him on and playing on his

248

sexual dependency? The picture, if true, did not please her. She knew, however, that she was like the girls in one respect: she *must* stay in charge of her life.

Sometimes she was afraid she had become, as Wrenshaw had said, terribly selfish, so concentrated on her work that everything else seemed no more than a distant sideshow she was only faintly conscious of. Why was she like this? She hadn't been like it in Ballyglin.

First, there was her last scene with Harry. Though she could never forget that day, her work was a way to dull the pain of memory; a way to justify herself to herself, to restore herself into the world.

Second, the terrible sin she had committed on the railway platform in Dublin in giving up her child. She fled from that moment still.

Third, and this was the most elusive and difficult, it was connected with her earliest thoughts and dreams, way back even before Harry had come into her life. Some nights, while she was on stage in her Dick Whittington costume, under the lights, with the orchestra playing below her and the press of people straining through the gloom towards her, she felt that this was, in some as yet unfinished way, a realisation of her vision of herself as Maeve, proud queen of old Ireland, Maeve the fearless, Maeve the noble, Maeve the resolute.

When Bríd returned at night, Isabella would be asleep, and she would tiptoe in, drop her clothes to the floor and creep into her own cold bed.

Tonight, though, as she climbed the stairs, depressed and irritated with Wrenshaw, confused in her mind, and came into the room, she realised with a slight shock that Isabella was crying. Bríd stood for a moment in the room in the darkness, unsure of what she had heard. Isabella was weeping quietly, as if she were ashamed.

'Isabella, what is it? What's happened?'

The girl did not reply.

Still uncertain, Bríd crossed to her bed. 'Isabella,' she whispered, 'are you awake?'

Isabella moved in bed, and Bríd heard a long sigh.

'Oh, Bríd.' Her voice sounded muffled.

Bríd was alarmed. She sat on the edge of the bed and rested her hand on Isabella. 'What is the matter?'

At last, after another long sigh, Isabella moved again, and then Bríd heard her voice, somehow far off and strained.

'I have a letter today, from Italy.'

'Yes?'

'Sandro – you know . . .'

Bríd knew. Sandro was her betrothed. He was the reason she was here – to earn her dowry. He was her cousin, a farmer's son, the embodiment of all the simple, uncomplicated life that Isabella represented to Bríd.

Isabella turned again in the darkness, reached out to Bríd, found her hand and held on to it.

'Everything is broken, finished. Oh, Bríd, what am I to do?'

'Finished! What do you mean?'

'Sandro can't marry. He has had a big trouble.'

'What? For God's sake, Isabella, what's happened?'

Isabella sniffed and was silent for a while, as if to collect her thoughts.

'Bríd, you know, like I tell you, his father has a farm, and Sandro, he's the youngest; we hope if I work and save money one day we can buy a farm. He's a very nice man, very good to me; we love each other very much, I never wanted another man. But now I have this letter today. First of all, their ox is killed, it slip and break its leg, and they have to kill it; and then, the pest comes on the vine. They have terrible trouble, and Sandro, he write to me and say he is going to America, and says goodbye, because is impossible we should be married now.'

Her speech broke down into sobs.

Bríd sat in the darkness holding Isabella's hand. Her own problems shrank to insignificance; she was strong, she would survive anyway, but Isabella had lived for Sandro, working and saving her little savings. She squeezed the hand, trying to think of some word of comfort which might be adequate to Isabella's grief.

'Oh, Bríd, what shall become of me now? I can never go back to Italy, I will never see Sandro again, I must stay always here in London . . .'

'Well, maybe Sandro would take you to America – would you go with him?'

'He already gone to America.'

'Isabella, I'm so sorry.'

It was inadequate, yet what else was there to say? She sat in the darkness holding Isabella's hand, thinking of the injustice of life. She would never see the man she loved again. Her whole life to live through, knowing that. Would she get another husband? Who knew? And in a foreign land, where she barely spoke the language?

Bríd bent over and clasped Isabella to her.

'Isabella, whatever happens, I will be your friend, never forget it.'

The run of *Dick Whittington* came to an end. Bríd said goodbye to

Madge and Ria, packed up her Irish colleen costume and left the Wellington.

The following afternoon, she said farewell to Isabella. They pledged eternal friendship. She wanted to say goodbye to the Maestro as well, and stood a long time outside his door, plucking up her courage to knock.

When at last she did, he was formal, distant; she felt she had never restored herself in his eyes, had let him down. He shook her hand and wished her well.

Then she was sitting in a cab, a trunk under her feet, on her way to King's Cross station to begin her tour with the concert troupe.

Chapter Thirty-Two

Before the concert tour was over, she received a letter from Albert Johnson; she was booked for a further three months of engagements in a variety of provincial music halls, and before that was over, there was an engagement in Edinburgh to look forward to. She queried nothing, took everything he sent, and went from job to job, feeling she had been in this business half a lifetime.

One bright May morning just after her twenty-first birthday, Bríd arrived in London early after travelling down by the night train. Her engagement was over, and she said goodbye on the railway platform to two colleagues she had travelled with, each in a hurry to dash off to their own home. Bríd took a cab and went to the lodgings in Buckingham Street which Albert Johnson had arranged for her. Other floors were taken by people in the theatrical profession. Mrs Walters, a widow who lived in the basement, cleaned and took laundry, cooked and supplied hot water in the morning, and was used to their late hours and free and easy ways.

Bríd's front room faced west and got the sun in the afternoon; it had a high ceiling with mouldings, and was comfortably if shabbily furnished. There was a marble fireplace with a large looking glass over it, an old Persian carpet, and several leather chairs and a sofa. Three long windows opened on a balcony over a quiet little street running down to the river. Standing on the balcony, as she did that morning, Bríd could see the multitude of little boats, some with red sails, others with tall smokestacks puffing black smoke.

Albert Johnson had fixed up an engagement for Bríd at the Oxford Music Hall, and she enjoyed a small triumph when she went in through that same stage door which she had once approached with such trepidation and uncertainty, and where she had once undergone such a humiliating interview. She shared a dressing room with another woman and came on later in the show; she had moved up into the second half.

One evening as she was changing there was a knock at the door and before she could answer it flew open and there was a mass of golden curls.

'Bríd!'

'Madge!'

Bríd leaped up as Madge flew into the room and into her arms. Madge the petite chatterbox, Madge the flighty, flirty, scatter-brained minx; Madge the pleasure-loving, amoral, sexy cockney.

Bríd clasped her tightly.

'Madge, oh, 'tis grand to see you! And you're looking well.'

She stood back and admired Madge's clothes, her billowing silk skirt and smart velvet jacket, and her pert bonnet with its lace frills. Madge perched herself on a chair and tapped her parasol against her dainty boot.

'Well, a person wouldn't say no to a drink, Bríd.'

'I have some port here, Madge.'

'Good. My doctor's ordered me to take plenty of port for my constitution. He says I'm anaemic.'

She shrieked with laughter as Bríd handed her a glass.

'Absent friends,' said Madge, draining her glass and holding it out for a refill.

'How's Ria?' Bríd asked as she poured.

'She's dead,' Madge said shortly. 'Consumption.'

'Oh, no!' Bríd said softly. 'Poor Ria. What a tragedy! When did she die?'

'Just over a year ago.' Madge's tone was brusque. She stared into her glass for a second, unwilling to discuss it. 'I knew she couldn't last. It was obvious.' She paused. Neither could face the other, and they sat in silence. 'Yeh, well. That's life, ain't it?'

Bríd at last tried to break the mood. 'Madge, dear, you're looking so well. You must be in love.'

'In love!' Madge laughed. 'Are you kidding? I'm in work! That's why I'm looking so well. If I am well; oh, another glass of port, dear, and I'll be myself again.'

Bríd refilled their glasses and the atmosphere lightened.

'What's the job?'

'New play: *All Change* – a comedy. I haven't told you, have I? I've given up the halls. Straight acting now, dear. And it's a stunning part: chance of a lifetime. Start rehearsals in a couple of weeks.'

She finished the port and then, as she lowered her glass, looked across at Bríd. A thought had struck her.

'You ever fancied acting?'

'Often. But I'm afraid I'll be touring for ever, hammering out the same old songs night after night.'

'Tell you what, Bríd, I know for a fact there's a part in this they haven't cast yet and they're looking for someone who can sing. Get your agent to put you up for it.' She thought for a moment, looking shrewdly at Bríd. 'You'd be ideal, with your voice. It's at the Royalty. Henry Burton's written it.'

Bríd was very interested. Ever since the night she'd seen W. G. Ross and his sensational performance of 'Sam Hall', the seed of an ambition had lain in her mind. Acting offered so much more scope than a concert platform. This could be a way forward for her. She had to give it a try.

Looking round the dressing room, Madge noticed a card stuck in the rim of the mirror on the dressing table. She plucked it out.

'Hullo, what's this?'

It was John Wrenshaw's visiting card. Madge turned it over. On the back was written 'See you on Friday'.

Madge looked up at Bríd, who seemed flustered.

'The bad penny shows up again.'

Bríd looked away. 'He called last week.'

'And you could deny him nothing,' Madge said with a knowing leer.

Bríd nodded, pained, remembering how the door had opened and he'd been standing there in evening dress, a cigarette in his hand, looking at her. After eighteen months he could still open a door and just stroll back into her life. She could not get past him. For all her brave talk when she was with him, she could not actually bring herself to say no.

Without looking at Madge, Bríd started tidying her dressing table and hanging up her costumes.

'He's no good, Bríd, I told you before. He'll never be any good to you. Why do you let him go on pestering you? Tell him to sling his hook.'

Bríd said nothing. Madge watched her, holding her empty glass in one hand, leaning on the dressing table.

'I know. He's got plenty of money and a big cock, and you just can't refuse –'

Bríd looked round sharply. Madge stared evenly at her.

'Well, anything else? Did I leave anything out?'

'Madge!'

She had been stung. But then – wasn't it true? She wouldn't have put it that way, but . . .

'You've got to make your own way. And you've got to keep your head. Or you'll end up in the gutter.'

'I know you mean well, but you shouldn't talk like that. Not even joking. It's not right.'

'But it's true.'

'No, it's not true!'

Yet she couldn't tell what the truth was.

Madge stood up and tied up the ribbon of her bonnet.

'It's your funeral. Anyway, get your agent to put you up for *All Change*. Might suit you, and it'd be fun working together.'

Bríd's turn came at last. She went down the corridor, through a door and on to the stage. There were three men, but she only noticed one of them, a man of about forty, very slim, with a mane of hair falling on either side of his bony face. He had strong eyebrows, which slanted downwards to either side, and a sharp nose. It was a striking face, once seen, never forgotten. This was Mr Henry Burton.

He came towards her immediately, took her hand and looked into her face, studying her closely.

'Miss Flynn, so glad you could come,' he said in a soft, fervent manner. 'We've invited you because we need someone who can sing really well, and Madge has told me about you. Have you done much acting?'

Now that she was here and had these men before her, a lot of her trepidation fell away. She stood on the stage, tall, sure of herself.

'I was the principal boy in a panto at the Wellington Theatre in the Waterloo Road once: Dick Whittington.'

The men looked at one another thoughtfully.

'The Wellington – a baptism by fire, truly.'

Burton became brisk.

'Now, would you like to read a bit for us, Miss Flynn? It's a new play of mine about a young fellow called Tom, who is a stockbroker and borrows money to gamble on the stock exchange. There are two young ladies in his life: a flighty one – a blonde, played by Madge, whom he is trying to impress – that's why he's gambling; and then there's another, Ethel, more serious. It's not such a showy part, I'm afraid; the blonde gets all the laughs, but Ethel gets him in the end. Now, at the end of the third act, young Tom hears Ethel singing at a party, and he realises she's the one for him, so the song's very important. It's the turning point of the whole story, do you see? He realises she's the one he really loves, and all the gambling and showing off isn't worth the candle. We'd like to hear you read a bit from the script.'

255

Burton handed her some crumpled sheets of handwritten paper. She spent some moments trying to make sense of them.

'Can you make out the scrawl? I'll read Tom.'

Bríd held up her hands. 'Mr Burton, you'll just have to give me a minute to look through the lines.'

'Take as long as you like. Wander around, feel free to use the stage. No hurry.'

Bríd walked about the stage, staring at the words. The handwriting was a blur to her and she could make no sense of the dramatic scene, who was who, and what the point of it was. These three strange men, the story of the play, the characters: she was in a daze. Nothing on the page made sense to her. She knew it had been a mistake to come.

Feeling suicidal, she said, 'I'm ready, Mr Burton.'

Burton loved to act, and even here on this morning he put as much into his reading as if it had been a first night. Bríd was uncomfortably aware of his enthusiasm as she groped for the sense of her lines, mispronouncing words, giving a wrong emphasis, losing her place in the script. She grasped the sheets in her hands, struggling to get through the lines. She'd look up and see him, his head a little bowed, peering intently at her from under his bushy eyebrows. He was nodding, with a humorous glint in his eye, enjoying the fun of playing a part.

She felt as if she had been hauled out of the sea after nearly drowning, gasping for breath, not knowing where she was, while around her strangers were smiling and cheering her up, making meaningless sounds of encouragement.

'I'm sorry, gentlemen, I'm only wasting your time. You must excuse me.'

She thrust the sheets into Burton's hands, gathered up her bonnet and gloves, and turned to go.

It was an intense embarrassment. At the Wellington, she had known where she was, and exactly what to do. Here, she simply appeared as a fumbling amateur. She hurried back along the corridor and through the stage door.

A few yards down the street Burton caught up with her and took her arm.

'Miss Flynn, not so fast! What have we done to offend you? I do apologise, whatever it is. Come back, do, I beg you.'

'Mr Burton, it was all a mistake; I apologise for wasting your time. Goodbye.'

She turned to go again.

'Miss Flynn, whatever is the matter?'

'Please don't mock me.'

'Mock you? I really don't understand. I insist that you come back. There has been a misunderstanding.'

She stopped, and suddenly felt deflated.

'Oh, there's certainly been a misunderstanding: me thinking I could act on the stage.'

He smiled into her face, and on an impulse took hold of her and held her for a moment at arm's length.

'Miss Flynn, it's a misunderstanding we can correct, believe me.'

She looked into his humorous, twinkling eyes.

'I don't understand.'

He led her back into the theatre, and they picked up the sheets and began again.

Later, as she was about to leave, Burton said,

'This is a cockney play, the characters are all Londoners. You'd have no trouble losing your brogue, I take it?'

'Tell me what you want me to do, and I'll do it.'

He smiled.

'We'll let you know in a day or two, Miss Flynn. Thank you for coming.'

Chapter Thirty-Three

If they offered her the part? She felt dizzy. She would kill anyone who stood in her way. Yet she told herself that probably nothing would come of it.

Wrenshaw called for her after the show on Friday. He was exactly the same, and she fell back into the same routine with him. Madge had been right. What was it? Throughout the months on tour Bríd had not been near a man, hadn't even missed it, yet as soon as Wrenshaw came near her, the shape, the height, the feel of him, her arm in his as they walked through the night streets – she couldn't explain what it was. She couldn't understand his hold over her. His smell? The glint in his eye? She didn't know. She didn't love him; yet she wanted him; wanted him holding her, making love to her.

In the morning, by day, away from him, she despised herself for it. He was worthless, she knew. Why didn't she just tell him to go away? However aloof she might be towards him, she knew that she would not tell him to go away, though, not tonight or tomorrow, nor at any other time he chose to come. They would have supper somewhere, he would be airy, witty, urbane, would pay for the supper, and then they would walk back to her lodgings and he would make love to her with effortless power, would spread her all over her own bed, helpless. Then he would go home.

Why didn't she just tell him to go away?

They had eaten supper and were walking back towards Buckingham Street, and were passing the coffee stall in Leicester Square where she had met him that autumn night. It looked curiously inviting, a little beacon of light in the darkness, illuminating the faces of a group of poor folk, some chatting to each other, others silently staring into the darkness as they stood clutching their cups.

They were just walking past when Bríd recognised a shabby, hunched little man with his hat pulled down over his eyes, and his collar turned up. There was something about his back and the set of his shoulders, and as they passed she looked briefly into his face.

'Maestro!'

He looked round abruptly. He was older, his face cast into lines of poverty and illness. He recognised her. For a moment they looked into each other's eyes, then he turned from her, put his cup back on the stall and began to walk away.

Bríd looked after him in amazement. 'Maestro!'

He walked on. Bríd broke free from Wrenshaw and ran after him.

'Maestro! Don't you recognise me? It's Bríd – your Bríd, who you were so kind to. Don't you remember?'

He looked into her face for a moment, nodded and said, 'Hello, Bríd', and then walked on.

'Maestro, wait, don't walk away! Wait!'

She caught him by the elbow and pulled him round to look at her.

'Maestro, I'm so glad to see you. I felt so bad when we said goodbye without making friends again. Won't you forgive me now?'

As she spoke, she was peering intently into his face, which seemed ill and old. He was silent.

'Are you living in Dean Street still?'

At last he spoke, in a hoarse voice. 'No, I'm not in Dean Street now.'

'Well, where do you live now? Somewhere nice?'

Again he was silent, the replied, 'I manage, Bríd, don't worry.'

He turned to go. Bríd again took him by the arm.

'Maestro, I can't let you go. You must come with us – we're just going back to my place. Come along and have a bit of supper.'

He allowed himself to be led back to where Wrenshaw was waiting.

'John, I must tell you, this is the kindest man in the world. He was so good to me, he taught me everything I know. Maestro Pertinelli, this is Sir John Wrenshaw.'

'Nice to meet you, old fellow.'

Wrenshaw was puzzled by this figure.

They got back to Buckingham Street and went up into her rooms.

'Glass of port, Maestro? John, help him off with his coat.'

Reluctantly Wrenshaw helped Pertinelli off with the frayed old coat he was wearing.

'I can't tell you how glad I am to see you again. I've thought about you so often, and I've felt so bad about the way we quarrelled. Have you forgiven me? John, pour the Maestro a glass of port. You must be hungry, I'm sure.'

She went down to Mrs Walters's kitchen and came back with some plates of cold meat, cheese and a bottle of pickles.

259

'It's all I could find at this hour, Maestro, but you're welcome anyway. Sit down.'

They sat round the table, and she helped him to the cold supper. The port was poured, and Bríd raised her glass to her old teacher.

'Come on, Maestro, tuck in now. Are you hungry?'

The old man made a deprecating gesture. 'Very kind of you to invite me, Bríd. I maybe take a little.'

'And drink up your port. Here's to you.'

They clinked glasses.

As he ate, Bríd watched the old man closely. He seemed smaller than she remembered, shrivelled, and his face looked worn and ill. As the port worked in him, hunger came, and he began to eat ravenously. Bríd was pleased. He had always eaten sparingly when she had known him.

'It's not much to offer you; of course I wasn't expecting you, or I'd have got you something special. I must tell you, John, Maestro Pertinelli is the best music teacher in London, he taught me everything. It was because of him I decided to be a singer.'

Wrenshaw looked with disbelief at this spectacle. In the twinkling of an eye she had whisked this old ragamuffin off the street and was fawning on him here in their sitting room, when he had been thinking of her bed next door. He was prepared to play along with her game for a while, but not for long.

As the supper progressed, she questioned Pertinelli about his life and what he was up to, but he was evasive; he wouldn't tell her where he was living, or whether he was still teaching.

When they had finished, she looked at the clock on the mantelpiece. It was nearly two o'clock.

'If you like, you could stay with us tonight, save you the trouble of going home.'

Wrenshaw made faces at her across the table, but she ignored it.

'I've got a spare bed. It's yours. You look tired. You don't want to have to drag yourself across London at this time of night.'

She took him to see her spare room. There was a bed in it, never used, and covered with clothes. She made it up, and the old man, although he protested, accepted her offer.

When they were alone together, Wrenshaw confronted her in a whisper.

'What are you doing, dragging that old tramp back here? He'll be gone in the morning, and take the spoons with him.'

'You have no idea. That man is a musician, he has the soul of an artist. He lives and breathes music. I can never repay him everything I owe him.'

260

Wrenshaw was taking off his clothes and getting into bed.

'Well, get rid of him in the morning, there's a dear. He makes the place smell.'

They were falling asleep when she began to hear groans and retching noises. In a moment she was out of bed and wrapping a robe round herself, lit a candle.

'Maestro, are you unwell?'

The noises continued. She opened the door and looked in. The old man had been sick on the floor and was lying in bed, his head thrown back on his pillow, his mouth open, looking like a corpse.

'Oh, my God!' She turned and threw open her own bedroom door. 'John! John! Run for a doctor. He's ill!'

Wrenshaw stirred in bed.

'John! For mercy's sake, don't lose a minute! Run for a doctor. He's very ill.'

Wrenshaw tumbled out of bed, into some of his clothes, and went out.

Bríd meanwhile had returned to the old man. He lay with his eyes closed, his face sunken with age, his thin hair scattered across his brow and bathed in sweat. She took the corner of his sheet and wiped his face.

'Oh mother of God, whatever are we going to do?'

Seeing the mess on the floor and down the side of the bed, she dashed down into the basement for a bucket and some water, and in a few minutes she was cleaning the carpet and wiping the bedding as best she could. Some disinfectant in the water helped to kill the smell of vomit.

The old man had gone off into a light doze, though he sometimes stirred. Bríd sat by him until Wrenshaw returned with a doctor. Mrs Walters knocked on the door, wrapped in a shawl, her hair in papers under a night cap. When Bríd explained what had happened, she went down to make a cup of tea.

The doctor was alone with the old man for a while. When he came out, he sat with Bríd and Wrenshaw in the sitting room.

'It's very simple,' he said. 'He hadn't eaten for several days. When he had supper with you, it was the first meal he'd had. His stomach couldn't take so much heavy food at once, and he brought it all up again.'

'Hadn't eaten for days?'

'He was starving. What have you been doing to him?'

'He's an old friend who I hadn't seen for a long time. We met him by chance this evening.'

'Well, he'll need nursing for weeks. Light food at first – porridge, cups of tea, broths. Build him up very gently. I'll call in again tomorrow.'

After he had gone, Bríd looked in to the Maestro's room again. The old man was asleep. She and Wrenshaw returned to their own bed.

During the next few days she spent all her free time nursing the old man. She was in and out of his room throughout the day with bowls of broth and cups of tea. She changed his bedding. He slept much of the time, but as the days passed, his face began to take on some colour and his cheeks to fill out. He felt stronger, though he was too weak to get out of bed.

As she sat by his bed, she slowly got his story out of him, how his pupils had fallen off one by one until he had none left, then how the restaurant had been sold and the new owner had wanted his apartment, and he had moved out into a room nearby, and how his savings had slowly dwindled until he had nothing left, and could see nothing before him but the workhouse. His piano had long since been sold. As he told her this, his eyes filled with tears, and she sat holding his hand and weeping too, to see this old man so helpless and so humiliated by his poverty.

She went to his lodgings to collect his things. It was a shabby little room in Soho, and there was almost nothing to carry, but to her astonishment, she found he had still kept the little Irish harp her mother had bequeathed to her.

She carried it back to Buckingham Street, together with his music books and the few other things he still possessed.

'I can't tell you, Maestro, how pleased I am to see my harp again. I brought it with me when I first came from Ireland, the only thing I brought, and now I have it again.'

The Maestro smiled at her.

'I never could bring myself to sell it. Somehow I think, One day, one day, Bríd will come for it.'

It was summer weather; the air was warm and soft. The window was open, and as she sat talking to the old man each day, Bríd would look out at the house backs and the slate roofs, and above them the blue sky, light and high. The air was still, the curtains would hardly move, and the weather gave a feeling of expansiveness and relaxation.

Wrenshaw had gone down into the country for a few days, leaving the two of them alone together in the flat. As the old man sat up in bed one morning, propped up on pillows, he was looking down, and his hands were playing with the edge of the sheet.

'Bríd, I'm worried.'

'What about?'

I'm afraid, maybe Sir John, he stays away on my account.'

'He's gone to the races.'

'*Sí*, I know; still, I'm afraid he does not like me very much. Bríd, I'm in your way. I got no right to ask you to look after me like this. I spoil your fun.'

'You were very good to me when I needed help. Don't say any more.'

'You are a young woman, Bríd, you got Sir John, I'm in the way.'

Mrs Walters knocked at the door.

'There's a telegram for you, Miss Flynn.'

The Royalty Theatre were offering her the part of Ethel in *All Change* at ten pounds a week, her costumes to be found. A script was in the post.

'Bríd, what did I always say? You will be a great actress one day.'

She looked into the old man's face, thinking, holding the telegram in her hand, looking down at it, and into his face again.

She went out to the post office and wired her acceptance of the part.

Chapter Thirty-Four

Next day Bríd received a letter from the Royalty containing the script. It consisted of a handwritten copy of her own lines, each speech preceded by half a line of the previous speech. Only Burton had the complete text.

Things between her and Wrenshaw seemed to be going on just as before. He made no explanations, he never apologised, he simply came and took her, and afterwards when he had gone, she racked her brains trying to discover what it was that made her yield to him so passively.

Ten days later she went to the Royalty to begin rehearsals. It was only on the first day of rehearsals, when the cast sat round in a circle reading from their parts, that Bríd heard the play complete. Bríd's Irish accent stood out among the others and she felt conscious of it every time she spoke. They had three weeks to get the play on and Burton sat at the front of the stage every morning in a long overcoat and a square bowler hat, directing the actors with infinite care and attention to detail. He had written the play, he had created the characters, and he knew how every part should be played. Sometimes, as they struggled with their roles, they were intimidated by this ability to demonstrate every character.

Bríd had difficulty with her accent. She had promised she would get a London accent for the part, and she felt that everyone would be watching her and wondering why Burton had given the part to an Irish girl.

Rehearsals finished at two, and the actors had the afternoon free to study their lines. Burton would stay behind, coaxing Bríd into the tight and harsh English vowels, so foreign to her ear.

'I'd be better with a pebble in my mouth.'

Even studying Italian songs with the Maestro in the old days had been no help. Their pure, open vowels were a world away from the

264

tortuous English sounds. In the music hall there had never been any problem; artistes came from all over the world and no one gave it a thought. But here in the theatre suddenly everything was so precise.

At the end of the first week she had become nervous and unsure how it would all turn out. She had made no headway with her English accent, which remained as awkward and stubborn as ever. There seemed to be no way into it for her.

There was much, too, in the play to absorb: so many moments where some nuance or phrasing was required that she could dimly perceive but could not as yet express.

Wrenshaw called for her after rehearsals that Saturday afternoon. It was a bright, hot summer day. They set off walking in a westerly direction through Soho and across Regent Street, heading for the park. She had her script in her reticule and Wrenshaw was going to hear her through her lines.

They had walked through Hanover Square and were just passing St George's Church when Wrenshaw said,

'There's a wedding on. Shall we wait and see the bride? Can you resist a wedding, Bríd? They say no woman can.'

They stood arm in arm in the summer sunshine across the road from the church. It was a society wedding and about to end, by the look of it, for several carriages were drawing up before the church. Bríd noticed the crests on their doors, and was about to remark that there was something familiar about them, when Wrenshaw called,

'They're coming out!'

Crowds were assembled on the steps, the doors thrown open. They could hear the organ playing the wedding march, and the bridal pair came out, blinking in the sunshine, stopping at the top of the steps beneath the tall columns of the church.

The blood drained from her limbs. It was Harry. Who was the woman? She looked familiar. Bríd had seen them dancing together at the ball in Castle Leighton.

The couple remained standing on the steps. There were a few cheers, and people were gathering around them.

'I must go,' Bríd said hoarsely and turned. Wrenshaw held her in a rigid grip. She looked quickly into his face. He seemed unconcerned.

'No hurry, Bríd; let's enjoy the spectacle.'

She couldn't move. He held her firm.

'Let me go.'

'No, Bríd, stay and watch the show.'

'I must go!'

'No, my dear, you must stay until the end; you must look, I say.'

265

Harry was smiling, the bride was smiling; Harry now kissed the bride, and the people about them cheered. They came down the steps and he handed his bride into the open carriage. Bríd now recognised Liam on the box. The bride was laughing and saying something, and then threw her bouquet among the bridesmaids. There was laughter and cheers. Liam whipped up the horses, and they pulled out into the street.

Wrenshaw held her so hard that she couldn't move. The carriage was driving up and past them. Harry turned back from waving, and was just settling the bride's dress round her in the carriage. He glanced up and saw Bríd with Wrenshaw.

Wrenshaw waved genially and called, 'Bon voyage!'

She had never seen such a look of surprise on anyone's face as she saw then on Harry's.

The coach rattled past.

She shook herself free, but in any case Wrenshaw had released her. She could hardly see for the blood pounding in her face, her ears, her brain.

'You did this on purpose.'

He was cool. 'You needed to know, my dear.'

'It was cruel.'

'It was the truth. Now you will be able to lay your head on your pillow in peace.'

'Oh, God, what a shock I've had! How could you do that?'

'Come on, let's take a boat out on the Serpentine. It's a lovely afternoon.'

He took her arm again and was about to walk on. She pulled herself free.

'You could have told me; could have broken the news gently. To bring me here like this, to lead me on, and never to say – Oh, you are heartless!'

'As I said a long time ago, I took you for a woman of character. Now you will be able to put Harry Leighton behind you for good. And not before time.'

'That's my affair.'

'And mine. Do you think I couldn't tell you were still pining for him? Brace yourself, you'll be the better for it.'

''Twas a mean trick to play.'

She was shaking with rage against Wrenshaw and shock from seeing Harry. Her mind was a cloud of memories, as if someone had shouted in a cave and a thousand bats were shrieking and flittering about her head.

*

266

Later Wrenshaw told her he had been to see Harry. Harry had told him about his time in India, in Rawalpindi, about expeditions to the Afghan frontier and skirmishes with wild mountain tribes, when they had had to fight their way to safety; about tiger hunts, boar hunts and pig sticking; about polo matches. She remembered how once he had said to her, 'I was always happiest on a horse anyway.' She drank in Wrenshaw's words, pressed him, insisted on every scrap he could remember. Wrenshaw, slightly ashamed of the shock he had caused her, obliged. Then he told her that there was some talk that Harry might be offered a government job in India and she tried to picture him all those thousands of miles away, married and soon perhaps to become a father, and building a life with his family in that strange new land.

She could not bear Wrenshaw to touch her, and after he had gone, in the utter desolation of the night, she stared up into the darkness and tried to take a grip on herself. She would never love a man the way she had loved Harry, and she wept helplessly in the darkness as she allowed herself to remember for a few moments the time they had been together. Yet she had too much strength, too much control of herself to let herself just go to pieces. She had to take command, to get herself up and force herself along the path she had chosen, whatever the cost.

She determined from that moment to put everything else aside, everything, Harry, Wrenshaw and all, and think of nothing but her work. She would do a London accent that would be indistinguishable from the real thing.

The following Monday she was back at work and a frenzy of anxiety swept through her as she watched the other actors and saw how they were polishing their performances, beginning to bring up a professional gloss, while her own performance was still in pieces.

She placed herself entirely in Burton's hands. Together they worked and she became a perfect mimic, copying his every gesture as he acted out her part, copying every nuance as he repeated her lines.

Bríd thought of nothing but this play. So great was her concentration that she mixed very little with the other actors. When they went round to the public house after rehearsals, she remained behind with Burton or, if he was elsewhere, working alone on the empty stage. The others found her a strange woman, difficult to get on with, rather reserved, with her mind entirely on her work. They would invite her to go out for a drink but she refused.

'Come on, Bríd, you mustn't overdo it. Give the old brain-box time to digest it all. Useless to force it.'

It was what Wrenshaw had said.

'It's all very well for you,' she would say, 'but I haven't the time. There's so much for me to learn.'

One afternoon Wrenshaw came along to find her, and she astonished herself when she told him she was staying behind to work. He seemed quite good-humoured about it and went off to the pub with Madge and the other actors.

One consequence of Bríd's efforts, which she had not foreseen, was that she made an enemy of Madge. When she had accepted the engagement, Madge had been assured she had the best part, the showy part, the part that got all the laughs. She was funny and pert; she knew how to win an audience's heart with a smile and a saucy laugh.

However, Bríd was now bringing to the part of Ethel a seriousness and a depth of feeling that threatened to throw her into the shade. At first Madge made light of it. She thought that once they had the audience in front of them, her expertise would show through and she'd have them eating out of her hand. But as she watched Bríd in rehearsals, she was irritated by the painful care with which she memorised every move, every step, every turn of the head, and moreover Bríd was effectively monopolising the actor playing Tom in order to extract every last ounce from their scenes together. Seeing all this, Madge became bitter and vindictive.

She went to Burton.

'This is supposed to be a comedy. She's turning it into a blooming tragedy, Henry!'

'Don't worry, Madge dear, I'll take care of that. Leave everything to me. You have nothing to worry about. You're going to be a sensation with the public, have no fear.'

Madge was not satisfied. Sometimes, during rehearsals, Bríd could hear malicious remarks coming from the darkness of the auditorium:

'Thinks she's Goneril.'

Or: 'Nose a little higher, dear.'

Or: 'Where *did* she get those boots?'

Bríd heard these remarks, and if she didn't always catch the words, she recognised the tone. She bit her lip and kept silent. Burton took a tolerant line. He would turn and say in a breezy fashion, 'Hush, everybody.'

Bríd was bitterly conscious of Madge's enmity and heard every taunt as if it were a lash. For a long time she simply could not understand it; she was only too aware of Madge's skill and personable qualities as a comedienne; she was conscious of her own awkwardness on stage and the strain of listening continuously for any telltale signs of County Roscommon in her accent. In the end it wasn't even the accent; a lilt, an intonation, a phrasing, anything

268

might give her away. She told Burton she wanted to be perfect. Nothing less would do. In the face of this, Madge's hostility was incomprehensible to her.

One morning as she was working on stage, she heard from the darkness of the auditorium Madge's voice in a stage whisper:

'Sure and begorrah!'

Followed by a fit of suppressed giggles.

Something in Bríd snapped and before she could think she marched down to the front of the stage, jumped down into the auditorium, walked quickly up to where Madge was sitting with three others and seized her by the ear. She tugged her out of her seat and down the aisle to where Burton had turned to watch.

'Mr Burton, I must request there is silence while we are rehearsing.'

She contemptuously let Madge go with a shove.

'You stuck-up Irish cow, I'll show you!'

Madge went for Bríd, but Bríd pushed her back. She was the taller of the two and had a longer reach.

'Girls, girls!' shouted Burton. 'That'll do! Come! Now, Madge, Bríd, an end to this! Madge, apologise for your nasty remarks. Bríd, apologise for hurting Madge's ear.'

The others were watching with open mouths.

'You vicious cow, I'll get you for this!' said Madge, breathing hard.

'Mr Burton,' said Bríd, her hands on her hips, looking very gravely at him, 'it's easy for her. She has the experience, I haven't. I have to get this part right and it's unprofessional of her to make fun of me while I'm working. You shouldn't allow it.'

Burton was taken aback by her high-handed manner. Madge burst into tears.

'It was only a bit of fun, honestly! Why does she have to take everything so blooming seriously? This isn't Shakespeare, for Gawd's sake. It's meant to be a comedy.'

'Madge, don't worry. The play's going to be fine, it's going to be a success, and you'll be a big hit. Trust me.' He took her in his arms and comforted her.

Bríd watched them with a dark look on her face.

'I don't interfere with her. Why can't she leave me alone?'

'Take a break, Bríd, everything's fine,' said Burton, looking over Madge's shoulder with a warning look in his eye.

The tension had passed but the friendship between the two girls was irretrievably destroyed. They could not speak to each other. Burton was very upset by this. It was essential for the health of any theatrical company, and for the success of the play, that everyone should be friends and should work together as a team. It was

269

fortunate for him that Bríd and Madge were seldom on stage together. He was unsure in his mind about Bríd, and couldn't decide whether it had been a good thing to engage her. She was an unsettling influence, it seemed, though he put it down to her worry about getting her part and her accent right, and he hoped everyone would drop their hostility and suspicion in the general excitement and tension of a first night.

Burton could also see Madge's point of view. Bríd was bringing a heavy, serious note to her character, which was justified to a certain extent by her contrast with Madge's feather-brained blonde, but sometimes he wondered whether Madge wasn't right, and Bríd was in danger of dragging the whole play down with a note of gloom. At the same time, some instinct told him Bríd was on the right lines.

By the time the first night came, Burton was as nervous as any of them.

In the event, his instinct was confirmed. Madge was brilliant, looked pretty, got all her laughs and had the audience eating out of her hand by the end of her first scene on stage. Bríd, by contrast, began quietly, not making any great impact on the audience, so that in her first scene with Tom she seemed a rather shadowy figure and the audience had no very clear idea what she was doing there.

Slowly, as the evening progressed, they became aware of her in spite of themselves. Bríd had the ability to be still on stage. It was one of her strengths. And what Madge had thought was a heavy and serious quality now appeared as intense sincerity. She stood, tall, still, in her dark dress and seemed to radiate an inner glow; her love for Tom, which had to be expressed in an oblique fashion because of Ethel's shyness, shone through to the audience and gave her an aching, poignant quality.

The song, at the climax to Act III, the moment in the play when Ethel feels free to express the strength of her love for Tom and the moment when Tom, so struck by her singing, at last realises that it is her he really loves, contained all this inner intensity, but now raised to a new level with the aid of music. Her voice soared through the auditorium and the audience was stunned. As they left the theatre afterwards, they could talk of nothing but Bríd's performance.

After the curtain had come down, she sat in her dressing room, ill with relief. When Burton came to congratulate her, she looked at him wanly.

'Did I get the accent right?'

He sat down close to her and took her hand in his.

'Bríd, my dear, you were exceptional. I never saw a debut like it.

270

Exceptional! I hardly know what to say. I never saw a performance of such power and intensity.'

'But did I get the accent right, Mr Burton?'

'Bríd, you were a born Londoner. I'd have sworn you'd lived here all your life.'

'That's good then.'

She burst into tears.

'Bríd, what's the matter? What are you crying for? You've just given the performance of a lifetime. You should be happy.'

'Oh, I'm happy, Mr Burton, I'm happy,' she sobbed, her voice muffled in her hands.

Chapter Thirty-Five

Burton threw a party on stage for everyone and there were numerous guests. Wrenshaw had come, but his natural detachment, his aloof manner, prevented him from effusive expressions of praise for her performance. Bríd, in her intense, wrought-up state, needed some warmth in return. She felt distant from him; the work, the concentration, the excitement, the whole backstage atmosphere, intruded between them. And she could not get over the shock of seeing Harry and his bride. It had set up a barrier between her and Wrenshaw.

Everyone else was crowding round, heaping praise on her, until her head swam with it. They seemed to run out of superlatives to describe her acting and singing, and she knew it had all been worth it and she was well and truly launched as an actress. From now on she could look forward with confidence to making a career. The play was going to run for months; she would be making plenty of money. On this wave of optimism and elation, she didn't mind Wrenshaw's coolness, and put it down to his typically English manner.

During the party she could see Madge surrounded by her friends and admirers; the hostility between them was a weight on her, and she would have liked to get back to their old friendship. But Madge would not catch her eye, and Bríd would not make a first move.

Wrenshaw had become friends with many of the actors during the rehearsals. On several occasions he'd come along to collect Bríd and when she'd been too busy he had gone to the pub with the others. He was talking to Madge now. Of course he knew nothing of Bríd's row with her. Why should he? Bríd had never bothered him with it. But then she'd spent very little time with him over the last two weeks.

It was a good party; there was plenty to eat and champagne was constantly pouring into her glass. Still, as the night wore on, the relief and exhilaration began to deflate and she felt tired and curiously alone. She looked about for Wrenshaw, but couldn't see him. No one knew where he was. Puzzled, but more tired, she suddenly didn't care anyway, didn't want to do anything but go home to bed.

She made her way back to her dressing room, exhausted, scarcely seeing where she was going. As she was passing Madge's dressing room she heard noises, scuffles, and Madge's voice, and from the sounds it could be only one thing: Madge was making love. Embarrassed by that sound, Bríd was about to hurry on to her own room when she heard Madge's voice, clearly excited in the sexual act, moan 'John' several times, as the heaving and sighing increased. Bríd stood still in the corridor, her face hot with amazement and shock.

The rocking and jolting of Madge's old chaise longue, her sighs and moans, and then again, 'Oh, John'; Bríd could hear it all. She stood, a cold shiver running through her body, and yet for a moment horribly fascinated.

The sounds intensified. They were coming to a climax. Bríd gathered her scattered wits, turned and hurried to her dressing room. She snatched up her shawl, threw it round her, pinned on her hat and hurried from the theatre.

She walked quickly through the streets. Sh couldn't believe what she had just heard; her mind would not accept it. Yet it had happened. Again and again, that horrid moment returned in her imagination, again and again she heard Madge's voice in that most intimate moment. Bríd turned her head from side to side as if she might shake off the memory. That word, pronounced like that, at that moment of extreme revelation and abandon. Wrenshaw on Madge's lips, Wrenshaw on Madge, in Madge, Wrenshaw – she couldn't think it, only hurry on.

She reached Buckingham Street and ran up into her room, throwing down her things, and went into her bedroom. The thought of sleep was impossible. She turned back into her sitting room. The room was silent. It was nearly three in the morning. She brought the candle to the table and sat down. The room seemed stark and bare, disturbed in the stillness of the night. She felt light-headed, unsure of what to do, restless, agitated.

Unable to be still, she rose again, and in an unconscious gesture checked her hair in the mirror. Her face was pale, her eyes staring.

At last she was turning to her bedroom again, when she heard a cab rattling in the street and a moment later a knock downstairs at the front door. At the sound every nerve jangled in her. She stood uncertain for a moment. The knocking continued. She went downstairs and opened the door.

Wrenshaw stood there, a shadow filling the doorway.

273

'You went off without telling me,' he said as he came forwards.

She turned and led the way back upstairs without saying anything. They came into the sitting room. Wrenshaw seemed as he always did, cool, immaculate. She was amazed at his self-possession. And yet she could not have been mistaken. She looked at him.

'I'm surprised to see you here.'

'What happened to you? You ran off without telling me.'

'I heard you with Madge in her dressing room,' she said at last.

There was a pause.

'Oh, that? Yes,' he said coolly, 'we were giggling together over something or other.'

'Something or other? Can you be serious? I heard you making love to her. Now please go. And don't come back.'

'Making love?'

'Fucking her. There was no mistake. Please go.'

'Bríd –' he turned on his most charming smile – 'don't get excited. I swear you're mistaken –'

'Go! John Wrenshaw, don't ever come back. Never. Never let me see you again.'

She crossed and opened the door. He came towards her, but she pulled herself back.

'Bríd, come, I swear it –'

'Get away! Never touch me, John Wrenshaw, I'll not endure it. Go, I tell you.'

All her tension, all her difficulties and frustrations, suddenly snapped in her. A fury, a wild, blind fury took her. She only wanted to eradicate John Wrenshaw, to wipe him finally out of her life.

'Bríd,' he said, and again reached out to take her in his arms.

She smacked him hard in the face.

'Have you no shame? Can you do it to her, and then come to me? Oh, get out – oh, God!'

She turned from him, tears starting into her eyes.

Wrenshaw put his hand to his cheek. He was stung. He went to take her arm, but she shook him off.

'Get out, you unspeakable –'

His cane was lying on the table. She snatched it up and turned towards him.

'Get out this instant, or I'll thrash you.'

As she lifted the stick towards him, he laughed, and as he laughed, her self-control snapped. She brought the cane hard down on his head. He staggered and she saw rage on his face.

'Now, by God!'

He quickly tried to seize her, but before he could stop her she struck him again forcibly.

'Brîd, by heaven! Stop this!'

He was furious, but again she slipped past him and hit him as hard as she could across the shoulders.

'Out! Out! Out!' she screamed. She threw open the door. 'Out! Out!'

'You'll pay for this –'

Again she struck him. He made another attempt to seize her but she was too quick and delivered a vicious blow to the side of his head. As he was distracted, his hand at his cheek, she pushed him with all her might through the door, and he tripped on the carpet and crashed down the stairs.

Brîd rushed out on the landing. Wrenshaw lay unmoving at the bottom of the stairs. She hung on the banisters looking down in the gloom. Then she heard Mrs Walters coming up from the basement.

'Oh, Mrs Walters, will you ever forgive me for making such a fearful racket? I'm so sorry, but it'll soon be over, and there's no cause for alarm.'

She ran down after Wrenshaw, stepped over him as he lay huddled at the foot of the stairs, and pulled open the door. She ran up to the cab rank in the Strand, and by good luck one cab stood empty, the cabby nodding over his whip.

Brîd looked up at him with a sweet smile. 'I wonder if you'd help me? 'Tis a gentleman who's had one too many and fell downstairs.'

She directed him down into Buckingham Street, the cabby came into the house, and together they got the barely sensible Wrenshaw down the steps and into the cab.

'The Albany,' said Brîd, and watched the cab drive away in the still summer night.

She turned and saw Mrs Walters standing in the doorway. Above her, the Maestro was leaning over the banisters.

'Oh, Brîd, I thought you was going to be murdered. Whatever's the matter?'

Brîd stood for a moment, breathing hard, her hands on her hips.

'Mrs Walters, I vow, no man will ever have power over me again.'

Chapter Thirty-Six

'You've nothing to worry about.'

Still he would not be settled. She wrapped the rug round his knees. The Maestro was sitting in the chair he liked by the fire. No fire was burning, since it was the middle of August, but even at this time of year, he seemed to feel cold. She tucked the rug round him.

'Mrs Walters knows about the macaroni. I explained to her carefully you don't like it overcooked. And I'll only be a few days. I'll send a telegram to let you know when I'm on my way home. You'll be fine, now.'

She bent and kissed the old man on the forehead.

'And maybe we'll go and hear Madame Patti when I get back. That'll be a treat.'

She smiled down at him and he looked up, almost like a child.

'Only a few days?'

'Yes.'

'Bríd –'

'Mrs Walters will take care of you. Sure, she loves you as her own, doesn't she?'

'Mrs Walters very nice, but –'

'I've got to go now, there's a cab waiting in the street. Look after yourself, and I'll be back soon.'

There was a knock at the door.

'Oh, Mrs Walters – will you tell the cabby to take this box?'

A few minutes later, with a sigh, she sat back in her seat as the cabbie whipped up the nag that was to carry her to the Euston Square Station.

Even when she was carefully stowed in a first-class compartment, the train was pulling up towards Chalk Farm, and she was staring out of the window, all the doubts kept forcing themselves back into her mind.

Should she be here? Should she be returning to Ireland?

For weeks the thoughts had revolved in her head. She forced herself for a moment to draw a deep breath, looking down at her lace gloves, her hands crossed on her cream silk dress, and try to arrange her thoughts.

A month ago she had found herself free for the first time in four years. Free: an alien concept, foreign to her. She was not free, could not be. At first she had felt guilty at not going to the theatre every day. No doubt Johnson would come up with something soon enough, and anyway most theatres were dark during the summer months. She could afford a few weeks rest. During the last two years she had earned high wages: ten pounds a week during the run of *All Change*, and then twenty-five for the play that followed it – another of Burton's 'cup-and-saucer' comedies. Money had been sent to Dublin regularly, and she had been able to buy herself some elegant clothes at last, had been able to dress as she had known she could ever since Harry had first taken her shopping in Regent Street, so long ago.

And then, as she was sitting in her flat in Buckingham Street one afternoon, the thought had come to her: she could go home. For a dizzy moment she had seen herself breaking the agreement and returning to Ballyglin. Lord, what a dust she would have stirred up! To step out of a carriage in Ballyglin in her cream silk dress, with her summer shoes, her parasol, and her straw hat with its streamers. For a second only she allowed her vanity to dwell on this picture, but it would never do. Nora had spelled it out to her clearly: her son was to be brought up in respectability, never to know the shame of his birth. That was the agreement; it was better for him. This was the message she had drummed into her own head whenever the pain of it surged through her again. Ballyglin was barred to her.

Well, but in disguise? Another dizzy moment: herself in a veil. Lord, how mysterious she would seem, a veiled woman; it appealed to the actress in her. But this was squashed too. How could she be serious? She had only to think of it for a second to see the absurdity of the idea. Standing on the green, surrounded by the entire population of Ballyglin, pointing, fingering her dress? They would see quick enough who she was.

Having once raised these thoughts, she was doubly depressed to have to suppress them again. But, as she had sat that sunny afternoon, looking up at the blue sky above the slate roofs of Buckingham Street, a new idea had come to her.

Not Ballyglin, no; but why not Boyle? On 15 August Patsy would take Nora to Boyle Fair; it was the Feast of the Assumption and

Nora's annual excursion to town – hadn't Bríd been with them herself all those years of her childhood? They would buy Nora her yearly treat – a new bonnet – and Matt, he would be four now: they would take him, for sure.

If she went to Boyle, no one would know her, and she would wear a veil to be safe. She would stay at the Prince of Wales Hotel – no one would ever know. She would be very careful. As this picture filled her mind, she knew she would do it. How could she not?

And now here she was in the train. The Maestro was safely tucked up at home. Mrs Walters would take care of him, she hoped. Mrs Walters was not the world's best cook, and the Maestro was fussy, but there was no helping it. Bríd must go, and that was all there was to be said.

She turned over her hands, studying her lace gloves.

What would he be like? She remembered a baby. Now he would be a little boy. The excitement kept crowding into her throat. Would he be like Harry, perhaps? Lord, what would Harry say if he knew he had a four-year-old son? Her agitation increased. What if Nora recognised her? She was breaking the agreement, wasn't she? Not precisely; she was not returning to Ballyglin, after all. Still, how would she feel if Nora recognised her? And if her little boy saw Nora talking to her, and asked who she was?

For a moment she squeezed her hands together in an effort to calm herself. Returning to Ireland was not a wise thing to do, that was a fact. But nothing would stop her doing it, no threat in the world could stop her now, now that she had in her mind the thought of seeing her son. Nothing in the world.

Late in the summer evening she had taken the train from Amiens Street Station, and was now gliding evenly through the Irish countryside. In August everything was at its loveliest, the grass at its greenest, the woods at their gayest.

Watching the crowds on the station platforms, though, came as a shock. The barefoot girls, holding babies in their shawls, might have been creatures from some distant planet, they seemed so strange to Bríd in her finery. And yet it was so nearly the picture of herself she was looking at. So close, and yet now so foreign – how odd it was!

And the men in their breeches and long-tailed coats, the blackthorn stick under their arms. As the train stood for a few minutes in the station, Bríd would stare across at the crowd on the platform opposite, so strange and yet so familiar.

It was dark when the train pulled into Boyle. Immediately she was approached by two ragged carmen holding whips, who competed with each other for her trunk.

'Wasn't it me was first, ye *umadaun*?'

'Oh, my lady, sure, isn't he the worst broken-downest car in the whole County Roscommon? A noted vagabond, your ladyship. If ye would only step this way –'

'Off with ye!'

The first ragged fellow had become aggressive and shoved his companion aside. ''Tis me for her ladyship. Now, won't ye follow me?'

'If you don't make up your minds soon, the pair of you, I'll carry it myself,' she said, laughing in spite of her weariness. 'You, my friend, pick up the trunk –' she pointed to the first of them – 'and carry me to the Prince of Wales Hotel.' She turned to the other and fished a penny from her reticule. 'Take this for your pains, friend.'

He touched his hat fervently. 'Your ladyship's the gentlemen entirely!' he called after her.

The hotel was thronged. She had forgotten how crowded Ireland always was. It was a good thing she had wired for a room. Everywhere men thronged the rooms and passages, shouting and calling, gesticulating. The manager was fulsome in his welcomes, bowing and rubbing his hands together.

'Your ladyship's welcome. We have kept the best room in the hotel for you; 'twas slept in by the Lord Lieutenant himself only last month. Here, Sean, take her ladyship's trunk – Sean!' He was nowhere to be seen. 'Your trunk shall follow directly, your ladyship. If your ladyship will follow me . . .'

Taking a candle, the manager, his coat shiny with grease in the flickering light, led her upstairs. The room seemed gloomy, but had long windows looking over the square.

'Ye'll have a fine view of the fair tomorrow, your ladyship.'

The novelty of being 'her ladyship' had worn off. The manager backed out, bowing, and left the candle flickering on the mantelpiece. She stood looking down into the square, tired, with her head full of rushing sensations, thoughts and memories. How familiar it was; how strange it was! How could she reconcile these two – her past, her present?

Down in the square there was a considerable amount of activity. Tents and booths were being erected; carts were rumbling in and men shouting as they bumped and lumbered past each other, backing horses, unloading timber, canvas, barrels. She looked down at the activity fitfully illuminated by pinewood torches, turning over the thoughts and impressions of this day.

Only a few miles from there, at that very minute, Patsy and Nora were preparing for bed. Already the little boy was asleep. How must he look now? A boy of four, asleep. She imagined the quiet breathing of a child asleep, the long eyelashes closed, the little hand perhaps clutching some toy. She turned from the window, paced slowly across the room; and she had returned for this?

At last she undressed and got into the bed. It was damp, even in mid-August. She was still unable to decide whether she should be here, what she should do if she saw them, what she should say if Nora spoke to her. Thoughts turning and turning, and herself in the damp bed; sleep would not come. And below the window the hammering and clattering, the sound of carts and the hooves on the cobbles went on through the night.

Morning came early, and she lay in bed, dizzy with fatigue, a headache splitting her brain, every limb aching.

Then it struck her that Patsy and Nora would come early; they always had when she had accompanied them. At this thought, she rose, and after splashing some cold water over her face, and dressing herself, she went down into the coffee room.

A clear sky promised perfect weather. The waiter was in jovial mood.

'A grand day for the fair, your ladyship.'

She smiled faintly, sipping her coffee. It tasted of washing-up water. The Maestro had exacting tastes in coffee and she had got into his way of doing things. This was barely drinkable. Still she drank it.

She had realised that her costume of the previous day had been far too fine for this little country town so this morning she was soberly dressed in a dark-blue costume and a bonnet with a long veil, which, as she drank her coffee, was thrown back.

The noise of commotion and bustle from the square reached her, and minute by minute there was more excitement within the hotel too. People were arriving for breakfast, and the two waiters were hurrying back and forth. It was still barely eight o'clock. Bríd tried to remember at what sort of time Patsy and Nora used to arrive in Boyle. And as she thought of it, she remembered Nora choosing a bonnet in the shop across the square. It all came back to her: how big the shop had seemed, how stern Nora had been with the girl behind the counter; how long she had spent and how many different bonnets she tried before she was satisfied.

Suddenly restless, Bríd decided to walk over and see if the shop was still there. Letting down the veil before her face and taking her parasol, she stepped out into the square.

The fair was now in full swing. At one side, a high platform had been erected in front of a tent, and there were several actors in a most extraordinary collection of costumes; bits of Roman emperors mixed with Egyptian princes and pirates of the Spanish Main. A barker was anouncing the imminent commencement of the tragedy of *Tamburlaine the Great*, the greatest prince of ancient time whose chariot was drawn by seven kings, whose hordes ravaged to the very gates of Europe and whose concubines were numbered by the score. She had to smile at this, wondering how this spectacle was to be presented when she saw but seven performers on the platform above her. Not far away in another tent there seemed to be a liberal dispensation of liquid refreshment even at this early hour. Seven bars and taverns also opened their doors on to the square. A strong man was proclaiming his powers and inviting competition from any comer. Everywhere entertainment was on offer to the holiday crowds.

On the opposite side of the square was the shop where Nora had bought her bonnets. Against its window Bríd and Molly had pressed their noses, staring at shawls brought from India, shawls which in those days had seemed of a richness and gorgeousness beyond description. How small the shop seemed now! How tawdry and dated seemed the fashions in the window! She smiled a sad smile to herself, and turned away, allowing herself to be wafted across the square as the crowd surged now this way, now that, not looking for anything, but seeing everything, and remembering so much.

Suddenly a coldness ran through her. They were there, not far away, looking at a stall selling sweets. Patsy, Nora and a little boy Patsy was holding. She couldn't see his face for he and Patsy were both looking at the stall, the boy was pointing, and they were discussing something. After negotiating with the woman behind the stall, Patsy picked up a stick of barley sugar to give the boy. For a moment during this, the boy looked absently round, and she saw his face clearly.

She went quite faint. Dear God, such a beautiful child! She saw Harry in his face in an instant, his blond hair, his pretty round cheeks and lips. She stared as if she could have eaten him, so hungrily did she yearn to run forward to take him and hold him.

This was too bad, but what could she do? They were there, so close, she had only to step forward, lift her veil and speak. Patsy and Nora, just as she remembered them, quite unchanged, yet so poor; how had she never known that before? They were poor folk, and she had been too, common people of the land, farmers.

But oh, the boy, she could scarcely bring herself to look at him, he was so beautiful. Now he laughed at something Patsy had said, and pulled at Patsy's hat for a jest. Tears sprang into Bríd's eyes as she

281

saw him laugh. Could she get close enough to hear them speak? All round her people pressed, passing and repassing between them.

The three of them moved on and she followed them carefully, wanting to get close enough to hear the boy's speech. He and Patsy seemed constantly in conversation, he pointing to things, nestling in the crook of Patsy's arm, one arm round Patsy's neck, the other pointing. Patsy was all patience, all attention. It was too much; Bríd's tears flowed fast, and she must reach up beneath her veil to wipe her eyes, for she could not see clearly.

They were before the theatrical booth, in a dense crowd now, and their attention was fastened on the barker above them, extolling the wonderful spectacle that awaited the lucky audience within. She insinuated herself through the crowd, almost holding her breath, until she was only a few feet behind them. The barker was repeating the speech she had heard earlier, but as he spoke Matt would turn and comment to Patsy, and Patsy would listen carefully to him. She could hear his little voice, the animation, the constant flow of new thought and change of subject of a four-year-old. It came as a shock to her to hear his accent; but he was an Irish boy, why had she expected anything different?

Watching Patsy and the boy, who seemed so close, like father and son in truth, she understood that there was no place here for her any more. If she did reach forward and touch Patsy on the arm, what should she say? And to take the child, as she had thought for an insane moment she might do, was impossible. A thousand times impossible. He was Patsy's shadow, they breathed each other's breath. There was no room between them for her. She stood outside and looked in.

She looked for a moment to Nora on the other side of Patsy. They were a family, the three of them, and there was no place in it for Bríd, except as a provider. She might send money, that much was permitted.

Matt turned again and saw her a few feet behind them, a tall lady in dark clothes and a thick veil. He had never seen a veiled lady before, and he was curious; he plucked at Patsy to make him look round. For a moment Patsy did look, and Bríd froze as he saw her, but he turned back to Matt and rebuked him for pointing at a strange lady, it was not polite.

A strange lady. She wanted to stay, to follow them; she wanted to run away. But she was rooted to the spot. The barker had finished his speech; some moved forward, others broke away. The little family had decided not to see the show, and turned aimlessly away. As they did so, Matt turned over Patsy's shoulder and looked at the veiled lady again with innocent curiosity. Then his attention was distracted and his glance moved away. She was, after all, only one woman in a crowd.

Part III
1875–77

Chapter Thirty-Seven

'Bríd, it's your turn to play.'

'What?'

She had been miles away. Isabella was looking at her with her soft smile.

'Would you rather do something else?'

Bríd roused herself.

'Oh – no, let me see.' She studied her cards, and eventually put one down on the polished table between them.

Dimly from the hall the grandfather clock chimed three.

'My trick. I'm in luck today.' Isabella tried to sound cheerful.

Bríd's gaze had moved past Isabella's shoulder to the garden. Her pretty garden. Years ago, when she had first come here, she had had gardeners in to remodel it. She had attacked it with all sorts of ideas: arbours, trellises, brick-paved walks, a little fountain. Now the garden looked unkempt, but it didn't seem important. She seldom went into it.

Her mind was wandering. She couldn't concentrate on the game, but she couldn't concentrate on anything else either.

'Are you bored? Would you like to rest?' Isabella looked at her with concern.

Bríd drew a breath. 'No. Let's see – is it me to play?'

'Don't you remember? I won the last trick.' She laughed.

Bríd threw down her cards. 'Good for you. Have 'em all.' She stood up. 'I'm going out.'

She walked across the room, then stopped by the piano, looking down.

'Do you want me to come with you?'

'No. Get my coat.'

As she went out into the hall, Isabella ran past her to the cupboard and brought out her new light summer coat.

'No, not that one. Oh, leave it! I'll do it myself.'

She pushed past Isabella and, thrusting into the coat cupboard, pulled out a man's navy-blue pea jacket, and pulled it quickly on.

'Surely you won't wear that old thing?'

'I'll wear what I like.'

She slammed the door behind her, went down the few steps, through the small front garden and into the King's Road. At the corner, she turned down the side street that led to the river.

It was a sunny afternoon, and after a few minutes the walking calmed her. She was already feeling guilty for her rudeness to Isabella. It was a wonder her friend put up with her moods sometimes. She walked faster, trying to forget it, looking down, her feet kicking out against her long, simple skirt. Better to walk, it soothed her; better to walk, her hands sunk deep into the pockets of her old seaman's jacket. She had wound a length of chiffon round her head and neck.

No one recognised her like this. She could be just an ordinary person walking through the narrow streets down to the river.

It was quite changed in the ten years since she had first come here. The riverside was opened out, and half of old Chelsea Village had gone altogether. Instead they had built a wide embankment with young trees and railings. She turned along the pavement.

Red-sailed wherries went past, and now and then a little steamer with its tall chimney stack belching out a stream of black smoke.

She had come here as a penniless girl with her lover ten years ago. She didn't think of it too often, tried not to. It was foolish, after all. And she probably could have forgotten him in the end, if there hadn't been the disastrous trip to Boyle.

She would never forget the journey back to London. She had not been able to help the tears; they would come. In the end she had sat in the train and just let them stream down her face. But by the time she had reached the Euston Square Station again, it was as if something, she did not know what, some little switch, had clicked in her. As she stood waiting for a cab, a voice in her had said, I will never weep again.

She had returned to her work. One play followed another. In the five years since she had been back, she had appeared in half the theatres of London. She had toured the provinces, she had taken a play to Paris, the only English actress ever to do so.

She had bought this house in Chelsea, two hundred years old, in mellow red brick on two floors, with a secluded garden behind. In this little oasis of peace and tranquillity, she would sit sometimes with Isabella and learn her lines.

Isabella had come to her soon after her return from Ireland. Bríd had gone round to Calvi's – which had been sold – and by a stroke of luck had been able to trace Isabella to another restaurant nearby and persuaded her to come to her as her companion.

So why was she she so rude to her this afternoon? What was wrong with her?

Her gaze swept across the wide expanse of the river to the line of trees on the opposite shore, thick with summer foliage in the bright sunshine.

Everything was wrong with her. That was the trouble. She could no longer see the point of anything. Night after night she went on, and for what? She still sent money to Ireland; it was ridiculous – Matt could buy the place by now.

How old would he be? Nine years old. Oh, but it was really too bad! He was nine, next year he would be ten, and the year after that . . . and every year she would try to imagine him another year older, begining to shoot up, becoming a young man, and then perhaps falling in love. And one day – who knew – he would be married. Somewhere, perhaps even in Ballyglin, he would come out of the church with a young bride on his arm, and the villagers would be there, Nora and Patsy would be there, they would cheer, throw rice, and there would be a party. All his life passing and she unable to be part of it.

And Harry would never know he had a son, though, when she came to think of it, he probably had several children by now. What did he look like now, she wondered.

Her thoughts wandered.

She had everything – and she had nothing. After the departure of Wrenshaw, she had never felt drawn to another man. Once at the beginning she had taken a lover briefly, but it had been meaningless, a sort of physical spasm, devoid of love; he had gone, and she had no more will to take another. Now only a ruthless discipline drove her on in her work, a fire burning in her that would not cool, yet all the time a sense of futility hung over everything.

She turned homeward; she must be back by four thirty.

When she let herself into the house, Mrs Foster set out a snack for her and Isabella, and they sat down in silence to a a piece of ham with a poached egg on it, and a cup of coffee.

At five thirty, Fred brought round her carriage and they set off for the theatre.

The gloom still hung about her; she seemed unable to shake it off this afternoon. As the carriage rolled up the Strand, she looked up and saw the front of the theatre plastered with posters; 'Miss Bridget

Flynn in *Mary Queen of Scots* – run extended by popular demand.' Repeated all down the front of the theatre: Miss Bridget Flynn, Miss Bridget Flynn . . . Her eye passed over it idly.

In her dressing room, Isabella set out her first costume and was brushing it as Bríd undressed. Sitting in her shift at the dressing table, she opened a box of powder. It was nearly empty.

'Did you get another box of *poudre de riz*?'

Isabella turned and drew in a sharp breath. 'Oh, Bríd – how stupid of me! Can you wait? I will run out now –'

'I told you last night! I told you! And you know you can't go out now – you've got to dress me. Have you got any brain at all?'

As they stared at one another, Isabella on the verge of tears, the door opened and a man was standing in the doorway. Bríd swung round.

'Haven't I told you a thousand times not to come in without knocking?'

He gave a comic smile, raising his eyebrows. 'That's what gives the moment its piquancy – you never know what to expect.'

He was quite unabashed. He came a step inside the room and closed the door behind him.

'And how are we tonight, girls, eh? All bright and cheery, I hope?'

Bríd turned again to the mirror.

'Bill, have you got any *poudre de riz*?'

'Breezy Bill' stopped. 'Now, I asks yer, I asks yer –' dropping into a cockney idiom – 'do I look like a bloke what uses powder dee rice? I mean ter say! What would the other fellers say, if they was to find aht I was using powder dee rice! I got my reputation to fink abaht, girls, do me a favour!'

Bríd couldn't help smiling.

'And what have you been up to, Bill?'

'A bit of this and a bit of that – more that than this, actually. Anyway, why don't you borrow some from Miss Charlton?'

'Isabella, run along to Flossy and ask her to lend me a little.'

Isabella went out without speaking.

Bríd poured herself a glass of port. 'Want some?'

'Thanks, but as you very well know, I don't touch the stuff – the result of a childhood conversion. I took the pledge at eleven.'

She threw back a stiff glass of port and poured another. 'It's good for the throat.'

'Whatever you say. Anyway, I can see you're in a hurry to get rid of me. See you on the green. Oh, by the way, I hear the Guv'nor's in tonight.'

As he went out, she turned to the mirror and smiled. Breezy Bill

290

Harris played Leicester to her Mary Queen of Scots, Petruchio to her Kate, Benedick to her Beatrice. Some said she had chosen him for his calves, and he certainly looked good in a doublet and hose.

And he was a tonic to her – better than port. He was not the world's greatest actor, but he had a bluff, manly quality and he looked good on stage in Elizabethan costume. Most important, he was unflappable, never gave her any trouble and never took offence. Whatever she wanted – or demanded, if she was in a bad mood – he fitted in with her wishes. He was soothing to be with, and he was funny. She smiled again, as she threw back the second glass of port.

Isabella came in. She had a screw of paper in her hand.

'Thank God for Bill! I think I'd throw myself in the river sometimes if it wasn't for him.'

In the looking glass she saw tears start into Isabella's eyes. Bríd leaped up and threw her arms round her.

'Oh, Isabella, forgive me! I wasn't thinking. Forgive me – really, I'm perfectly hateful nowadays.'

Isabella drew away and blew her nose. 'It's all right, it doesn't matter, really.'

They looked into each other's eyes.

'I don't know where I'd be without you, Isabella. You won't ever leave me, will you? Not even when I'm in a such a hateful mood? Sometimes I don't know what I'm saying, I don't.'

Isabella helped her into the stiff, heavy costume of black velvet with silver trimming, doing up the hooks and eyes and the innumerable, fiddling little tie strings which held the complicated costume together. Then Bríd sat again at the dressing table and Isabella pinned up her hair tightly against her head before fixing the wig over it: the red wig of Mary Queen of Scots.

The moment had passed, the tension had eased between them, but still, as she was leaving the dressing room, she took another glass of port, and she saw the look of concern in Isabella's eyes. She said nothing but gave her a defiant look before going up to the stage.

The taste for port went back a long way. She had first drunk it when sharing a dressing room with Madge and Ria, who used to get through bottles of the stuff. It had never affected their performance, and it was as if they did not *need* it but drank only for the sheer fun of it. But then it seemed in those days that life was just a huge game, in which they held all the winning cards.

Bríd had not drunk for the fun of it, not for a long time. She told herself she did not drink, or not much; it was just for her throat, or some other excuse – it was a cold night or it helped her to relax. She wasn't afraid of the audience the way some actors were. She didn't drink for that; she didn't drink, she told herself again – or else, well, everybody liked a drop now and then. The bottles stood on the dressing table, she didn't count them. She wouldn't let herself notice.

And anyway, it wasn't that she *needed* a drink. If she had an odd glass of port, well, it was just, well, it did help to deaden the pain a little. She felt as if she were going through her life with a knife stuck in her side, a constant pain, as if she could never stand upright or draw a full breath. A drink helped to dull the edge. That was all there was to it.

Anyway, it didn't interfere with her work – which was what mattered.

But as she was coming off afterwards, just walking into her dressing room with Isabella behind her, George Thompson came in and he was very loud and angry.

'You've been drinking!'

She swung round. She was quite in command of herself; she always was – in front of the audience or George Thompson. She looked at him haughtily.

'So what if I have? What's it matter? The audience don't see it.'

'I see it!'

'Go to hell!' She turned away.

'That's where you're going, Bríd, if you don't get a hold of yourself.'

'Have I ever let you down?' She was pulling pins out of her wig. Isabella was helping her.

'Not so far.'

'No. And I never will. When have I ever missed a performance?'

He threw his arms up in a gesture and turned away for a moment. George was hot. There was perspiration on his forehead. He turned to her again, his tone gentler.

'Bríd, I've seen it before. Believe me, I know. You think I can't see the signs?'

'They can't see the signs – which is what matters.'

'You need a holiday.'

She turned to him as Isabella eased the wig off her head and set it on its block on the dressing table.

'You have a nerve. You work me like a packhorse, making money for you. When did I last have a holiday? I'm your gold mine, aren't I? And when have I ever let you down?'

Breezy Bill was in the doorway. The row was audible all down the corridor.

'Go easy, Guv'nor.'

'And please don't shout at me, because I won't stand for it. Now get out of my dressing room. This is not a public highway.'

'And where's your evening gown? We're going to Lady Westlock's tonight.'

She dropped both hands on the dressing table. 'Oh, God!'

'Don't tell me you forgot?'

'Yes, as a matter of fact I did forget. Isn't that a tragedy? Anyway, I haven't the faintest desire to go to Lady Westlock's or anywhere else. I'm going home.'

'You're going to Lady Westlock's whether you like it or nor. You've accepted, and I know for a fact that HRH is coming tonight especially to meet you.'

She drew a long sigh. 'Fine. Now get out of my dressing room.'

She shut the door behind them.

'I'm sorry, Isabella, I'd completely forgotten. I have to go. You can have the carriage to take you home.' Isabella began undoing the hooks and eyes down the back of her black gown, the gown in which Mary Queen of Scots had gone to her execution. Bríd looked at herself in the mirror with a sarcastic expression.

'We can't disappoint the Prince of Wales, can we?'

If it hadn't been that Thompson had accepted on her behalf, and that it was considered bad form to turn down an invitation when the Prince of Wales was going to be present, Bríd would have gone home to bed. What did she care anyway? He probably only wanted to get her into his own bed. He was notorious for it.

'We're not staying long,' she said to Thompson as they sat side by side in his carriage.

'All right, all right, you may say it's boring but it matters – never think it doesn't. You're part of society – and society is powerful. It's part of your reputation and reputations pull people into the theatre. So just grit your teeth, be nice to people, and don't touch any more drink tonight. That's an order.'

'I'll have a drink if I want.'

'You won't – if I have to pull the glass bodily out of your fist myself. I don't mind making an exhibition of myself, but I'm not having *you* do it.'

'What are you afraid of?'

'I don't have to spell it out.'

Lady Westlock's house overlooked Park Lane. By the time they arrived it was after midnight and the ball was well under way. On this warm summer night, the windows above them were open to the night air, and people were standing on the balcony. Carriages were still drawing up at the door.

Thompson and Bríd went up the wide stair and were announced at the door. Lady Westlock, who spent most of her time in the country and claimed to be more at home in a farmyard, was there to welcome them. She was in London this season to launch her second daughter.

'So glad you could come. Angela's here somewhere – she's dying to meet you. HRH hasn't come yet. Everyone's on tenterhooks. Oh, I say, are you hungry? You've been working all evening, haven't you? Supper will be served shortly.'

Supper was served and Bríd was very hungry indeed. She and Thompson lost no time in making for the buffet. A manservant passed them with a tray of champagne and she took a glass.

Thompson gave her a look.

She raised her eyebrows and looked directly into his face as she drained it, replaced it on the tray and took another.

'Champagne is customarily drunk at balls, I'm told. And you're such a stickler for *form*, aren't you, George?' she said sarcastically.

'I'm watching you.'

'Watch me. I'm not running away. Ooh, have one of these – they're delicious.' She thrust a canapé at him.

Thompson drew a sigh and took the morsel.

'Good, eh? Caviar vol-au-vent. I'm glad you brought me, George. Perhaps we can enjoy ourselves after all.' She took another glass of champagne.

'Bríd, I warned you. If you go near that stuff again, I shall physically prevent you.'

'That'll be exciting. Let's create a scandal, George, liven up the party.'

'He's here.' Thompson was looking over her shoulder. She took advantage of his distraction to empty her glass.

'Oh, goody.' She put the glass down. 'Now the party can really begin.'

The Earl of Westlock was at her shoulder.

'Miss Flynn? May I present you to His Royal Highness.'

She swung round. 'I'm ready. Where is he?'

She swayed very slightly.

'It's rather warm in here, isn't it? Now, where is he? Your whoness –' She hiccupped. 'Your Whoyal Righness, I'm ready. Georgy, lend me your arm, it's rather stuffy. Oh, drat!' She put on a cockney accent. 'Nearly tripped over me gahn –'

The short, plump, bearded figure of the Prince of Wales was before her.

She smiled. 'Afraid to curtsy, your H'ghness – might not be able to get up again.'

She hiccupped and giggled. The smile on his face was just beginning to set into a frown.

'So here you are,' she went on as Thompson tried to take her arm. She shook him off.

'Well,' she went on, looking round, and flourishing her arm. 'See anyone you fancy, old feller? They say you have an eye for the ladies, what? Rumour has it. Whoooo's it to be tonight? Hmm? Can't be me, I'm afraid. Frankly, I'm too tired. Just too tired.' She waved her arm again and, losing her balance, fell into Thompson's arms.

All around her conversation had stopped and everyone was looking at her.

HRH turned away with complete dignity and began talking to someone else as if nothing had happened.

Chapter Thirty-Eight

Bríd leaned on the rail, looking down at the crowd on the open deck below her. For a moment, forgetting Isabella and Bill beside her, she was hypnotised, watching the pushing, heaving, gesticulating, weeping, crying, calling, laughing, cursing crowd, yet feeling strangely detached, as if, like some God of old, she were looking down on the puny strife of mere mortals.

The liner had left Liverpool the evening before and now this morning was at anchor in Queenstown harbour in southern Ireland, its last stop before America.

Forgetting Bill and Isabella, she watched, unable to pull her eyes from the scene, fascinated in a way she had quite forgotten. It recalled so much to her, memories of her childhood in Ballyglin, memories of the fair, of hagglers along the roadside, of Gypsies, of young farmers in a fight she had once seen.

There was a young man taking leave of his mother, she hanging on him and calling aloud to heaven to protect her boy, raising her arm aloft as she still held tight to him, and he, desperately trying to stop himself breaking into tears, was imploring her not to cry for him – sure, wouldn't he do well, why shouldn't he? Nearby, a young couple had their arms round one another and were staring back at the hills in the distance, as if trying to print on their memory this last sight of Ireland. Three men passing a bottle among themselves were laughing and talking loudly, as if emigrating to America was something they did every week, and trying to smother the feelings welling up inside them at this moment of leaving their own country for ever.

Now a fiddler started up, and three couples began an impromptu jig. And throughout the crowd, as Bríd's glance passed over them, was a heaving and pushing, a restlessness, people afraid to sit down, afraid to settle for fear they might miss something, some last moment before the ship weighed anchor. A young man was forcing his way up the gangplank, pushing past other poor folk still coming aboard, past porters carrying boxes and bundles, and holding a large black object above his head, something she could not at first recognise. As he rejoined his friends, there was laughter, and she saw now that it was a large piece of turf, and she heard him distinctly saying, 'I said I'd be buried beneath my native sod!', wrapping it in a blanket.

'Takes you back, does it, Bríd?'

'Every Irishman knows about the pain of parting,' she said without looking up. 'There isn't a family in Ireland that doesn't have relations in America.'

Suddenly she could stand no more.

'Excuse me.' She turned away from Isabella and Bill and wandered along the side of the ship looking away across the harbour to the hills beyond. The last of Ireland. She wondered whether this might be the last time she saw her native country too.

Bill looked at Isabella. 'What's the matter with Bríd?'

Isabella shrugged, though she understood very well.

Bill drew a breath. 'Well, I'm glad we're here, I can tell you. It was a stroke of genius of the Guv'nor. I always wanted to see America. They say they serve the biggest steaks ever seen, and every mod con too, by all accounts. And it'll be good to get away from the Smoke for a while, eh? You glad you're going, Isabella?'

'Oh yes, and I think it will be best for Bríd too.'

'I should say. The way she was going on – between you and me, Isabella, she was heading for the edge. One more episode like that one at Lady Westlock's, eh? Know what I mean?'

Isabella nodded. 'Poor thing! I felt so bad, Bill – there seemed to be nothing I could do. Nothing. It was – you know – she was tired of life, I think. Nothing to enjoy any more.'

'Beats me. She's got everything she could want, I should think.' He took out a cigar. 'Well, like I said, the Guv'nor's done the right thing. America! The land of the free!' He lit his cigar. 'And the money's supposed to be very good.' He raised his eyebrow with a significant look. 'Know what I mean? We could all come home happy men. And Bríd will be a new woman, you mark my words. Everyone will have forgotten the little misunderstanding at Lady Westlock's.'

A hooter sounded and an officer appeared below them, shouting, 'All ashore that's going ashore!' This only served to renew the crying and lamentations, the calling and the hugging and kissing, the sons torn from their mothers' arms, the lovers torn apart, the fathers kissing their little ones' heads.

'Poor devils,' Bill muttered. 'Glad it's not me, I can tell you.'

Isabella went in search of Bríd and found her at the far end of the ship, staring across the bay towards the hills.

'Bríd, can I do anything for you?'

'Oh, no thanks.'

She turned to Isabella with a gentle, mournful smile.

The ship pulled away from the quayside and made its way out of the harbour. As she began to meet the Atlantic breakers and the strong wind from the ocean, Bríd's spirits rose. She stood at the prow of the ship, her face to the wind, and breathed deeply. It was good to break right away, to set off for something completely new, an adventure.

From the moment Thompson had suggested an American tour, her spirits had risen.

They would be the first theatrical company to visit America since the Civil War, and they would be a novelty. When Thompson had closed the deal with Colonel Watney, the American impresario, Watney assured him that her name was not unknown in America, and he could promise them a profitable tour. That was good enough for Thompson.

That evening they sat at dinner in the saloon with the captain. Over the table hung a tray on chains holding all the salt and pepper pots, the sauce bottles, the vinegar and horseradish sauce, and as the ship rose and fell gently through the long Atlantic swell, this tray swung back and forth between the guests on either side.

'Dash me,' Bill said. 'I reached up to put back the sauce bottle and the wretched thing had swung to your side, Bríd. Wait – here it comes.' He deftly replaced the bottle. 'Could make a feller perfectly dizzy. Hasn't taken away your appetite, then, Bríd?'

But the sea had given her a good appetite, and Isabella thought she was looking more cheerful than she had for a long time.

The following morning the sky was grey and overcast, and the wind carried spray with it. But inside there were always faint nauseating smells, cooking, oil or the acrid smell of coke, so she preferred to be on deck, even though, at the end of October, it was now cold in the wind. She wrapped herself in a thick overcoat – she had been told to bring plenty of winter clothes – and installed herself in a wooden deck chair with a script for *La Tosca*, a new play, translated from the French of Sardou, which they had been rehearsing.

It was impossible to open the script in the wind, however, and she was content to sit and stare out to sea, to feel the damp wind on her face and let her mind wander, thinking over the sight of the poor emigrants on the decks below, the wasted years behind her, as she saw them, and the new land ahead. Thoughts followed each other through her mind with no special pressure, and all the time she felt relaxed and glad to be there.

She was alone on that side of the ship, but after a while two men appeared at the corner of the deckhouse, coming towards her, bending into the wind. One was an elderly man in a long overcoat, holding on to his hat with one hand, and the other, in a jacket and bowler hat and clutching an armful of rugs, was expostulating with him. As they got closer, she was able to hear what they were saying.

'You'll catch your death of cold, sir!'

'Nonsense, Meredith! I've never taken the least care for my health and I don't intend to start now! Besides, no one is going to care much whether I live or die anyway.'

He stopped.

'I am going to sit by this young lady. I am sure she won't object to an old man for company?'

He stood tall and slender over her, touching his hat as he spoke. She could only stutter that she would be delighted.

The valet fussed about the old man as he lowered himself into the deck chair beside Bríd, tucking him in from all sides with shawls and plaid rugs.

'Give one of those to this young lady. I am sure she needs it more than I do. No, my dear, take it, I insist. You must keep warm. It doesn't matter about me. Meredith, wrap one of those about the young lady's skirt.'

As the valet placed the thick, fleecy rug over her legs, tucking it in with practised efficiency, the old man went on,

'You mustn't mind Meredith, my dear. He worries about me. I tell him he shouldn't. At my age I've stopped worrying, I assure you. I'm eighty-seven years old, and if I can't do what I want now, when will I?'

He smiled benevolently.

'Oh, but I beg your pardon, I believe you were reading. Do forgive me for interrupting. Really, I am such a foolish old man, please excuse me.'

Everything about him had a quality of understated elegance and wealth. His speech too had a delicate modulation, as if even his accent were expensively hand made by craftsmen.

'I believe you are the first American I have ever met,' she said smiling.

'Really? Well, that is a good omen, a very good omen indeed. I hope it may augur well for your visit to my country.'

'I'm sure it will.'

'May I ask where you are going?'

'Oh, we're on a tour. A theatrical tour. And, let me see if I can remember, we are going to New York first, then Brooklyn, Pittsburgh, er, Philadelphia, Washington, Baltimore –'

'Land sakes!'

'–Chicago, Cincinnati, St Louis, Detroit, Toronto, Boston, and finally back to New York again. I think I've got them in order. The tour will take us up to next April.'

'So you are an actress? Well, this is an honour. My! Er, may I enquire your name, young lady?'

'Bridget Flynn.'

'*The* Bridget Flynn?'

She laughed. 'I believe I am the only one – so far.'

'Oh, well now, I saw you in London. Do forgive me for not recognising you at once. What was it now? No – don't tell me. Drat it, my memory is not as good as it was.' He appeared to be racking his brains. 'Oh, now I remember, it was in *Mary Queen of Scots*. Of course! And to think I never recognised you – but you had red hair, I remember distinctly.'

'A wig,' she said quietly.

'Oh, I see. Yes, of course. Well, Miss Flynn, I can confidently predict you have a great success ahead of you in my country. And your first visit too, my, my.'

The valet reappeared round the corner of the deckhouse, holding down his hat against the wind.

'I really must insist you come inside now, Mr Sherborne. Mrs Halifax would have my hide if she knew I'd left you out here to freeze to death.'

'Oh, drat Helen! That's my daughter. She rules me at home with an iron rod. But I'm not at home now, Meredith – and Mrs Halifax will never know!'

He levered himself with difficulty out of his deck chair and was about to go.

'Do forgive an old man. I believe I have not even introduced myself. William T. Sherborne the Third. I hope we may be able to continue our little chat – tomorrow perhaps?'

The following day they did indeed meet again, and took short walks round the deck, he resting on her arm while he told her about himself. He was the retired president of the City Bank of New York, he said. His son, William T. Sherborne the Fourth, was now in charge, and he himself was just an old hulk washed up on the beach and drying in the sun. Although it wasn't very sunny, he pointed out, looking up. 'Nothing to do but pester pretty young ladies on transatlantic liners.'

He had travelled, oh, all over, he forgot where, and sometimes he had been able to bring home a few things. He particularly liked England. His own home on Fifth Avenue, he said, was modelled on the Duke of Devonshire's home where he had once been a guest. 'Derbyshire – have you ever been there, Miss Flynn? Reminds me of Vermont.'

So he chattered on, and she was very happy to have him leaning on her arm. His old-fashioned courtesy made a relief from the boisterous high spirits of the theatrical company.

On the last evening on board before they docked, he spoke to her after dinner, and his manner had become grave.

'My dear Miss Flynn, the captain tells me that we shall be docking very early tomorrow, and you may wish to be on deck to see the ship steam up the Hudson River. It is quite a sight, I assure you. I am not an early riser, so, in case we don't have an opportunity to speak again . . .' He looked closely into her eyes. 'Before I go any further, I want you to promise me faithfully one thing.'

'What thing?' she said, slightly alarmed by his solemn manner.

'I want you to promise not to say anything when I hand you this small package.'

She saw he was holding a little brown paper package in his wizened hand. She looked down.

'Very well.'

He placed the package in her hand, and she untied the ribbon and unfolded the paper. Inside was an old red Morocco leather jewel case, and when she opened it she saw inside a necklace of beautifully matched garnets. She drew in a breath.

'Remember! You promised!'

He placed his hand on hers, looking into her eyes, and said, 'They belonged to my wife. And there is something about you that reminds me of her. Please! Don't say a word. You promised!' She had been about to speak. 'Believe me, I cannot please you in giving them to you as much as you will please me by wearing them.'

At last she said, 'I will wear them. They are quite beautiful.'

She fixed them round her neck, and he sat back a little on the padded bench where they had been sitting, and looked at her for a long time. Then she leaned forward and kissed him lightly on the cheek.

'Thank you,' she whispered. 'They will remind me of you and of our talks together.'

*

301

The next morning she was up at dawn, and stood at the rail as the ship passed through the mouth of the majestic Hudson River, with its wooded hills on either side. As they sailed up towards Manhattan Island, the water was covered with little craft, steamboats belching black smoke, pretty yachts and big-sailed wherries. The flags at their mastheads reminded her that they really had arrived in America.

A tall graceful steam yacht was brought alongside, and a plump, short man hurried up the steps which had been lowered down the side of the ship. He was buttoned tightly into a frock coat, and had a big moustache and goatee beard. He shook hands with Thompson, who had been standing with Bríd at the rail, and was immediately introduced to her as Colonel Watney.

'Miss Flynn, it is indeed an honour to welcome you to our fair country. The *Columbia* awaits your pleasure – may I escort you? It will be so much easier this way, and you'll be able to avoid all the inconvenience of the public customs formalities.'

As she went down into the yacht, she looked back at the faces of the immigrants lined along the rail and staring at the millionaire's yacht. What would their reception be like, she wondered?

'And as for the reporters,' said Thompson, 'be nice to them. They can make us or break us. Watney warned me. The best thing is to get them over and done with first. Not too early for you?'

It was still before eight in the morning. Bríd felt perfectly composed; in fact, after the ten days at sea, she felt better than she had for years. And she had touched nothing stronger than a glass of white wine with her dinner. She thought of this as she watched Thompson and Colonel Watney pouring generous glasses of brandy and water and handing round dishes of fried chicken.

Bríd decided to charm the reporters.

'Now, gentlemen, I am completely at your disposal, so fire away and don't spare me. This is the first time I've visited your country, and I'm looking forward to it. You know, I'm an Irishwoman, and many of my fellow countrymen have settled in the United States, and out of the wealth they have made here, they've been able to send money back to the old country that has been the breath of life to many poor families. On behalf of all of them, I want to thank you.'

This took them by surprise, but was very gratifying too, and they warmed to her immediately. Still, Bríd found their questions unlike anything she was used to. They only seemed interested in her private life. Was she planning to marry? Was there any special beau in her life? Did she have many beaux? What was her favourite colour? What was her favourite flower? Could she tell them about her home in

London? How did she think she would suit in America? Was she expecting a friendly reception?

Oh yes, she was sure she would love America, she had such warm feelings for America and had wanted to come here for many, many years – in fact, she would have come before if the pressure of work in London had not prevented her.

In the end, as they were approaching the pier head, Watney took over, thanked the reporters and told them he was sure readers would receive a fair and impartial account of the tour, according to the highest traditions of the American press. By the time the yacht was moored it seemed that the gentlemen of the press were well and truly on their side.

'So long as nothing goes wrong, Bríd,' Thompson whispered to her, as they watched the pressmen trooping off the yacht and away down the pier.

Colonel Watney's coach was placed at her disposal and the three of them were conveyed to her hotel.

During the twenty-minute journey, she was staring out of the carriage window, her eyes taking everything in. The streets were muddy, but the sidewalks were well built. There was a tremendous air of bustle as they made their way away from the dock area and into town. It seemed as if ships were tied up from every country on earth, even Chinese junks. Well, it was quite different from London, she said, as the Colonel leaned over and asked her again what she thought of New York.

They arrived at the Hotel Dam and were about to go in when the Colonel suggested she might like to lift her skirt just a little. Looking down she saw that the doorstep and threshold were yellow-brown from the quantity of spittle that was drying on it. 'Another time, I suggest you use the ladies' entrance to the side, Miss Flynn. It is more commodious and hygienic.'

Coming into the hotel lobby which was large, high and furnished in a rich and exotic taste, she was met by a blast of heat. It had been colder outside than in London, and the Colonel said they had already had their first snowfalls, so she was grateful for the warmth.

A black porter came forward to conduct her to her suite, and she was astonished when she was ushered into the 'elevator' and they were whisked up to the next floor. Nothing like it existed in London, she told the Colonel and he was highly gratified. 'I believe you, ma'am. And there'll be a few other surprises before you're through, I'll wager!'

A door was opened and she was ushered into a spacious, light room, where flowers awaited her. Thompson said he was returning to the ship and Isabella would be along later with the rest of the luggage. She was left alone to explore their suite. Two bedrooms opened off the parlour, and there was a bathroom with hot and cold running water; an electric bell could summon the maid. Without doubt it was all well appointed, she thought as she threw up the window, but it was also the hottest room she had ever been in. The first thing she enquired of the maid when she summoned her by the electric bell was, 'How do I turn down the heat?'

Isabella arrived exhausted later that morning, and Bríd made her sit down and take her boots off while she sent for a cup of tea for her. Coffee it had to be. 'We're in America now, Isabella,' Bríd said.

Isabella plumped back in her chair. 'What a city! *Mamma mia!* I've never seen such a bustle! It makes Regent Street look tame.'

After lunch Thompson reappeared and the three of them went round to inspect the Park Theatre. Bríd was favourably impressed. As good as anything we've got, anyway, she thought as she stood on the stage, looking round at the circles of boxes and the seats below them. 'I say – they've got no pit! Who's going to sit in all these stalls seats?'

'In the orchestras?' repeated Colonel Watney beside her. 'Well, now, don't you have no fears on that score. With your name on the boards outside, Miss Flynn, I ain't counting on no empty seats nohow!' He burst into a hearty laugh and clapped her so hard on the back, she almost toppled forwards into the orchestra pit.

'Pleased to hear it,' she muttered.

As she saw later, her name was already plastered all over the front of the theatre – which was on Union Square, she was told, as she struggled to get an idea of the geography of the city, right on the corner of Broadway and Thirteenth.

'Thirteenth what?'

He laughed. 'Why, Thirteenth Street, of course – where was you brung up? You won't have no trouble finding your way round our fair city, Miss Flynn, if you just hold on to one simple fact: the streets run across, and the avenues run up and down.'

'Well, that's two facts – but I hope I'll remember.'

'That's my girl!'

They had a week to prepare the four plays they had brought with them: *Mary Queen of Scots*, *Much Ado About Nothing*, *The Taming of the Shrew* and *La Tosca*. They had played all these in London over the last four years. Thompson had some of his scenery brought over, and was busy overseeing the carpenters in the theatre constructing additional pieces.

*

304

The following afternoon Bríd and Isabella went out together to look at the shops. Not far away, on Broadway between Eighth and Ninth, they found A. T. Stewart's, a palace of a store, like nothing they had ever seen, and lit by electricity. They wandered through the departments, riding up and down in the 'elevators', giggling at the novelty ('Paper bags! Whatever next!'), turning things over, and admiring the alacrity of the girls behind the counters, who all seemed so willing to please, with nothing of the sullen manner of the average London shop girl. The girls here were pretty and had excellent teeth, Bríd noticed, and were so bright and helpful it was a pleasure just to stand talking to them.

Everyone wanted to know what they thought of New York. 'Ain't it the greatest city on earth? Mind, I ain't ever been to London, or Paris or any of them other cities, but I'll bet a dollar they can't compare with New York!'

And Bríd, from her own limited knowledge, was inclined to agree. It was quite overwhelming, only it was very hot inside the store, and in the end she and Isabella had to get out into the air again to breathe.

'I'd die in there if I had to stay in there all day, I would! How can they stand it?'

When they got back to the hotel they found Thompson. He was angry about something, and it didn't take him long to come out with it.

'They'll have us over a barrel, Bríd. Damn it! It's the one thing I didn't foresee!'

'What?'

'Ticket touts! I saw them this morning, a ragged army camped out on the steps. The moment the box office opened, they were there buying up the house. Half the tickets gone, to my knowledge. You know what it means? Once we open, they'll be at the door offering those tickets for twice the marked price. I was all for tearing into them, but the Colonel – and God knows what regiment *he* was ever colonel of – the *colonel* tells me there is nothing he can do. It is their God-given right as native true-born Americans to buy tickets if they feel like it, and sell them again if they feel so disposed!'

He turned away, stamping about the room.

Bríd and Isabella watched him anxiously.

'Is it going to harm us?'

He stopped and looked down at the carpet.

'No way of telling at this stage. We'll have to wait and see what sort of advanced publicity the newspaper boys give us. At least you gave them a good buttering-up.'

Chapter Thirty-Nine

'Well, Bill, I hope you're satisfied?'

Isabella smiled at him slyly.

'That is without a doubt what I call a beefsteak,' Bill said, as he cut into it. On the plate before him lay what appeared to be approximately half a cow. 'Dash it – the tenderest bit of beef I ever ate and that's the truth.'

'Don't speak with your mouth full!'

It was midnight on the night before they opened, yet they had only just sat down to dine; Thompson the taskmaster had at last relented and let them out after a day of rehearsals.

'But, blow me, it's a German restaurant. I've never seen so many Germans in my life. Did you know there were Germans in America, Isabella?'

'And Italians too, I believe,' she said wistfully.

Bríd reached over and touched her hand, and Isabella looked up at her. Somewhere among these sprawling millions was Sandro, her once betrothed.

'Eh? Oh, I dare say, and Norwegians, Roosians, Jews and all. Well, they're certainly doing us proud.'

'Would you like some iced water?'

'Who'd have thought it, eh? Iced water. Mind you, it's all the heating, if you ask me; drives you to distraction, don't it? And talking of iced water, the wine's good, too. Did you know the Americans made wine, Bríd?'

Bill cut himself another large mouthful of beef.

'Well, if it's going to be like this all the way round, I for one am glad I came.'

Bríd was further down the table with Thompson.

'So long as you can fill your face three times a day, that's all that matters to you, it seems?'

'Steady on. A man of my figure needs a lot of stoking. No need to pass personal remarks on it. It's all very well for you ladies, you've got your waists to think of, but spare a thought for me. Thirteen stone; it's got to be supported somehow.'

Bill Harris was impervious to first-night nerves. The theatre was sold out, all the press and many of the most influential citizens, the mayor and millionaire industrialists would be there the following night, but so long as he got three square meals a day, Bill was imperturbable.

It was after two when they left the restaurant. Turning up the collars of their coats against the icy wind, they hurried the few yards to their hotels. The men were in a separate one nearby.

Bríd threw herself into an armchair and was easing off her boots.

'Are you nervous about tomorrow night?' Isabella sat oposite her in front of the fire.

'Hmm? Not really. I expect I'll get a few last-minute butterflies in the stomach, that's all. I remember, when I started, how terrified I used to be. But now somehow I don't seem to care all that much.'

'Are you glad you came?'

'Aren't you? I think it's wonderful. Such an adventure! And the people are so friendly, everywhere we've been. We've only been here a week, and already so many invitations! Once we've got the plays on and running, we must try to see more of the city.'

The following night, a blizzard whipped down Broadway and round Union Square. Sitting in her dressing room watching the snow flurrying past the window, Bríd wondered whether anyone was going to brave such bitter weather to see them.

Thompson came to her room ten minutes before curtain up, and was gloomy.

'They're still dribbling in, but the house is only half-full at the moment. Keep your fingers crossed. The press are here, anyway – I've been pouring champagne into 'em for the last half-hour. By the way we needn't have worried about the ticket touts. Apparently, it's quite normal!' He shrugged and made a grimace.

The orchestra struck into the overture and the curtain went up. Bríd was not in the first scene, and stood at the side of the stage listening for any response from the audience. It was very quiet, ominously quiet, except that the doors were opening and shutting continuously, and she could feel the freezing draught as the icy wind swept in from the street. At the end of the first scene there was no applause. In the gloom of the half-light at the side of the stage, the actors looked at one another. It didn't bode well.

Then she was on, and she could see straight away that there were quite a number of gaps in the audience. She hoped it was the weather and not indifference that was keeping people at home. As the scene ran on, she could feel a drag in the audience, a lack of response, a stillness and quiet which alarmed all her keen instincts, and when the curtain came down for the interval, there was only a spattering of applause. She met Thompson in the wings, with his hands in his pockets.

'It's a frost! It's a damned frost!' he muttered.

Seeing Thompson so down had the contrary effect on her, though, and she squeezed his arm.

'Don't worry, Georgie. If we aren't a hit tonight, it won't be for want of trying! You watch me.'

'Good girl!'

A spirit of defiance inflated her. She and her friends hadn't come all these thousands of miles to die a slow death on the Broadway stage. If they were destined to go down tonight, they would go down fighting.

There was an extra electricity in her movements as the curtain rose again, a quickness in her step, an alacrity in her responses, a fire in her eye, a crackle in her voice, a defiant spirit as she turned on her accusers in the great trial scene, swishing her skirt about her, standing erect, proud, noble, even in the moment of her condemnation. She still had no idea what effect this might have out front but she would let them see what she was capable of tonight.

At the final curtain, the audience at last gave their verdict. The applause was deafening. The audience rose, clapping their hands up in front of them, crying out 'Bravo!', quite unlike a London audience, quite unlike anything she had ever known. Standing in front of the footlights, bowing or making curtsy after sweeping curtsy, the actors were stunned with the response.

'I can't understand. They were so unresponsive all through the evening.'

'Well, Miss Flynn, that's our American way. We like to make up our minds about a show first, and then let the performers know what we think at the end.'

'I wish you'd told me me before. It would have made our work a little easier, Colonel Watney.'

The next morning flowers were arriving, notes of congratulation and invitations to dinner. The newspapers were very complimentary indeed.

' "'Oh, I love America,' Miss Flynn told your correspondent,"' Bríd was reading out over a late breakfast. ' "'Your American audiences are so discerning!' " Which they are, only I don't see how the reporter could know what I thought of them, seeing I gave that interview a week before we opened!'

By the time she had finished reading it, she realised that three-quarters of the interview had been invented by the reporter.

'Well, they certainly have a very free press, that's for sure. The freest on earth – for they write just what they like!'

Then they sifted through the invitations. One was from William H. Block.

'The coke millionaire,' Thompson told her. 'We'll accept that one. He's supposed to have a very fine art collection.'

And so, four nights later, when the theatre was closed for a night while the scenery for their next play was being erected, Bríd and Thompson were driven up Fifth Avenue through the snow. As the carriage stopped, she looked out at what appeared, in the dim light from the streetlamp and through the swirling flurries of snow, to be the castle of a medieval German knight: spires and turrets, crenellations, battlements, narrow lancet windows gleaming with coloured light. The door loomed above them, studded oak with an enormous iron ring hanging on it, and gargoyles leered down on them from either side in the gloom.

In the lofty hall a stone staircase rose, twisting round to a sort of minstrel's gallery with a fretted oak balustrade. A dignified footman took their coats, and they were led to the baronial hall, where, in front of a log fire big enough to have roasted a whole company of heretics, stood a short, stubby man with a bulbous nose and a fierce expression, in evening dress. She was introduced to William H. Block.

Around the wall she had already had time to notice many works of art. After they had been served drinks, and before dinner was announced, Mr Block could not resist pointing a few out to her.

'A Rembrandt, Miss Flynn. A self-portrait.'

An aging man with a haunted look in his eyes gazed at them from a foggy darkness.

'And Boucher, these four panels. Though perhaps not quite for a lady's eyes?' He leered at her. The panels represented pastoral scenes in which young ladies disported themselves in various stages of undress.

Over dinner he pointed to a large silver structure which dominated the centre of the table, a riot of Bacchic revellers, nymphs, dryads, a drunken Hercules, satyrs with vine leaves in their hair and tambourines in their hands, their heads flung back in a drunken orgy.

'See that epergne? Looks kinda familiar, don't it? I should just say it does! By no less a hand than the great Cellini, and copied from the original by the artist himself! Had it shipped from Paris. Expense is not an object, Miss Flynn, when Mrs Block commands, as I am sure you understand. You are a woman yourself!'

Indeed I am, she thought.

One day they made a party, hired two carriages and rode through Central Park. The park had only recently been laid out, so the roads and pathways had a raw newness and the trees had barely taken root.

Colonel Watney was very proud of the park.

'Pretty good, eh, Miss Flynn? Two and half miles long by three-quarters of a mile wide. Kinda throws some of your old parks in the shade, don't it? Eh?'

She had to agree that it was indeed very impressive, though privately she believed it might not have come to rival St James Park or Hyde Park *just* yet.

The streets on either side of the park had all been laid out and were numbered, as they could see by the signs at the intersections – but there were not yet any houses built on them. Here and there, scattered across the wasteland of empty lots, rose a solitary mansion.

'It is a growing city, Miss Flynn. In thirty or forty years, this will all have been built up. Why, every year folks are moving uptown. You've seen for yourself that many of the big stores are already moving on up to Thirtieth and Fortieth. It's only a matter of time. And when once the cream of society takes the plunge, why, then everyone else just follows right along!'

They acted in New York for a month, and their reception was very warm indeed. She did not think she had ever met such a kindly people, so ready to throw open their homes to them, so ready to embrace new ideas, new fashions, always eager for the latest, whatever it might be. She found them very well mannered, too, and well educated, especially the girls. In England, the daughters of wealthy families and the aristocracy were in general ignorant to a remarkable degree, and had a knowledge of nothing in the world outside horses and dressmaking. The American girls were otherwise, and they were quite ready to converse on any topic, not afraid to show off what they knew, as well as having an armoury of witty expressions which she had never heard before and which sometimes reduced her to fits of laughter, to the bemusement of her hostess.

Then it was time to board the train for Philadelphia. Colonel Watney had engaged a private train of five carriages for the actors, the orchestra, the dressers and the lighting and scenery men, plus two boxcars for the pieces of scenery Thompson wanted to bring with them. He had written ahead to the theatres with instructions to construct various pieces which it would have been too cumbersome to carry.

They thought they had a private train, but they discovered that the Americans had only a very hazy idea idea of what the word meant. Conductors, guards, officials, waiters and other staff wandered quite freely through the carriages, and when Thompson in an impatient fit pointed this out one day, the conductor looked at him in astonishment.

'What do you want to be private for?'

There was something suspicious and un-American about privacy, it seemed.

They had to be careful in Philadelphia. The city considered New York as its rival, and Thompson was afraid that if rumour of their success in New York reached the city, their reception might be correspondingly cooler.

Fortunately, things went off well. They found the old Puritan ways still lingered on in Philadelphia; it had a sedate, churchy manner, the citizens were neatly dressed, and life had a decorous quality quite at odds with the bustle and energy of New York.

In Washington the President attended a performance of *The Taming of the Shrew* and afterwards told Bríd, 'I laughed till I bust my buttons!'

And then they were back in the train again, for days at a time sometimes; watching all day as the country, farms, forests, sheer wilderness, flowed past their window, going to sleep and in the morning raising the blind to see still more, now rolling hills, now some marshy river valley. She was staggered at the sheer size of America, crawling through the mountains hour after hour, vista after vista of tree-covered peaks unfolding, then coming down gradually at last to the plains and seeing in the distance the afternoon sun flashing on a great river winding away lazily in the incredible distance. The country unrolled, it seemed, endlessly; always some new mountain range, some broad new river, the name of which she had known hazily in the back of her mind but never imagined she would actually see.

City followed city, until the effect became quite blurred, but everywhere there were friendly welcomes, and they found their audiences always so well educated; people would quote Shakespeare to them at receptions they were invited to, or query whether a certain incident in *Mary Queen of Scots* was quite historical.

They came to Pittsburgh by night, and the sight of the whole plain covered by furnaces, the flames shooting up into the night sky, was quite extraordinary – as if there must be enough steel here for the entire world. Again she thought, This country must surely one day become the biggest and most powerful on earth.

When they arrived in Chicago, it was early in the new year, and the weather was bitingly cold. The next morning, struggling down the street from the hotel in the teeth of the wind, Bríd was certain her nose would freeze solid and just chip off! But if the temperature was forty below, the welcome was as warm as it had been everywhere else.

One day she was taken to visit the stockyards, and even though she had thought she was hardened by now to the sheer size of everything, she was once more staggered by the thousands upon thousands of steers penned up, the cacophony of lowing and bellowing and shuffling; the great marshalling yards and the long lines of refrigerated boxcars.

'No wonder the steaks are so big,' Bill muttered. 'They could feed the whole world from here, I should think.'

When they approached the slaughterhouse, Bríd wanted to hurry by. Looking in briefly, she saw men who seemed entirely covered in blood, wallowing in blood; blood on the walls, on the ceiling, blood washing down through sluices in the floor. Steers were urged into a pen, stunned by a man holding a kind of pistol, upturned by a tackle, whisked into the air by their hind feet, whirled along and then shot down a chute, where these men waited with their great knives, and in a matter of minutes the animals were reduced to horns, hides, bones and meat.

'Oh, for goodness sake, show us something else!' she cried.

The following morning in their hotel room a small parcel arrived for her. Throughout the tour, letters, flowers and other gifts had crowded into her room. She turned the package over. It was not franked, so it must have been handed in to the hotel by hand.

She opened it and found inside a small jewel case. There was a note: 'An admirer hopes Miss Flynn may graciously condescend to accept this trifling expression of his esteem.' No signature.

Isabelle was watching as Bríd opened the case. It contained a pair of earrings with the most exquisitely matched flawless diamond pendants.

For a moment neither spoke. At last their eyes met.

'An admirer? Isabella, I can't accept these – they must have cost a fortune!' She turned them in her fingers, watching the diamonds flash, and mesmerised for a moment. 'Who on earth could have sent such an expensive gift?'

Chapter Forty

Through January, February and March the tour continued – Detroit, Toronto, Boston and New England – and everywhere they went, the mysterious admirer followed.

Another jewel arrived, a bracelet in gold, chased filigree work set with an uncut ruby. She stared at it. How much could it have cost? She held it to the light and was mesmerised by the rich wine colour of the stone. She put it on her arm, took it off again, then put on her earrings and, turning her head, watched as they caught the light and flashed – flames of purest fire.

Then another small package and she opened it with trembling hands – what was he going to dazzle her with now?

Opening it, she found a ring set with a large diamond surrounded by emeralds, and slipped it on her finger, turning and holding it to the light and then looking again at the box and the little note: An admirer hopes that Miss Flynn may graciously condescend to accept this trifling token of his esteem.

Trifling token! The jewels that lay in her lap were the gifts of a prince – at any rate an American prince, a millionaire many times over.

These packages too had been handed in to the theatre. That meant that her admirer was following her from town to town. At night during the play her eye would range across the audience, the row upon row of faces eerily lit by the reflected glow from the stage, all staring hypnotised at her. Which one was her wealthy admirer? She would glance up at a box. Was that a man's hand she could see resting on the balustrade? Was her admirer sitting there in the shadow watching her?

Isabella took a lighter attitude.

'Why worry? You have an admirer – I should think you do! You probably have thousands!'

313

'But these things,' Bríd would say, picking them up from her lap. 'How can I accept such things when I don't even know who has given them?'

Isabella would laugh.

'*Cara*, if a man wants to give such a gift to the lady he admires, why should she not accept it?'

Bríd was not convinced. Accepting such a gift put her under an obligation, she feared – especially if the gift came from an admirer.

She thought of old William T. Sherborne the Third. She might have been inclined to think he was her admirer if it were not the for the fact that this admirer was following her about. In any case, Mr Sherborne would surely have come to see her.

She gave strict instructions to the stage doorkeeper. 'If any small packages for me are handed in, make sure you find out who they're from.'

But when the next one arrived, the doorman was unable to help. It was a boy from the Washington Hotel, he said, and he had no idea who had sent him.

They were due to leave town the following morning, and she had time only to walk briefly to the Washington Hotel and through the lobby once before she had to return to the theatre.

The theatre company returned to New York finally at the beginning of April, and already there were signs of spring. There was a lightness in the air and an intoxicating clarity in the light. It gave a heavenly lift to the spirits after the long days and nights of travel through the heavy snow and blizzards.

Coming down from Boston through New England, Bríd had admired the little farms with their white fences and red-painted barns; the villages with their white clapboard churches and prim steeples; everything neat and respectable. Now the untidy bustle of the city surrounded them once more.

They were to play *Much Ado about Nothing* in New York for three weeks before returning home. She wrote a short note to Mr Sherborne and was invited to tea one afternoon.

The carriage brought her to what she took at first to be an English country house, the residence of a duke perhaps, only, instead of being set in a spacious park where deer grazed, it stood in a side street just off Fifth Avenue.

The ducal theme was continued inside, where all was hushed. She could have been in a gentleman's club in St James's, she thought, as the butler led her through panelled rooms hung with heavily framed portraits and over broad Indian carpets past full-sized classical statues and a magnificent ormolu French eighteenth-century clock, until they arrived in a smaller and snugger parlour.

William T. Sherbourne had been asleep in an old leather-backed chair in front of a little fire. He hauled himself from the chair with difficulty, but expostulated when the butler went to his assistance.

'No, damn it, Wilkins, I'm not such an old wreck that I can't get out of a chair. All my servants have strict instructions from my daughter to treat me like an invalid, Miss Flynn, but I won't have it! Now then, Wilkins, you just attend to your duties. Miss Flynn is no doubt dying for a cup of tea – isn't that so, my dear?'

She smiled as she took a chair opposite him.

'Now, let's make ourselves snug! Have you had a successful tour? You have? I'm not surprised. The American people are hungry for culture, Miss Flynn! They snatch at it whenever they get the chance. Of course, here on the east coast we're doing fine, but in the newer cities, still young, you see, still growing, finding themselves, I fear things may be be just a little rough at the edges. Did you find it so? Oh! But I see you are wearing the garnets. My! They certainly do become you.'

This was the lead-in she had been waiting for.

'They are most beautiful, Mr Sherborne, and I shall always be most grateful –'

'My dear, please don't say another word. I would like to have given you more, believe me.'

She changed the subject.

During the last New York engagement, no new jewel arrived. Bríd thought she might have left her admirer behind at last. Perhaps he had tired of her? But one afternoon, walking up Fifth Avenue, she went on impulse into St Patrick's Cathedral, and all her suspicions were renewed.

She had taken to going to Mass again over the last few years. When she was young, it had meant little to her, but now she found the consolation so many others had found before her, and breathing the incense-laden air, as she stepped into the deep gloom of the interior, she thought, wherever she might be in the world, she only had to step into a church to feel at home.

She made her way down the aisle towards the altar with the little red light of the host glowing in the dark, and the rich, deep colours of the windows reaching down in dim shafts of light from high above. Somewhere she heard a shuffling of footsteps and two women whispering together, and she noticed a woman hunched in a pew to one side.

Bríd entered a pew and knelt in prayer.

At first her mind was empty, and she was content to allow the great peace that the church held out to flow silently into her soul until she relaxed, felt calmer and more tranquil.

Even so, worries began filtering into her mind. What about the future? Back to London? More of the same? More work, night after night coming home at midnight, making a life for herself in her Chelsea home? She had everything, didn't she? And yet in some way that it was not easy for her to tease out, what did she have?

Her life was empty. Why did she go on? What was she doing it for? Of course she was sending money to Ireland; Matt would be well educated, no doubt, and would perhaps go to the university, have some respected profession, perhaps even make a name for himself. She rejoiced in the thought. Yet she would never see him, never share in any of his triumphs or trials ... She banished the thought, and waited till her mind should settle again.

She would never see Harry again either. She glanced up into the gloom above her as the memory of him came to her suddenly. She seldom thought of Harry now, not by day. By night, in the early hours when she could not sleep, it was another matter.

She drew a deep breath; it did not do to harp on the past. What was the use of it? Better to get on, to work, to establish herself, to fortify herself against the world. So the thoughts went round in her mind, always coming back to the same spot. There was within her still an emptiness that she simply no longer knew how to fill, and she felt she had become no longer a woman but some kind of automaton, wound up by an invisible hand and unwinding day by day, whirring and clicking as her life unwound within her.

Her attention was distracted. From the corner of her eye she noticed a dim shape moving away between the pillars. She turned her head. A man had been watching her. The door at the far end opened briefly and he passed out.

Was she being followed? Spied upon? Clutching her skirt about her, she rose and made her way out into the daylight again and looked around.

The street was busy as always and crowds hurried past her along the sidewalk. Her heart was beating, and she had a sense of foreboding; something was in the air. She should have asked Isabella to come with her. She must not go out alone again. She turned back towards the hotel.

She tried to shake the mood off. It was all imagination. In any case, was it not a woman's due to receive homage from men? Flattery, compliments, gifts? Why did it agitate her?

316

Because these gifts were so expensive. Any one of those things could have kept Patsy and Nora in comfort for the rest of their lives. Giving a gift like that to a woman gave a man power over her. That was what unsettled her.

An invitation arrived. One of many, but this was perhaps special. Mr Vanderbilt Jr was throwing a masked costume ball. She and a friend were invited. It was to be three days after the end of their run, and she had a few days off before the company returned to London. She would go with Thompson.

She looked forward to dressing up. Oddly, despite the years of make-believe on stage, the pleasure of seeing herself in graceful historic costume never diminished. But masked? She would have to select something appropriate. She was put in mind of one of the old Maestro's favourite operas, *I Puritani*, in which the tragic figure of Charles I's widow, Henrietta Maria, escapes from a Roundhead castle disguised in a bridal veil. Bríd would go as Henrietta Maria. It was a lovely period and she could have something modelled upon a Van Dyck portrait, an elaborate, stiffened lace collar, a wig of massed curls, a puffed skirt, high waist and low-cut décolletage. And she would put on a French accent; that would fool everybody.

She would wear her new jewels, Bríd thought dreamily. All of them. Why not? She was quite sure the belles of New York would shine on that night. They knew how to dress themselves and they had the money to do themselves justice. She had Ireland's reputation in her keeping.

So, on the Wednesday night towards ten, a soft evening of early spring, with the balmy smell of blossom in the air, she and Thompson were deposited at the doors of the Vanderbilt residence. George had entered into the spirit by dressing up as a Cavalier.

She had seen some palatial homes on Fifth Avenue but the one which rose before them was perhaps the grandest of them all. Modelled on a Renaissance Italian palazzo, it proclaimed its owner a prince indeed, albeit a merchant prince. Going up the steps and into the brightly lit hall, easing their way through crowds of laughing guests, Bríd could see no hint of the origins of his money. Rich Flemish tapestries hung on the walls, lit by gilded sconces. Around her the guests swirled; Turkish sultans, Roman emperors, Spanish courtesans, Marie Antoinettes by the half-dozen, a Queen Elizabeth or two, a Sir Walter Raleigh here, an Eleanor of Castile there, and all masked, so that there were constant shrieks of amusement and recognition – 'Oh, Randolph! I never thought!' 'Well, sir, the doublet and hose sure looks good on you!' 'Is that? It can't be! Teddy, you old devil! Oliver Cromwell, eh? Suits you, you old scallywag!' Vivacity on all sides, and the clinking of champagne glasses.

They found their way into the ballroom, a vast salon made to seem even bigger by the mirrors which almost covered the walls, sending reflections of the enormous candelabra back through multiple reflections into infinity, an endless regression of light on every wall.

In the centre of the floor an artificial lake had been created, on which half a dozen swans seemed perfectly at ease, and into which a fountain tinkled among ferns.

Dancers already occupied the floor. Thompson and she danced twice, and then found seats in an anteroom.

'I'm not much of a dancer, Bríd. I'm sure one of these tycoons or their sons will give you another whirl round the floor.'

'Oh, come on, Georgie! I'm dying to dance! I haven't had a dance in ever so long. I don't even remember the last time we danced.'

But Thompson sat down and mopped himself.

A callow young man dressed dashingly as a French revolutionary of the *Directoire* period, with cut-away coat, a huge sash of red, white, and blue round his waist, and tight pantaloons, appeared before her and invited her to 'tread a measure'.

It amused her to try out her French accent. He was impressed.

'Hey, gee, are you foreign?'

'Per'aps – eet may be!' she hinted.

'May be, huh? Now just let me see, my fair maid – from which country do you hail? Erm, you English?'

She couldn't help laughing, but then retained her gravity.

'Eengleesh? Wiz such an accent? What can you be theenking of, *mon brave*? Surely you yourself are from *la belle* France?'

'Oh, sure.' He laughed too. 'So you're French – for real, huh? Gee, if that don't beat everything.'

Later, when they had been helping themselves to delicious ice creams, she noticed a tall man who was not in costume, but wearing immaculate evening dress.

'Someone's not playing by the rules, George.'

The masked gentleman approached her as she was putting down her ice-cream dish and in a serious, quiet voice invited her to honour him with a dance. There was something a little forbidding about him. All his attention seemed focused on her as if the entire object of his evening had been just this moment as he escorted her back into the ballroom.

He took her in his arms and they moved round the floor for some time in silence, until she wondered whether he was going to say anything at all, or whether she should tease him with her French accent. Yet something about him hinted against it.

Then, as they danced, he turned her hand slightly in his own and was studying the bracelet on her arm.

'A pretty trinket.'

'Oh . . . yes.' She was not sure how to go on.

'From an admirer perhaps?'

'Perhaps.'

'An admirer, let me see.' He paused, looking away over her shoulder as if recalling something, and then back into her eyes. ' "An admirer who hopes Miss Flynn may graciously condescend to accept this trifling expression of his esteem?" '

The room had become very hot all of a sudden. There was something very strange here, and she was feeling giddy.

'Who are you?' she said hoarsely.

'Can't you guess?'

'How can I?'

'Oh, you know me well enough, Bríd.'

'Do I?' She felt tight in the throat.

'You know me very well.'

She couldn't stand any more of this. She wrenched a grip on herself and, disengaging her hand, reached up and pulled away his mask.

It was very strange indeed; it was the strangest moment of her life. For that second she did not know where she was, which country she was in, what day it was, what time it was, which was up, which was down. He had to catch her as she lurched in his arms, staring into his face.

'Garrett!' she breathed.

Chapter Forty-One

It wasn't him, it couldn't be – but it was. He had caught her easily and went on with the dance, moving her in spite of herself, as her limbs responded automatically to his movements and the distant music of the orchestra.

For some seconds they continued to dance as she stared at him, her mouth frankly gaping with shock.

'But *how*?' Her voice was hoarse.

He allowed a tiny smile to pass across his face.

'Take your time, Bríd. We have plenty of time. All the time in the world. Thank you for wearing my jewels.'

'But Garrett . . .' Her strength was returning. '*Here?* I mean – you must explain. I never had such a shock in my life.'

'I'm going to explain, don't worry.' His accent, though recognisably Irish, had acquired an American inflection which must have fooled her when he first invited her to dance. 'Bríd, I must tell you, you've given me genuine pleasure. I don't go into playhouses as a rule, but I just couldn't keep away.'

'Oh.' Her voice was small, far away. 'Thank you.'

His glance was caught by someone over her shoulder, and he called, 'Don't worry – we won't be late!'

She did not have the strength to turn her head to see whom he had been talking to to wonder – late for what?

The dance ended and he escorted her back to George Thompson.

'I have to leave now. But I'll call on you tomorrow afternoon if that would be agreeable?'

'Oh yes,' she breathed faintly, 'I believe I'm free . . .'

'We might drive out somewhere – what do you think?'

'I'd like that . . .'

Garrett slipped away and was swallowed up by the crowd.

She sat down heavily beside George, who turned.

'You look as if you've seen a ghost.'

'I have. Would you get me a glass of water? I don't think I could stand up at this moment.'

After she had swallowed the water, she said weakly, 'George, do you think we could go home now? I've had enough for one night.'

'For heaven's sake, what's happened?'

'Don't ask me. I'll tell you later.'

When they got back to the hotel, it was nearly two in the morning. None the less, Bríd knocked on Isabella's door. They had a suite with their rooms opening off a common parlour.

'Isabella, are you awake?'

Isabella appeared in her nightgown with a robe over it, and her long hair in plaits over her shoulders.

'What is it? Are you all right?'

'I'm not sure. Do forgive me for waking you at such an hour, but I must talk to you. The most extraordinary thing has just happened. I can still hardly believe it. In fact, I can't believe it. Sit down, Isabella, let me hold your hand and recover myself.'

'Are you ill? Do you want me to fetch you a doctor?'

'A doctor? No, it's not my body. My mind – I'm not so sure. I can hardly tell you. A man . . .'

'Yes?'

She squeezed Isabella's hand tightly.

'Isabella, there was once a man. Oh, many years ago, before I ever went to London, in the village in Ireland where I grew up. A man who wanted to marry me. He was very proper, very respectful, he courted me according to the rules, we walked out together. He was a farmer, prosperous, respected – he was the best match in the village, and if I had been any other girl there I would have accepted his proposal the moment he offered it. But my head was filled with all kinds of foolish dreams, I was certain there was more in store for me. And when Harry, you know, who was so lovely, so handsome on his horse, when he noticed me and talked to me and when he kissed me – I remember it to this moment – of course, this other man, so proper, so dignified, just flew out of the window.'

She paused.

'Well?'

'Oh, I won't go through it all.' She gripped Isabella's hand so tightly that Isabella had to take her hand in her own and ease it.

'Go on.'

'It was so complicated. This man, well, he forced me to agree to marry him.'

'How?'

'He found out I had been going with Harry and he threatened to expose me and shame me before the whole village. I would have been ruined unless I promised to do as he asked – marry him. So I promised. Then – you know it all, Isabella, I told it all to you years ago – I ran away to be with Harry, leaving Garrett, this man. Later I heard he had left the village. It was said he had been in such a state of rage and violent despair that it was thought he might do away with himself – or someone else. Then one day he left. No one ever knew where.' She paused looking up into Isabella's face.

Isabella understood. 'Until tonight?'

Bríd nodded, looking down, her hand still strongly grasping Isabella's.

'And he is the man – the admirer?'

She nodded again, still looking down.

'I met him tonight – not an hour ago. I'm in such a whirl. He didn't stay long, but he's calling tomorrow afternoon to take me out.'

'But Bríd, those jewels – he must be very rich.' Isabella smiled at Bríd. 'Very rich. How did it happen?'

'I don't know! We only spoke a couple of sentences. Oh, Lord! I don't know what I am going to do. Should I return the jewels to him?'

'What? Why?'

'Those jewels are worth a fortune, you know that yourself. How can I accept them? I mean, if I keep them, it is as good as saying – well, as good as saying . . .'

'I see. And you don't want him to think that you are willing to accept his attentions?'

'I remember when he was courting me. He's a very powerful man, Isabella. He wanted me very badly, I felt as if he wanted to take me over. To absorb me into himself, to make me part of him. I didn't want that. I didn't want it even before I met Harry. I don't mean anything against him. He's a good man! Any other woman would snatch him up, believe me.'

'So you were never in love with him?' Isabella asked quietly.

'Never.' She was twisting her hands together now as she tried to think it all out.

'And what are you going to do?'

'I don't know.'

'Will you go out with him?'

'I must. I treated him so badly, Isabella. It's the truth, I left him, I ran away, I humiliated him in front of the whole village. He must resent it still. I should have thought he would want to kill me instead of sending me jewels. I must go with him and try to make it up to him a little.'

*

322

The following morning she woke late with a headache. It still seemed as if it must have been a dream, yet it was not a dream. Garrett was real – and he was coming to see her in a few hours, to take her out. Her mind cast round restlessly, thought chasing thought. She must look smart for him. What should she wear?

She seemed to have no energy, and at last ordered something to eat in the room.

Isabella came in and sat on the side of her bed as she nibbled some toast and picked at some fruit.

'*Cara*, you must eat a little more. You look pale this morning.'

'Do I? Oh, God!' She sipped her coffee.

Isabella reached across and touched her hand.

'Bríd, listen to me. First of all, if you did not wish to marry him, it was wrong of him to try and force you. So you were within your rights to go away. Second, if a man gives a lady a jewel – or two, or three – contrary to what you think, it does not impose any sort of obligation on her. He wishes to give a jewel – so! If she chooses to accept it – so! That is the end! *Basta*! But you must eat your breakfast. You will be no use to anyone if you are fainting through lack of food.'

Thus encouraged, Bríd finished her breakfast and ordered the maid to run her a bath. Then Isabella did her hair for her and helped her into an afternoon costume: a jacket of russet-red velvet trimmed with fox fur, and a skirt of ruched satin, taken up behind her in a fashionable bustle. And on her head, a little hat with a small veil.

When this ensemble was complete, she surveyed herself in the mirror and tried to breathe some confidence and hauteur into her manner.

There was a knock at the door and the little black maid handed her a note. Mr Doyle was in the lobby and looking forward to a jaunt in the country.

Some last-minute instinct warned her against the elevator, so Garrett first caught sight of her at the head of the staircase, where, with a true actress's skill, she was able to descend slowly towards him, the fullness of her skirt taken up in one hand and a tiny parasol in the other. She looked superb, and she could read the reaction in his face, though he was a man always in control of himself.

He was elegantly dressed in dove grey for an afternoon's ride. Outside, a groom was holding the leading rein of a beautiful pair of black horses harnessed to an immaculate phaeton, an open two-seater riding high on its springs.

Garrett handed her up into it.

'I thought we might go over to Long Island and down the coast a little way?'

She nodded, scarcely able to muster speech.

They crossed through lower Manhattan to the Brooklyn ferry, and were carried to the Long Island shore. Flicking the whip, he soon got them beyond the swathes of new housing under construction, up and over Brooklyn Heights, with its pleasant, tree-lined avenues, and out among the fields and small villas looking down over the bay, where a bright April sun glinted on the water. The ships passed each other in the distance like toys, sending up little plumes of black smoke which would be caught by the afternoon breeze, and many small sailcraft were leaning into the wind, their sails straining and billowing. It was a heavenly day, and she cheered up to be out in this splendid little carriage, bowling along behind two well-fed horses.

Garrett looked at her at last and smiled a small smile.

'You've been wondering how I did it?'

She nodded.

'I do owe you an explanation, I admit. I thought you were going to pass out last night.' His attention was distracted by the horses and he took them in hand to bring them round into a new lane. 'Yes, I owe you an explanation.'

'Garrett' – her voice was hoarse – 'I think I owe *you* an explanation.'

'All in good time.' He smiled again. 'In fact, thinking about it, you did me a favour in one way. If you hadn't run off as you did, I would never have come to America. And we wouldn't be here now. Are you comfortable, by the way? Not too breezy for you? Yes –' he gave a little flick of his whip – 'we would be living in Ballyglin, we would have our children, we would have our farm, we would go to the fair in Boyle. All very snug. Do you ever go back to Ballyglin, Bríd?'

'No.'

'Why not?'

'I can't explain.'

His eyebrows rose but he said nothing. Then he went on.

'Well, like many another Irishman, I came to America. To Boston. And like many another I was taken in hand by the local boss – lent money and found a job. I went to the Midwest to build the Central Pacific Railroad. Some men drank, some killed each other, some got killed or injured. I worked hard, I watched my step, and they made me a ganger. The men, let's say, respected me. I became foreman of the section. I soon had a bit of money set by. I paid off my obligations back in Boston. Then I invested in stock, just a little at first. But I soon found out how the railroad company made its money – not through the passengers or the freight. Land, Bríd. The government gave them ten square miles of land for every mile of track laid, on alternate sides of the line. Now, that land wasn't worth a cent when there were only Indians on it, because there was no way of reaching it. But once the railroad came through, it was another matter. Well, I got the map and I studied it hard. I sold my stock and went into land. The railroad company had ten square miles on one side; I bought the ten on the other side, at two dollars fifty an acre. I followed that line, buying here, buying there, and after a while, as the settlers came down the track looking to farm, I sold. That land now sold at forty dollars an acre.

'It was dangerous work. The settlers didn't always like it. Someone had told them two fifty, but when they arrived they found it was forty. It was legal, but I carried two Colt revolvers on me.

'Well, the railroad was completed and I was back in Chicago, not sure what to do. But I saw an article in a newspaper one day about the amount of beef coming through the stockyards. Thirty-five thousand head in 1867; seventy-five thousand in '68; three hundred and fifty thousand in '69. I leased a fleet of refrigerated boxcars and started dealing in beef, shipping it east from Chicago. I couldn't go wrong. Everything kept going up and up. I leased stockyards. I bought out rivals. One unfortunate gentleman fell in the mincing machine.' He glanced at her and grinned. 'Only joking – but it was getting like that. Men would do anything – *anything* to cut out a rival, Bríd.' He thought for a moment, studying the backs of the horses. 'Anything. You needed to keep a cool head. And you needed a sharp eye for figures. You have to keep your eye on the ball, never let up for a second, and be prepared for anything.

'If you want to, you can make a fortune in this country. America's been good to me.'

Chapter Forty-Two

'At first I wanted to kill you – and him, that arrogant Englishman. Then I only wanted to forget you, pretend you had never existed. I could do that only by leaving Ireland, making myself in a new image – I wanted to make an entirely new me, to obliterate everything connected with you. All my hatred and bitterness gave me energy, it made me hard. I would do anything, drive any bargain, let nothing stand in my way. It was my way of wiping you out of my life.'

He looked down, his face shadowy in the soft lamplight.

'But I guess that after ten years, when I allowed myself to think about you, I found I didn't hate you any more. I had been too hard on you, had forced you to agree to marry me.' He paused again, looking away as he thought. 'I was so sure we were made for each other that I was ready to force you; I was convinced you would come round to my way of thinking eventually.' He looked up into her face. 'It's I who ought to ask your forgiveness.'

She could not think of anything to say to this, and there was a silence in the air between them. Around them other diners chatted; waiters hurried between tables.

He had brought her back to the hotel early in the evening and given her an hour to change. The restaurant was only a block from the hotel; the food was excellent, but she was not thinking about food.

All afternoon they had talked; hours of talk to tease out the years between them, each telling their story or such part of it as they chose. She said nothing of Matt, of course, and as they filled in the missing years, and drank a glass of wine and then another, the revelations and confessions went deeper, becoming more serious.

What a handsome man he was! He had hardened into a man, come into his rightful self, and there was nothing of the peasant about him now, nothing of the Irish farmer any more. He was a man of business, a man who gave orders affecting thousands, a man whose bank-rolls were long and complicated, who had accountants bowing and nodding, secretaries taking notes, managers asking for orders. She pictured him in that bloody charnel house in Chicago, the bellowing of the cattle, the harshness of it, the brutality. It was awesome – and he owned a good part of it. He told her his company was called Anchor Beef and Canning, and on her travels she remembered seeing boxcars with an Anchor symbol painted on the side, boxcars passing her one by one till she was weary with counting. He was a director of the New York and Erie Railroad Company, too.

This was the man sitting across from her, toying with a fork, his other hand in his pocket as he sat back, now looking up at her, now away across the other tables. A waiter approached and was clearing the plates, and they discussed an ice cream or just a cup of coffee, and all the time her head held a cloud of thoughts and impressions.

'You have nothing to be forgiven,' she said quietly.

'I haven't forgotten, Bríd. I wanted you so badly I would have killed to get you. I would have killed him. He had gone before I could get at him.'

'Garrett, there is something I must ask you. Soon after I left Ballyglin, Lord Leighton was murdered. Did you have anything to do with that?'

'No. My quarrel was with his brother. I might have joined the Fenians all the same, if you hadn't gone. After that I didn't want to stay in Ireland.' He was silent for a moment. 'I did kill a man once. When we were building the Central Pacific. We had come over together on the boat, we had travelled out west together. I'd lent him money. We worked alongside one another at first, laying tie-beams. Then they made me foreman. We'd been friends – now I was giving him orders. The company was in a hurry and there was a bonus for me if I brought the work in ahead of time. I pushed the men pretty hard, and I could see he didn't like it. He had his pride. Finally, one night when he'd been drinking, he lashed out at me; took me by surprise and sent me sprawling. I rolled over and as I looked up he had an iron bar in his hand, raising it over his head. I didn't wait; I had my revolver out and he was dead before I'd even thought about it.' He paused. 'I killed a fellow Irishman, Bríd.'

'In self-defence.'

'Oh, I've excused myself, of course, told myself all the reasons why I couldn't have done anything else. It doesn't lessen the fact that there's a family in Ireland that had to mourn a son. I decided from then on that violence isn't the way. Killing only begets killing. Daniel

O'Connell was right: Ireland's freedom is not worth the price of one man's life.'

As he looked away from her lost in thought, she could see how that incident had burnt into his mind. She wanted to get away from it, to change the subject.

'Still, you've come so far and made such a success. You could never have done all this if you had remained in Ireland.'

He made an effort and pulled himself up. 'No – and you could never have done all that you have done, either.'

He looked carefully into her eyes, and she was on her guard. Conversation became difficult between them as she sensed that he had things on his mind to do with her, and she was afraid that he would utter them, because she was not yet ready to give any answers.

'When do you return to London?'

'We sail for Liverpool on Monday.'

'Can you postpone it?'

'Oh, let me see – well, no, not really. In fact, not at all.' She was awkward. 'We're playing another month at the Adelphi when we get back and we must re-rehearse our productions.'

'Do you ever think of giving up the theatre?'

'Often. But what would I do?'

'Marry?'

'I don't think of that any more,' she said softly, looking down. 'I don't think I could now. I have my house in London, I have furnished it with great care. I have Isabella and we're very snug together, I assure you.' She looked up and smiled at him, a bright, false smile.

'Hmm. Monday? Will we meet again before you go?'

'Oh yes,' she said readily, 'if you wish it.'

'What I was thinking of was that, with all your months of work behind you, you might like to get away from the city for a couple of days. Maybe a run up to Newport? Have you seen it?'

'No, what is it?'

'Newport? A very pleasant little place on the coast, where some of the New Yorkers have their seaside cottages. You'd like it. Will you come?'

'Very well. When?'

'Tomorrow. Then you can come back on Sunday for your departure on Monday.'

'That would be nice. Thank you.'

It was generous of him to invite her, and she still felt that she owed him her time so that they could straighten things out between them. He relaxed and smiled.

That night as she undressed, she could not stop thinking of

Garrett and the man he had become. He was a tycoon; he could raise his little finger and thousands of men and their families might be affected. That was what that aura about him meant: power. Like some magnetic field, which drew lesser bodies into its sway, as he moved through the city, men, women, stock markets, railroad companies, farmers thousand of miles away, all were affected by him.

That was it. She felt herself stiffening, rebelling against his power. The pattern was repeating itself as it had done in Ballyglin.

Still, in a way, she couldn't help being impressed.

In the morning Thompson was at the door. He was holding papers.

'Just settled the accounts with the Colonel, Bríd. Good work! And he wants us to come again.'

She thought, Come again, Garrett would like that . . .

'Let me see.' She took up the accounts. 'Total receipts four hundred thousand dollars.'

'Of which a tenth share goes to you. Reckon four dollars to the pound: ten thousand pounds. Not bad, eh? One of these a year and we could all afford to retire in a few years. If we were the retiring type, which you're not.'

'Don't bet on it.'

He looked at her sharply.

'Are you?'

'Georgie, I've got to the point where money has ceased to mean anything. I've got more than I need. I've got more than I would need if I lived to be three hundred. I can never spend it all. So what am I doing it for? It's not vanity, I got over that years ago. Oh, of course, now and then it's fun to dress up, fun to be admired. But going on night after night, the same plays, I don't know . . . Sometimes I think if someone said, "Come for a round-the-world trip and forget the theatre", I don't know but I might not take him up.'

'Who? Who's offering?'

She laughed.

'You looked so worried! No one! I only said that if someone were to offer, I might be tempted.' She sobered up, staring at him. 'Where would you be without me, eh? Where would you get your next star? You'll have to be looking out for one eventually. One of these days you're going to want someone younger than me, aren't you?'

Thompson was now gazing out of the window.

'That's just it. I get plenty of girls coming to me. Thousands, throwing themselves at me, making flattering offers. But a woman like you – they're not so easy to find.' He swung round. 'So promise me, no more talk of retirement for the time being – all right?'

She laughed. 'Don't worry. There doesn't seem much prospect of it at the moment. What else would I do?'

The door opened as she said this and Isabella came in. She walked through the room past them to the closet to hang up her coat, and Bríd noticed something strange in her manner.

Thompson gathered up his papers. 'Well, I'm off. See you tonight.'

'No, you won't.'

'Eh?'

'I'm going out of town for the night.'

'Out of town? Where?'

'Newport. Wherever that is.'

'What on earth for?'

'Don't ask. But I'll be back in plenty of time for the boat.'

As Thompson went out, Isabella came back into the room and sat in a corner. Bríd turned to her. She sensed something was wrong.

'Where have you been?' she asked brightly.

'I have been very foolish,' Isabella said softly.

'What on earth do you mean?'

Isabella drew a big sigh, looking away, and at last said, 'They told me downstairs that there was, you know, some Italian people living here in New York, and I thought what a good idea to visit them. The man at the desk told me how to get to the Italian district, and I found it very easily, not far from here. A poor quarter, of course, but suddenly I found myself among my own people, everybody talking Italian, all the shops, everything written in Italian, and the little businesses, the tailors, dressmakers, cobblers, barbers, everybody Italian, and it was all so jolly and pleasant, so nice to see them all . . .'

She faltered, then suddenly buried her face in her hands, sobbing.

Bríd crossed quickly to her.

'Isabella, what is it? I beg you, don't cry!'

She knelt at her friend's knee, taking her hands in her own and unwinding them, and then threading her arms round Isabella's neck and holding her close.

'What is it? Surely it is not such a bad thing that they're so happy? Did you wish you were among them?'

Isabella shook her head, still uncontrollably sobbing; after a while she began to regain control of herself and pulled away.

'It was very stupid of me, I know.' She heaved up a sigh which shook her whole body. 'Very stupid. When they told me about the Italian people, I thought of Sandro – that he was in America and that maybe someone had heard of him, or might have an idea where he might be. But, Bríd, when I got there it was like – I might as well have walked into Naples and asked where was Sandro. Thousands and

330

thousands of people – how could I ever find him in such a crowd and crowd of people?'

Bríd pulled an armchair across to where Isabella was sitting by the window, sat beside her and took her hand.

'Isabella, don't forget, I will always be your friend. I'm so, so sorry about Sandro, but we can be happy together, I promise you.' She held on to Isabella's hands, looking earnestly into her eyes, filmed with tears.

Isabella withdrew one hand and wiped it harshly across her eyes.

'I'm sorry. It's all so long ago. He must have married many years ago, Bríd. I am sure he is somewhere far off, maybe in San Francisco, with his wife and family. What would he want with me?'

She lifted her eyes to Bríd in a bleak look of hopelessness.

Bríd's own gaze fell. But she held tight to Isabella's hand.

Garrett called for her the next morning and together they went to Grand Central Station and settled themselves in a train.

American trains did not have first, second and third class, which would have been un-American and contrary to their notions of equality. In theory all were equal. In practice, however, there were also Pullman's 'Palace Hotel' cars; Garrett and Bríd made themselves comfortable.

In the early afternoon, they checked into the largest hotel she had ever entered. She thought she had seen some large and elegant hotels in the cities they had visited, some hotels better equipped, more technically advanced than any other in the known world. But here at Newport, the hotel was in a class of its own.

'You could play a game of football in the ladies' drawing room,' she told him after she had been to her room, changed her clothes and washed her face. They had separate rooms, that was understood.

Then they walked together along the seashore. Away ahead of them on the cliffs she could see the residences of wealthy gentlemen. And as they got closer she remarked them more and more, because she could begin to appreciate how big they really were.

'There appears to be some money in Newport. I wonder who lives here?'

Garrett laughed. 'Those are the "cottages".'

'Cottages? They're enormous!'

'That is how the man of wealth speaks. He has a "little cottage down in Newport", but everybody understands exactly what he means.'

Again, as on the day he had taken her out in his phaeton, it was heavenly to be beside the sea, with the bright, clear sky above them.

Bríd felt there had never been so much light; the great vault of the heavens was simply filled to bursting with radiance; light spilling out, light all about them. Coming from the foggy islands off the coast of Europe, knowing only the infinite shades of grey which that climate afforded, she found the light here intoxicating. She rejoiced in it, her spirits rising, and she threw her arms out, breathing in the salt air.

'It's glorious here!'

Garrett walked beside her in a light-grey suit, a soft felt hat, a hand in his pocket and a walking cane in the other.

After the long, involved conversations they had had, the unravelling of the past, their talk this afternoon was light and inconsequential. They discussed the "cottages"; he told her who owned which, and which he had been invited to. In fact, he had been invited to quite a number.

'You remember that ball at the Vanderbilts'? That kind of thing. The rich at play. To be more precise, the sons and daughters of the rich, and their mothers, determined to make everything a success. The fathers have usually lost the art of enjoying themselves. It's a mistake I don't intend to make.'

That evening as she dressed for dinner, looking at herself in the mirror as she hung the diamonds in her ears, she asked herself the inevitable question: What does he want? To seduce me? On the face of it, the answer should be yes. We have gone away for a night; we are in the same hotel, we are about to dine together, and no doubt wine will be served, there will be soft lights, amusing, flattering conversation. These are the traditional ingredients, the normal prelude . . .

Yet he had made not the slightest overture of any kind. Not the merest touch on her arm; never a long lingering look into her eyes; not once had he made any kind of leading remark or suggestive hint. She had no idea what he was up to, but he was up to something, that was certain. He had pursued her with single-mindedness since Chicago. He had spent a king's ransom on jewels for her, and he had monopolised her time since they had met. He dictated to her. There was something in the air, but what it was she had no idea.

They dined well. The conversation again was light and inconsequential. By some mutual understanding they kept away from the hot, dark area that still lay to be explored between them, and at last, after a pleasant evening, parted for the night.

The following morning they again took a stroll by the sea, and, arriving back at the hotel, sat on the covered veranda and ordered lunch. All the time Garrett was charming and attentive.

332

The sky was clear, high and blue; the breeze stretched the American flags on their poles; the bright sunlight glinted on the breakers; and out on the water great pleasure yachts bent into the wind, their sails filled. It was all quite beautiful.

As they ate lunch, she at last found out what he wanted. He was looking carefully at her.

'I'm going back to Ireland. The market's at a high just now; right time to sell. I'll never have such a favourable time. America's a grand country, Bríd, the land of the future. But I'm an Irishman, and I belong to the old country. I'm going to build myself a house in Ballyglin – something special – and I'm going to settle. I've made my fortune and I'm going to spend it in the village. I could do a lot of good there with a tenth of what I've made. What do you think?'

She was taken completely by surprise, and could hardly speak at first. Then she began to see what was coming.

'Oh yes, Garrett. I think it's splendid.'

'But there's one thing missing. After all, what's a house without a mistress? Hmm? A poor place. A woman is the life of a home.' His voice was soft, caressing, as he leaned in towards her, his eyes on hers. 'Who is to furnish it, arrange everything, order the servants? How am I to entertain my friends? Who is to welcome my guests? A man dreams of a home to come back to, Bríd, when he's been wandering the world alone for years, always on the move, in lodgings, in hotel rooms, always eating alone in restaurants. I've dreamed of a home of my own and a wife to welcome me, dreamed of us being together, and in the evenings, when we've had dinner, dreamed of sitting by the fireside and being able to look up and see – you.'

An involuntary thrill ran through her. She couldn't help it; as Garrett spoke these words, she felt herself responding. His voice had become low and hypnotic, and the image he conjured up was so vivid to her that despite all her efforts her imagination warmed to the picture he painted.

'All through the years, it's been you, Bríd, always you. And extraordinary though it seems, I knew we'd come together again. I just knew it had to be. Call it fate, call it anything. We were made to be together, you and I. It was as if all the time I was making the dollars, I was making them for you, so that one day I would be able to stand before you and claim you as my own. No one, not an English aristocrat nor anyone else, would be able to push me aside, but I would stand before you and claim you in my own right.'

A home and to be married, to be settled with a regular, respected place in society. And perhaps later a family ... She could feel him drawing her. At last, swallowing, she was able to break his look.

'You must give me a little time to think about it, Garrett.'

'You're leaving on Monday. Will you give me an answer before then?'

'I will.'

'All ashore that's going ashore!'

'For God's sake, they're casting off in five minutes. Where in heaven's name can she be? If she isn't here in one second, I'll tell the captain to delay sailing.'

Thompson stood on the upper deck with Isabella and Bill Harris. All three of them scanned the quayside for any sign of Bríd. Among the crowds, the piles of boxes and rolls and bales, the last-minute bustle and preparation, there was no sign of her.

'Who is this Garrett, anyway?'

'A friend.'

'And why did she have to go off with him this morning, for heaven's sake?'

'I don't know. He said he was bringing her to the ship. I thought she would have been here before us.'

'There she is!'

An open two-seat carriage was nosing its way through the crowd towards the ship. Bríd was turning to Garrett beside her and saying something, then reaching behind her for a handbag, shaking hands with him and getting out. She looked up towards them, waved gaily and hurried up the gangplank.

Two minutes later she was among them, and already the ship was casting off. The great hooter startled them, and was followed by the throbbing of engines as the ship began its manoeuvring away from the quayside.

Bríd leaned over the rail and waved to Garrett, who waved back, then was turning the heads of his pair of black horses.

'Phew! Bríd, please, I beg you, please, don't ever do that again.'

'Wherever did you get to?'

'Oh, it was nothing!' She laughed. 'He wanted me to see a little more of the city before I left. And there were a couple of things I wanted to buy. It was most pleasant. Isabella, have you sorted out the stateroom?'

'Stateroom! Never mind about the stateroom!' Thompson burst out. 'Do you know you've nearly given me a heart attack? Another two minutes and you'd have been left behind!'

'George, calm down. You really shouldn't worry. Everything's fine. Come along, Isabella.'

She smiled at him and disappeared through the door with her companion. Scarcely were they out of sight of the two men, however, than Bríd stopped. Isabella turned and saw that the gay smile had been wiped off her face.

'Isabella.' Her voice was tight, as if she could not breathe. 'Oh. Wait. Come this way.'

They were in the saloon. Waiters were setting out the tables for dinner.

'Let's sit here. Oh, God, I hope I've done the right thing.'

'Bríd – you don't mean?'

She nodded. 'I've married him. Just now. He didn't even have time to kiss me. And I don't even know whether I wanted him to.'

'Bríd –'

'I couldn't decide. All night on Saturday night and then again last night, I couldn't sleep. Should I accept – or what should I do? Then it came to me. Everything was clear. I have lost Harry for ever. I must face that. Seeing Garrett somehow made it real. Then, you see, I thought, if I return to Ballyglin, I would see my little boy. Going back as Mrs Doyle would somehow be different – not as if I were just going back for myself, do you see? Going back with him, it would seem more natural. And my aunt wouldn't be able to reproach me.'

'Yes.' Isabella faltered, and looked up mildly into Bríd's face. 'And do you – do you love him?' she asked softly.

Bríd looked down at her hands, gripped together tightly.

'I respect him, you know, and I thought, with time, I might grow to love him . . .'

Chapter Forty-Three

She had told Garrett she must be able to continue with her acting. Yet only a day or two earlier she had told Thompson she was bored with it. What did she want? Making conditions with Garrett was tantamount to saying, 'I must have an escape route', or frankly saying, 'It'll be a sort of halfway marriage, an on-off marriage.' She was not committing herself to him truly heart and soul.

Garrett had been kind and understanding, agreeing to everything she said. Yet he seemed to want her so certainly – just as he had done before. It was difficult to stand in his way. He was like some great American locomotive pushing everything before it, plunging headlong on its way. And then she thought, Garrett has everything and he could have any woman he wanted; why does he put up with my conditions and uncertainty? Why does he want to marry a woman who is not in love with him?

Leaning on the rail the next morning and staring at the horizon, she was still plagued by doubts. What had she done? Given away her freedom, her independence. He had told her he would let her work in the theatre, but would he, once he had her in Ireland in his new house? If she told him she was going back to London, what was to stop him from simply saying no? He could do it – he was a man capable of dragging her home from the railway station by her hair.

Still, there was no shame in being Mrs Garrett Doyle.

He is a good man, she would say, he wants to do good things in Ballyglin. He may be powerful but he is not cruel, is he? She couldn't be sure, but she thought not. Not cruel – only passionate. And anyway there was something admirable about a man who loved her as much as he did. Why couldn't she love him in return? In her cheerful moments, she decided to make a very strong effort to return his love. With time, she might come to love him indeed.

By night she dreamed of Harry. Why did the dream come back to her so persistently? Harry was nothing – a wraith, a phantasm, long dissolved in the mists of time, far away and married to someone else.

She would wake feeling low and depressed.

Then there was George Thompson; she had better break the news to him.

She waited till after dinner, and made sure he had a couple of brandies inside him.

'Married? You're joking! When?'

'In New York, just before we left. I told him I would be happy to be his wife, thinking vaguely, you know, a year or two years' time – whereupon he pulled the licence out of his pocket and drove me to St Patrick's. I didn't have much say in the matter. Anyway, George, don't worry. I've told him it is not going to interrupt my career.'

'Did you? And what did he say to that?'

'He agreed.'

'Really?'

'Really, I swear it.'

'Good Lord!' George emptied his brandy glass. 'Give me another. Well – where are you going to live?'

'In Ireland.'

'In Ireland! How can you continue to act if you're living in Ireland?'

'George, calm down. I'll come over – or we may come together and spend so many months in London, working for you, and then return to Ireland for the rest of the year. Why not?'

George looked gloomy.

'I don't like it. Husbands never like their wives to appear on the stage if they're not in the business themselves. They get jealous of other fellows ogling them. And with good reason.'

'What good reason? There won't be any good reason in my case, I assure you!'

'Bríd, why did you do it? I told Colonel Watney we're going back to New York next autumn.'

'I won't be able to, George. Sorry.'

Even when they were deposited at the Chelsea gate by Fred, and Mrs Foster opened the door to them, and they were kissing cheeks and taking off coats and hats, and sitting in her own drawing room, sipping a cup of tea; even as she rejoiced to be back in her own house, to sleep in her own bed, she would look up and think, I'm married! What have I done? I'm going to live with a man who's almost a stranger!

And in a moment of panic, she would think of some harebrained

337

scheme. She would wire Garrett and tell him the whole thing was a ghastly mistake, beg him to forgive her and pretend it had never happened. But it was out of the question. She was married. And she knew that he would hold her to it.

So what was to be done? She walked through her house, and now everything in it looked precious. She looked through the window into her garden, at the paved walks, the arbours, the trellises, the little fountain. She had never loved it so much. She walked round her drawing room, touching things – her grand piano, her little harp, still there after all these years, the long portrait of her on the wall as Mary Queen of Scots by Mr Whistler, the little Moroccan table, the easy chairs in Spanish leather, the carpets – everything chosen by herself, everything placed just where it was by herself. She had created this room, this air of pleasing harmony, this oasis of tranquillity where she could come after work, after all the excitement, all the nerves and high spirits, the fear and uncertainty.

There was no need to give up her house, she told herself. He had agreed that she could continue with her acting. It would be her London home, and she would travel between Ballyglin and here – it ought to work very well, she told herself brightly. Many wealthy families had two homes – what was so strange about that?

But Garrett wouldn't want to live here, she suspected. Would he begrudge her the time away from him, now that he had her?

She turned to her loyal shadow.

'This will always be your home, Isabella, as long as you want it. I don't know yet how things are going to work out in Ireland.'

She suddenly had a vision of meeting Garrett at the railway station, taking fright, and jumping on the next train back.

She had a letter from him. It was warm and friendly.

Ballyglin, May 1876

It is wonderful to see the old place again [he wrote], though it's in a sad state of repair. It's strange how the memory plays tricks. I thought I remembered the village quite clearly, yet when I walked through it a few weeks ago, it looked so poor and small. Well, I don't mind that. It's why I came back. But it makes me angry to think that some English family has had it all these years, owned every house and cabin in the village, and let it sink to this condition. The English have a lot to answer for.

The morning after I got back, I met one man – old Liam O'Conor do you remember him? He showed me how the thatch was rotted through on his cabin and let the rain in, and I asked him

338

why he didn't write to the landlord? 'Write?' says he? 'Me write – that never held a pen in me hand in me life!' 'Well, speak to Kemp,' I told him. 'Oh, very likely! Very likely that Mr Kemp would trouble his head about the likes of me,' says Liam. It was the same wherever I went. A terrible lowness of spirits, as if there was nothing in the world to hope for, but only to crawl through it as quickly as one could and make way for someone else.

There is some sign of struggle in Ireland all the same. The Land League has appeared and is campaigning all over the country for the three F's: to give the farmer security of tenure, to compensate him for the work done on his farm, and for fair rent. It is early days yet but I think with a bit of energetic support things might just be beginning to move. The English government, though, is massively indifferent to the Irish people. I can see it so much more clearly than the people here, who are used to it. I plan to get involved myself, once we are settled in ourselves.

Well, I am not idle. I am busy making arrangements for our future home, and counting the days till you'll be able to join me. We're going to make a fine couple, Bríd, I know it, and I think you'll have reason not to repent of your decision. Once you're here, we'll have our honeymoon right here in Ballyglin and I shall be able truly to make you my wife. I think you'll be pleased with the arrangements I've made. I've had some very satisfactory ideas about our house. Once you're here you'll have a completely free hand to arrange everything to your satisfaction of course.

When the villagers found out I had got married, they were agog to see my bride. 'All in good time,' says I, 'you'll have your fill of her when she gets here', and wouldn't say another word – so they're filled with curiosity to see who I am going to produce for them. What a shock when they set eyes on you, eh?

By the way, I have seen Patsy and Nora and they're both well. There's a little nephew lives with them – apparently his parents died of cholera – Matthew, a lively boy, you'll like him. I didn't tell them about you – it'll come as a surprise eh?

Things are going on very well here. Everywhere I go in the village I see scope for improvement. What do you say to a bridge on the river, eh? Instead of the ford? And I can see a new school building and a reading room. And I've told Father Geoghegan to go ahead and order stained glass for all the windows of his church. But there's more to be done yet. That's just to be going on with.

Take care of yourself now, Bríd; I think of you every day, and thank God that allowed us to meet again after so many years, and then gave you to me. I love you, and I intend to see that you will not have cause to repent of your choice of a husband.

Her heart had beaten when she got to the mention of Matt. A boy of ten; Garrett had not seen any resemblance to her – yet why should he look for any? And yet, one day, perhaps many years hence, she might have to break the news to him – and what would he say?

A few weeks later she found herself on the train once more pulling out of the Euston Square Station. Boxes corded and locked were stacked in the guard's van, and she was wearing a new silk dress, mauve gloves on her hands and an elegant hat. She must go back in style; Garrett would expect no less, and she had decided to do him proud. He should have no cause to find fault with her.

He had told her to take the night packet from Holyhead, so that she would get to Ballyglin by daylight, and eventually her train pulled in at the little station early on the following afternoon. She adjusted her hat, pulled on her gloves, smoothed down her skirt.

Garrett was waiting on the platform. He too was carefully and soberly dressed, and held a bowler hat in his hand. As he greeted her, he leaned forward and kissed her on the cheek. After the boxes had been unloaded and entrusted to a carter and his waggon, Garrett handed her into a two-seater gig, and they were off on the road to Ballyglin.

Once they were out of sight of the houses clustered by the station, she reached her hand to his face, drew him to her and kissed him full on the lips.

As they drew apart, she said softly, 'I owed you that. I'm sorry it was so long delayed.'

They kissed again with passion, hungrily, and she felt the rush of blood, the need surging within her after so long, as Garrett crushed her in his arms and kissed her strongly until she felt herself melting into his arms, swallowed up into his greater presence.

At last they separated.

'I'm glad you're here. I always knew that sooner or later everything would come right between us,' he said gently, his arm round her shoulder.

Her heart was beating, and she realised she had made the right decision that night in New York. Obviously they would have to get to know one another but the basic thing was right between them, of that she was sure.

As they drove along the familiar road, she drank in the trees, the fields and far off the Curlew mountains, so long remembered. He talked. As he had told her in his letter, there were many things to do here, but he had made a bit of a start. And as for the welcome back he had received, 'They couldn't have been more happy to see me if I'd been the Pope himself, Bríd!'

'Where are we going now?'

'Well, I think I've found us suitable accommodation. You'll see.'

He looked at her and grinned, a little mischievously.

Eventually she saw they were approaching the village.

'We're going back to Ballyglin? I don't understand.'

'You'll see. Don't worry.'

Then the wheels were splashing through the ford, and up into the village green, and the entire village was waiting to greet them. She looked at Garrett.

'You told them?'

He smiled slyly. 'They would never have forgiven me if I hadn't.'

'Garrett, you might have warned me! What do you want me to do?'

'Nothing at all – just look beautiful and smile at everyone.'

'Welcome to Mr Doyle and his bride!'

The villagers crowded round and burst into cheers.

God, how poor they were! Scarecrows in ragged clothes with bare feet, the women with coarse blankets over their heads, their faces burnt and gnarled from years of working in the fields. And everywhere around her, ragged and run-down little cabins, piles of manure before them, a pig here, chickens there, a goat by Mrs Carruthers's Stores and Bar.

But the warmth! The cheering!

'Won't you favour us with a word, Garrett?'

Garrett stood up.

'Friends! Thank you for your welcome! You know all the years I was away in America, never thinking I would be here again one day, I never forgot my native home, the place where I was born. And I never thought that one day I would bring my bride home, and hear all of you welcome her with such warmth.'

Bríd sat beside him, smiling and nodding to them, and wondering whether anyone would recognise her. In her silk dress and hat, she might have come from a different planet.

She saw Nora and Patsy. Nora had recognised her, but amazingly no one else appeared to. Patsy was just as he had always been; Nora too. And the lad beside them: he was bigger now, of course, but she recognised him.

He was so like his father. Surely someone *must* have seen the resemblance? She squeezed her handkerchief in her hand as she smiled.

'Garrett, for God's sake, let's get on!' she whispered. 'I can't bear this!'

Everyone had their fill of cheering, and of course no one expected *her* to say anything. It was quite sufficient for the bride to sit beside her husband and smile inanely. But Bríd was cursing under her breath. It was just like Garrett to want to show her off as his trophy, another one to set beside the others. And there was that beautiful boy among them cheering as loud as any, and not knowing why.

At length, when her face was aching with smiling, Garrett sat down again, whipped up the pair of grey horses before them, and amid a renewed outburst of cheering they rattled up through the village. Her last glimpse was of Nora's face and the serious look in her eye.

'Garrett, you might have spared me that!'

He was pleased with himself and smiled as he gave the horses a flick with his whip.

'And where are we going? Garrett, where are we staying tonight? Why can't you tell me?'

'It's a surprise. You'll be pleased.'

She couldn't think where they could be headed. There was nothing up this way. Still he kept the horses at a smart trot, and after another twenty minutes she was in an agony of impatience. It was as if they were heading towards Castle Leighton, but she could hardly believe it until Garrett was turning the horses through the gates. To her absolute astonishment the old gatekeeper came out and opened the gates for them and in a moment they were bowling down under the old avenue of elms which she remembered so well.

And now they came out into the broad gravelled sweep before the house, and it rose before her in all its old glory; the great portico of white marble columns, the spacious steps rising to the great front door, and the curving wings to either side.

Garrett pulled up at the steps, and already the door had opened and O'Flaherty was coming down towards them, and Liam was running from the side by the stables to take the horses' heads.

Now O'Flaherty was helping her down, but Garrett had leaped out easily. Coming round, he took her hand and wrapped it under his own arm, as if for safekeeping.

They were ascending the steps where the door stood open to them. O'Flaherty was saying, 'Welcome home, sir, welcome home, madam.' It was a dream. Still Garrett would not look at her; looking straight ahead, holding her arm tight under his, he steered her through the tall entrance hall and into the dining room.

The table was laid for them in readiness.

'O'Flaherty, take Mrs Doyle's coat. Would you like to wash before dinner, my dear?'

She stared into his face.

'Garrett, you must explain! Why are we here? Where is the Earl? Where is his family?'

'It's very simple –'

'Have you rented the house from them temporarily?'

Garrett looked round the room and drew a breath, inflating himself with pride and pleasure. This was a moment he wanted to savour.

'Oh, better than that. Much better than that.'

She stared at him.

'You mean . . .'

'I've bought it.'

Chapter Forty-Four

She sat heavily in one of the dining chairs beside the table.

Beyond the table through the window the demesne stretched away and she stared out for a long moment before turning to him.

'You can't,' she said weakly.

'I have. It's done, signed, sealed, red tape, sealing wax, lawyers' fees, engrossed on parchment, all regular. It was worth it, eh? It cost me, but I didn't begrudge a penny.'

'But why? I don't understand – the Earl . . .'

'The Earl was in a poor way, Bríd. On the verge of bankruptcy, every foot of land mortgaged. I'd got my lawyers on to it long ago and bought up the mortgages cheap – oh, they were glad to compound with me, you bet – for a shilling in the pound sometimes. When I had all the mortgages in my hand, I went to the Earl and told him, "I want you out." And he was very glad to go. Glad to get out of the place. He had no love for Ireland – never did, him or his family.'

But Harry did – he had told her. She couldn't believe it: he had evicted Harry from his home, the home he loved so much.

'How could you? It was despicable. Oh, God, I hate you!'

'It was poetic justice!' He stood large over her as she rested her arm on the dining table, tears smarting in her eyes. 'The old rotten, corrupt rule swept into the ash pit by American money. A new era in Ireland! It's a proud day.'

'You're heartless! I loathe and despise you! Did you ever think how they would feel about having to leave their home? Did you? They have lived in this house for two hundred years. Didn't you think of that? They loved this house! It was theirs, everything here belonged to them, collected by them, treasured and handed down through the generations! Did you have no respect, no heart, but just to walk in and coldly buy them out? Flash your dollars in their face and tell

344

them to get out of the house they have lived in for two hundred years? How could you?'

'What is the matter with you!' He was upset and angry. 'What do you care about the Leightons – any of them? Don't tell me you're still in love with that little *jackeen* of a Harry Leighton – not after all these years?'

'He's a gentleman and he has feelings – he would never have thrown a family out of its home!'

'*What?* Are you crazy? The Leightons have thrown families out of their homes by the score! Don't you know anything, Bríd? They were notorious during the famine! I told you before: families thrown out to starve under a hedge, winter, summer – it made no difference to the Earl of Elphin! And you feel sorry for them?'

She got up suddenly and rushed to the door, and then turned to O'Flaherty, who had been listening with open mouth.

'Mr O'Flaherty, where is my room? Please show me to my room now.'

The tears still wet on her cheeks, she took up her skirts and fled towards the staircase, not wanting to see Garrett's face or hear him.

O'Flaherty was torn, then he hurried before her.

'If you'd follow me, madam.'

She would not look back but hurried up the stairs, the great curving marble steps with their iron-filigree balustrade. O'Flaherty opened a door, and she found herself on the threshold of a large ornate room with a high ceiling and moulded cornices round the walls, hung with faded red silk, and with a large canopied bed to one side. Beyond the window lay the tangled, wild countryside of Ireland.

She threw herself on the bed and let the tears come.

She lost all sense of time. Her sobbing exhausted itself and she lay, her face buried in the counterpane of the great bed. There was silence in the room. She opened her eyes, thinking, I have married him, I have to spend the rest of my life with him. Why not run back to London now? I could be back in the morning.

She turned her head slightly. Garrett was standing close to her, holding a cup of tea in his hand. He looked down at her in silence for a moment, seeing the tears still wet on her face, the puffy eyes. Then he brought up a chair and sat close beside her, and held out the tea.

'I expect you're tired from your journey. Drink your tea, then try and sleep for a while.'

She pulled herself up on one elbow. Gathering her strength, she looked into his face.

'Garrett, I shall never forgive you for this. I can never stay in this house.'

He ignored this.

'Drink your tea,' he said quietly again.

She dashed the cup from his hand on to the carpet. There was a clatter of crockery. Garrett saw the concentrated look of hatred in her eyes before he bent and picked the pieces up. He looked thoughtful as he turned to the door.

'I'll send a maid with some hot water. Go to bed and sleep. You'll feel better.'

Her mind was a blank, and she continued to stare at the rich silk wall coverings, tracing the spiralling patterns up the wall. There was a faint tap at the door and a girl of twelve came in with a can of hot water in one hand and Bríd's travelling case in the other, and crossed to the washstand.

'Will I help you undress, madam?'

The young girl's innocent face checked her mood.

'Thank you,' she said, all feeling exhausted in her.

The girl helped her out of her dress, her stays and petticoats. Standing at the washstand in her shift, Bríd washed herself. She changed quickly into a nightgown the girl had taken from her travelling case, and climbed into the high bed.

'Will I bring you a hot-water bottle?'

'Thank you.' The bed was cold and she shivered.

The girl went out quietly. Bríd stared up at the canopy above her, thoughts running round in her head, round and round to no avail. Garrett could afford to be gentle with her – didn't he have all the cards in his hand?

The girl returned with the hot-water bottle, and Bríd moved to one side to allow room for it in the bed with her.

'Thank you. You may go now.'

It was so silent here. She had grown used to the distant rumble of street noises in cities, but here there was a deep, deep silence. Even the melancholy sighing of the wind in the trees outside only magnified the profound silence which welled up and filled the room. She stared up.

What was she to do? Garrett had bought the house, and he was unlikely to sell it again to satisfy a whim of hers. She had better face that. It meant she could either stay or go. But she knew why she had come, and nothing had changed that. Seeing Matt this afternoon had confirmed it in her. Nothing was going to stand between her and her son now. It was going to be difficult, and there would have to be diplomacy and tact, subterfuge even. But she would do it.

Her heart raced at the thought of the boy now only a few miles away, in the little cottage with Patsy and Nora. And she would see them again, perhaps tomorrow, perhaps the next day. But soon. She fell asleep.

When she awoke it was dark. She had no idea what time it was. The house was preternaturally silent, only that faint sighing of the wind, and for a moment she started up in fear. What should she do now? Then she remembered seeing a bell pull at one side of the bed; finding it in the dark, she pulled it.

Eventually there was a knock at the door.

'Come in.'

O'Flaherty appeared with a candle.

'O'Flaherty, what time is it?'

'Nine o'clock, madam.'

'Where is Mr Doyle?'

'I will see, madam. I believe he may be in his study.'

'No – if he is busy it doesn't matter.'

She was at a loss.

'Would you like me to bring you up something to eat, madam?'

'Yes.' Now he mentioned it, she was ravenously hungry.

'Very good, madam.'

He came across the room, lit the two candles which stood on the table beside the bed and went out.

She didn't allow herself to think about Harry; to think that he would never again enter this house – his own home. It was unforgivable in Garrett. Why couldn't he have built himself a new house? He had bought this house deliberately to spite the Leightons and to show off to Bríd his trophy. Yet, it was true, if Garrett hadn't bought it, someone else might have.

There was another matter which she had better face up to. Garrett was a man, and tonight he would want to exercise a husband's prerogative; and she would have to do her wifely duty. She had considered it when she been thinking the matter over in New York, but it had all seemed a long way in the future. She had pushed the thought aside and told herself vaguely that she could cope somehow.

Well, tonight it must be. If he came through that door now and wanted to get into this bed with her, how could she refuse? That was what marriage was supposed to be for.

However, there was one thing she had decided upon. There were to be no children – not yet, not until she was clearer in her mind what the future was going to be. The means to prevent it existed and she had them in her travelling case. Garrett would have to put up with it.

*

347

Strangely, however, he did not come to her room that night. The following morning when she ventured downstairs, she found him at the breakfast table, calm and pleasant. He did not mention the previous evening; he hoped that she felt rested, and his low-key politeness drew the sting of any resentment that might have lingered in her. It was impossible not to be polite in return. He himself had to go to Boyle on business today, but he had left orders with Liam to show her a little gift he had for her.

As she sat at the table, he rose, gave her a little peck on her cheek and went out.

'See you this evening. Will you speak to O'Flaherty about dinner tonight?'

It was impossible to fight him while he was like this.

She drew the napkin from its ring and looked about her. All the old furniture was still here, the paintings on the wall: sporting pictures, fox hunts, race horses. The Earl did not seem to have taken anything from the house. Behind her stood a broad mahogany sideboard, and she was sitting at one end of a twenty-seat dining table where two place settings had been arranged. The remains of Garrett's breakfast had not yet been cleared away.

A footman came in.

'Will ye have your breakfast now, madam?'

'Micky O'Sullivan! Don't you recognise me?'

'I beg your pardon, madam?'

She laughed. 'You don't remember Bríd Flynn all the years ago?'

'Bríd Flynn – is that you? Should I ever forget you? Is it yourself? Holy mother of God!'

'And do you remember the night I waited at this very table itself, and poured wine all over the tablecloth?'

'Did ye now? Well, well! Bríd Flynn, and now Mrs Garrett Doyle. What a transformation.' He checked himself, and once more assumed a grave manner. 'Well, now come on, madam, eat this up before it's cold. Will ye take tea or coffee?'

'Coffee, please, Micky.'

He went out, and as she began on her rashers and eggs, she thought how extraordinary it was that when he was a boy Garrett had punched Micky once coming out of church because he had teased her and pulled her hair, when she couldn't have been more than ten years old. And now Garrett was a millionaire and owned the village, and Micky was his footman.

As she ate her breakfast, she remembered Garrett's words: speak to O'Flaherty about dinner. She was the mistress of this house – all of it. Remembering so vividly the night when she had waited at table, remembering the corridors, the kitchens, the outhouses, the servants, cooks, footmen, O'Flaherty – how august he had seemed to her then, how majestic – she pulled herself together and, when she had finished her breakfast, she set out on a tour of inspection of her new home.

Room opened into room; heavy varnished doors, the red drawing room with its broad sofas in heavy gold brocade, old French carpets on the floor, a marble fireplace, large paintings on the walls. The yellow room, the music room, the west room, the master's study, the office. Girls were tidying and dusting. They stopped and curtsied to her as she entered.

She passed through the invisible door in the entrance hall and down the stone steps to the cool brick-paved corridor below. Voices could be heard and the clattering of crockery and utensils. She went into the kitchen. O'Flaherty and several women were at the large kitchen table.

They got hurriedly to their feet.

'It's all right, Mr O'Flaherty – and all of you. Sit down. I'm afraid I have interrupted your breakfast.'

'Oh, that's no trouble at all, madam. Can I be of any assistance?'

'Mr Doyle asked me to speak to you about dinner tonight.'

'There was never any need for yourself to come down here, madam. You had but to ring, and I would come to you in the drawing room.'

She realised her faux pas and for a moment felt awkward. But then she thought, Wait a minute, I am not going to be dictated to by 'form'.

'Never mind about that, Mr O'Flaherty. Will you just introduce me to this lady here?'

'This is Mrs Flanaghan, your cook, madam.'

'How do you do, Mrs Flanaghan.'

She sat down at the table.

'Now what do you recommend for dinner? I'm new here and I haven't had the time to find everything out. What's good just now?'

Mr O'Flaherty looked at the cook and winked.

Later she explored the stables, and found Liam and two other grooms busy. Liam was brushing the coat of a large chestnut cob.

'Oh, Mrs Doyle, Mr Doyle has something for you.' He was flustered. 'Now let me see – he gave special orders about it. You were to wait on the front steps, madam.'

There was such a look of anxiety on his face that she had to give in gracefully.

'Very well, Liam. I shall do as you ask.'

And five minutes later, as she stood all alone on the steps beneath the lofty portico, breathing the heavenly freshness of the morning air and looking across at the elms in their summer green, there was a clatter of hooves, a rumbling of wheels, and at the corner from the stables appeared Liam perched up before a small upright carriage, and with a glossy black horse between the shafts.

As the carriage drew up before her, she saw that it was new, painted a rich maroon and embellished with gold scrollwork; the brasses gleamed, the leather harness was all new.

Liam leaped down and opened the door. On the door among the elegant scrollwork was her own monogram, BD.

'If you would care to look inside, madam?'

The interior was immaculate with comfortable velvet cushions.

'Mr Doyle's compliments, madam, and he said it was a wedding present from himself.'

'It's beautiful.'

After lunch she could wait no longer. Today it had to be, now. And she would go in her new carriage. Why not? Garrett would expect her to use it; he would require his wife to travel in style – that was his way.

She was plagued by doubts: was this the right time to go? Should she write a letter first? Make an appointment? Invite them to tea? Should she walk? Wear old clothes? Would they feel awkward having her in the house?

Would Nora refuse to speak to her?

She thrust all her doubts aside. She would go now, and she would ride in Garrett's gift. It was a splendid gift; she had a carriage in London, too, but this was much smarter. She was not made of stone; it was a handsome gift. But then Garrett was a generous man; always had been.

She changed her clothes. She wasn't going to dress down – that would have been insulting, as if to say, 'I don't want to show off in my finery before you, so I've just huddled into my oldest things.' No, she would dress as she normally did: pretty stylishly, she had to admit, looking at herself in the mirror.

Rattling through the lane as she approached Ballyglin, she re-hearsed in her mind all the things she wanted to say – her excuses. Garrett had asked her to be his wife. She had accepted. Garrett wanted to live in Ballyglin, and as his wife of course she would accompany him. How could she do otherwise? What was she supposed to do? Refuse his hand because of a legal document ten years old, lying in the safe of some lawyer in Dublin?

She had broken her word, though; that was the fact. Her oath.

Nora would want an explanation; and Bríd had none. She wanted to see her son again: that was the whole of it. After she had sworn she wouldn't.

The carriage came down the narrow *bohreen* near Ballyglin, and now here on the left was the farmhouse. Liam pulled up and Bríd looked out.

How small it looked! How old! The thatch was grey, with a little wisp of smoke at the chimney. The ground before the door was dusty and away on either side spread a tangle of briar and thorn, of grass and bramble.

'Wait for me, Liam.'

She knocked, as if it were quite normal, as if she might have been any neighbour calling for a chat or to borrow a teaspoon of sugar, and in a moment Nora opened the door.

Chapter Forty-Five

Nora did not smile. Her eye flicked to the carriage behind Bríd and then she stood aside.

'Come in.'

The smell of the peat fire in the kitchen evoked such a powerful memory that Bríd felt quite faint.

Patsy was pulling himself from his rocking chair by the fire.

'Bríd – Mrs Doyle, I should say; we never thought you'd come.'

'Uncle Patsy!' She flew across the room and took him into her arms.

'Bríd, be careful now – your new gown, don't get dust on it. I hardly like to touch you now, and you such a fine lady. Nora, can't we find a chair for Mrs Doyle?'

'Uncle Patsy, call me Bríd, I beg you! I'm still the same old Bríd, you know!'

'Well, Bríd, here's you such a fine lady, and the carriage in the *bohreen* there, and married to Mr Doyle –'

Bríd swung to Nora, who had still not spoken.

'Aunt Nora, will you not say hello?'

Nora's face would not move.

'What am I supposed to say? Welcome home, that is no home to you – nor has been these eleven years?'

'No home?'

'No home, Bríd, and well you know it. There is the whole world for you to roam in – and you had to come here.'

Bríd was flustered and began fiddling with her gloves, easing them off her hands and undoing the drawstring of her cloak,

'You'll let me sit down a moment and talk, Aunt Nora. I've thought of you so often. Wondered how you were.'

Nora, still wooden, made a slight nod of the head, and Patsy took it as his cue.

'Bríd – Mrs Doyle, madam, you've got me all muddled. Oh God, there's no chair proper to a lady –'

'The chairs are good enough for her, Patsy, don't act the fool. Sit down if you're going to.'

'Aunt Nora, you know I didn't mean – I'm not going to be any trouble, I swear it. Only, naturally, I was curious, just a little, to know how Matthew might be getting along.'

'He's fine.'

'Yes, of course, I'm sure, I'm sure, and then since Garrett, Mr Doyle, decided he wanted to return to Ballyglin, I thought you might not mind if I was to ... well, you know, just call in, just once in a while ...'

'Call in?'

Bríd hurried on, afraid that at any moment Nora would order her out of the door. She sat at the table with Patsy opposite, while Nora remained standing, unwilling to unbend or offer her any hospitality.

'Of course, there's no question – I mean, the secret will be safe with me till my dying day, don't fear that.'

'Safe? For how long?' She leaned forward on the table over Bríd. 'I must say, you have the cheek of the devil to come in this house after so long. After you swore before the lawyer and took your Bible oath never to come here again.'

'But Garrett –'

'Never to come here again! After I explained to you so carefully that it was for the boy's best interest never to know the shame of his birth. You sinned, Bríd, and you had to pay the price. Now, because you've made a good match, you think you can forget the promise you made. You think that now you've money and are living in the big house above, you can push us aside and forget your oath. Well, now you listen to me, Mrs Doyle. I have cared for that boy these ten years, in good times and bad, and Patsy has been as good a father to him as any that breathed. What father could you have given him, eh? Eh? A fine upbringing he would have had with you – wouldn't he? These ten years he's had the best we could have given him, he's wanted for nothing –'

'I know, Aunt Nora.'

'And nobody – not you or anybody – is going to interfere now. He's ten years of age, he's still young, and I will never, never allow you to come in here and ruin it.'

'Ruin it? Aunt Nora, why should I want to ruin anything?'

'And what would he say if I was to tell him you were his mother – have you ever thought of that? He'd ask me who his father was, wouldn't he?'

'Aunt Nora!' she screamed out. 'Aunt Nora, I never said I would take him away! I won't take him away! I swear it upon my honour. And I will never, never tell him who I am! I won't! All I ask is to visit him maybe now and then – you know, just a little visit maybe from time to time. And I'll tell him I'm his aunt, come back after all these years. I can say, I don't know, I could say I was from another branch of Uncle Patsy's family or some such, that has been away and now come back. Why should he suspect anything? Don't be too hard on me, Aunt Nora. I've thought and thought about Matthew, I've paid for my sin over and over since, don't you think I haven't? Don't be hard on me! You could just let me see him, just a little – couldn't you?'

Tears were starting into her eyes.

Uncle Patsy rested his arm on hers.

'Of course you can see him. We trust you, don't we, Nora?'

'I don't trust you,' Nora said strongly. 'You say that now, but what when you've spoken with him, and maybe taken him for a little walk or two? Next maybe you'll take to visiting, eh? And the folk in the village seeing you coming and going, you in your fine carriage – are they stupid? That's Bríd Flynn that was, they'll say, strange she's for ever coming and going from the Byrnes'. And they'll be reckoning on their fingers – for there's nothing so strong as curiosity – they'll be reckoning up and saying to themselves, "She went rushing off eleven years since, and now here's this lad, and him just ten years old, and she can't keep away from him." And then the next thing you know, there'll be talk, and one day at school some little lad will shout it out – because the children always hear these things.' She paused. 'Is that what you want?'

Bríd stared up at her, white-faced.

'Don't take on too hard, Bríd. Nora's exaggerating.'

'Am I? Let Bríd answer that.'

The door opened and Matthew burst into the room. Seeing a strange woman, he stopped and looked round at Nora and Patsy.

'Aunt Nora, there's a fine carriage in the *bohreen*.'

Patsy for once took charge of the situation.

'Matt, here's your aunt come to visit, that we haven't seen these many years. Will you say hello now to Mrs Doyle?'

She could see the trepidation and uncertainty in his eyes as he took in her fine clothes.

'My aunt?'

'Call me Aunt Bríd, Matthew.'

'And is that your carriage outside?'

'It is.'

'Can I have a ride in it?'

354

Bríd laughed. 'If you like.'

'Now?'

Patsy interrupted. 'I'm sure your aunt will let you ride in the carriage, Matt, but you'll take your tea first. And you'll take a cup too, Bríd?'

She nodded, unable to take her eyes off Matt.

'Matthew, I was just thinking that maybe you like sweets – is that possible?' She smiled impishly.

'What sweets?'

She had fished a paper bag from her pocket. 'I just happened to have a bag of bullseyes here – isn't that strange now?'

His eyes were glued to the bag. Bríd was acutely conscious of Nora watching her, but she was not going to be deflected.

'Will you have one? Or perhaps you had better wait till you've had your tea. Isn't that right, Aunt Nora?'

Nora grunted, and began to cut slices of bread and spread them with butter. Patsy made a pot of tea. Bríd watched as Matthew disappeared into what had once been her own room, to deposit his satchel.

'It's a pity we didn't know you were coming, Bríd. Nora would have baked you a cake.'

Nora raised an eyebrow at this but said nothing. As Matthew returned, Bríd turned to him.

'And you've just come from school, have you, Matthew?'

'Yes.'

'Yes what?' Nora interjected.

'Yes, Aunt,' the little boy said meekly.

Patsy laughed.

'Why didn't you say I had another aunt, Aunt Nora?' said Matt.

'You see, Matt, I've been away for many, many years, and I've travelled so many places, to London, and America –'

'You never went to America, Bríd?' exclaimed Patsy.

'That's where I met my husband.'

'In America?' Matt's eyes glowed. All boys knew that America was the Promised Land. Many of them would go to America, and all of them had heard fabulous stories of America's marvels. 'Is it true they have lifts to lift you up inside the house so you don't need stairs?'

She laughed. 'Yes, it's true, and many, many things. Some houses don't have fires at all; they have pipes filled with steam running through the house to keep them warm.'

'You never say so,' Patsy breathed.

'And trains in the middle of the street to ride through the town?'

'Streetcars. Yes, you don't have to walk anywhere if you don't want to, Matt. You needn't ever walk at all, if you had a mind to it.'

355

'And everybody a millionaire, they said.'

'Not everybody. Maybe no more than here, but it's easier to become a millionaire in America, that's for sure.'

'That'd be grand,' the boy breathed, gazing at her over his teacup. 'Now will you give me a ride in your carriage?'

'If Nora will permit it.'

Nora raised her eyebrows and shrugged. 'So long as you're not too long.'

They rode in the carriage – but not through the village, despite Matt's violent protests. 'Why can't we go through the village, Aunt Bríd?'

Nevertheless he was well pleased with his ride, and when half an hour later they were back at the cottage and he was about to leave, he said,

'Will you come again, Aunt Bríd? I did enjoy that.'

'If you wish it,' she said sweetly, her heart beating so violently that it took a very great effort to smile normally round at the three of them.

She took her leave, kissing Patsy, though not Nora.

As the carriage swayed back up the *bohreen*, she could scarcely keep the tears from her eyes. Such a darling boy! And all the years she had missed, so many years, day upon day gone for ever, and she never able to make it up any more.

But she would see him again. She didn't care what Nora said, what anyone said; let the gossip be what it might, she would see him, if Nora barricaded the door, yet she would see him.

That evening Bríd and Garrett dined in solemn splendour, the candle-light glinting on the silverware and the polished mahogany table. The clinking of cutlery on their plates, the sound of wine pouring into a glass, the ticking of the clock, every sound served to underline the deep silence of the house.

'I'm having some friends to dinner on Saturday, Bríd. You'll be in charge. You can spend what you like and I know you'll make it look good, my dear. This will be our first dinner party.' He sat back in his chair and smiled. 'I've been looking forward to this moment: you and me inviting our guests to dinner. You at the head of the table, good food, the best wines. You'll do us justice.'

That night she again slept alone in the giant bed, and as she fell asleep she thought, not of Garrett and his dinner party, but of Matthew in her carriage, his childish enjoyment of the fittings, and wanting to ride up with Liam; and she all the time wanting to burst into tears or sweep him into her arms, or both, and holding herself in only by an enormous effort of will.

The next morning, however, she summoned the cook.

'The master is having ten guests to dinner on Saturday, Mrs Flanaghan, and we must do him proud. So, let me see, we can start with turtle –'

'There's no turtle to be had in Boyle, madam.'

'Really?'

'You'd have to chase to Dublin for a turtle.'

'I see. So what can you suggest?'

'Why not a salmon?'

'Why not? Excellent suggestion. A salmon à la Genevese, a red mullet and a spring soup.'

'Mullet is good, madam.'

'Then, for the entrées, a calf's liver and bacon *aux fines herbes*, a chicken vol-au-vent, pork cutlets and sauce Robert, and grilled mushrooms.'

The cook was uncertain.

'I think I'd better be writing all this down, madam.'

'Don't worry, Mrs Flanaghan, I've written it here. Now, second course: a saddle of mutton, half a calf's head, tongue and brains, roast pigeons and ducklings, a braised ham and asparagus.'

'Very good, madam.'

'You cooked for his late lordship, did you not, Mrs Flanaghan?'

'I did, Mrs Doyle.'

'And how was he – demanding in his tastes?'

'His lordship had a very refined palate, Mrs Doyle. He knew his food and drink, and nothing was too good for his guests.'

'And nothing is too good for *my* guests, either, Mrs Flanaghan. For the third course, sponge-cake pudding, charlotte à la vanille, gooseberry tart, cream, cheesecakes. And an apricot-jam tart. Finally, a dessert and ices to round off.'

She handed over the menu, which she had written out. 'There will be twelve at table, and we shall dine at eight. Will you ask Mr O'Flaherty to come and see me?'

She made a tour of inspection of the wine cellar with O'Flaherty. It gave her a strange feeling to stand in this chill, dusty cellar where she once first tasted champagne, and the bubbles had run up her nose.

'These were his lordship's wines, madam. When Mr Doyle bought the house, the wines came with it. His lordship had very good taste in wine.'

Bríd made a selection for the dinner, and O'Flaherty looked at her with respect.

*

357

Garrett dressed carefully, and before his guests arrived he came into Bríd's bedroom and inspected her. He approved her choice of gown.

She could see in his eyes, even before he spoke, the pleasure it gave him to be here with her, where her clothes, underclothes, stockings, shoes and all the intimate paraphernalia of a woman's bedroom lay scattered about. His eyes drank her in.

'A man would have to travel a long way to see such another sight,' he said softly, almost with a sigh of satisfaction.

Garrett's guests were all men, important men, and they arrived by carriage. Bríd offered them champagne. As the candlelight flickered on her diamonds, the talk was all of county business, politics, the price of wheat, the price of livestock.

She had rehearsed her staff in their duties for the dinner, and O'Flaherty was a veritable sergeant major, so that when the guests had all sat down, and he bent at her shoulder and asked with creamy smoothness, 'Shall I serve dinner, madam?', she could glance at him with a regal dignity and give the tiniest nod.

Garrett at the bottom of the table looked up between his guests. He let his eyes run over the great dishes, the heaps of pigeons and ducklings, the puddings and pyramids of piled fruit, the flower arrangements and epergnes, to rest on his wife in a white gown, fitted tightly over her figure and cut to do her ample justice, low on the shoulder. To see her perfect skin and the plump rise of her bosom, the flash of her smile as she turned and made a remark to a guest or indicated a dish further down the table, to see the diamond flashing fire at her ear as she moved her head, and the soft light of her dark eyes, all was a deep source of pleasure and contentment. Garrett had come a long way, and at a moment like this, with the most important men in the county seated at his table and his wife doing the honours with grace, wit and aplomb, his heart was full.

As the guests left, they too were full of her praises. As they stood at the door where the carriages stood waiting on the gravel in the darkness, they would grasp his hand and tell him, 'Doyle, you've a wife in a million. You're a damn lucky fellow – mind, no more than you deserve!'

It was on this tide of good will and wellbeing, with a good dinner and several glasses of wine inside him, that Garrett was carried up to her bedroom.

Bríd had already gone upstairs, and he went up calmly, judging that the time had come.

In her bedroom – their bedroom, he told himself – she was removing her jewels. She turned as he came in.

He crossed to her, took her gently in his arms and kissed her.

'You looked like a goddess,' he said softly, looking into her eyes, 'More beautiful than I have ever known you. I fell in love with you all over again. They were all mesmerised by you, but I most of all. I never saw such a vision of loveliness, and I thanked God that He had given you to me.'

With his arm round her waist, he led her to the bed and laid her gently down. Kneeling beside her, he kissed her, gently at first, then with the passion stirring in him, kissing her face, her neck, running his lips over her bosom. Easing the strap of her gown over her shoulder, he pulled the dress away from her breast, his lips all the time kissing and caressing.

'Wait,' she whispered, sitting up.

She left him and crossed quickly to her dressing closet, the small room where her clothes were hung up. She got out of her gown, pulling hurriedly at the hooks and eyes, the drawstrings, petticoats, stays and her drawers, until there was a white heap of clothes on the floor about her. Shrugging on a night wrap, from a drawer she took the little metal box labelled *Fleurs d'Aphrodite* which she had bought in Bond Street. Opening it and lifting one foot on to a chair, she prepared herself for what was to come.

Garrett had undressed and was in the bed. She blew out the candles and got in beside him. He was ardent, quick and strong, his mouth, his hands everywhere about her. Garrett knew women, he was experienced, she could tell immediately, his hands cupping her breasts, then taking a nipple into his mouth, sucking, caressing, his hands never still, always moving about her. For all the strength of his passion, Garrett was in control of what he did; he was content to take his time, to bring her to her climax before taking his own.

The only problem was, she could not respond. She knew what he did, knew it all, but it did nothing to her. If it had been another man, if it had been Harry now in this bed – his rightful bed – she could have yielded herself to him and never wanted to stop. She would have made love to him all night long, and watched the dawn break still cradled in his arms.

Garrett was over her now, entering her, slowly at first, working on her. It was all power, she told herself. This was Garrett at his favourite sport, manipulating her, using her, making her conform to his will. It was the ultimate expression of his power – to watch a woman melt under him into helpless ecstasy. She would not. It was not that she was frigid; she did feel something, a sort of physical spasm; but it was not she that moved beneath him.

She knew he was coming from the urgency of his gathering movements and then that last helpless sprint when he was no longer in control, until finally he was still, subsiding gradually on the pillow beside her.

They lay a long time in silence, until she thought he was asleep.

'It meant nothing to you, did it?' he said expressionlessly.

She was silent. At last, very quietly she said, 'I can't help it. It's not something you can command. I expect I'm tired.'

He moved away in the dark, getting out of bed.

'No, Bríd, not tired. Indifferent.'

She saw a crack of less than darkness where the door opened, then he was gone.

Chapter Forty-Six

She slept little that night, and as dawn broke she stared at the crack of light between the curtains as the same thought ran through her mind.

I can't help it if I don't love him.

Yet when she thought further she said to herself, I didn't love Wrenshaw either, yet he could make me come and come again. What's wrong with me? Garrett is my husband, I owe it to him. It's a wife's duty. I must do the best I can. I will try, even if I have to fake it. He's a man, he's entitled to a loving wife.

Then she would turn over and say, I told him when I married him I didn't love him. He's only got himself to blame. I can't change the way I am, can I?

Then, after a while, It's my fault though. I should never have married him if it hadn't been for Matt. Still, it wasn't fair to him. But he was so insistent. I did tell him I didn't love him.

Then she would turn over again and repeat, He *is* a good man. I'll do the best I can. He's worth a thousand of Wrenshaw any day of the week. I could fling myself into bed with Wrenshaw, who isn't worthy to clean Garrett's boots, and I can't even take to the trouble to make Garrett happy. What's the matter with me? If I have to fake it, so be it. He was utterly humiliated last night, I know he was. I can't think what he'll say to me this morning.

When they met at breakfast she found him courteous, though perhaps a little strained, and she guessed he had slept as little as she had. Nevertheless, though conversation between them was fitful, there was no hint in his manner of what had passed between them.

It was Sunday morning and they were going to church. She had dressed carefully, smartly yet soberly, in gloves, a bonnet and a perfectly fitting coat in royal blue.

'Are you ready for church this morning?' he asked suddenly, breaking the silence as they stood together, both rather stiff and formal, on the steps in the sunlight. 'You'll have to take the place of honour, you know.'

He had ordered her little carriage round, and, seeing Liam up on the box, the smart paintwork and her monogram BD inscribed on the door, she felt a rush of gratitude again to Garrett for his kindness. On an impulse, sensing his unhappiness, as they sat together in the carriage, she slipped her arm through his and pressed it, smiling to him.

They rolled down through the village to the new church, rising gaunt and grey among the little houses of the village, with many of its windows still boarded up.

The villagers hastened to make way and to greet them with reverence, as if they were indeed the heirs to Elphin. Garrett was affable, stopping to chat to a man here, a woman there; everyone wanted to catch his eye, and give him a smile or a nod. They passed Patsy and Nora with Matt, and Bríd smiled at them; Matt was wriggling with excitement.

Bríd felt acutely the pressure of their attention as they made their way down the aisle and as she took her place in the front pew she thought, They're all watching me, and I can imagine what they're saying to each other: 'Who does she think she is? I remember her when she was Bríd Flynn, and no better than she ought to be. She ran off, didn't she? That was never explained properly.'

She pressed her lips tightly, took her gloves off, opened her prayer book and studied it hard.

After Mass, as everyone was scattered about on the muddy turf outside the church chatting, she couldn't resist taking Garrett by the arm, interrupting his conversation, and introducing Patsy and Nora again.

'And this young gentleman is my nephew, aren't you, Matthew?'

'I had a ride in your carriage!' Matt said.

'I paid Aunt Nora and Uncle Patsy a visit the other day, Garrett,' she explained hastily, 'and Matthew wouldn't be satisfied till he had ridden in the carriage!'

She laughed nervously and Garrett watched her until she was suddenly afraid of what he might say, but he only smiled.

'Will you give me another ride?'

Bríd looked at Garrett. 'Shall he sit up with Liam as far as the farmhouse?'

'As far as the castle, if he likes. Liam can bring him home again afterwards.' He smiled to her and she felt a gush of relief and gratitude.

They were about to go when Father Geoghegan touched Garrett's sleeve.

'Mr Doyle, if I might have just a word. I've been in touch with the firm of Baxter's in London, and they are sending a man over to measure the windows and to prepare sketches. I took the liberty of giving them some idea of the themes I want depicted. Because of your more than munificent gesture, I shall be be able to plan something on a lavish scale. I have had a letter from the Bishop too expressing great interest in the work. Once I have had an opportunity of talking to the artists, I hope to wait on you with some sketches to give you an idea of the kind of thing I have in mind.'

'I shall be very interested to see your plans, Father Geoghegan, but I leave it entirely in your hands.'

'God bless you, my dear sir.' Father Geoghegan shook him warmly by the hand.

They rode home, Matt up outside with Liam.

'We are going to Ballinasloe Fair a week on Saturday,' Garrett said. 'In the long run I want to have a first-rate stable of horses. For the time being I shall buy myself a couple of good hunters and a hack or two. We'll have to see what we can find. I want you to have a horse too. There's no life in the Irish countryside if you can't ride. Would you like that?'

'A horse of my own? I should love it!'

'I've been looking forward to seeing you on a horse. I can imagine you.' He laughed with pleasure. 'Have you ever ridden?'

'Never.'

'No matter. You were born to sit on a horse, Bríd.'

Bríd thought of the fox-hunters she had seen flashing past her when she was a girl, the cruel glamour of the ladies in their hard hats and their perfectly fitting habits. Oh, she would look good in a riding habit, make no mistake about that!

As they arrived at the house, Matt jumped down from the box, his eyes alight with excitement.

'Liam let me hold the reins, Aunt Bríd!'

Liam, behind him, winked over his head.

'Come inside for a glass of milk and a biscuit, then Liam shall take you home.'

For an intoxicating half-hour they sat together in the red drawing room in two easy chairs by the window. He wriggled and sipped his glass of milk, and then looked shyly at her and asked if he might have

363

another biscuit. She laughed and said of course, only he mustn't have too many or he wouldn't have any appetite for his dinner, and at every moment she wanted to snatch him into her arms and hold him for sheer joy.

That afternoon, while Garrett was out in the farm on some business, she stood in the empty drawing room, staring out across the demesne and the trees, and feeling all the time the silence like some immense shroud descending over her until it threatened to smother her.

He has the patience of a saint, she thought. Why does he put up with me? He could have had any woman he wanted. He's a millionaire, he's young, he's good-looking, he's as brave as a lion, he's generous, there's no side to him, the servants adore him. Any other woman would be on her knees night and morning thanking God she's got him.

Then, after another turn through the large, empty room, I must be crazy. And I must be the most ungrateful woman that ever lived. He's bought me a beautiful carriage for my personal use; he's given me the most gorgeous jewellery; he's going to to buy me a horse to ride; he treats me like a queen, always asks my opinion about things, gives me a free hand in the house, never counts the money – he left the dinner entirely to me to organise.

She stopped at the window and clasped her hands tightly together. I resolve – again – to be a good and dutiful wife. So far as I am able. Then her hands would drop. But oh, it's lonely here. The silence drives me crazy. And Garrett's out all the time. And when did I last have a good laugh? Bill Harris could have me in stitches. And how is Isabella getting on? I must write her a letter. Come to think of it, George will want me back in London sooner or later.

But always the same thought came round to the same place. It's not my fault if I can't love him, is it? I do my best.

On a bright morning of July they went to Ballinasloe Fair. The entire town was overflowing with men, women and horses. Copers leading big, mettlesome hunters and shouting incoherently to 'Keep away now!' as they pushed their way through; vendors of apples and pigs' feet; knots of old women in capacious blue cloaks with large hoods who would not budge out of anyone's way, not even for Garrett and Bríd in their smart open gig. 'For the love of God, ladies, is a man to get to the fair this day or not?' Garrett called to them.

Garrett is too good-natured. I should like to see a London cabby here, she thought, he would soon cut his way through this!

In a field immediately outside the town, horses were being put through their paces, and men on great hunters were busy facing them at a makeshift fence of turf and sticks to try them. At either end of this temporary barrier, crowds of men and boys shouted and hooted encouragement.

Garrett recognised several men, and she saw how respectful they were, raising their hats, and he as affable as ever. Everywhere there were horses – grey, chestnut and black. She saw a man slapping another on the hand, saying, 'And there'll be two sovereigns back now, for luck!'

Eventually they found themselves in front of a large, strong dapple grey. Garrett bent to run his hand down the hind legs and then across the rump, digging his thumb into the muscle, all the time expressionless but watchful. He checked the neck, the placing of the head and the strength in the forelegs.

The coper watched carefully as Garrett made his leisurely examination. 'That's a horse in a thousand, Mr Doyle. Look at the chest on him! He'd carry you thirty miles and never pause for breath.'

'What are you asking?'

'Ooh.' The coper drew a sharp breath. 'As to the matter of guineas now.' He ran his hand over the horse's shoulder, patting and smoothing it as if to draw attention to the beautiful proportions of the animal. 'There you put me to it, Mr Doyle. We've got to be talking a hundred guineas at the very least – and that's in honour of yourself returned from America, and a man of some consequence in the county now. I've refused a hundred and twenty this morning for him.'

'If you refused a hundred and twenty this morning, why are you offering him to me for twenty less?'

'On account of yourself, sir, and in hope of a long and fruitful association to come. I wouldn't want to lose your valuable custom, Mr Doyle.'

Garrett mounted the strong, handsome animal, and Bríd couldn't help admiring the way he sat, as if he and the horse were moulded together. He took the horse through the field at a gallop and, turning, cleared the hedge and back, and so at last drew up again to where they were standing.

'What do you think, Bríd?'

She laughed. 'He looks lovely, Garrett.'

'He's a year or two older than I would like –'

'Old? A four-year-old, Mr Doyle. His grandsire was the General and he lived to forty. The grandest horse in the barony. The family was that heartbroke, they gave him a wake when he died.'

'Nearer seven, I should say,' Garrett repeated coolly, still looking the horse over. 'But he might live to thirty. Call it ninety guineas and you've got a deal. What do you say?

Garrett held out his hand and the man slapped hands on it without saying a word.

Garrett bought two other horses at the fair. Once more he turned politely to Bríd.

'Have you set eyes on anything you fancy?'

'They're all lovely.'

He laughed. 'Oh, Bríd, you've got to have the devil's own eye open here. They'd scalp you as soon as look at you. There's no race on earth for trickery to touch horse dealers.'

Garrett found her a lovely chestnut mare called Diamond, three years old, which was guaranteed to be 'gentle as a dove! A perfect lady's horse, never fear!'

As Garrett was writing out the cheque, resting his chequebook on the mare's rump, a new thought entered her mind. She clasped his arm.

'Garrett, let's buy a little horse for Matt too. I'll pay for it. Really; I should so love it. We could learn to ride together.'

He would do anything to please her, it seemed, and a little, patient old nag, Maisie, who had seen her best days and only wanted a quiet life, was purchased for ten.

All the way home Bríd could think of nothing but herself and Matt riding together. She planned to look superb in a perfectly cut black habit, with the handsome boy at her side, her son, though no one knew it. That did not matter. She would be so proud to see him; he deserved a horse of his own.

Garrett always had such an air of authority, of being a man in control of his own life, that it came as a shock to see him in quite a black mood one evening when he returned from a meeting in Athlone.

'The *American*!' he muttered, leaning on the mantelpiece and looking down into the empty grate.

'What?' She looked up.

'I overheard Langan in the Queen's Hotel in Athlone – you may remember him, he was here to dinner two weeks back – calling me "the American". Oh, I know how they think! Where did he come from? Who are his people? No family at all. A "vulgar *arriviste*" whose father never owned a foot of land in the county, and now throwing his weight about with his American dollars. God damn them and their snobbery – men who were never out of the country in their lives! Men who have never earned a penny by their own hands!

The country's rotten with snobbery, jobbery, place-hunting, currying favour with the Lord Lieutenant, kowtowing to the Viceroy for the chance of a title or a place at court. They think they have the whole country neatly parcelled up between them. You can imagine what they think of me, when I stand up in the council chamber to make a few mild, well-intentioned remarks . . .'

She thought, Yes, I can just imagine Garrett's mild remarks.

'Men who've sat down in this house, Bríd! Men who've drunk my wine and eaten my food! Hmph! Well, all I can say is, thank God for the secret ballot. Votes can't be bought any more. I'm standing for Parliament, and I'm coming forward as the people's man, an Irish Nationalist. That'll put their noses out of joint.'

He chuckled, his good humour restored.

Bríd did not give Garrett's plans as much thought as her own. The following morning she was on her way into Ballyglin to put her proposal to Nora.

Nora was not enthusiastic, but Bríd bore her down; and Uncle Patsy was on her side.

'No one will suspect anything, Aunt Nora. He'll come to me in the evenings or at weekends – who's to know? The castle is three miles from here.'

'Word will get round.'

'And suppose it does?'

'I thought I had spelled this out to you before, Bríd?'

'All right, all right. But the people have seen him with me at church, and him riding up with Liam on the box. Has anyone said anything? Has he come in asking awkward questions?'

Nora grudgingly sat, but did not reply.

'And they won't, I know it.'

They also discussed the fortune in the Dublin bank that the solicitor was keeping for Matt. Nora was defensive.

'I can't spend money on him here – it would look odd. But he'll go to the Christian Brothers in Roscommon when he's eleven.'

'And he can go to the university! And he will have a profession. Aunt Nora, he'll be a gentleman!'

So Matt first came to the castle. Liam helped him on to tame little old Maisie, and Bríd sat rather less readily, on her chestnut mare, and they were led round the paddock at a walk, getting the feel of it, with Liam making encouraging remarks. Bríd kept smiling nervously at Matt, who was grinning and laughing with glee.

He came again in the light evenings, and then at weekends. It was a drug with her; she only wanted him to come again; she was indifferent to the horse she sat on, but cared only for the sight of him on his own, and how much more quickly he picked it up than she did. She was so proud of him, how bold he was, how ready to progress, to go faster.

'Let me off the leading rein now, Liam!'

Bríd cried out with a rush of anxiety, 'No, Liam! Not until he is absolutely ready!' Liam would smile good-naturedly.

But the evening did come when Liam let him off the leading rein. Matt rode round the paddock and kicked his little heels into the long-suffering mare's sides until she broke into a trot. Bumping up and down as he trotted round, he laughed with childish glee at the speed.

'Dig in with your knees, Master Matt!'

Chapter Forty-Seven

The months passed away into autumn, and she saw less of Matt, just a visit at weekends. The season for parties and dances came, and she and Garrett were regularly invited out. The priest came one day with his drawings for the new windows in the church, and another time an architect with plans for the new school, and there was talk of a bridge over the river in place of the ford.

Time passed. Garrett came again to her bed, and she did her best to fake it (as she put it to herself), but she couldn't. If the feeling was not there she couldn't act it. Strange that she who had made her living out of faking emotions could not fake this one.

Garrett seemed to have accommodated himself to this. He was not a man to confess to a weakness or a deficiency, and only seldom did his irritation or frustration show through. She trembled, though, to imagine how it would be if it did, and asked herself again, Why does he put up with me?

She thought of London. How she missed the theatre! There was precious little excitement in being the most glamorous woman at a county ball, and she was fiercely aware of the stares and comments of dowdy landowners' wives and the catty looks of their daughters. Everyone was respectful to Garrett – to his face. But she remembered what he had said about Mr Langan in Athlone, and she developed a sharp nose for hypocrisy. The little world of county gossip! She remembered her London theatre life, the thrill as she went out to face a glittering metropolitan audience. Looking round the town hall one evening, listening to the wheezing and scraping of the local band, seeing the laughter and drunken frolics – for things got pretty rowdy as night drew on with figures slumped in evil-smelling passages and bouts of fisticuffs in the doorway – she thought, And I'm the woman who could once make a fool of the Prince of Wales, reduced to this. I'm a long way from home.

And that was it: this was not her natural home. Garrett was not her natural husband. She suffered him to make love to her; she went through the motions of being his wife; and sitting through yet another of those county balls, she thought, I'm keeping my side of the bargain: Garrett came back to Ireland determined to cut a figure here and to use his dollars to improve things; he wanted to be the big man, and he wanted a glamorous wife. I've done my duty, I've done everything he could ask – outwardly. And he comes to my bed and I allow him to . . . well, do whatever he wants. What more can he ask?

There were great oceans of time when she would wander through the empty rooms, staring out at the eternal trees, the eternal grass, listen to the eternal wind, or watch the eternal rain. The only thing she could hang on to was Matt, and in that winter, with its short days, its long evenings, the incessant rain, she saw little of him.

Nora had at last put her foot down: she must ration even this short amount of time with him. Nora was always afraid to hear the question: Why was Mrs Doyle so interested in the boy?

So she would wander through the house, her mind full of thoughts for them both, and at dinner she would have a faraway look in her eyes, which, one evening, caught Garrett at last on a raw nerve.

'Thinking about London?'

'Hmm? No.'

'You'd rather be there, wouldn't you?' She saw the resentment in his eye. 'Don't bother to deny it. You hate it here. You're bored with me.'

She was caught out, startled by the bitterness in his tone.

'You'd even rather be with your little nephew than me. You're always talking about him.'

With a huge effort she tried to turn the conversation to a lighter note. 'It was so good of you to buy him a horse Garrett; I shall always be grateful. It gives him such pleasure.'

It didn't work.

'If it hadn't been for him, you would have gone back to London by now.'

'I told you when I agreed to marry you that I would have to return to London sometimes.'

'Well why don't you go?'

She stood up.

'That will depend on my manager. I leave my business affairs to him.'

She turned away and would have swept grandly out of the room, but he thrust his chair aside, loudly scraping it across the floor, and came across very quickly, taking her arm.

'God damn you! Your business manager? What about your husband?'

'Don't touch me!' She shook herself violently free.

'Answer my question!'

'What question?'

'Bríd I'm your husband, I'm entitled to your affection.'

She stopped, thinking, then looked down.

'I do everything I can to be a good wife to you. Don't ask for more.'

She wired to Thompson, and received an answer that he was working on a revival of *Mary Queen of Scots* for the spring. She wrote to Isabella and had a letter from her. It was wonderful to hear about Chelsea again. Isabella had had a very quiet time of it, missed Bríd awfully and would love to see her again. The house was fine; she looked after the garden, and took walks by the river. But it was lonely, too, though she sometimes saw Bill Harris, who was appearing in a revival of *The Lyons Mail* successfully.

Garrett announced plans to modernise the house. There was something frenetic about his energy which made her feel horribly guilty. She knew now he was doing all this to drown his unhappiness, and that she was to blame.

Nevertheless he was full of bustle and plans. There were to be bathrooms, with a bathtub and running hot and cold water. He had fittings imported from America. What had been her dressing room would become her bathroom.

In the basement a boiler was installed, and coke was delivered from Galway. Garrett had also had a gas generator fitted and some of the principal rooms were installed with gaslight.

Bríd preferred candles and would never use the gas when Garrett was not at home.

The construction of the new bathroom necessitated the rearrangement of the dressing room and her bedroom. The chests of drawers were brought into the bedroom, the wardrobes moved, floorboards taken up, holes knocked in walls. She moved into a different bedroom to avoid the upheaval and hoped that eventually all would be worth it.

One afternoon the workmen were at work upstairs, there were bangs and thumps echoing in the house, shouts and calls, men carrying pipes and fittings up and down stairs, and Garrett was in high spirits. He was happiest when there was business in hand, new ideas and improvements. She was in the drawing room, trying not to listen, when the door opened sharply and he was in the doorway.

371

She saw instantly he was angry.

'You whore!' His voice was tight.

Startled, she shrank from the implied violence.

'You confounded, damned whore!' Crossing to her, he slammed the door behind him. 'No wonder you haven't conceived. You never had any intention of bearing me a child, did you?'

'What do you mean?' she said weakly, looking up at him, terrified for the moment.

'This is what I mean! This! This!' He thrust the tin box under her nose. *Fleurs d'Aphrodite*. 'This disgusting French filth! God, I could never have believed it, you degenerate, foul slut! You worse than whore! You've cheated me, Bríd. You don't love me – and you're cheating me out of my children.'

He snatched her up out of the chair.

Even in her terror, paralysed with guilt as she was, she tried feebly to assert her dignity.

'Have you been looking through my things?'

'Is it likely? No, Bríd, like a fool I trusted you! And like a whore and a slut you cheated me! This fell out of a drawer as the men were carrying it out of your closet.'

'I told you when I married you that I didn't love you,' she said weakly, still fighting to assert herself as best as she could.

'You didn't say when we married that you would never bear me children. We are married. Do you know what that means? What is a marriage without children? Are you afraid it might ruin your figure? Or interfere with your career?'

He shook her in his arms, then thrust her violently back down into the chair.

'Bríd, I loved you! Slut, whore that you are, I followed you, gave you everything you asked, anything I could think of. But still it wasn't enough. You took and took and took – and gave me nothing. In spite of all, I hoped and hoped that once we had a child it would bring us together. Can't you understand that?' He was almost in tears. 'And all the time you were cheating me with your filthy French contraptions!'

His anger now was worse, stronger.

'Well, we'll see about that.' He snatched up the box and flung it violently through the room. 'You'll have my child, Bríd, oh yes, oh yes, you'll have my child. In the teeth of your despite.'

He wrenched her out of the chair, flung her to the floor and threw himself down beside her, snatching at her skirts.

She rolled away quickly and leaped to her feet.

'Would you rape your wife?' she screamed.

He was on his knees, looking up at her.

She saw him mastering himself. But she saw still the heightened colour in his cheeks, the brightness of his eye and the laboured breathing. He stood slowly, never taking his eye from her. She waited, ready at any moment for him to spring on her again. He straightened his jacket, then turned to the door. At last, as she was still expecting him at any moment to come at her again, he stopped, his hand on the doorknob, and turned slowly to her. There was such a look of awful solemnity in his eye that she was more terrified than ever.

'No, Bríd, you need never fear that.'

He went out, and she burst into tears. She stood in the middle of the great room with her hands over her face, feeling the shock working its way through her body with racking, shaking sobs. For an endless time, it seemed, a time impossible to measure, she sobbed until at last she grew still again. Slowly her eyes opened and she was looking through the window, across the demesne.

Like a sleepwalker she moved to her desk, where she sat down and took up a telegram blank. Her hand shaking, she wrote,

To Mr George Thompson
Adelphi Theatre
Strand
London

Am returning to London. Bríd

Chapter Forty-Eight

'Phil! You've lost weight! And you're looking so well. That German spa has worked wonders.'

Phil was in fact plumper than when he had worked at the Wellington. He had also grown a large moustache. Bríd turned to the merry young lady on his arm.

'And this must be Sally. Phil has told me so much about you.'

Sally was a Lancashire lass. 'Aye.' She squeezed Phil's arm. 'He took the starvation cure, didn't you, love? And the mud baths. Ooh, you had a lovely time, wallowing in all that mud. Second childhood.'

Bríd had bumped into Phil a few weeks previously one morning in the Strand. He was now rich and successful. He ran a string of music halls in the north of England, he had told her, was married and had two children. From this mountain of security and happiness he could afford to look down on the world with a benevolent smile.

'Lambert!' Bríd turned from Phil and Sally to greet a small, elderly man, frail and white-faced, but exquisitely dressed, who bent to kiss her hand.

'My queen,' he breathed. 'At such moments words fail me. Bernhardt is annihilated. My dear, I sat *entranced*! You are alone, *alone*! Thank you –'

'Lambert, you old silly, take this –' she gave him a glass – 'and drink some of this,' pouring champagne into it.

The elderly man turned to the half-dozen others in the little dressing room.

'Ladies and gentlemen – if any there be in this temple of art – will you raise your glasses with me and salute a true artist, a priestess of the Thespian muse! To Biddy!'

Bríd couldn't help laughing, as glasses were raised about her. 'Thank you! It's wonderful to see so many old friends tonight.' She turned. 'Come on, Georgie, your glass is empty. Can't have that.'

'No thanks, Bríd.' He covered the top of his glass with his hand. 'Had enough for one night.'

'Don't be a spoilsport. Drink up!'

Overriding his protests, she tipped champagne into his glass. 'Who else? Oh, there's mine. Nearly forgot. Forget me own name next.' She had mimicked a cockney accent. She giggled, then drew a deep breath. 'Oh, you can't imagine how nice it is to see every one like this. It's been such a long time, you can't imagine. You're all so kind, and I'm sure I don't deserve it. I really don't.' She laughed again and was surprised to feel a smarting at the corner of her eyes. 'No, it is really more than I deserve. Oh, for goodness' sake, lend me a hanky, some-body. Forgive me – Georgie, take this bottle and fill every glass in sight. I want everybody to be happy, I do, I do.'

She sniffled into the handkerchief which an admirer had proffered her. At this moment three men in evening dress crowded in at the door.

'Miss Flynn, may we intrude?'

'Come in, Lord Mottram – and who's that? Anyway, come in, all welcome. Bella, give Freddy and his chums something to drink. Every-body's come tonight! It's wonderful, all old friends. Don't mind the deshabille, I don't!'

She was dressed in a frayed dressing gown to her ankles and but-toned to her neck, with what appeared to be a turban round her head. Near her, on a block on her dressing table, sat the red wig of Mary Queen of Scots.

She looked round the crowded dressing room. This was better, wasn't it? She did at least know what she was doing here. This was her place, after all. Since her return to London six weeks earlier she had thrown herself into a round of entertaining and being entertained and was out almost every night after the show.

She had not written to Garrett, nor received any message from him. The morning after that last appalling scene, she sat in her car-riage, her travelling coat buttoned up, her hat pinned on, her gloved hands clenched together in her lap, frozen with resolve, while Liam strapped a box behind the carriage. Then Garrett had come quickly down the steps and looked in at the carriage window. Fixing her with his eyes, he had said, with a terrible seriousness, 'If you ever mean to come back, come back as my wife.' In that last look, behind the will, the strength of him, she had seen a terrible pain, which she had tried to forget in the rush of travel, in the arrival in Chelsea, in her greet-ings, in the hugs and kisses with Bill and George and the others – tried to forget, yet could not forget. That look hooked into her like the line of a distant fisherman, so that an invisible thread bound her to Ireland, to Garrett, and, turn where she would, would not let her be free.

She had used him wretchedly: the thought burned into her, and all the friends, the admirers and colleagues, all the nights out after the show, the parties, the late dinners, all the bottles of champagne, were a vain attempt to postpone, ignore or somehow blot out the fact that her life would not be straight before her until she had settled with Garrett, cleared and understood whatever life remained to be lived between them.

She had tried to write to him; sat down and started many a letter. None had been finished. She could never bring herself to say quite what she knew he wanted to hear. He was a man; he was entitled to a wife, and she had no right to make conditions with him. If ever she were to return it must be, as he said, as his wife: he had the right to her full loyalty, her undivided self. She was utterly confused.

'What's this rumour I hear about *The Fair Rosamund*?' Bill Harris was before her.

'Ssh. Hush-hush. Anyway, nothing's been decided.'

George Thompson had overheard. He glanced suspiciously at her and she caught his look.

'Nothing has been decided, has it, George?' She turned back to Bill. 'But if it ever does go ahead I'm sure Georgie-Porgie will consider you for the part of Henry. Though I'm not sure you're old enough.'

'Eh? What's that mean? There are beards, aren't there? A dab of grey at the temples, a few lines round the eyes –'

'Biddy, I've booked a table at the Café Royal.'

'Freddy, you think of everything. And I was ready to eat the carpet. Bella –' She was interrupted by the boy from the stage door who had entered unnoticed and was offering her a card.

'Gen'l'man asks if he might speak with you, Miss Flynn.'

She turned, a glass of champagne in her hand. 'Show him in. Show 'em all in!'

She took the card he was holding and turned it over. It read only: 'Earl of Elphin'.

She stared at the card for several seconds. As she grappled with its simple message, one part of her brain was telling her that the Earl of Elphin was dead. She had read about it in the newspapers a month ago. Another was struggling to tell her that if that were the case then at this minute Harry was just outside waiting to speak to her.

Harry here? After so long? She stared up in despair. Oh, Harry, why now? Why now, when I'm not dressed, and I can't think straight, and there are all these people talking at once?

'Biddy, your glass is empty. Here. Now listen, Motters is having a few friends down at the weekend and you're positively invited. Have a few larks, what? Remember that time you pushed him in the lake?'

What will he want? And why has he come *now*?

'Just so long as you keep your roving hands to yourself, my boy.'

'Biddy, *Brigitta*, when, *when* are you going to bring back *Much Ado*? It was your play. I came to see you in it fifteen times –'

In any case, it can only be a social call. For old times' sake. Out of curiosity. He'll probably have his wife with him, to show her off – like Phil. And his children too, most likely.

Sally was beside her, as if reading her thoughts. 'Since I've had the children I've given up the halls. I miss it sometimes, though. Coming here tonight and smelling the grease paint brought it all back.'

It was him. Just the same. Exactly the same, exactly. She recognised him at once. How brown he was, suntanned – he must have got it in India. Was he just a little thinner, leaner? He was a man now, of course, not a boy. And in evening dress; how well it became him! One could tell at once that he was an aristocrat. Immediately.

Harry was standing at the door, uncertain whether to enter. The room was crowded. He was raising his hand to knock at the open door.

'Lord Elphin! Do come in!' She pushed her way through to him. How was she to address him after all this time? 'Bella, give me a glass. No, do come in, I beg you. Such a lot of old friends tonight, what must you you think? Come in.'

She shook his hand. He was staring concentratedly at her, then remembered himself.

'Bríd, Miss Flynn –' He looked round embarrassed at the noisy crowd about him, then coughed. 'Not sure what to call you . . .'

For a moment they stared into each other's eyes, then he broke the look. 'Saw your play tonight. When I saw your name at first I couldn't believe it was you. Still can't, actually. Been out of the country, you see. But I met Wrenshaw at the club –'

George took her arm. 'Bríd, for heaven's sake, keep mum about *The Fair Rosamund* for the moment. I still haven't got the money sorted out.'

As she was distracted, Lord Mottram held out his glass, and without thinking she filled it. The champagne bottle was now empty and as she held it out to Isabella she noticed her arm was shaking.

'Bella, is there another bottle left? Let me have it, there's a dear.'

She heard behind her Lambert talking to Harry.

'I told her, Bernhardt is *exploded*! Do you know she took *Much*

Ado to America? A *succès fou!*' He turned to Bríd. 'My dear, "A star danced, and under that were you born"!'

Bríd laughed, catching Harry's eye. 'Lambert is my *cavaliere servente*, aren't you, Lambert?'

The old man knelt with surprising agility and and kissed the frayed hem of her dressing gown. 'My dear, I am your *slave!*'

Harry was looking intensely awkward.

'Bríd, Miss Flynn, dash it, I was wondering –'

Someone took her arm, and she turned.

'Phil, you're not going so soon?'

'We've got an early train to catch. Sally can't wait to get back to the children.'

He kissed her cheek and for a moment she looked into his eyes. 'It's been lovely to see you again and I'm so glad everything's worked out well.'

Phil understood her and smiled.

But what shall I say to him? And what must he think to see me like this in a theatrical dressing room and in rags? Oh, God, after so long and to come back now?

Harry was watching her, unable to intervene as her attention was distracted. As Phil and Sally left, she turned and was near him again. She smiled, and he smiled too, with difficulty.

'I was wondering whether we might meet. There's – there are things I'd like to discuss.'

Someone was already dragging at her elbow. She smiled again, achingly, into his eyes, and murmured, 'Oh Harry, do you think it would be wise? Hmm? After all this time?'

He looked down, speaking with difficulty. 'I have to speak to you.'

'Listen, everybody, time to go! Leave Biddy to get dressed in peace. We'll wait for you at the stage door. Come on, the Café Royal awaits!'

There was a fresh commotion and Harry looked round in alarm as men began making their way towards the door. In the upheaval she half turned to him and said softly, 'Oh, well, if you must, you must. Shall we say Brompton Cemetery next Sunday at three?'

'I'll be there.'

'Isabella, hold my hand.'

They had just got into her carriage and Fred was pulling out into the street. It was after midnight, and dark inside the carriage.

'The most extraordinary thing has just happened. Either the most wonderful thing, or the most terrible thing, I don't know which.'

'Bríd, what are you talking about?'

'That gentleman, this evening after the show – so stiff, so English, who stood there looking solemn and awkward?'

'Yes.'

'Bella, that's him.'

'Who?'

'Harry.'

Isabella put her other hand on Bríd's. 'My dear!' she breathed.

'I can't believe it.'

'He looked so distinguished, so handsome.'

'Do you think so?'

'Oh, yes.'

'Oh, I think so too.'

'And he's come back?'

'His father died, and Harry has come into the title. And he came to see me. After all this time, he still thought of me. It was his father came between us.'

'I think he still loves you, Bríd.'

'How do you know?'

'Why would he have been so awkward? He was nervous, of course.'

Bríd laughed. 'Oh, I think he just felt out of place in that backstage atmosphere.' She thought for a moment. 'Why do you think he came to see me? He's married, you know. Oh, Lord, and so am I.'

'Are you going to see him again?'

'Yes.' She squeezed Isabella's hand tighter. 'Whatever shall we talk about? After so many years? Oh, Isabella, I really must keep a hold on myself. We are both of us married now – and he has a family, I'm sure he does. It would be foolish . . .'

But once she began to remember, it was all coming back, everything that had ever happened between them, in a terrible rush.

She saw Harry as he had been that first time she had ever seen him. Lying on the kitchen table, his face white, his head caked with mud on one side, twisted at an angle; and then in her bed, unconscious, his steady breathing, and then when he got down from his mare in the *bohreen* and kissed her without asking, took her and kissed her with such feeling . . . and then – oh, but why go through it all,? And yet she could not but go through it all, every scene, and, brightest of all, the afternoon in that little hut, when the rain had poured down outside, and the fire had winked and glowed, as if the whole world were shut out, and the two of them together.

But then there had been the terrible injustice; how could she ever forgive that?

Of course it had been his father who was to blame. Harry would

379

never have abandoned her if his father, with his family pride and hateful snobbery, had not forced him. But could she ever explain to Harry the pain she had suffered? Make him understand how she had taken the broken pieces of her life and, with such difficulty, with so much hard, laborious care, built herself together again, made herself into what she was?

It seemed to her that they would be talking to each other across some impossibly deep gulf of understanding. Was there to be a way of crossing it?

Did he want to? She had no idea. Why had he come tonight? Just so he could return to his wife and lay his head on his pillow with an unruffled conscience? A man in his position, Earl of Elphin, married, no doubt with beautiful children? A whole career of life – they were far, far apart, impossibly far apart.

Yet there was – after all the weeping, after the thinking, the reasoning – the simple truth at the bottom of it all, that she had never loved any one else. She had seemed that evening no doubt to have everything she wanted, and outwardly that was true: she led an enviable existence, she was a society figure, people recognised her in the street, she had more money than she could ever spend.

Everything was there, except that one thing – she loved him, and they would, could, never be together.

Chapter Forty-Nine

'Help me, Isabella, this hat won't stay on. Silly thing!'

'Oh no, Bríd, it's most charming.'

Isabella fitted the hat at the front of Bríd's head, the tiniest straw hat with long pink ribbons hanging down behind.

'Why is it called a Dolly Varden, anyway?'

'I have no idea, I am sure.'

Bríd turned away from the looking glass before Isabella had finished pinning the hat on to the massed coils of her hair.

'Oh, Isabella, will it look odd?'

'It will look wonderful, *cara*, only keep still!'

Bríd turned again to the looking glass as Isabella went on spearing the little straw confection on top of her head.

'It should be tilted as far forward as possible – just so long as I can still see, that is. It says here that the Dolly Varden hat should sit so far forward over the brow, it must seem as if it started at the tip of the nose!'

Isabella, in silent concentration, drove more pins through Bríd's hair.

'It is so unjust! Why did Harry have to come back *after* I'd married Garrett? After all these years! There's some fate that hates me, I know it. If God was just, how could he play such an unfair trick?'

She pulled down the tight little jacket in lovat-green velvet with lace at the wrists and neck. It had been made to fit like a skin over the corset which sculpted in her waistline.

'But I'll tell you this. Married or not, if Harry wants me, I'll go to him, and the world can think what it likes.'

She stared at herself in the looking glass. 'That can't be right!'

Isabella adjusted the hat again. *'C'est très charmant!'*

'It's absurd!'

'No, *cara*, that's how it's supposed to look.'

Bríd looked glumly at herself. 'That's the trouble with being away in Ireland – I've got completely out of touch with the fashions. Are you sure that's right?'

Harry was carefully dressed in a grey morning suit. He had agonised over the cravat, and made his man tie it and re-tie it four times; he had found fault with his boot polishing, and had spent twenty-minutes choosing cuff links – in fact, he thought ruefully, his behaviour would have done credit to a debutante attending her first ball.

And he had been here twenty minutes already, with no sign of Bríd. Had he mistaken the place, or was there another gate? Or had she meant a different cemetery? And why a cemetery, anyway? A bizarre place to meet, he thought. He had taken his gloves off, put them on again, then surreptitiously bent and given his boots another quick polish with his handkerchief; it was absurd.

Families came and went, and there was a flower stall at the gate, where a man was doing brisk business. Harry's thoughts were interrupted by his cries of, 'Best hothouse flowers! They're lovely!' He turned away, and at that moment a black carriage drew up, the coachman got down to open the door, and Bríd stepped out. Harry's heart missed a beat.

She smiled to him as she turned to speak to the coachman, who had taken something from the back and handed it to her. Then she came quickly towards Harry, holding a small gardener's basket filled with bunches of flowers.

'Have you been waiting long? I'm so glad you could come. You must be wondering why I asked you to meet me here. You see, I've been away, and there is a little duty I must perform, and I thought it would be a quiet place where we could talk.'

She spoke quickly, nervously, smiling at him. They turned into the cemetery.

Harry was unable to put any coherent thought into speech; everything was in fragments. He was glad to see her so cheerful, and it was easier to let her speak without interruption. He still found it difficult to look directly at her, and tended to look away – at the gravestones, at people setting flowers in urns, at the trees coming into leaf, or simply down at his boots.

'You've been away from London so long, it must seem strange coming back.'

He searched for words. 'Felt deuced chilly when we first landed,' he said at last.

'Do you feel more at home now?'

'Oh, rather.' He coughed, then rallied. 'It was good of you to meet me. I was afraid you might have thought it impertinent of me to ask . . .'

He was at a loss. She tried to seem brisk and light-hearted.

'This way.' She steered him into another walk. People were everywhere about them, tidying and tending graves, setting out fresh flowers.

'Aren't you going to ask me why we've come here?'

He coughed. 'A relative?'

'Harry, and my entire family in faraway Roscommon?'

She smiled at him, but sensed the tension between them. He looked down and they fell silent; her heart was beating and she clutched herself together inwardly. Everything would soon be clear between them and she would know the best – or the worst. In her nervous state she was prattling at him, she could hear it. Yet she had to know what his feelings were, and she needed him to take the lead, to show her how much of her own feelings she could reveal.

But now she stopped at a grave planted with a profusion of flowers. The headstone was an elaborate Gothic edifice, exploding into miniature spires and finials.

Harry bent to read the name.

'Sacred to the Memory of Tommaso Pertinelli, who departed this Life aged Sixty-Seven Years . . .'

It didn't mean a thing to him. He looked at Bríd. 'A friend from the theatre?'

She stared at him. 'You mean you don't remember? Harry, you introduced us. The Maestro in Dean Street – surely you remember?'

'Good Lord! Well, he was only a name to me, you know. We never met.'

She had put down her basket and taken from it a pair of rough leather gloves.

'He's been dead three years now.' She was pulling on her gloves. 'He was very good to me, Harry; the only man in London who helped me, when I badly needed help. I could never have done it without him. He got me started. And I'm afraid I didn't repay him very kindly.'

'What do you mean?'

She took a little gardener's fork from her basket.

'He wanted me to go on the operatic stage. But I was so desperate to make a start – anything to earn money – I insisted on going into the music hall. It hurt him.'

'Surely it was your future – your life?'

383

'But he had given me so much, invested so much hope in me, you know. The idea of me singing popular songs in the music hall made him very unhappy. In fact, we quarrelled over it.'

She knelt and began digging and rooting among the plants, turning over earth, pulling out weeds.

'I'm sure you can get men here to do that for you.'

She smiled up at him. 'I like to do it. I feel I'm keeping in touch with the old Maestro. In any case, I'm an Irishwoman, and we have a great affection for graves, you know.'

'Do you?'

'Did you never see families in Ireland making a picnic on a grave-stone? To let the old ones know they hadn't been forgotten, make them feel they were somehow still part of the family?'

'I don't think I ever did.'

Bríd bustled among the plants, pulling out some unhealthy-looking specimens and taking fresh ones from her basket. For a while, as she recalled the Maestro, conversation had been easier between them. Without looking up at him, she said,

'Now, Harry, tell me what you've been doing.'

Bríd had planned this afternoon carefully. They had such important things to tell each other; things for good or ill. It was possible that her whole life could be made or destroyed this afternoon; possible that they would fall into each other's arms, or walk coldly away, never to meet again. She trembled to think of it. This was why it was best to meet in some neutral place.

'Well, I was in India, mainly. I got on to the Viceroy's staff, so there was quite a lot to do, making the Viceroy's life easy for him. He was very appreciative when I left, I must say.'

'And you were married. Do you have any children?'

'My wife is dead. She died in childbirth.'

She stopped, looking up. 'Oh, Harry, I am so dreadfully sorry. How long since –?'

'Eh? Oh, four years last March. That's the trouble with India – deuced hot, hygiene not very reliable. Some infection, you see, in the – well, I won't go on.'

She had stood up. 'Harry, you must have been destroyed!'

He looked at his boots, prodding vaguely at the grass with his walking stick.

'Left me deuced low for a while, I must admit. In the end the only thing was to get on with my work, try to forget.' He coughed. 'But that wasn't the reason I asked you to meet me. You see, Bríd, I always felt I treated you unfairly. Left you in the lurch, so to speak.'

'It was a very long time ago –'

'I've never had the chance to really explain how it was. The fact is, Bríd, I was confused. I had borrowed a large sum of money to bring you over to London. It was Wrenshaw's idea, actually, and my father knew nothing of it. But very soon afterwards – soon after Edward's death, I mean – he found out. The Jew had come round to the house and demanded his money with a vast amount of interest, and so of course I was hauled up, and the whole thing spelled out: the family was in difficulties; Father was appalled I had borrowed on a non-existent security. I was the heir to the title and Stella was an heiress; I knew Stella wanted to marry me and it would set the family on its feet again.'

'You don't have to go on,' Bríd said softly. 'It really doesn't matter now.'

'Deuced difficult position, to tell you the truth. I didn't want to leave you a bit, but what could I do?'

'Never mind, Harry,' she said hurriedly. 'It's all over now – long ago. Oh, I can't tell you how pleased I am to see you again, and to know you're well, and an earl now – imagine!'

'Yes.' He was still looking down. 'Yes, funny business. The stupid thing is that marrying Stella didn't actually make any difference in the end. Her money didn't save the house. Father sold out. Some American wanted to buy it – can't think why. Draughty old pile, never liked it myself.'

'I thought . . . I thought you liked Ireland, Harry?' she said tentatively.

'Oh, I like the riding well enough, you know, and some of the Irish I got on with well enough – comical old characters, some of them.'

He looked up at her.

'It's not that. Bríd, I wanted to say – well, wanted to apologise, I suppose, for the way I behaved. Been on my conscience rather.'

He looked into her eyes and she saw the perplexed look, the little-boy-lost look she could remember from years ago.

She touched his arm.

'That's very sweet of you, Harry. There's nothing to apologise for, you know. I understand how it must have been for you.'

She knelt again among her plants and went on digging, uprooting old ones and bedding in young fresh ones, her fingers quick and expert.

Harry suddenly burst out, awkwardly and vehemently,

'I swear I'm not trying to justify myself. I treated you quite unforgivably. I hope that perhaps you can understand my situation –'

She looked up, startled and moved by his tone, and for a moment their eyes locked. Then he seemed to panic, and looked down at the dead flowers.

'Shall I – shall I take these? I expect there's a bin somewhere . . .'

Flustered, she caught his tone. 'Yes, over there.' She laughed awkwardly. 'This London soil is guaranteed to kill any flower stone dead.'

He took the dead flowers and crossed to a rubbish bin.

She was beating a little dust from her elegant skirt. She pulled her heavy leather gloves off and stowed them in her basket, then turned to Harry.

'That's better. I feel the old Maestro will sleep easier now.'

She took his arm, and they began to walk away back up the long path towards the gates. She could sense his awkwardness and it infected her, but she fought it.

After a while Harry said, in a more relaxed tone, 'But you know, you haven't told me how you are.'

'I'm very well, Harry.'

'And you're married?' he asked in a light, offhand tone.

Now it was her turn to look down.

'Yes, Harry, I'm married.'

'Ah.'

'And since you mentioned him, I should tell you I married the American who bought your home.'

He stopped. 'I don't believe it.'

'It's true.' She forced herself to smile at him, and they continued walking. 'Though I had no idea he was going to buy it when we were married.'

'Good Lord! You in the old place! Do you know, I'm rather pleased. But whatever made you marry an American?'

'He's not an American – he's an Irishman who went to America and was very fortunate.'

'Made a million, d'you mean?'

'Yes.'

'Well, I mean to say, what are you doing over here in London if your husband's in Ireland? Does he mind you coming over here to act?'

'He said I could if I wished.'

Harry make a comical face and whistled. 'Rum go, and no mistake.'

As they reached the gate, Fred brought Bríd's coach forward.

'Oh, I say, look here, you're not going already?' He took her arm, and for one mad moment she thought he was going to kiss her just as he had done years ago – not wait for permission but just snatch her into his arms and cover her face with kisses. But as she turned, smiling, he hastily let go of her, as if he might have offended her.

He coughed. 'I was just going to say; that is, I wondered whether you'd care to have tea with us next week? Mother is very keen to meet you. She got rather excited when I said I knew you.'

She regained her composure. 'I should love to meet your mother, Harry.'

As Fred was pulling away, she looked out and waved to Harry who stood by the gate. He seemed curiously sad.

Later, after she had changed into comfortable old clothes, she went down to the new embankment and walked under the trees, staring across the river and thinking over their meeting.

That last glimpse of Harry troubled her. When at last she forced herself to recognise it, it was that he looked somehow, well, he could have been any City businessman, in his grey suit, the tall hat, the cane, the spats. What had she expected? The Harry of her memory was a knight on a white horse, an officer in long boots with a cavalry sword, irresistibly glamorous. It was puzzling and upsetting. She had looked for that Harry but she could not see him in the uncertain man who stood with her by the grave.

She felt disloyal and ashamed to think so, and her hand strayed to the little gold locket she still wore round her neck. There had been something about that last glimpse of him which was – she hated herself for thinking the thought – really rather conventional.

But it didn't matter if he was after all quite an ordinary, normal man. That didn't make any difference, did it? To her he would always be special; that went without saying.

And yet, oh, dear, running over their conversation in her mind, there had been something lacking. She had been waiting and waiting for that spark to leap between them, when they would look into each other's eyes and know they still loved each other; she had longed and longed for him to throw aside his cane, throw aside her basket of flowers and take her in his arms, and instead he had hummed and hawed, stared at his boots or over her shoulder.

It was very unsatisfactory.

Chapter Fifty

Perhaps it had been her fault. Had she been too brisk or bright in her manner, afraid to give him an opening? He said he had come to apologise; he was hardly going to seize her and kiss her in a public cemetery in any case. He did not know her feelings. It was all her own fault. She ought to have helped him more.

She thought it might make things easier between them if she were to write to him before going to his house.

Dearest Harry,
May I call you this? You have been dearer to me than my own life for these last twelve years, and now at last I can address you directly instead of in my thoughts; it warms me just to write the words.

Dearest Harry, are you pleased to see me again, as much as I was to see you? There were so many things I wanted to say to you – and so many things, I am sure, that you wanted to tell me. Oh, the letters I have written to you in my thoughts over the years, often wondering where you must be, and every night praying that you might be well and happy. I was so sorry to hear that your wife had died and I do sympathise with you in your bereavement. It is doubly tragic that a young and beautiful woman should die in bringing forth a child. I wanted to reach out and touch your hand when you told me. Do forgive me if I seemed cold or indifferent; I was no such thing, but after so many years, of course, it is not easy for us to talk – at least straight away.

'That is why I am writing this letter. You will have it well before next Sunday, and I hope you will have time to consider what I am saying.

Harry, I am yours if you want me. I have never loved anyone but you. I do not love my husband, and only married him for reasons which I will explain to you some day. I do not have any compunction about leaving him – that is what I want you to understand. As a Catholic, of course I can never be divorced, but my husband lives in Ireland and I know he will never disturb us. If you can devise any means by which we can be together, I ask no more in this life.

    Bríd

She wrote this hastily, scarcely read it through, and sent it off.

After she had sent it, however, she began to have doubts. She owed it to him to tell him about Matt. But how could she tell him, when they could never take Matt from Patsy and Nora? And what would he say when she told him she had given away her baby? Would he blame her?

In her more cheerful moments she told herself that they had plenty of time before them. Obviously they could not overcome twelve years of living apart immediately, but they would be able to go on meeting and would be able to straighten everything out little by little.

Over the days before the Sunday, images constantly intruded on her thoughts; distant memories, hazy images of Harry twelve years ago, and then the sharper memory of the awkward and unsatisfactory meeting at the cemetery.

It was a strange feeling indeed to arrive at the house in King Street St James's, the house she had walked past so many times without ever going inside, the house outside which she had stood and wept, thinking of Harry inside with his tyrant father.

Now here on this May afternoon Fred brought her to the steps, she descended from her carriage, the butler opened the door and Harry was there to escort her into the drawing room.

The frail, white-haired figure of his mother rose from a chair and extended a withered hand. The room was large, high-ceilinged, with plaster mouldings and trailing vine decorations. Family portraits hung on the walls, and a flower arrangement stood in the empty fireplace beneath a marble mantelpiece. Heavy swags obscured much of the light from the windows.

Harry was nervous.

'Dunne – tea, if you please!'

'Very good, my lord.'

The butler bowed obsequiously out.

Bríd perched on the edge of a chair and they made small talk. Very small talk. The Countess was graciously pleased to say that she had seen Bríd in *Much Ado About Nothing* and thought it one of the best Shakespearean performances she had ever seen. She considered herself something of an expert in these things.

'And you are Irish by birth, Elphin tells me. Strange, I could detect no trace of an accent.'

'No. It's a trick we have in the theatre, of changing our accents.'

'Ah. Indeed. I am afraid that is something I could never do.'

This sort of apparent confession, which was actually a boast, was the pattern for the conversation during the afternoon. The Countess let Bríd know, subtly but clearly, that she was privileged to be allowed through these hallowed portals, and that for an actress to be noticed by a peer was a great honour – which she was not quite sure that Bríd fully realised.

Tea was served. Pretty Sèvres porcelain plates and cups, a silver cake stand, lace-fringed napkins, everything was of the choicest. As she took tiny bites from wafer-thin cucumber sandwiches, Bríd watched Harry watching his mother.

'Can I help you with that, Mother? Oh, do be careful, Mother, I fear it may be too heavy for you. Let me –'

Mother would admonish her son, 'No, Elphin, I am perfectly capable of pouring tea. Have you asked Miss Flynn whether she would like another cucumber sandwich?'

At first she thought she had misheard, then Bríd understood that his mother was actually addressing her own son by his *title*. The tea-table ritual was insufferable, and it was absurd to see Harry dancing attendance on his mother.

As Bríd was about to leave, Harry became nervous. He came down the steps with her as a manservant went to find Fred in the mews.

'About your letter.'

'Yes?' She turned quickly.

'Could we meet somewhere to talk about it? In the park tomorrow morning? Would you mind? Impossible to talk here, with Mother inside –' he nodded his head – 'and servants and so on.'

He looked terribly uncomfortable and she felt sorry for him.

'Of course, Harry,' she said softly.

'On the bridge in the park tomorrow at eleven – would that be convenient?'

It was a slightly misty morning as she stood watching the swans and ducks gathering about an old gentleman who was standing on the bank and scattering bread crumbs. The sight of their squawking and pushing, and the way the ducks bustled in between the swans who towered graciously over them, helped to still the beating of her heart.

Eleven o'clock. She looked away across the water towards the Horse Guards rising through the trees, glorious in their fresh leaf, as the mist was slowly burned off by the strengthening warmth of the sun.

It had been a rash letter, she realised now. She should never have sent it. It had probably embarrassed him. It wasn't a woman's place to tell a man she loved him, even if he knew it already. In any case, he knew she was married. And he was a peer of the realm. It was out of the question, she convinced herself, and turned along the bridge again.

Still, in spite of all, there was something in her that hoped against hope that her Harry – the real Harry – would take her into his arms, tell her he loved her, and insist that they must be together for ever and let society do its damnedest, he didn't care.

He was coming. Again, he was dressed like a City gentleman in the hat, the gloves, the spats. It didn't suit him! She wanted him to come to her as she remembered him, as a cavalry officer in his green and gold uniform, so handsome, so adorable.

He stood before her and sheepishly offered her his hand. Why didn't he take her and kiss her? It would have been so easy. There was no one around. He had but to step forward, put his arms round her, draw her to him and cover her lips with his own.

He withdrew his hand hurriedly after they had shaken hands.

'Thank you for coming. Deuced difficult to talk at home, as you can imagine. Look, I can't stay long – got to go to the Lords this morning to discuss my induction ceremony. Taking my seat tomorrow, you know.'

'Oh, Harry, I am sure you'll look splendid in your ermine! To think of you in the House of Lords! Goodness, and there will be so much that you can do. I am sure that you will make your mark!'

'Eh? Oh, don't know about that. To tell you the truth, I'm only doing it to please Mother. She won't be satisfied till she sees me in my robes. Don't care for it myself.'

'I see. Harry –'

'Yes. About your letter. Of course, I appreciate your writing. Decent of you. To tell you the truth, Bríd, I'm not sure what I'm going to do yet. Not for the time being. Going to stay in London for a bit, get my bearings, then look about for somewhere to settle.'

He would not look at her; he would look at his boots or across the lake. She felt ill. Why wouldn't he look at her?

'Of course we could never live together,' he said in a sudden burst, and at last plucked up the courage to look into her eyes. 'Mother would never have it, Bríd. She wasn't pleased when I showed her your letter, I can tell you.'

For a second her mind was a blank.

'You showed her my *letter*?'

He was taken aback by her tone.

'Well, of course, I had to discuss it with her. She would have to live with us, you see.'

She was left without words.

'Could hardly leave Mother on her own, could I?'

Bríd could not speak.

'Mind you, that doesn't mean we couldn't see each other now and then, does it?' He smiled furtively. 'We could meet, have discreet little dinners together, you know. Go for little trips together – maybe go to the continent now and then. Eh?'

She couldn't speak. She was still thinking of that snobbish, stiff-backed, narrow-minded old woman reading her letter.

'What's the matter?' He had now noticed her expression.

Staring at him, she saw inside his eyes a little man peeping out cautiously. This was not her Harry; not this puny mother's boy, this conventional, ordinary man without a spark of fire or imagination.

'I say, are you all right?' He was worried. Still she couldn't speak. She couldn't – not ever, no, not ever again. Show her letter to his mother?

In a trance, she held out her hand.

'Harry, you will be late for your appointment.' Her voice was without expression.

'Lord, so I will – good thing you reminded me. When shall we meet?'

'We won't meet.'

'Eh?'

'Goodbye, Harry.'

'What –'

'Goodbye, Harry. Go now or you will be late.'

'Not meet?'

Her hand was held resolutely out, and his at last grudgingly met it. They shook hands, looking at each other for one last moment, into each other's eyes, and understanding each other rightly now. He coughed.

'Oh, er, right you are. Yes, suppose I had better – well, goodbye then.'

He turned awkwardly and began to walk away from her through the park in the direction of Westminster. As she watched him walking away, there was nothing special or important about him at all.

She watched him until he disappeared. He did not look back. Then slowly she turned, her eye moving across the lake, the trees and the ducks and swans. The old gentleman had gone now.

The ducks preened themselves in the morning sunshine; a swan waddled ungainly down to the water's edge, slipped into the water and moved graciously away across the still surface.

She couldn't think yet. At last she began to walk, crossed the bridge and turned along the water's side, towards the palace. The trees were in their freshest leaf, the sky high and blue above her. Yet her mind still refused to function. She stared ahead of her, seeing only that last sight of Harry as he walked away, never looking back, never wanting a last glimpse of her. She had told him to go, and he had meekly obeyed her and walked away, in his neat morning coat and his umbrella.

She kept rerunning the scene in her head, hearing his words over and over, the grotesque, impossible words, and at last had to understand that this was her Harry, this was the man she had remembered in her night thoughts, lain awake thinking about, hoped for, looked out for, gone to bed with Wrenshaw to hear about, the man she had dreamed of, had wept over, sighed for; this was the man she had humiliated and angered Garrett for; argued with and shamed him for.

Twelve years! And for that! The realisation sank and sank into her mind. Twelve years thrown away – for that! Twelve years of weeping and hoping. For that! How was it possible?

She began to walk faster and faster towards the palace, trying to wipe out of her memory the ruinous folly of those years. For that – and she had rejected and humiliated Garrett for *that*! Garrett, who was worth a thousand of him!

She turned once more, looked away along the length of the water glinting in the bright morning light, her mind clearer, then reached up to her neck, unclasped the little gold chain and holding her hand out, let the chain with its little locket slip through her fingers and down into the water. It made hardly any splash.

Chapter Fifty-One

She went about in a daze. How could it have happened? How could she have been so stupid? She wanted to beat her head against a wall, she wanted to weep or cry aloud, and did neither. She felt utterly worthless. Who could be interested in her weeping? How could she insult Isabella by confessing her own folly? She seemed annihilated from the earth, worthless, futile, aimless. She heard the applause at the end of the play every night with incredulity: what on earth were they clapping *her* for?

But oh, the waste of it! And what was she to do now? What was there left to do with her life?

More plays, piling up money, getting older alone? With no hope any more, nothing left to live for except to get richer? She had no vanity left; she didn't care whether she appeared on stage or she didn't. She didn't care for society. The only thing left to her was to be near Matt – yet how could she return? How could she have the impertinence ever to appear before Garrett again? Stand on the steps of the castle? 'Garrett, I've been a fool; please take me back. I'll do anything you ask, I'll scrub the floor for you, wash your shirts, bear your children, only have me back.'

Impossible. She could just see the look of contempt in his eye. She had used him shamefully; oh, God, how he must hate her now!

The play finished, and as the summer wore away she wandered round Chelsea like a ghost. She did not know what to do. She might as well jump in the river for any good she could ever do in the world again, that was the truth of it; she was just a nuisance, a waste of space. Why didn't she get out of it?

In the end she realised she would have to return to Ireland. There was nowhere else for her to go.

It was the middle of October when at last she made up her mind. Isabella went with her; she was going to need moral support. She had no idea how Garrett would react when she arrived and she did not dare tell him she was coming. She would have to stand on the doorstep and pray that he did not just order her to be thrown out.

They were married, she kept telling herself. 'Come back as my wife,' he had told her; surely he would not throw out his own wife? But she wasn't sure.

She armed herself with gifts. A new shotgun for Garrett, as well as lots of other things, a bridle for his hunter, cravats, watch chains and other trinkets. He was not a vain man, but he did like to dress well, to uphold his new status; there was never anything negligent or careless about him. She thought she had gauged his taste.

And she had bought for Matt too. What could she buy for an eleven-year-old? Anything! The difficulty was not to buy too much; she must be sparing. She saw Nora's eye every time she handed over the money in the shop, and she knew what Nora would think. What would the village say? What would the other children think – his playmates? Bríd forced herself to moderate her enthusiasm.

Late at night, tired, dishevelled and grimy from their endless train journeys, they arrived at the little station and saw all their boxes, parcels and packages unloaded from the guard's van till they formed a heap on the platform. The train pulled away, puffing steam, and disappeared down the track, leaving them in absolute darkness.

'What a welcome for you, Bella! If you'll wait here, I will walk into the village and see if I can rouse anyone to carry us to Ballyglin.'

Leaving Isabella alone with the luggage, Bríd walked into the nearby village. It was a windy night, with the taste of incipient storm in the air. She prayed it would not rain while all her luggage lay on the railway platform. She made out the shapes of trees lashing and beating against one another, and barely visible clouds hurrying through the sky.

She wrapped her cloak more tightly round her and bent into the wind. At last she came to some little cabins, and as she approached she saw a light in one, and then could hear voices. She pushed open the door and found herself in a little bar. She smelled the peat-smoke and the dried earth floor.

'I wonder – gentlemen, excuse me. There was no car at the station to meet the train. Do you know of anyone who could give me a lift to Ballyglin at this hour?'

A dozen or so men were drinking by the light of two guttering candles. They all looked up. If she had come down from the moon they couldn't have been more surprised. She looked round at them helplessly, at their gnarled, potatolike faces, ragged breeches, swallow-tail coats and pot hats. One of them started up.

'Was there never a car to meet ye, me lady? Seamus, where would Art Foley be now, think ye? If ye would only wait one minute, me lady, I'll go and see if I can't dig out Art Foley, and he'll carry ye to Ballyglin, never fear.'

'Thank you. I have some boxes too.'

'He'll be with ye directly.'

The man hurried away in the darkness, and Bríd walked back to the station.

Isabella was still waiting on the platform. She huddled her cloak round her.

'Who's there? Bríd? Is that you?' Her voice was shrill.

'Yes, it's me. A man has gone to find us a car.'

'Oh, Bríd, I was so afraid waiting here in the dark. Why did you leave me alone? I've never been so afraid in my life.'

Bríd laughed. 'I'm sorry. I supposed I'm used to it. You had nothing to fear. The people are the kindest on earth, and they'd turn themselves inside out to please you. Really.'

Twenty minutes passed and they heard the sound of a horse, and a man appeared in the gloom on an old sidecar.

'We have a lot of luggage.'

Art Foley scratched his head.

'Ah, well, never fear, me lady, I'll get it to ye first thing tomorrow. We'll just stack it in the station house here for now.'

Amazingly the little station house was not locked, and the three of them carried all the boxes and parcels inside.

'Now where to is it?'

'Ballyglin House. Castle Leighton that was.'

'Mrs Doyle, is it? God forgive me, I never knew ye in the dark. Come now, me lady, up with ye and your friend there, and we'll have ye home in a twinkling.'

All the way home she could think only of Garrett. She felt she could stand anything so long as he didn't shout at her. Tired but nervous, she shivered in her cloak as the old sidecar lurched and swung through the dark lane, and Art Foley kept up a running commentary.

'Mr Doyle – now there's a gentleman for you! We had Father Geoghegan offering up thanks in the pulpit for his new windows as if he was the Pope himself. And the school he's after building. And now a new bridge, me lady. And him that will drink with any man. Open-handed. "D'ye never wish ye was back in Americky, Mr Doyle?" says I. "Ah, there's a great country, boys," says he, "I've seen the future.

But I never forgot the old country," says he. And he didn't! He made his millions, and he's come back to spend 'em in poor old Ireland!'

She had no idea what time it was when they finally arrived, but thanked God there was a light at the drawing room window. Garrett must still be up. It occurred to her only then that he might have company: perhaps his political and business associates, all the hard, successful men who had sat at her table. Perhaps a woman? Bríd had been away six months – why should he wait for her to return? He could have taken a mistress; why should he wait six months in enforced celibacy? A man like him? She had refused him children – might he not beget a child by some other woman? She could hardly complain if he did.

Together in the darkness Bríd and Isabella climbed the steps while Art Foley waited, the horse shaking its head and stamping sometimes on the gravel. Bríd rapped on the door and it seemed an age as they waited, clutching their cloaks about them, before they heard a bolt being drawn back. Bríd shivered with nervous apprehension.

A crack appeared and they glimpsed the flickering of a candle.

'Who's there?'

'O'Flaherty, it's me, Mrs Doyle.'

'Mrs Doyle? Glory be, at this hour?'

He threw open the door.

'There are some things in the car, and would you settle with the driver?'

'Yes, madam.'

'Where is the master?'

'In the drawing room, madam. If you would follow me.'

'Come with me, Bella.'

Bríd ushered her in. Across the marble hall O'Flaherty's candle guided them in the darkness. O'Flaherty opened the door.

'In you go, Bella.'

So long as she had Isabella with her, Bríd thought, Garrett couldn't shout at her.

Two candles had burned low on the mantelpiece. They flickered with the draught from the door. The fire was a mass of glowing turf. Garrett was standing with one foot on the fender, an elbow resting on the mantelpiece. He was holding a whiskey glass.

As the two women entered he looked up, but did not react or make any move towards them.

For a moment he and Bríd looked at each other. Bríd could make out no expression in his look. At last, conscious of Isabella beside her, she assumed a businesslike manner.

'Bella, I should like you to meet my husband.' She advanced a step.

397

'Garrett, this is my old and dearest friend, Isabella Moretti. I have invited her to stay with us for a while.'

Her tone forced him to come forward. Bríd could feel herself shaking. Garrett gave her a questioning look, then turned gravely and politely to Isabella and shook hands with her.

'You're very welcome to Ireland, Miss Moretti. He turned again to Bríd. 'Why didn't you wire you were coming? I could have had someone to meet you.'

She swung aimlessly away. 'It was no bother. I got a man from the village to bring us. O'Flaherty is bringing in our things.'

There was an awkward silence. Bríd kept waiting for some reaction from Garrett. At last he said, 'Well, you're both very welcome, I'm sure. O'Flaherty!'

The butler was at the door.

'See that a room is prepared for Mrs Doyle's friend.'

'Yes, sir.'

Bríd turned quickly. 'She can have the room next to mine, O'Flaherty.'

'Yes, madam.' He bowed himself out.

'Well, Isabella, come and warm yourself at the fire.' Bríd's tone was bright and artificial, and she was trying to avoid Garrett's eye. 'Would you like something to eat? Or a drink?'

'I think I'd just like to go to bed, if that is convenient, Bríd.'

'Yes, I think I will too. We're both done in with travelling.' She hesitated before turning to Garrett again. 'Would you excuse us?'

He raised his eyebrows ironically and she could see he knew exactly what was passing through her mind.

'We can find our own way.' She took a candlestick from the mantelpiece and conducted Isabella to the door. She turned.

'We'll see you in the morning?'

'Very probably,' he said, still with that ironical expression which discomfited her.

After she had shown Isabella to her room, Bríd returned to her own. O'Flaherty was fussing about the bed, turning down the coverlet. To her surprise the fire was lit and the room pleasantly warm and inviting.

'The fire was already lit?' she asked absent-mindedly as she dropped her cloak over the back of a chair.

'The master always kept the room warm and ready against your return, madam,' O'Flaherty said as he finished turning down the bedcover.

Soon after he let himself out, and she threw herself into a chair and stared into the fire, almost too tired to undress.

However, while she was wondering at the strange fact of Garrett having the fire lit like this every night, the door opened and the man himself appeared. He closed the door quietly behind him and stood looking down at her.

'I'm surprised you didn't have more consideration for your friend. She'll be sleeping in a damp bed tonight.'

She started. 'Oh, but O'Flaherty –'

'Don't worry. He's taking her a hot-water bottle. Well!' He came over and, throwing himself into a chair opposite her, crossed his legs and looked at her calmly. 'The village will be pleased to know you're back. You've been much talked about.'

He paused, but she could think of nothing to say.

'Not that they asked me directly. Not to my face, you understand. No one actually had the guts to look me in the eye and ask what had happened to my wife . . .' He was silent again, still looking at her. 'But now and then I'd hear a whisper, just occasionally a snigger behind my back. You can imagine the kind of thing: "Garrett Doyle's wife has run away. The *Big Man* couldn't control his own wife."' He paused and then went on, still in a light, ironical tone, 'Yes, it's been a long summer, never knowing whether you intended to come back or not. Why did you?'

She was brought up short by this, and fumbled for a reply. 'I don't know exactly,' she said in a low voice. 'I suppose because – because this is my home now.'

He raised his eyebrows. 'Are you sure? Do you know – or only suppose?'

She vainly attempted a lighter note. 'Well, you know, the play ended –'

'When did it end?'

'Oh, in July.'

'July? It's October.'

'Yes.' She flailed about. 'I know. But there were things to do, I mean, various matters to arrange, and so on . . .'

He let her grind to a halt.

'So you were occupied with "various matters" in London for three months, and then "supposed" you might as well come back to Ireland?'

'Oh, Garrett!' His irony was crushing her. Garrett would give nothing away, however; as she turned to him she could not meet his gaze, and looked again to the fire.

'It seemed best,' she murmured at last.

She was conscious of him watching her. He seemed to be thinking.

There was a faint knock and the door opened an inch.

'Will I undress you now, madam?' A diminutive girl peeped in.

Garrett stood up. 'You're tired. Go to bed, and I'll see you in the morning.'

Without saying anything more, he went out as the little maid came in.

'Bring me some hot water,' Bríd said wearily.

'Oh, but madam, your new bathroom –'

'What?' Bríd turned, and opened the door of what had once been her dressing closet. It had been transformed. The walls were covered with white tiles. There was an enormous bathtub with brass taps, a wash-basin, a water closet. Beautiful fleecy towels hung ready on a mahogany rail and she ran her hand along them as she gazed about her. She turned on a tap and water thundered forth. It was immaculate, every detail beautifully finished.

She looked back at the bed turned down, the fire burning, the room warm and welcoming. He had done all this, never knowing whether she would return.

In the morning they all three sat down to breakfast. Having Isabella at the table made things easier; it gave Bríd the opportunity to explain everything, and they could make conversation together. Garrett was polite and affable, but Bríd still had no idea what was going through his mind.

He said they had made a start on the bridge, and he was going down to inspect the work that morning. Would the ladies care to accompany him?

Of course they would. Having wrapped themselves in warm clothes and thick cloaks, they drove down into the village.

The bridge was barely begun. At the nearer side large piers were being constructed, and men were heaving blocks of stone into place; earth had been shifted, and the bank dug away to provide a new approach. At the further side, men were engaged in sinking piles which would eventually form a coffer dam, to allow the piers to be sunk into the riverbed. Bríd could see from the scale of the work even at this stage that this was going to be a substantial bridge.

'We've been held up by the weather. There's been heavy rain over the last ten days. The coffer dam was completely washed away last week, which set us back. By the way, this is Mr Daley, the architect.'

He was a neatly dressed, clean-faced man from Dublin, a city type.

'The construction was delayed unfortunately, Mrs Doyle; this is summer work. I advised Mr Doyle to postpone the construction until next summer, but he was anxious to press ahead.'

She understood all right.

'Garrett, I had no idea! It'll be enormous. Ballyglin will have the best bridge in the west of Ireland!'

As she laughed she caught his eye. He was laughing too. He seemed so easy as if, to all the world, everything was right and comfortable between them. And it was not. The thought frightened her.

It began to rain, and she turned to Isabella.

'My dear, let us get back to the carriage. I want you to meet my little nephew.'

Garrett looked up as he heard this.

'We'll see you at dinner tonight?'

He nodded and and turned back to the architect.

Liam brought them to the little farmhouse. Bríd introduced Isabella to Patsy and Nora, and they waited until Matt came in from school for his midday dinner.

'I've been up to the castle while you were away, Aunt Bríd. Mr Doyle lets me come and ride Maisie as often as I like.'

Seeing Nora about to serve their simple stew, Bríd made ready to go. It was on the tip of her tongue to say, 'You have all that money in the bank – why don't you give him something better than that?' but she knew what Nora would say, so she pulled on her gloves, they made an appointment for Matt to come up to Ballyglin House, and she and Isabella made their own way home.

It rained all that afternoon and evening. Garrett came in, in boots and heavy waterproof coat, shaking the rain from his dripping hat and bringing a breath of cold wind in with him.

Waiting for Garrett to change, they sat in the drawing room, listening to the wind whistling round the house. Isabella was overawed by such bleak weather.

'It seems so much wetter and windier here than in London. I've never been to the country before. It's so raw and wild.'

'I know. It can drive you crazy sometimes, especially if you're alone.'

Garrett, now in evening dress, joined them in the drawing room for drinks before dinner. He was the perfect host, and made intelligent and urbane conversation with Isabella, drawing her out about her home in Italy. He was light and witty, and watching him Bríd wondered afresh at his power of self-command.

Isabella was very impressed with him, Bríd could see.

After dinner they returned to the drawing room, and Isabella took up some needlework as they sat and talked round the fire. So long as there were the three of them, they could converse like civilised human beings, pleasantly and rationally, and Bríd was spared the looming silences and the probing questions that developed when they were alone.

Garrett picked up a newspaper. Sometimes he would look up at her over it and she would ask herself, he's thinking something, but what?

'I saw Matt this morning,' she said brightly. 'He told me you invited him to come up and ride his mare while I was away. That was kind. That reminds me – those things we brought him from London, Isabella. They've come up from the station. We can go down tomorrow and give them to him. He'll think Christmas has come early!'

They laughed.

Later, Isabella packed up her work basket, wished them good night and went to her room. Bríd and Garrett were alone together, and she sat staring into the fire.

'Yes,' Garrett said casually, looking over his newspaper after a long silence, 'he came often while you were away. He missed you.'

She looked up quickly.

'He was always asking after you,' he went on. 'Wanted to know where you had gone. When you were coming back.'

He had lowered his newspaper. Bríd could feel herself colouring. She could not meet Garrett's eye, and turned back to the fire.

After a long silence in which she was conscious of Garrett watching her, he said, 'He's your son, isn't he?'

He knew instantly by the guilty way she started that he had hit the truth. At length, in a breathless and hoarse voice, she said, 'How do you know?'

He was looking steadily at her, 'And Harry Leighton is the father?'

She nodded.

'I thought so.'

Garrett put down his newspaper and leaned forward, his elbows on his knees, his eyes glowing with concentration. Whenever he looked at her like that, she shrank under his scrutiny, but he would not let her go.

'You gave him a son, Bríd but you wouldn't give me one.' His voice was quiet but insistent. 'Can you imagine what that means to me? You lay with him – that little runt – you gave him your body, you bore him a son. Think what that means to a man. Try to imagine what it is to be a man and see the woman you love give birth to your son, and to hold that son in your arms. Try to imagine it. And try to imagine how a man feels when that woman refuses – or worse, tricks him out of it.'

His gaze shrivelled her as she sat staring into the fire. She wanted to say, 'You're worth a thousand of Harry Leighton!' But if she did it would sound selfish and calculating, as if, having finished with Harry,

402

she had hurried home to make sure of Garrett. And it wasn't like that at all. She had her dignity, a bit of it at any rate, and at last she tried to return his gaze.

There was such a seriousness in his eyes that she might as well try to look into the sun. She searched and searched in her mind for something to say to him, but could find nothing.

At last he stood up and turned to the door. He was about to go out, but at the last moment turned again and shook his head slowly.

'You're such a fool, Bríd. You had everything, and you couldn't see it.'

Chapter Fifty-Two

What was she going to do?

She turned over in bed, staring up into the blackness as the wind whistled and whirled round the house and she heard the sudden lashing of a gust of rain and the rattling of the window.

Garrett had understood her completely. He had guessed simply by watching her that Matt was her son. She felt helpless.

She had returned to Ireland intending to come to an understanding with him and believing that she still exercised a certain influence over him. Even if he had shouted at her, he had still loved her, after all, and he had said, 'Come back as my wife . . .' At first she had dared to imagine he still felt for her, and reminded herself of the new bathroom, the warm fire that had greeted her. But it seemed he wasn't interested; seemed he had finally lost all hope of ever making her love him; she had heard the weariness, the finality in his voice when he said, 'You had everything . . .'

She turned over. It was so cruel. Garrett seemed to grow in her eyes at the very moment she saw him withdrawing from her. What a fool she had been to take him for granted! Yet she felt powerless to act. After the way she had behaved towards him, how could she approach him? She no longer held any territory of her own in their relationship; nowhere to stand and assert herself. She held all the cards once; now she had none.

It rained all the next day, and all the day after that. In the village the thatched roof was blown completely off a house. Garrett had a temporary tarpaulin covering lashed on immediately. Work was suspended on the bridge and the men were put to doing repairs to storm damage.

Materials had to be brought from Boyle. It was market day and despite the high wind and constant rain, Garrett told her he was going in to buy materials for the repairs.

'I'll come with you,' she said, on impulse. She wanted to be part of the work.

'I want to come.'

'Do you? It's terrible weather.'

Isabella stayed behind.

They took Garrett's gig with the hood up. It was quicker and lighter than the carriage, and less likely to get bogged down in the muddy tracks. Liam came along behind with a cart and horse.

The river was swollen.

'Garrett, we'll never get through!'

'Oh yes, we will,' he said calmly and drove the mare straight into the river. Bríd looked down frightened as the water reached to the horse's belly and swirled and eddied about them, muddy and turbulent. It was difficult, but they managed to get across.

All the way into Boyle it rained, and when they arrived, rain poured down on the market, which continued despite the weather.

Men stood gloomily about in the downpour with animals, their heads hanging glumly enduring the incessant rain.

It had always been the same. She could remember such scenes from her childhood. The fair went on as if the rain were not there; it had to. Farmers and their wives, their sons and daughters, huddled with their heads bowed, their clothes plastered to their backs; still they bought and sold, hands were slapped, calves and lambs driven away, geese traded. Wives with blankets over their heads stood with baskets on the ground at their feet holding a dozen eggs or a few cheeses. The square was a mass of churned-up mud and dung, and the air was filled with the lowing of young calves and the dismal sounds of lambs taken that morning from their mothers, and from somewhere the boastful but pathetic cry of a cockerel.

Men escaped into the taverns on the square, and she went into one with Garrett.

The parlour was hot and damp; steam rose from men's overcoats. Garrett had a heavy rubber-proofed overcoat, a memory of his railroad days when he had been a section foreman and would stride along the tracks with a gun at his belt, keeping men at their work.

After a midday meal, Garrett went down to a factor's to order building materials, and Bríd was crossing the square to a shop when she saw Patsy.

'Uncle Patsy! Stop! Uncle Patsy, you're soaked to the skin!'

He laughed. 'Never fear, Bríd, aren't I well used to it?'

'For heaven's sake, come inside! You'll catch pneumonia!'

'Oh no, we've got to be getting back.'

405

'You're not alone?'

'Nora and Matt are just finishing. They'll be out directly.'

And at that moment Nora and Matt came out, buttoning themselves up and hoisting umbrellas.

'Aunt Nora, you're never going to walk back in all this rain?'

'How else do you suppose we'll get home, Bríd? Not all of us have carriages to ride in.'

'Aunt Nora, you must come with us! You can't possibly walk. You must, I insist!'

'We'll walk. Come, Patsy.'

'Well, at least let Matt come with me!'

'Matt can walk with Patsy and me. He's not a milksop!'

'Aunt Nora, I never said he was! But in all this rain, surely you'll let him ride inside with us?'

'He'll walk. Come, Patsy.'

Bríd tried to catch her arm, but Nora shook her off, and then turned sharply again.

'Ye'd have us always beholden to your charity, wouldn't you? You'd buy off your guilt and shame, is it?'

'What? Aunt Nora! Buy off? But haven't I put by all the money for Matt – that you were happy to have?'

'Happy? Happy? You think we need your money – is that it?'

'No . . .' She was uncertain, but could feel the force of Nora's bitterness. 'No, it's not that, Aunt Nora, only – all those years ago when we made the agreement –'

'Which you broke!'

'Yes, I know. Still, I did try to put by the money.'

'We don't want your money, Bríd! Take your money – I have never touched a penny of it. Take it, keep it, and leave us in peace. Matt has never wanted for anything; he's had as good a home as any in the townland. And you've done nothing but bring trouble and discord since you returned.'

'What?'

The handle of the umbrella was slippery in Bríd's hands. Patsy and Matt were standing a few yards away; Patsy was looking away embarrassed, but Matt was watching them both anxiously.

'Aunt Nora!' she screamed. 'How can you say such things?'

''Tis better the truth should be spoken, Bríd. Come, now.'

She turned away from Bríd and the three set off in the downpour in the dim light of the autumn afternoon, and were soon lost to sight among the farmers and their cattle.

Bríd watched them until they had disappeared. Rain dripped from her umbrella and she reached up a wet hand to wipe away her tears.

It was as if all the years of resentment had boiled over in one speech. Aunt Nora hated her. She had never had a child of her own, and the coming of Matt had been a gift of heaven. But Bríd had never conceived the depth of her bitterness and animosity.

At last she turned to find Garrett.

He was in the building contractor's yard with Liam, trading for timber and tarpaulins, ropes, sacks of nails, tools and other implements for emergency help for the village.

An hour later they set off for home.

The rain showed no sign of abating, but the hood of the gig kept off most of it. Garrett's hat was pulled down well over his brows, and in the dim light under the leaden clouds, it was difficult to see his face. The lower part of Bríd's skirt was soaked, and she was damp and cold at her neck and wrists. She shivered.

They did not speak, and she thought he must be thinking of the work ahead. Liam was behind them in the cart with the timber and tarpaulins.

Far away ahead of them she saw a flash of lightning and soon after came the rumble of thunder. She huddled into her sodden cloak, hunching her head down between her shoulders and staring out at the dim landscape.

She was still running the horrible scene with Nora through her mind, when Garrett unexpectedly spoke.

'Bríd, I've been thinking.'

She looked up.

'It came to me last night, after I'd gone to bed. You married me to be near your son, didn't you?'

She said nothing.

'I understand. Why shouldn't you? You're a mother, and maybe it was your only way back to him. And it's why you came back this time, too, isn't it?'

She was still silent, not looking at him but searching for an answer.

'Did you see him – Harry Leighton – while you were in London?'

'Yes,' she said, dully.

Garrett was silent for a long time, staring ahead at the horse trotting before them.

'You can go if you want to. Go for ever, I mean. I won't hold you back. I've spent my life chasing you, but nothing worked; I can see now it was never meant to be, and do what I might, I could never force you to love me if you didn't want to. So, if you want, you can go. Ask your aunt to let you take Matt with you. I'm going to sell the house, maybe go back to America.'

With every word he spoke she felt a stiff, deathlike inertia in her

407

body, as if she could never rouse her spirits again. All she could think was, I caused this. I have given him all this unhappiness. It has all been my fault. And she felt within her the most enormous tenderness, wishing she could reach out her arms and take him into her embrace and comfort him like a little child who has fallen over and scraped its leg, holding, comforting it, and kissing it better. But Garrett was a big, strong man, and his unhappiness was gigantic, overwhelming, and who was she, after all that had happened between them, who was she to dare to reach out to him? What an impertinence! He would only recoil and stare at her, and think it must be another of her tricks, that she wanted something else out of him.

The rain beat against the canopy, and she felt colder and colder as the wetness infiltrated itself through her clothes to her skin, till she was a block of silent, cold misery.

A million years seemed to pass before Garrett spoke again.

'Think it over and let me know what you decide.'

She wanted to cry out, 'No Garrett, no!' but the words would not form themselves.

They were approaching the village. Through the driving rain, she began to make out people on the riverbank and the half-built piers of the bridge, and then they could hear shouts. Within a few moments, as Garrett brought the gig to a standstill, she could see the river, now hugely engorged, thickly swirling with mud and branches of trees, frightening in its primaeval potency.

For a second she gazed into the swift, black stream, then she made out on the opposite bank a knot of men and women, and among them Patsy waving frantically and pointing.

Old Danny Keogh rushed up to them.

'Oh, Mr Doyle, is that you? Praise be! 'Twas Mrs Byrne there, trying to cross, she slipped and was carried down. There, d'ye see, beyond . . . And young Master Matt is trying to save her!'

Bríd saw where a tree, fifty yards further down, had half fallen into the river, its roots gouged out by the force of the water. Two figures were tangled among the branches.

Garrett sprang out of the gig and ran. Bríd followed behind him as quickly as she could, clutching her wet skirts.

Matt was in the branches, clinging low over the water and stretching down towards it. Bríd saw a movement, a hand reaching up, and thought she heard Matt shouting, but amid all the shouts of the villagers on both sides of the river, the incessant noise of the wind and the rain, and the heaving and thrashing of the trees about them, it was difficult to make it out.

Garrett ran to the tree, throwing off his heavy waterproof. He

408

began making his way among the branches, quickly and skilfully, but his own weight had a catastrophic effect. The tree gave way and both he and Matt were precipitated into the swirling water and carried downstream.

Bríd screamed and ran down past the pollard willows to where she could see Garrett wrestling with the water, clinging on to Matt and managing to hold his head up. Then she saw there was a third figure, who had to be Aunt Nora, struggling in the current.

Garrett had got Matt now more securely, and as they were carried beneath another tree, he reached up and grasped a branch. Immediately, three men, who had been running along the bank, plunged half into the water, holding on to branches, and were pulling them clear. Garrett was shouting, 'Take the boy!'

They had Matt securely and were bringing him on to the bank. Bríd flew to him and clasped him to her, and was looking earnestly into his face as the others clustered round.

The boy was dazed, covered in mud, spluttering and trying to regain his breath.

'Are you all right, darling?'

'Oh, yes – oh, Aunt Nora . . .'

Then he fainted.

She screamed, and clutched him to her again.

'There, Mrs Doyle, don't fret yourself now. He'll come to.' Hands were all about her, taking him from her grasp to lay him on the wet grass.

'No, bring him to the gig – bring him now! We must get him inside immediately; he's soaked through. We must get him into the warm somewhere!'

Willing hands were lifting Matt, who began to stir again, and he was carried to the gig. She snatched up Garrett's waterproof and wrapped it round him.

'Never worry now, Mrs Doyle, ma'am – he's safe and sound, ye see.'

She looked round. 'But where's Mr Doyle?'

There were still half a dozen men on the riverbank shouting and calling, and one of them leaning out from an overhanging willow.

'This way, Mr Doyle, sir, now –'

She ran, and saw Garrett was in the river, fighting against the powerful current, and holding a black figure in his arms.

She couldn't believe it. He was right out in the middle of the flood. He must be carried away at any moment. She screamed.

'Garrett!'

But her cry was simply lost in the wind and the shouting.

The river was perhaps four or five feet deep, but the force of it kept pushing him off his feet, and he was struggling to lift Aunt Nora, who appeared quite limp in his arms, so that it was almost impossible for him to make any headway.

'Garrett!' she screamed again. Suddenly she had never wanted anything so much in her life as she wanted him to be safe.

'Help him, someone! Oh, God! Help him!' she screamed.

And she plunged forward to the river's brink, wading down into the soft mud of the riverbank.

A chorus of men were around her, hands pulling her back.

'For God's sake, Mrs Doyle, you'll be carried away yourself!'

'Mr Doyle's got her – never fear!'

'Garrett! I'll help!' Her face was so wet with rain and tears that it was difficult to see, and she would have slipped into the river but for the men holding her back.

Garrett was gradually making ground, but then suddenly he lost his footing in the soft gravel of the riverbed. He sank up to his neck in the water, still clutching the black, inert form of the woman.

'Garrett!' Bríd screamed again.

But still, indomitable, as if he were charmed or of more than human strength, he regained a footing, though carried several yards downstream. Fortunately he seemed to have found a slightly shallower, firmer bank, and waded at last ashore, grasping the body of Bríd's aunt. Hands were ready to take her from him and lay her on the grass.

'Oh, Garrett!' As he helped lay down the body of Nora, she flung her arms round him.

'Oh, thank God! Thank God! I thought I had lost you! Oh, God, I was never so frightened in my life! Oh, Garrett!'

He embraced her and she looked up into his face. The hair was plastered about his head, water poured from every part of him, and there was a muddy streak across his face.

'Look to your aunt Nora.'

She turned quickly to where a group of the villagers were kneeling round the body on the grass.

'What'll we do? She's not breathing.'

Bríd knelt beside Nora's body and lifted it in her arms, shaking it. As she moved the body, water poured from Nora's mouth and nose.

'Send for Dr Fitzgerald.'

'Seamus went for him already – but he's from home.'

Garrett knelt by Nora's body, turned her over and began to try lifesaving movements across the upper back, pushing down hard against the shoulder blades. Water trickled from her nostrils.

He stopped at last and, looking up, took Bríd's hand.

'I think it's too late.'

He got to his feet, put his arm round Bríd's shoulder, and the two of them looked down at the inert body spreadeagled on the muddy grass.

Chapter Fifty-Three

Bríd stared down at the sodden body on the grass as the realisation of the truth filtered through her.

Around her, all was bustle and organisation. Garrett was shouting orders; a rope was thrown across the river and secured to a tree so that they could bring over the horses and gig, and then the cart.

The body of Nora was carried across and laid on the ground. The villagers crowded round, staring down at it, crossing themselves. Patsy, turning his hat in his hand over and over, was repeating, 'Oh, God, what a day of it! What's to become of us all?'

But Garrett, as soon as the cart had been got across, had everyone busy unloading the materials for the repairs. Then the body of Nora was lifted on to it and driven up to Patsy's house. Bríd got Patsy up with Matt on the gig and Garrett drove them quickly to Ballyglin House. The rain was still pelting down as they approached the dark shape of the house, and all of them were soaked to the skin. As soon as they came through the door, Isabella and O'Flaherty began fussing about them.

'O'Flaherty, tell cook I want hot soup brought up immediately. Isabella, will you take Matt up to my room and put him into a hot bath? Uncle Patsy, you come with me and and we'll find you somewhere to wash, and some dry clothes.'

Patsy, still confused, was turning to the door. 'I must go to Nora –'

But Garrett took his arm.

'Nora is being taken care of, Patsy. You come with me and we'll get into dry things first, or we'll neither of us be any use.'

Once they were all in dry clothes, and Matt wrapped in a dressing gown after his bath, they were given hot soup in front of the fire in the drawing room. Only Garrett went out again to return to the village and organise the repairs. Some of the houses had holes in the roofs where thatch had been blown away.

Matt was put to bed. Bríd remained in front of the drawing-room fire with Uncle Patsy and Isabella, waiting for Garrett. Patsy was feeling very awkward in some of Garrett's clothes, and would pick at the material of his sleeve and run his finger round his neck in the unfamiliar fabric of the shirt collar.

'In the morning I'll go down and get your own clothes, Uncle Patsy, and we'll arrange about Aunt Nora.'

He was still too stunned to think, fidgeting in the chair and repeating, 'What a day of it! And Nora gone, she that was a prop to me. Bríd, what's to become of us now?'

She would mutter reassuring things, and reiterate, 'Garrett will know what to do.'

But later, after she had put Patsy to bed, she could not keep still, and wandered from room to room waiting for Garrett. That last sight of Nora kept intruding into her imagination, Nora sprawled awkwardly on the muddy grass, Nora wet and bedraggled, Nora dead. And the memory of their argument ran again through her mind. She felt that she was in some way responsible for Nora's death, though she couldn't think how. The worst thing was that she should have died before they could be reconciled.

It was midnight before Garrett came home.

Bríd ran to the door and flung herself into his arms.

'Oh, Garrett, are you all right?'

'Yes.' He seemed surprised. 'Why? I've been putting tarpaulin covers on the roofs. I told you.'

'Are you tired? Do you want something to eat?'

'Don't bother the servants. I had something in Mrs Carruthers's. Why?'

'Oh, Garrett, don't scold me. But I was so frightened this afternoon. Only promise me you won't go away; promise you won't sell the house.'

He seemed slightly amused, but also very tired.

'I won't if you don't want me to.'

She pulled his face to her, kissing him full on the lips.

He chuckled. 'Wait! Let me get out of these wet things.'

O'Flaherty was with them and took Garrett's waterproof, then Garrett put his arm round her shoulders and they walked into the drawing room. She turned at the door.

'O'Flaherty, bring Mr Doyle a large whiskey toddy.'

'Yes, madam.'

The fire had sunk into a glowing heap and the two candles on the mantelpiece had burned low.

413

'It seems a sacrilege to feel glad at this moment, with Nora dead. But seeing you safe, and Matt safe, I can't help it. Garrett, I kept thinking when you were in the river, If Garrett is safe I'll be such a good wife to him, I'll do everything I can to make him happy. Oh, Garrett, I've been so wretched to you! Oh, Garrett, don't ever leave me!' She clasped her arms round him.

His arm rested on her shoulder. 'Don't worry about that.'

He sat in a large chair by the fire, and she knelt by him.

'When I saw you there this afternoon I realised everything suddenly. How unkind I'd been to you, how stupid and unfeeling; how wretched you'd been and all through my fault . . .'

He ran his hand over her hair.

'And then, seeing you with Matt in your arms, I realised how you were a thousand times better a father to him than any other man could possibly be – and to think I had wanted to deprive you of your own children. What a faithless and cruel wife I have been to you!' She felt tears smarting in her eyes. 'And seeing you in the water, I swore and prayed that if you would only be saved, I would be a good wife to you and give you children and care for you and look after you in every way I could . . .'

He laughed softly, seeing her so wrought up. Curling his arm round her shoulders, he pulled her to him and kissed her.

'Never fear, Bríd, we'll be a grand husband and wife from this out. There'll be never such a happy couple in Ireland. We'll be the envy of our friends. I always told you we were made for each other. Maybe we're too much alike for you to see it. We're kindred spirits, Bríd.' He kissed her again gently. 'You've given me a long run, my lady – but it was worth it.'

The door opened; Bríd sprang up to meet O'Flaherty and took the silver tray from him.

'Thank you, O'Flaherty.'

He bowed his way out. She carried the big steaming tumbler to Garrett and knelt beside him. Before she would let him take it, they kissed, slowly and lovingly.

'Oh, Garrett, I do love you.'

She proffered him the glass, and he sipped it, looking into her eyes, then made her sip it too and kissed her again caressingly as he took the glass from her wet lips. And so they kissed and sipped the hot drink, always looking into each other's eyes, and all the time feeling a powerful electricity generated between them, a force of desire and attraction. Bríd felt an insupportable need grow in her body till she could hardly breathe, and her hand holding the tumbler began to shake. Garrett drained the last of the toddy and rose, lifting her with

414

him when she could hardly stand. He kissed her again tenderly, kissed her face as she held it up to him, her eyes closed, the blood pounding in her throat, and ran his fingers through her hair.

'Let's go up now, Bríd,' he whispered as he held her.

She shuddered with desire for him, and whispered to him as he still held her close,

'Oh, Garrett, if you don't make love to me this instant . . . There is such a debt of love I owe you.'

'The night won't be long enough or dark enough for what we have to give each other.'

He lifted her easily in his arms and carried her up the broad staircase, her arms twined round his neck, as the wind still sighed and groaned round the great house.

The weather had eased on the following day and Garrett was in the village throughout the day, securing and making fast where some coverings had gone astray. Liam was sent in to Boyle to bring back provisions and supplies for the families that had been left destitute by the storms.

Arrangements were made for the wake and funeral for Nora. Garrett ordered some bottles of whiskey and a barrel of porter to be brought to the cottage, and Mrs Carruthers and two friends came up to lay out the body.

Nora lay on top of her bed in her bridal dress, and two candles burned at either end. The house was swept and cleaned. During the day neighbours came to view the body and pay their respects.

Bríd with Isabella and Mrs Flanaghan came down from the big house with a large cauldron of mutton stew and other provisions, including oatmeal loaves, the round loaves which broke into four pieces.

As evening drew on, the cottage began to fill up with men in awkward black suits and women loosing the shawls from their heads. As each entered, they would salute those in the cottage, 'God save all here.' Greeting Patsy, they would throw their arms round him, consoling and commiserating with him. Then they would go into the bedroom and comment on Nora's appearance before returning to the kitchen and taking a seat on a bench.

Garrett had set the barrel of porter on the table and, as they returned from the bedroom, would offer them a glass of spirits against the cold. The neighbours sat round the wall on benches, talking as the noggin of porter passed from one to the next. Garrett had also brought in a store of clay pipes and these lay on the table with tobacco available to anyone.

Patsy had watched the preparations in a state of apathy until at last Garrett put a pipe into his hand and made him light it. Patsy smoked it, staring into the fire.

''Tis the first time ever I smoked a pipe of tobacco in this house,' he said at last.

'Is that so, Patsy? How can that be?' said a neighbour, pulling on a pipe himself.

'Herself would never allow it; she could never abide the smell.'

'There, now. And isn't a pipe a great comfort in the world, when we're seated easy?'

'It is.'

'She was a woman of great strength of character, so she was.'

There were murmurs from the others. Patsy stirred himself.

'Mrs Carruthers, will you take just a suppeen of whiskey? And Mrs O'Conor? And you, Michaeleen Brannagh?'

He went round with the bottle, pouring for each a long glassful.

Mrs Carruthers shifted her pipe in her mouth and spat into the fire.

'I mind the day you was married, Paudeen.'

'I can see it myself as if it was yesterday,' said Patsy.

'She made a fine, tall bride, taller than yourself, I remember,' Mrs Carruthers went on. ''Twas said no one in the seven parishes round would have her for her scolding tongue, but I never agreed with that. She was a clever woman, would make a fine wife for any man, Patsy, and you were the lucky one that caught her.'

'I was never thinking to be married,' said Patsy dreamily, ''Twas herself told me, "Patsy you and me had better be getting married, I'm tired of waiting."'

There was some laughter around the room, which was full now, men and women drinking from the bucket of porter as it passed round, and smoking their clay pipes.

'Was that the way of it, Patsy? To think you might have been a bachelor man to this day if Nora hadn't taken you in hand. She was a great blessing to you. 'Tis no matter for her scolding tongue. There was no woman in the townland would drive a harder bargain, Patsy; she saved you a mint of money, I'm thinking.'

'She did,' said Patsy.

'And a handsome woman in her youth, I remember her well. She would walk throught the village in a red dress, driving the geese to Boyle Fair, her long black hair streaming down her back, like Queen Maeve herself. And bold. Do you mind the time, when 'twas a hot summer and her the young colleen still, she would pull up her skirts and wade in the river, for the cooling of her legs? Do you mind that now, Mrs Casey?'

416

'Oh, she cared not a straw for what the people might say, Mrs Carruthers. The men was afraid of her. That's the truth of it. Was you not afraid of her yourself, Patsy?'

Patsy took the pipe from his mouth and looked round at them, a melancholy smile on his face.

'To tell the truth, ladies, when I was a younger man, I was maybe just the merest little bit afeared of her. For she was a powerful bold woman, no one can deny. But in all the years we was married I grew out of fearing her, do you see? Knowing her at close hand, like.'

They all nodded.

'Ah, knowing her at close hand, 'twould be so.'

'Knowing a body so many years, you find out the, so to say, inner side, or the secret side of them,' said Mrs Carruthers, ''tis the mysterious way of marriage. One person can never say that another body be married well or ill, I'm thinking. For how do we know what do be passing between the husband and wife in the evenings by their own fireside?'

'That's very true, Mrs Carruthers,' said her neighbour, Mrs Casey, 'and for all we know, when Patsy and Nora was alone together, she was as soft as milk, and as pliable to him as he could wish. Was that the way of it, Patsy?'

'I can't deny it.'

Patsy sighed, and took another glass of whiskey.

Bríd stirred the stew.

'Will you take a bowl of stew, ladies and gentlemen?'

She began to fill bowls on the table and the villagers came forward to take them.

In the dim room, by the light of the fire and two candles on the table, the villagers made hunched, dark shapes on their benches, the men in their black suits, the women with black shawls round their shoulders. As they ate the stew, silence fell.

'Mrs Doyle, 'tis the best bowl of stew I tasted this many a year. Mary, why ever can you not make a stew the like of this?' an old man said, turning to his wife with a mischievous smile on his face.

'If you was to give me the piece of mutton that went into it, then I might be after cooking you such a stew. But I do believe your pockets are stitched up, for the few pence that ever I get from you.'

There were smiles and chuckles at this. The man looked round, grinning sheepishly.

The door opened and a young lad of eighteen came in. There was a fiddle under his arm.

'Sean, is that yourself to give us a tune? Come in and welcome.'

417

'God save all here,' said Sean. 'Patsy, my heart goes out to you. Is it Nora within there?'

He went briefly in to the bedroom. When he returned, Patsy offered him a glass of whiskey. The other people were finishing the stew and putting the bowls on the table.

'Sean, *acushla*, will you give us a tune to raise our spirits?'

Sean posted himself near the door to what had been Bríd's room years ago, and struck up a reel.

Bríd went into the bedroom where Nora lay by the light of two candles. Two old ladies sat on stools, crooning and keening to themselves. Staring at the floor and, clasping their hands round themselves, they took no notice of her.

Nora lay still, her eyes closed, her bony features relaxed in a noble expression of repose. She had been a handsome woman, Bríd realised for the first time. This was the woman who once drove her geese across the village green, proud in her red dress, the men frightened of her; now she lay still as a stone, grey in death. The awful mystery of it flooded into Bríd.

She felt a touch on her arm, and Garrett was beside her, with Matt. The three of them stood silently looking at the body of Nora. Then Matt looked up at Bríd and said,

'What'll we do now, Aunt Bríd?'

And Garrett, looking into Bríd's eyes, said to him, 'You're coming to live with us, Matt.'

'And Uncle Patsy too?'

'And Uncle Patsy too.'

As they stood in the dim light of the candles, the reel next door finished and the voice of an old man rose, quavering, in an Irish song. The desolation in the song, the bleak sadness of it, captured all the finality and hopelessness of death.

She reached across behind Matt and took Garrett's hand.

Epilogue

Bríd turned in her saddle.

Matt was coming up the hill behind her, and, watching him, she thought what a handsome young man he had become. He was twenty now and home for the long vacation. How well he sat his horse, and how fortunate she was in her eldest son, she thought. At home that afternoon, she had left her three other children. Matt always held a special, secret place in her heart, and since he had gone away to the university, she treasured the moments when they could still be alone together.

He joined her and together they urged their horses up the hill, and came out on the wide open hilltop, and so to the old stone circle – the Fairy Ring. Around them, the countryside stretched away, the pocket-sized fields, the patches of gorse and bog, the copses, all the tangled, wild countryside of Ireland. And in the distance to the west rose the Curlew Mountains, glowing in the bright summer afternoon.

Somewhere overhead she could hear a lark. She looked around, and took a deep breath.

'I often used to come here as a young girl.'

They sat silent, gazing across the open miles of countryside, enjoying the wide emptiness, the great space of air and cloud around them.

'Aunt Bríd, did you . . . did you ever know my mother?'

He looked at her innocently, openly.

She was taken aback and looked away. For a second it was on the tip of her tongue to tell him the truth.

'Yes, Matt,' she said at last, still not looking at him.

'What was she like?'

'Oh, goodness! A bit like you.'

He laughed slightly.

'I mean, was she beautiful?'

'People said she was.'

419

'It's strange, you know,' he said thoughtfully, 'never to have known one's parents. Like Moses, being found in the bulrushes, going through life an orphan. Other fellows at college introduce me to their people, and – well, I suppose I feel set apart. Don't misunderstand me, Aunt, you and Garrett have been like a father and mother to me; I couldn't ask for more, you know. It's just that, once in a while, I wonder, that's all.'

She was still looking away from him and something about her frightened him.

'Oh, I say, are you all right?'

She turned, her eyes glistening, and looked at him, and the young man was embarrassed.

'Oh, Matt, do forgive me. It was just something you said, that's all.'

'What about?'

'Nothing, nothing; I'll be all right in a moment, I promise you. Just a passing thought. Give me a moment and I'll be myself.'

But he pulled his horse closer to her.

'No, what is it? You must tell me. I look on you as a mother, you know that. I couldn't bear to see you unhappy. Do tell me what upset you?'

'Please, don't ask me, Matt. It won't do, really.'

She rallied, and taking her reins in, turned the mare's head.

'Come on, let's get home. They'll be wondering where we've got to.'

She urged her mare into a gallop and Matt followed, and together they rode away over the brow of the hill and so were lost to sight.

1921 04 5

FEB 0 8 1997